DEAD HOUSE

A ZOMBIE GHOST STORY

KEITH LUETHKE

OTHER LIVING DEAD PRESS BOOKS

CHRISTMAS IS DEAD: A ZOMBIE ANTHOLOGY
BOOK OF THE DEAD: A ZOMBIE ANTHOLOGY
BOOK OF THE DEAD 2: NOT DEAD YET
THE ZOMBIE IN THE BASEMENT (YOUNG ADULT)
THE LAZARUS CULTURE: A ZOMBIE NOVEL
RANDY AND WALTER: PORTRAIT OF TWO KILLERS
END OF DAYS: AN APOCALYPTIC ANTHOLOGY VOLUME 1 &2
DEAD WORLDS: UNDEAD STORIES VOLUMES 1, 2, 3 & 4
FAMILY OF THE DEAD
REVOLUTION OF THE DEAD
KINGDOM OF THE DEAD
THE MONSTER UNDER THE BED
DEAD TALES: SHORT STORIES TO DIE FOR
ROAD KILL: A ZOMBIE TALE
DEADFREEZE, DEADFALL
SOUL EATER, THE DARK
RISE OF THE DEAD
DARK PLACES
VISIONS OF THE DEAD

THE DEADWATER SERIES
DEADWATER
DEADWATER: Expanded Edition
DEADRAIN, DEADCITY
DEADWAVE, DEAD HARVEST
DEAD UNION, DEAD VALLEY
DEAD TOWN, DEAD SALVATION
DEAD ARMY (coming soon)
COMING SOON
BLOOD RAGE by Anthony Giangregorio
LOVE IS DEAD: A ZOMBIE ANTHOLOGY
DEAD HISTORY: A ZOMBIE ANTHOLOGY

DEAD HOUSE: A ZOMBIE GHOST STORY

Edited by Anthony Giangregorio

Prologue

The rain fell in blinding sheets along the stone structure of Dead House.

A black creek flowed across the neglected front lawn, it didn't bother to puddle in the small cavities of earth lining the upturned soil, as the house wouldn't allow anything so violent like running water to end its travels there. Dead House didn't sleep as most homes do. It wasn't content to sit on a lonely hill and watch. A deep seeded evil breathed within the heart of its structure, its foundation; aged and bitter, it waited.

Brilliant lightning struck a nearby oak tree, severing a limb with the rage of Achilles' own fury. But, as with all living things at Dead House, the weathered oak gave a silent shudder and dug its twisted roots deeper into the tainted earth.

From outside the mansion, came a mournful wail, the cry following the thunder like a phantom to then die among the pouring rain.

Gnarled limbs poked from the ground like two bent poles. The limbs became arms, flailing and swaying in the wind. Then a round, ragged head forced its way through the wet, loose soil. Yellow eyes flickered within sunken sockets. The hunched figure clawed its legs free with long overhand strokes. It plucked a worm free from the soil and dropped the wiggling crawler into its greedy mouth. Crooked teeth chewed, a low moan of pleasure seeping from its lipless mouth. Lightning flashed. The misshaped figure produced a wailing moan. It lurched forward like an old man too stubborn to use a cane and before making for the tree line, it gave the crumpled house a hard stare.

A single candle was lit in the fourth floor's window, the flickering flame giving Dead House the appearance of a one-eyed beast gazing into the night.

Content, the twisted figure pushed through the dense tree line and lumbered onto the road.

Chapter 1

As the rain continued to pour outside, Victor Leeds, a nineteen year old Delicatessen manager was closing up for the night. He'd busily scrubbed the metal countertops, put the bread in the refrigerator, swept and mopped the floors, and wrapped the Boar's Head meat and cheeses when Jimmy Vahaugn decided to order an Italian combo. Jimmy had poked through Nick's Deli for nearly two hours now. He read the newspaper, bought a pack of gum, and made small talk with every customer until Victor pulled the **Closed** sign down. And now he wanted a large sub.

Victor leaned over the countertop. "What's wrong, Jimmy?"

Jimmy gave Victor a look of confusion. "What're you talking about? I want an Italian combo. I'm a hungry man."

"That's not what I meant," Victor said. He gathered a soapy dish rag from a bucket under the counter and swept away a few crumbs he'd missed. "You've been hanging around here for hours. Why don't you go back home?"

Jimmy's balloon belly shook as he spoke. "I would, but the crazy bitch I married threw me out."

Victor nodded in understanding. Everyone in Stormville knew the wrath of Jimmy's second wife of twenty-three years. One time, Victor witnessed her beat the umpire's head in with her heavy purse because he declared her only son, Mick, out on his third strike. Mick was never allowed to play little league baseball again. He grew older and headed out west. Then there was the time she called the police on the fourth of July. The neighborhood had gathered in the local park to shoot fireworks, like they did every year when the cops showed up. They had to confiscate each firecracker, bottle rocket, Roman candle, and M80 in sight. Only in New York could such a tragedy occur. The sudden burst of memories came to a halt. Victor feigned a smile. "Fine, I'll make that combo for you, but you've got to leave after that, all right?"

Jimmy patted Victor on the cheek. "You're a good kid. It's no wonder Nick lets you run this place."

Victor cracked a slight grin. He grabbed a fresh rye sub roll and went to work. "You still like it the same as always, right?"

"Sure do. You make the best." Jimmy took a seat beside a stack of newspapers and stared out the window. "Nasty weather isn't it?"

"You bet," Victor agreed as he unraveled a chunk of provolone cheese. "I haven't seen this much rain since last week."

"I guess that's why they call it Stormville," Jimmy joked.

Victor faked a chuckle. He'd heard the joke one two many times. But he humored Jimmy with a nod. "Good one." Victor turned his attention to the meat slicer. Carefully, he placed the chunk of provolone on the slide and secured it with the barbed holder. He cut a quarter pound, thin sliced of course. Next he wrapped the cheese back up with clear plastic and put it back into the refrigerated case. Victor repeated the process for the sharp cheddar, salami, pepperoni, smoked turkey, and honey ham. He dressed the sub with pickles, lettuce, tomatoes, and then splashed on the oil and vinegar. "All done, Jimmy."

Jimmy dug his piggy fingers into his pocket and yanked out a faded twenty.

Victor shook his head as he wrapped the Italian combo in deli paper. "It's on the house."

Jimmy shoved the twenty onto the counter. "What're you trying to pull here? Is my money different from everybody else?"

"We'll call it a down payment then," Victor said with a sideways smile. "You've been entertaining the customers for hours. It's good for business. Now take your sub and get out of here."

Jimmy took his twenty back and put the Italian combo under his arm. "You're a good kid, Victor. I'll see your tomorrow." With a wave and a shuffle, Jimmy left Nick's Deli to be swallowed by the night.

"Bye," Victor waved. With the place finally empty, he busily worked to clean his mess; swiping handfuls of meat and cheese crumbs into the garbage can, then wiping down the slicer for the second time.

Thunder shook the Deli as the storm raged on. Victor jerked his head around in time to catch a flash of lightning race across the cloudy sky. In that moment, he caught sight of a humanoid shape, slowly dragging itself toward the deli's front door.

Victor darted around the counter and locked the door.

The shape lurched forward, not deterred in the least. It was a lithe figure with long wet hair and bright eyes.

"We're closed," Victor proclaimed. "Come back in the morning." He ignored the customer's advances and went back to his duties.

A soft tap rapped the entrance.

Victor pawed the .38 special under the counter. He'd never used the handgun before. His fingertips ran along the walnut stock.

The rapping came again.

"Go away," Victor said.

3

Two smooth hands pressed on the glass and a familiar voice beckoned. "Victor, I know you're in there. Come on and let me in."

Victor's hand fell away from the pistol. "Lynn? Is that you?" He stormed around the counter and peered through the door's thick glass. Lynn Watterson's bright blue eyes greeted him. She was soaked from head to toe.

Victor unlocked the door and stood back so she could enter.

"What are you doing here, Lynn?"

Upon entering, Lynn threw her arms around him and planted a kiss on his cheek. Her tight blue t-shirt and matching gym shorts were soaked, but underneath he felt a surge of warmth. "Thanks for letting me in."

"I didn't know it was you." Victor pulled away from her. "You're soaked."

Lynn brushed her long blonde locks behind her back. "Duh, it's pouring rain outside."

"I can see that." He locked the door behind her and went back to cleaning the meat slicer.

Lynn chased after him. "Do you need some help?"

"Sure," Victor replied and gave her a wet dish rag. "Wipe down the newsstand."

Lynn raised an eyebrow. "How 'bout a please?"

"Please wipe down the newsstand. I would really appreciate it."

Lynn blew him a kiss. "Thank you." She moved around the counter and ran the cloth over the metal stand. "You know I didn't come out here to do this, right?"

Victor was quiet for a moment. "Why did you come here?"

Lynn stopped cleaning. She spun about slowly and looked him in the eyes. "I wanted to talk to you."

Victor pressed the rag over the sharp blades of the slicer. He turned away from her. "I'm very busy."

"I know," Lynn pouted. "Every time I call you're never home. And when you are, your father always says you're asleep."

Victor nodded. "I work."

"And I go to college, but I still make time to see you."

Victor faced her. "What are you getting at, huh? You said we're just..."

"Friends." Lynn finished for him. "I know. But I've been doing a lot of thinking lately. I miss going out to eat with you. I miss our walks in the park. I just came here tonight to tell you that I care for you, too."

"But..."

Lynn put a hand on her hip. "There's no but. I want to be your girlfriend."

4

Victor swallowed a lump in his throat. He wanted to leap over the counter and kiss her, suck her warmth and love out in one long embrace. But his body was encased in iron. He didn't move an inch. "What about David?"

"What about him?"

"Aren't you two an item?" he asked with crossed arms.

"We were, sort of." She avoided his stare. "He asked me out to a few movies and I said yes. We never did anything. Then one day he tried to kiss me and I told him no."

"Ah," he said. "So you ran away."

Lynn shrugged. "He wasn't my type."

"And I am?"

She studied him for a long moment. "I was wrong about you. I came here tonight to apologize and ask if you'd like to be more than friends."

He put his dish rag in a dirty hamper. "Look, it's getting late. Why don't I walk you home?"

She frowned. "Don't I at least get a yes or no?"

"We'll talk on the way." He darted across the counter and opened the door for her. Outside, the rain struck the ground like a million pins.

"After you," he instructed.

"Thanks, are you sure that you don't have an umbrella back there somewhere?"

"Positive. Why didn't you drive?"

"I don't like to drive," she snapped.

Victor took the dirty rag from her grasp and tossed it onto the counter. "I don't like to work but I still do it."

Lynn stuck her tongue out at him. "It's healthy to walk anyway."

Victor closed and locked the deli's door behind them. The night was bitter, the cold snapping at his collar. "I'd rather not walk tonight," he said softly, more to himself than to her.

"I don't think you have a choice, mister." Lynn wrapped an arm about his waist. "Care to take me home?"

Victor saw a hint of mischief gleaming in her sea blue gaze. He blushed in the dark. "Sure."

Together they walked down a lone, curvy road. The rain pounded on their heads; the thunder crackled and snarled in the black sky above. But Victor and Lynn soon found themselves smiling at each other as they went.

"I can't believe you walked through this mess," he said.

"I wanted to see you," she said and squeezed his arm. "I really think I made a mistake in not taking you up on your offer before. I do want to be your girlfriend."

5

Victor gulped. His hands began to tremble. "What about your parents?"

Lynn's charming smile faded to a thin hard line. She stared at the twisted road ahead. "They said you're not ambitious enough. Boys your age should be in college."

"I didn't want to go," he said. "I'd rather go to the library and study alone than have some old fart teach me about something I'll never use in the real world."

Lynn tightened her grip on his arm. "And I understand that. But my parents don't."

"What's with them?"

"They want me to date lawyer's sons and med students. But I don't want that."

Victor laughed. "Do you want a deli manager?"

"No. I want you." She pressed her body close to his. She wrapped her arms around his neck and leaned in. "Kiss me, Victor."

And he did. Their embrace was a long one. The rain splattered like a song and the night was filled with renewed hope.

She pulled away first, then bit her lower lip and grinned. "I liked that."

As he eased into her, he kissed her again, deep and lovingly. The lightning flashed over the tree line, making her jump.

Victor chuckled and held her close. They melted into each other and hugged.

"I never want to let you go," he sighed. Her body was wet and warm in his arms.

"You don't have to," she whispered in his ear.

Lightning darted across the night, illuminating a farmer's field across the road.

Lynn tensed suddenly. "I think I saw someone watching us."

"Where?" Victor broke away from her and spun around. All he saw was darkness.

"Over there," she said and pointed toward the field off the road.

Victor peered into the inky blackness and caught sight of a vague humanoid shape. "Is someone there?"

Lynn was shaking in his grasp. "I don't like this at all."

The lightning blazed once again and the figure standing there had vanished.

Victor called out. "Jimmy? Is that you?" He waited for a reply. When none came, he took a few steps back.

"Who's Jimmy?" Lynn asked with a hysterical laugh.

"He's a local customer. I made him a sub. He left before you arrived." Victor took her by the hand. "I don't think that was him, though."

Thunder roared above them like an angry lion. Another bolt of lightning dazzled the dark clouds. And in the brief flash of light, the figure appeared again.

To their amazement it was closer this time.

Lynn's hand broke from Victor's as she fled down the road. He chased after her, glancing over his shoulder only to see the shadowy figure now standing in the rain in the middle of the road.

Their fleeting footsteps pounded on the concrete as they raced. The rain slapped at their faces as the storm carried on. Lynn was about ten feet from Victor when he called after her. "Lynn, I think he's gone, whoever he was."

She twisted her head to see him. "We're okay," she gasped, slowing down to a slow walk to wait for Victor to catch up. Her breath came out in heaves as she halted and wiped strains of golden wet hair away from her face.

Victor stopped beside her. He coughed twice, then filled his lungs with air. "I think we lost him."

"Who was that?"

Victor shrugged. "I don't know. I didn't get a good look."

"Neither did I." Lynn used the back of her hand to wipe her eyes. "I feel really silly right now."

"How come?" he pried.

"Because it's probably just Jimmy eating his sub in the field, or someone out for a midnight stroll in the rain."

Victor lifted his hands and water droplets tumbled off in beads. "But it's raining," he said, as though this explained everything.

She gave a girlish giggle and hugged him. "I just got scared, okay? Who goes for a walk in the rain in the middle of the night?"

Victor rubbed her backside. "That's okay." He cleared his throat. "If it makes any difference, I was a little shook up, too."

"A little?"

"Yeah," he replied. "Just a little."

Lynn nudged him with her elbow. "Come on, hero. Why don't you finish walking me home."

Victor's hand intertwined with hers. He gave her a quick kiss on the cheek, then they began the journey once again. In the distance, slithering footsteps followed after the couple.

Victor stopped abruptly. He and Lynn exchanged glances. He eased her down the dark road, wanting to keep going. "Let's keep moving."

But Lynn remained, her feet firmly planted on the slick concrete. "No. I want to see who it is."

Victor took her hand and pulled like a child eager to leave the church before mass was over. "I don't think that's wise. It could be a mugger."

Lynn giggled. "A mugger? Here, in Stormville? You've been watching one too many horror movies."

The footsteps became louder as the stranger got closer. Not far off, in the dying light of the thunder storm, a bipedal outline could be seen. Whoever it was wore ragged garments; trails of ripped pant legs blew in the wind like waving snakes. The figure came within twenty feet of the couple before disappearing into the gloom.

"Where'd he go?" asked Lynn.

Victor could feel her trembling. He put his free hand around her shoulder. "Jimmy!" he called out. "Is that you?"

A bolt of lightning stripped away the night sky, offering enough light to see the figure approach. It was a gaunt woman with chin length hair and glowing orbs for eyes. She stumbled as she lurched within reach of them.

Victor leaped back two feet, but Lynn remained rooted to the spot.

The woman dragged herself toward Lynn and groaned.

"Get away from her," Victor said in a harsh whisper. "There's something wrong with her."

Lynn took a step forward. She extended her hand to the woman's clay-colored face and ran a finger along her jaw line. The woman spread her mouth wide and gave a Cheshire cat smile. Her teeth were stained yellow and black.

Lynn jerked her hand away and squeezed her finger as though it were in horrible pain. Victor grabbed Lynn and shoved her in front of him.

"Run, now!" he yelled.

Lynn did as he instructed and fled into the night. Victor faced the twisted being in front of him. The wide smile on the woman's face had vanished. He stared into her sunken eyes.

"Stay away from me," he warned.

The woman moaned and lurched forward, reaching for him with a skeletal hand.

Victor dodged out of her way by a fraction. He spun around and ran after Lynn, not daring to look back, because if he did, he knew the dead woman would be there wearing that awful smile.

Chapter 2

Victor sat on Lynn's front porch, panting for breath. He forced air into his lungs and waited for the pounding in his chest to fade. Lynn leaned against the house with her eyes closed. Sweat and rain clung to her face and neck like she'd just finished running a marathon through a hurricane.

And she did, thought Victor as he rubbed his sore calves. His shirt, pants, shoes, and even socks were wet. He stared at Lynn; her golden hair was a tangled mess. Her t-shirt hung limp, and her right hand was grayish black. At first, Victor thought it was only a trick of the light, until she opened her eyes and slid her hand behind her back.

She looked at him for a moment before speaking. "Thanks for taking me home. I'm glad you were there."

"Yeah, no problem." Victor turned his attention to the road. "I think..."

Lynn's voice interrupted him like a sharp knife slipping between his ribs. "I don't want to talk about it. As far as I am concerned, we didn't see anything, okay?"

Victor snapped his mouth shut and gave a silent nod. He peered into the dark and wondered if it was looking back.

"I think I'll go home." He rose to leave but Lynn put a warm hand on his shoulder. "Did you want to talk some more?" he asked.

"No. I just want you here for a little while longer."

Victor held her close, but never took his attention from the patch of midnight beyond her front lawn; past the freshly mowed grass and hand painted mailbox where the darkness waited and grinned.

"Are you mad at me?" she asked.

"Why would I be?"

"It's just that...never mind. I don't want to talk about it." She broke away from him and rubbed her right hand. "I feel sick."

"Should I get your parents?"

She shook her head.

"Can I see your hand?"

Lynn took a step back. "It's sore." She cradled her hand to her breasts. "If I show it to you, do you promise you won't touch it?"

"I promise," Victor said. "Let me see it."

Lynn offered her hand to the porch light. It had the color of naked clay.

His mouth dropped. "We need to get you to a doctor."

"I'm fine." She tucked her hand behind her back. "The soreness is going away."

"Is that the hand you touched the woman with?"

"Look, Victor, it's getting late. I think you should go now."

He frowned. "Can I call you tomorrow?"

Her upper lip curled. "Do you still have my phone number?"

"I do. You wrote it on a napkin in black ink."

Lynn leaned into him. "Well, in that case, you can call me anytime." She gave him a lasting kiss, and stumbled to the front door.

"Are you sure you'll be okay?"

She directed her attention to a sudden burst of light from the living room window. "That's my mom. You'd better go; quickly before she sees you."

Victor gave her a kiss. He knew better than to stick around any longer. "Take care of yourself."

"I will. Goodnight." She pulled a set of keys from her pocket, unlocked the front door, and stepped inside.

Victor watched her go. He stood in the porch light's glow, looking at the road ahead. His house was a ten minute walk through steep hills and blind curves. He stepped off the porch and into the rain. He left Lynn's gravel driveway at a slow gait, and picked up his pace when his feet struck pavement.

The porch light faded behind, enveloping him in a sightless blanket of swaying trees and darkness. He walked for a time until he heard footsteps not of his own.

Then he ran.

Chapter 3

Kirsten Tucker peered through the backseat window of a Subaru Forester and watched the rain storm in awe. Lightning blazed across the dark sky in dazzling yellows and whites; the rain fell hard and fast, clinging to ancient trees taller than she'd ever seen before. Kirsten combed back her long, jet black hair and smiled at the night.

This place was a fresh start. A new beginning. A town where nobody knew her past and she could work on her future. Kirsten crossed her legs and pulled down her short pleated skirt. She silently cursed herself for getting dressed up in her gothic slut outfit: combat boots, fishnet stockings, short skirt, and a black tank top that showed off her belly button piercing. But, then again, one never knows when Mr. Right could come galloping along on his white horse. She laughed to herself. At age twenty, she didn't care if he came riding a donkey. As long as he was handsome and knew how to respect her. Kirsten went back to watching the storm. The towering trees swayed overhead like walking giants as her father sped down Route 52.

"Slow down," Lisa said, Kristen's stepmother as she gripped the dashboard. "Or pull over somewhere until it stops raining." Lisa wrapped her arms around her waist as though she was cold. "You're scaring me, Trevor."

"It's only a little shower. I've driven through worse." Trevor turned to Kirsten for a split second. "Do you remember our vacation in the Catskills?"

Kirsten gave him a knowing smile. "How could I forget? You drove through that hurricane with no trouble."

Trevor laughed. "That's my girl. You didn't complain once the entire trip."

"I was only five," Kirsten replied.

Lisa tapped her husband on the arm, and then pointed to the road ahead. "Focus on the road."

Trevor's grin faded. He braced the steering wheel and tried not to go over the white line on the road. He was a tall muscular man at fifty-four. His gray hair was slicked back like Eddie Munster, and he wore prescription glasses on a prominent Italian nose. "I can't believe I'm moving back home after all these years."

Lisa rubbed his leg with a finely manicured nail. She leaned her slim body against the passenger seat in an attempt to relax. "It's definitely not like Knoxville."

Kirsten almost snapped at her but bit her tongue instead. She'd lived fourteen years in Knoxville, Tennessee, and six in Stormville, New York. Though the memories of her childhood days in New England eluded her at times, she was pretty sure Stormville had been better than Knoxville.

The small city was bitter with raging football fans parading around in bright orange hats, shirts, car flags, and anything else a price tag could fit on. Not that football bothered her, or the fans, it was the drunken frat boys sporting orange shirts calling her 'Baby' that she hated. Her mind drifted to the night her best friend Kelly dragged her to a party at The Fort. There were all sorts of guys hitting on them when they entered. One even slapped Kelly on the butt. Kelly giggled at the gesture and went about drinking from a keg. Kirsten never drank. She had once in her teen years when Kelly broke into her parent's liquor cabinet, but she didn't enjoy the taste, or the after effects. At The Fort, everyone was drinking, and nobody wore black. Kirsten was out of place there. She tried to find Kelly after a frat boy laughed at her, but her best friend was lost in the crowd. Kirsten poked her head in nearly every room when a large man grabbed her by the hair and tossed her into one. They were alone. He locked the door and went for her. Kirsten yelped and screamed, but the man clamped her mouth shut with a giant palm, then ripped her shirt off and fondled her breasts. That's when Kirsten knew she'd be raped unless she tried everything she could to escape. She kicked, bit, and shrieked through his mighty grip, but the man was too strong and pinned her down on the bed. He was unbuttoning her pants when Kirsten found a pencil amidst the dirty sheets. It had no tip, but she put the writing tool to work. With one quick jerk of her hand, Kirsten thrust the pencil into the man's ear until it was embedded halfway in his canal. He immediately screamed and let her go. Kirsten raced out of the room, out of The Fort, and drove herself back home. She never went to another party again. Kelly called her two days later and said she was sorry, that she didn't know. It ended up she was giving blowjobs to men in the bathroom that night.

Kirsten crossed her arms in the backseat and sighed. "I never liked Knoxville anyway."

Her father smirked.

Lisa gave a little pout. "It was a home. Don't you think you'll miss it?"

"No. I have Dad and you. What's to miss? Going to a different church every Sunday? God knows there's only about five on every street."

Trevor laughed. "We just wanted you to get a taste of each religion. Now you can pick one for yourself."

"What fun," Kirsten said. "I think I'll take the middle path."

"Don't worry," Lisa said. "It won't be hard to choose in New York. You're either Catholic or Jewish."

"Or Buddhist," Trevor added. He pulled down a lonely back road and decreased speed. "We're almost there."

Kirsten pressed her nose to the glass. "Where's Dead House?"

"It's here somewhere," answered Trevor.

Lisa gave a confused look to her husband. "What's Dead House?"

"It was built by a medical doctor who used the house as a temporary morgue for the town."

Lisa watched the dense forest whip by. "Why would they do that?"

"The town or the doctor?" Kirsten asked, as she searched for the mansion through the rain.

"Be nice," Trevor instructed.

"The doctor did it as a favor to Stormville because Dead House isn't really a house; it's a four-story mansion."

Lisa nodded in conversation but she really didn't seem to be paying attention. "You seem to know a lot about this place," Lisa said.

"It's haunted by ghosts," Trevor said.

"Really? I should've known," Lisa taunted and shook her head. "You need a boyfriend, Kirsten."

"No thanks. I'd rather have an education and a job to support myself than some guy always trying to get into my pants."

Lisa chuckled.

"Honey," said her father. "There's a nice boy out there for you some-where."

"Anyway," sighed Kirsten as she changed the subject. "Dead House was where you went to before the cemetery. People say it's haunted because a few of the bodies disappeared before burial."

"How nice," Lisa said. "And where is this place located?"

Trevor spoke before Kirsten could. "Only a few miles down the road. A family lives there now." He patted his wife's thigh and gave her a wink.

"When were you two going to tell me this?"

"Busted," Kirsten laughed

Trevor's made a frown. "It's nothing to be worried about dear. Just a little house in the country." He drove through a bend in the road and came upon the beginnings of a ten foot high, chain-link fence. "We must be getting close."

Kirsten sucked in her breath as the road curved. The car sped on-ward.

13

Dead House rose from the forest like the neglected tombstone of a slain elder god. Kirsten could make out the side of the stone structure just before her father made a sharp right. "Hey, drive back please."

"Not tonight," Trevor said. "You'll have plenty of time to look at it later. We do live here now, you know."

Kirsten slumped in her seat. "I know." She crossed her arms and caught candle light flickering in one of the windows.

Trevor drove faster and Dead House was gone, swallowed by the dark and rain. "Our house is down Ritter Road." He made another right turn. "Are you paying attention, dear? You'll be driving down these streets tomorrow."

Kirsten feigned a smile. She gazed out the window and wondered what life would be like in this small town.

Chapter 4

Randolph Leeds was one-eyed, crippled in both legs, and angry as hell. He sat in his wheelchair, studying germ strains in the basement, what his son referred to as the deep dungeon, when the doorbell rang. He jerked his head from the microscope at the sound. "Victor! Answer the door."

The doorbell rang again and again, like a hammer falling on solid steel.

When his son didn't reply, Randolph knew his son had fallen asleep in his bedroom; which was a bad sign, as he hadn't slept there since the sudden death of his mother ten years ago. Randolph called for Victor one last time, and unsuccessful, he wheeled to the intercom and broadcasted his voice through all four floors of Dead House. "Victor, this is your wake up call. Be a good boy and go answer the door before I go out there with a bat."

The doorbell still continued to ring.

"Dammit!" Randolph wheeled out of the basement and onto the ramp. He stopped at the service elevator and got in. "Damn that boy." He pounded his fist onto the button for the third floor. The elevator shuttered then slowly rose. He cracked his knuckles. He could still hear that droning, ringing sound throbbing in his head. It was akin to listening to that God-awful music his son listened to every night.

What was it called again? Beats? No. Techno, or trance, some garbage like that, he thought.

The elevator doors parted and Randolph wheeled himself to the front door. Through the barred window at the side of the door, he could see a tall woman and a man, the couple both dressed in black; their faces wore the pain of a thousand deaths. The pale-faced woman stabbed a long finger against the doorbell.

Randolph unlocked the door and spat at them. "What the hell do you think you're doing? I'm not deaf, you know."

The man and woman wore surprised expressions. The woman leaned over. "I'm sorry to trouble you, sir. Is this the home of Victor Leeds?"

Randolph raised an eyebrow. "Depends, what do you want?"

The woman tried to speak but her voice broke. "My..."

A large hand fell on her shoulder.

The man, gray-haired and worn, spoke softly. "Our daughter died this morning. She came home last night after visiting Victor at the deli. We just wanted to speak with him."

Randolph nodded. "How'd you get in? I've got a gate, you know."

The woman began to sob.

"It was open," said the man. He held onto his wife and let her cry on his shoulder.

Randolph glanced past the couple and saw that his front gate was indeed open and unlocked. "Damn that boy." He swung open the front door. "Why don't you two come inside while I fetch him."

"We don't want to bother you, Mr..."

"Randolph Leeds." He offered his hand in greeting.

"I'm Jack Watterson, and this is my wife, Rosemary." The man shook Randolph's hand as his wife turned away.

"Well, come in already," Randolph said. "Have a seat in the living room and I'll be right back." He directed the couple to a large red couch and wheeled back to the elevator, glancing up to the ceiling as he rolled along.

"You'd better hope you're in your room boy, or they'll be hell to pay."

*   *   *

Victor was sound asleep in his childhood bed when a loud rapping shook the bedroom door. He wiped the yellow crust from his eyes and slipped out of the small bed. After finding his way home the night before, Victor went to his old bedroom, let his feet dangle off the edge, and laid awake inhaling memories from the past. His boyhood football trophy still sat on his wooden desk along with action figures of Anakin Skywalker and Darth Maul. Posters of Transformers and X-men adored every wall. And the portrait of his mother, her brown hair and blue eyes watching over him as the sandman took him away to the land of dreams.

"Victor! Open this door!"

Victor rolled out of bed only to find he'd fallen asleep with his clothes on. A groan escaped his dry lips as he stood up and went to open the door.

His father stared up at him with his single eye. He spoke in a calm and sad voice. "So...you are in here."

"Yeah, well. I wanted to be."

His father turned away. "I'd never thought you'd sleep in here again."

"I needed too. I'm sorry, Dad. I just. . ."

Randolph raised a hand to silence him. "There're some people downstairs who want to see you. Do you want me to run them off?"

"Who are they?" Victor yawned and stretched his stiff limbs.

His father's old anger came back. "How am I supposed to know? They're in the living room; said something about you being with their daughter last night."

Victor's back went ridged. "Oh, no. Lynn's mom?"

"Some guy, too. They look really upset. I'll go with you." Randolph wheeled down an adjacent hallway. "Wash your face first. You look like someone smeared mud on it."

Victor eased from the bedroom and went to the bathroom. He could hear his father grumbling as he forced the wheelchair into the elevator. Victor splashed his face with cold water, then followed after him; the entire time a tight knot formed in his lower belly.

Lynn's parents were here to see him. What could they possibly want? To harass him about being with their only daughter no doubt. But when Victor approached the couple, he knew this wasn't the case. Jack Watterson and his wife were dressed in black. Dark shadows clung about them like a rain cloud ready to burst open. Lynn's mother, Rosemary, held her head on her husband's shoulder, and when she looked up, her face was harsh and full of vigor.

"There he is. There's the murderer."

Victor stopped short. "What?"

Rosemary rose from the couch and raced for him. "You killed my daughter! You killed her!"

Victor stumbled backward from her advances as he caught sight of his father leaving the room. "I didn't kill anyone. I saw your daughter last night. I walked her home."

"In the rain! What kind of stupid boy are you? She got sick and died because of you." Rosemary launched herself at him with her long black nails. Victor grabbed her hands by the wrists and wouldn't let her move.

"Lynn's dead? Is that what you just said?" Victor asked.

Rosemary screamed and thrashed in his grip like a hooked shark.

Her husband barreled forward and pulled her away from Victor. "That's enough!" He held onto her as sobs assailed her body. He matched eyes with Victor. "Why did you make her go out in the rain?"

"I...I didn't." Victor's voice betrayed him. Tears streaked down his cheeks. "She's really...dead?"

Rosemary shrieked. "Yes, she's dead, you bastard! You killed my daughter!"

The blast of a shotgun deafened the room as bits of plaster fell from the ceiling. Randolph Leeds wheeled himself into the living room with a double barrel directed at the ceiling. "I think you two should leave."

Jack Watterson's eyes widened at the sight of the shotgun. He silently nodded and ushered his wife out of the front door, the couple quickening their pace as they left the property. Rosemary looked back and captured Victor's attention. "I'll be back! Do you hear me? I'll be back!"

Randolph fired off another round into the air and the two ran off. "Crazy bitch! Stay off my land!" He jerked his single eye at Victor. "What was she babbling about, huh?"

"Lynn. She's dead. I just saw her last night." A wave of shock froze Victor in place. He closed his eyes and fought back his sorrow.

Randolph patted him on the back. "Dead, huh? It's okay to cry about that, son. Why don't you lock the gate up and get some rest."

Victor's lower lip trembled so he bit it. He walked into the morning sunlight and down the cracked driveway.

Lynn. Beautiful, carefree, Lynn was dead. The thought was a dagger in his heart. He'd loved her. He'd kissed her. And now she was gone. Victor rubbed his eyes. He noticed a patch of disturbed earth on the lawn. The grass was withered and large clumps of soil were heaped in a pile, but there was no sign of any digging tools or equipment. It was as though the ground had simply erupted. He pushed the image of mutilated earth and upturned soil away. *Lynn's lithe body will be put in dirt just like that.*

"Food for the worms," his mother once told him. Victor pressed on. He walked to the end of the driveway, grabbed the gate, and swung it shut.

Lynn's parents were drifting down the road, Rosemary clutching her husband like he was a life raft. Victor watched the couple until they vanished, then he went back to his room to be alone with his grief.

Chapter 5

While Victor Leeds sat on his childhood bed and wondered how God could take away someone as kind and full of promise as Lynn; Kirsten Tucker was on a quest in her new home. Three stories of unexplored territory lay at her feet. She strapped on her combat boots, put her long black hair into a pony tail, and in faded blue jeans and a lacy black t-shirt, she set about her task.

The interior of the house was cold and stale compared to her old home in Knoxville. Instead of carpet, she now had hardwood floors. The kitchen was smaller and with fewer cupboards. And every window view was of a lush, untouched forest. Kirsten started in the kitchen. Her stepmother and father were out grocery shopping, so she knew the refrigerator was bare. The kitchen led to the dining room where a large glass chandelier dangled. Kirsten flipped the switch on the wall and only half of the lights flickered.

"Great," she muttered and walked through the large empty space of the living room. The movers said they'd be coming at one in the afternoon, by her watch they were late by twenty minutes. She couldn't wait to fill their new home with furniture, a blaring television, computers, and décor. The more she explored the more she felt like she was looking at the fleshless skeleton of a skinny guy. Her boots echoed down the hall and creaked as she raced upstairs.

Three bedrooms, one with pink walls, the other in blue were enormous and devoid of humanity. She'd claimed the biggest room last night and fell asleep on her air mattress while listening to crickets and owls. For a moment, she had pictured herself in her old bedroom in a deep slumber, only when she awoke did she realize she'd staked the pink room as her own. And pink was not her favorite color, by far. Her father's laughter had bounced around upstairs like a phantom's howl. Kirsten shrugged. She didn't plan on living here long. At twenty years old and with an Associate Degree in English from Roane State, she wanted out. When the computer was set up she'd hop on the internet and find the closest university to flee to. Not that her new home was that bad, but she needed a place of her own, away from her loving father and pushy stepmother. And Kirsten was sure they wanted some time to themselves anyway. But for the time being this house and its pink bedroom were hers.

She checked out all the closets and the bathroom's medicine cabinet, but discovered nothing of interest. She went back downstairs and unlocked the basement door. As far as she knew, nobody had ventured down there since her father had checked out the house months before. The minute she swung the basement door open, a stale stench like that of moldy books stung her nostrils. She coughed and flipped on the nearest light switch but nothing happened. She went upstairs, searched through her luggage and found a flashlight. She tested it on her bedroom closet first; the small light came on with a push of the plastic tab. Satisfied, she bounded back downstairs and ventured into the basement.

Her light shone on a narrow passage fitted with wooden stairs and flanked by cobweb-strung brick walls. She tried the first step and the wood sagged slightly under her one hundred and twenty pound frame, but didn't give way. She went down the staircase slowly, and when she reached the bottom, her heart was throbbing.

"That wasn't so bad," she said to herself. The flashlight scanned over stacks of cardboard boxes, an old pool table, piles of random paperback books, and a blue dress. She circled around the heap of boxes and ran a fingertip along the edge of the pool table. Her finger came back imprinted with a dust smudge.

"Gross," she said and wiped it off on the blue dress. Unlike everything else within the confines of the damp basement walls, the dress wore no sign of age. As Kirsten drew closer, the soft fabric took on shape and form. Where flat silk and white lace connected a smooth arm took shape, then long legs touched the ground, and a head of black hair darker than hers grew within seconds.

Kirsten screamed, but no sound escaped her mouth. The blue dress took on the shape of a lithe female form. She could see her arms and flawless legs, but the head was entangled in dark hair. The flashlight shook in her hand. Kirsten fought the urge to run, so instead she took two steps forward.

The woman in the blue dress raised her head and then Kirsten did scream, because it was a fleshless skull. Long arms shot out at her. *"Kirsten, my darling, it's been so long."*

"Nooooo!" Kirsten shrieked as withered hands curled about her neck. She could feel the putrid stench of a thousand years decay pour out of its hollow mouth. Kirsten jerked her body and swung the flashlight repeatedly into the phantom's backside.

"Honey, that's no way to treat your mother."

"Let me go!" Kirsten cried.

Footsteps shook the ceiling above her as dust rained down on her head. The basement door was swung open with a crash. "Kirsten? Are you down here?"

"Dad, help me!" She thrashed in the woman's grip but couldn't manage to pry herself free.

Within moments her father was racing toward her. "Honey? What's going on?"

Kirsten realized she was screaming and stopped. The blue dress hung around her like an aloof lover devoid of life, empty.

She batted the garment away, ran by her father and upstairs.

But even as she did, telling herself she had imagined it, the voice of the woman echoed in her head.

It was indeed that of her mother.

*　　*　　*

"Here, take some of these." Trevor held out three purple pills to his daughter and a tall glass of water.

Kirsten lay sideways on the mattress in her pink room. She twisted herself from him and faced the wall.

"Sweetie, it's for your own good," her father pressed.

"Leave me alone."

Trevor sat down on the mattress and rubbed her shoulders. "Now you know I can't do that. You're my daughter and I love you."

"I love you too, Dad, but go away. I don't want any pills."

"Kirsten, we've been over this before."

"I know. I'm tired of taking pills for everything. If I'm sad I take a pill. If I'm stressed I take a pill. If I'm in pain I take a pill. I'm so damn sick of it. I'd rather let my body and mind heal by themselves. Maybe I'm sad, stressed out, or in pain for a reason and I should deal with it instead of swallowing another stupid pill."

Trevor took his hand off her shoulder. He placed the glass of water on the floor. "I understand, honey. I really do. But you need these pills. Everyone goes through rough times when they need medicine, but very few people see their dead mother in the basement of their new home."

Kirsten let two tears trickle down her cheeks. "Her face was a skull this time."

"A skull..." Trevor trailed off.

"Yeah, that's a good sign, right? I mean, she always comes to me whole like she once was. Maybe she'll eventually just shrivel down to nothing and disappear."

Trevor wrapped his arms around his beloved daughter and held her tight. "It wasn't your fault. I know that you blame yourself, but I don't

21

understand why? We've seen so many doctors and head shrinks, suffered all the tests, and nothing has changed, has it?"

Kirsten sniffed. "I'm sorry, Dad. I'm so sorry." She burst into tears.

Trevor let her cry. He curled her up into his chest as he did when she was a child, rocking her back and forth.

"I miss her," Kristen said, laughing and crying at the same time. "Lisa is okay but I really miss Mom."

"I miss her, too." Trevor clenched his jaw and sealed his eyes, forcing the pain in his heart to wither down to a dull throb.

"She was my best friend. Remember that time when we got ice cream and I dropped mine," she asked.

Her father gave a little smirk. "I wasn't going to share with you."

"Mom did."

"She had a good heart. And she loved you very much."

"But I couldn't save her. It was my fault. I wrecked the car and couldn't help her."

Trevor raised his hand to silence her. "You did your best."

"No I didn't. I should've..."

"Enough. I'm not talking about this anymore," he said.

Kirsten swept away from him and crossed her arms. "Fine."

"You aren't responsible for what happened and that's that. Now take your medicine please and get some rest."

"I don't need it."

"Kirsten, you do need it. And if you don't take it like you should, then how do you plan on attending a university?"

Kirsten sighed. She rolled over. "Fine, I give." She took the pills from his hand and washed them down with a glass of water. Then she closed her eyes and lay on her back. "Now leave me alone."

Trevor kissed her forehead. "Thank you, sweetie. Things will get better, I promise." He rose from the mattress and went to the door. "Lisa and I are having lunch in a little while if you want to join us?"

She didn't respond immediately. She cupped her hands over her stomach and breathed in deeply. "No thanks. I want some time alone."

"Okay." Trevor shut her door and went downstairs to the kitchen. He heard Lisa using the can opener. When he reached her, he found three plates set out on the counter. "Kristen won't be joining us. She needs her rest," he said.

Lisa nodded as though she'd heard this response before. She poured excess water from a can of tuna into the sink. "Did she take her medicine?"

Trevor leaned against the refrigerator. "Yeah, but not without an argument."

Lisa emptied the tuna fish into a serving bowl. "Can you hand me the mayonnaise and relish?"

"Sure." Trevor reached into the fridge and grabbed the two items. "I'm worried sick about her. These...images, visions, or whatever the hell they are, set my nerves on edge."

Lisa rubbed his back and confiscated the relish and mayonnaise from him. "Have you thought about it?"

"About what?"

"What we talked about last night."

Trevor slammed the refrigerator door. "I'm not locking her up in a damn crazy bin. She's my daughter. Not some wacko."

Lisa continued making the tuna fish sandwiches, never looking him in the eye. She reached for the Jewish rye bread. "Would you like yours toasted or not?"

"You think she's crazy don't you?"

"I don't think that. But she does need *professional help*, dear?" Lisa asked.

Trevor heaved his chest outward and crossed his arms. "Professional help." He lingered on the words like they were a deadly poison. "Let me tell you something about professional help. I took Kirsten through a long series of shrinks and doctors with lots of special papers on their walls from where ever. They drugged her, made her draw pictures, and said she needed this or more of that. One night, she climbed on the roof of our old house and tried to jump off. By chance I saw her standing there. She said she hated being probed by all the doctors, hated their large stale offices, cozy couches, and unwavering voices. They couldn't help her so she wanted to jump. I promised her we wouldn't see anymore doctors then, and that I'd take care of her." Trevor cleared his throat. "She said okay. I kept my promise. We never saw another doctor again."

Lisa had watery eyes. "You never told me this."

"She didn't want me to."

"Why?"

"She didn't want you to feel sorry for her," Trevor answered. He sank against the fridge and sighed. "I love my daughter, Lisa. And I respect her for not jumping off that roof. Had our positions been changed, I think I would've taken the fall. I don't see how she can deal with those haunts, those visions."

Lisa put two slices of bread on a pair of plates, then added the tuna. "She's a strong girl. I love her, too. But I'm thinking of the future. You can't take care of her forever. What happens when you pass and she has nobody to help her?"

Trevor's upper lip rose. "She'll always have someone to turn to. People, even strangers, help one another everyday. I'll make sure she has proper care."

"And what about us? I want to retire one day. Sip a few margaritas on the beach with you by my side. Just you and me."

Trevor ran his fingers through his hair in frustration. "We'll worry about that when it happens."

Lisa finished making the sandwiches. She gathered the plates and faced her husband. "I won't wait for you, Trevor. I've been hurt before and I don't intend to be hurt again."

"She'll overcome this. I have faith in my daughter. Why don't you?"

Lisa closed her eyes and shook her head. She forced the tuna sandwich on Trevor. "Here's lunch."

Trevor took the plate. "Thank you."

Lisa put her plate down on the counter. She walked out of the kitchen, swaying her arms.

"Aren't you going to eat that?"

"I'm not hungry," she said and disappeared out the back door.

Trevor took a bite of the tuna sandwich; the mix of relish, mayonnaise, and tuna was delicious.

He ate lunch in silence and stared at the kitchen wall.

Chapter 6

Victor sat on his front porch with a cold glass of lemonade. The water beads from the cup rolled over his hand and splashed on the concrete between his feet. Victor hadn't taken a sip from the glass in over an hour. He simply sat on the porch and watched the living world pass him by. Far in the distance, children played, their gleeful laughter drifting on the summer wind. The afternoon sun was making its way west over the mountains, and it filtered through the twisted oaks lining Dead House. He soaked it all in, trying to drown himself, but the children's laughter faded, as did the light. He brushed off a fire ant climbing up his forearm, then set his drink down as he heaved a long sigh. In his mind, he wanted to scream.

Didn't the world know Lynn was dead? Didn't the children and the sun? Did God? Or did they know and not really care. Life goes on forever doesn't it? Victor pressed his palms to the sides of his throbbing skull.

"Lynn," he whispered.

Behind him, the front door swung open. Randolph rolled his wheelchair out, stopping short of the porch steps. "Another sunny day," he sneered.

"Yeah," Victor said.

"Don't take it too hard. It'll rain again soon."

Victor slumped forward. "It was raining when Lynn and I kissed last night."

His father cast his only eye downward. "She meant that much to you?"

Victor caught a tear dribbling down his cheek and quickly brushed it aside. "She did. I loved her. I loved her for a long time."

Randolph nodded, his features taking on a harder edge. "I won't lie to you, son. That pain in your heart won't ever heal. It's like when your mother had disc surgery on her back. She was never the same again." Randolph placed a hand on Victor. "All you can do is remember the good times and go on with your life as best you can. And if you cry, then cry. If you laugh, then really laugh." He took his hand back. "I'll be here for you, son. That is until I die myself." Randolph gave a throaty laugh.

Victor found himself laughing, too. "Dad, don't say things like that. I'm sad enough right now."

"Nothing lasts forever, son, except that damn shining sun."

Victor shook his head. He rose from the porch and gave his father a hug. "Thanks, Dad."

"Sure thing. Now wheel me back inside, would you? I think I heard the phone ringing."

Victor picked up his lemonade and placed it in the wheelchair's cup holder. The he pushed his father back inside, locking the door behind them.

Randolph spun the wheels of his chair and sped into the living room. He snatched up the phone with one hand and seethed into the receiver. "Who's there?"

Victor's stomach turned. He had a feeling the phone call was for him, and nothing good would come of it. He headed for the stairs and had reached the fourth step when his father called out. "Victor. You've got a phone call."

"Great," Victor muttered as he clomped down the stairs and into the living room where his father held out the phone for him. "Who is it?"

"Why don't you ask him yourself," Randolph spat and handed the phone over.

Victor pressed the phone to one ear and spoke into the receiver. "Hello?"

A gruff male answered. "Is this Victor?"

"Yes it is. Who is this?"

"This is Jack, Lynn's father. I was calling to apologize for this morning. I'm terribly sorry about everything. Especially the way my wife acted."

Victor cleared his throat and didn't respond for a moment. He took a deep breath and spoke calmly. "I didn't kill your daughter, sir. After I walked her home she said she wasn't feeling well, but I never expected her to die."

"Neither did I, or my wife," Jack said. He blew his nose into the phone.

Victor could picture the large man standing in the kitchen with his shirt unbuttoned and tears pouring down his cheeks. The large father figure reduced to a shaking, crying thing. Victor held back his own sadness.

"I'm sorry for your loss, sir. I loved her. And I asked her to be my girl-friend last night. She said yes."

Jack blew his nose again before speaking. "I've never had a problem with you, Victor. I've seen you open and close the deli nearly everyday on my way to and from work. You're a good kid. I can see why she said yes."

The pain in Victor's stomach sank even lower. He found himself nearly breaking down on the phone. "Thanks."

Jack coughed a few times. "I'd like you to come to the funeral."

"What about your wife?" Victor asked. The question spilled out of him like a poisonous copperhead waiting to strike.

"She's not very fond of you I'm afraid. But I know Lynn would want you to be there."

"I'll think about it," Victor said.

"It's going to be held at the cemetery in Carmel."

"The one across from McDonalds; yeah, I know the place. Thanks for calling."

"I'm sorry again for all the trouble we caused. Please come. It would mean so much to me and my wife."

Maybe he was telling the truth, Victor thought, but he knew Lynn's mom wouldn't be too pleased if he went, no matter what Jack told him now.

"We'll see," Victor said. They said their goodbyes and Victor hung up the phone. He'd felt like he'd just got knocked around by Mike Tyson. His stomach ached, his arms began shaking, his back felt sore, and his heart pounded.

He went to the refrigerator for a glass of milk. When he reached in and found the smooth white container, an image of last night came into focus. The dark figure of the woman that had stood before Lynn, peering at her through twin orbs far back in the decaying skull. The woman's skin was the same color as milk, almost like unmolested clay, like a corpse. Lynn had reached out and touched that pale flesh, and now she was dead. Victor shut the refrigerator door. His stomach gave a gut wrenching churn.

That walking corpse last night had followed them. Lynn touched it, and the corpse had grinned. Victor shook the image away. He recalled how Lynn's hand turned the same color of that thing. But Victor didn't want to think about that so he marched toward his sleeping quarters. Not where he'd slept the night before, but where he'd laid his head for the last ten years. Stepping inside his bedroom, he paused. His desk was lying on its side, various works of fantasy from Terry Brooks, C.S Lewis, and J.R.R Tolkien were scattered across the floor. He backed out of his room and ran to the basement door, then down the stairs.

"Dad?"

No answer emitted from the deep dungeon, only the constant drip of a leaky faucet and the occasional squeaking mouse.

Victor leaped over the last five steps. When his feet pounded the basement floor, he heard a door creak shut.

"Dad? Are you down here?" His feet crunched on a crumpled piece of paper with ink drawings and runes inscribed in the margins. He continued, only to discover a long trail of discarded, hand written notes and computer print outs leading to his father's work room. Victor clenched his fists and fought the urge to run back upstairs. He stepped on the papers and walked into his father's office. The dangling light bulb illuminated a broken chair, shattered beakers, and no sign of his father.

He searched under the desk and in the closet, but only found rat traps and a ragged coat. Something had happened when he was on the phone with Lynn's dad. A robber or vagrant had broken into the house and kidnapped or murdered Randolph Leeds.

"No... it can't be." Victor clawed the side of his head. "He has to be here somewhere." He stormed out of the work study, to then search every inch of the basement, as he worked his way upstairs. Dead House remained a dark, empty shell. After two hours of running through the house Victor slumped over on the couch.

It was true, his father had vanished.

* * *

"I'm going out," Kirsten called as she held the door open with her right black combat boot.

"Okay, honey," her father answered from somewhere in the house. "Don't get lost, and be back before nightfall."

"I will. I love you, Dad. Bye Lisa." Kirsten closed the door and walked into a breezy afternoon. Her long hair flowed in waves behind her. She quickly tied it into a pony tail and walked by the movers. They'd arrived over an hour ago, two men in a gray truck. One man was dark skinned and thin, while the other man was white and overweight. Both of them stared at her as she passed. Kirsten ignored them. She lowered her black skirt, making sure it was covering her underwear.

The black man whistled. "Hey, girl, where do you think you're going?"

Kirsten continued on her way. "Out, so fuck off."

The white man chuckled. He set down a large box marked for the kitchen. "She's sure got a mouth on her, Lenny."

"Damn, right," Lenny said. "I bet she knows how to use it, too."

The white guy laughed harder. "Hey, girl, why don't you come over here and give us a hand on this job." He made a jerking motion to his crouch.

Kirsten quickened her pace. Her hand slipped to the small of her back where she stored a long knife. "What did you say, asshole?"

Lisa's voice fell on the conversation like a judge's gaffe. She stood in the garage with a wood handled axe. "Is there a problem here, boys?"

The two men saw her hard stare, then the axe. Lenny shook his head. "No problem at all, miss. We were just finishing up."

Lisa rolled the axe in her palms. "Good." She took a step toward them. "I think you two have done enough for today. Why don't you put the rest of those boxes in the garage and leave."

Both men agreed and went back to work.

Lisa lowered the axe as she walked by the men without a glance.

"Thanks," Kirsten said and meant it.

"Don't mention it." Lisa set the axe beside a slender birch tree. "A word of advice."

Kirsten leaned in.

"Dressing like that will only attract the wrong kind of guys."

Kirsten rolled her eyes. "It's hot outside. I'm wearing my skirt. Is that okay?"

"It would be if that skirt wasn't ten inches above your knees. And your pink underwear is showing."

Kirsten's fists tightened. "You're not my mom. I'll wear whatever I please."

"You're not decent. If you're trying to impress a guy by wearing those clothes, all you'll get is scum like them." Lisa motioned to the movers with her middle finger. "A nice guy would either be too embarrassed or think you're a slut." Lisa sighed. "You're a pretty girl. And smart. You don't need to show off like this."

Kirsten seethed through her teeth. "I'm grown up. I can make my own decisions. In four months I'll be twenty-one." Kirsten stormed past her. "And maybe I don't want a nice guy. What's he going to do for me? Nice guys put up with everyone's shit. Why would I want a weakling like that?"

Lisa picked up the axe. "Fine, do what you want. You're right, I'm not your damn mother," she hissed.

"No, you're not. And I don't need your help either so back off." Kirsten stormed down the driveway, kicking small rocks as she went.

Lisa closed her eyes and huffed. When she opened them, her stepdaughter was gone. "Just a little while longer," she said to herself.

Lisa raised the axe above her head and brought it down on the birch tree, making a large gash. Two more strokes and the tree fell over.

* * *

"Damn, bitch," Kirsten cursed as she walked down the lonely street. The road was curvy and not well paved. She kept her head lowered, muttering curses as she quickened her stride. Every now and then she lifted her head to the sound of a hooting owl or woodpecker.

The sunny afternoon was eaten by darkness before her eyes. Undeterred, she marched onward, passing houses set far back in the woods, singing creeks, and a moss-covered shed.

"How could she say that?" she asked herself. She had no idea where she was going nor did she care. "I'm not sluttish looking. Maybe a little Goth, but not sluttish." Kirsten felt a cold breeze of air slide across her naked thighs. She braced herself from the cold and walked on until darkness swallowed her. Her thoughts were jumbled: Lisa's comments, the movers, and the vision of her dead mother, played in her head like a deck of cards scattered on the floor.

The day had started off so fresh and full of hope only to end in turmoil. She held in a scream of frustration. What was Lisa thinking? Didn't she have enough problems? She wrapped her arms around herself. She was just about to head back home when a terrible moan came from the sparse field to her right. She froze. Her first instinct was to run but instead she stayed positioned with cemented legs and listened, scared yet fascinated.

The wail came once more, horse and throaty; it was followed by a desperate cry for help.

Kirsten arched her neck, goosebumps spreading across her arms. "Who's there?" She slipped the long knife from her back. "Answer me."

"*Help me.*"

The voice was soft and full of despair. Kirsten stepped into the field. "Hey, where are you? Come out or I'll cut you." Kirsten sliced the air with a flick of her wrist. "If this is a joke you'll pay for it."

"*Please...*"

Kirsten searched for the speaker of the disembodied voice. The weeds in the field were tall and thick, nearly reaching her chest. She parted the tall grass and pressed through the darkness. "Hello?" The field yielded to a square metallic lump. She paused, not sure of what action to take.

Suddenly, a cold hand clamped down on her ankle.

She let out a piercing scream as she jerked her leg away to see a crumpled man at her feet. His black suit blended in with the dark so well she could turn around and look upon him again and he would disappear. "Hey, are you okay?"

The man withdrew his withered hand and looked up at her with one eye. "Please, help me."

Kirsten kept a safe distance. She brandished her knife as a warning. "What happened to your eye?"

The man gave a pained look as he strained to see her. He dragged his feet along the ground behind himself like they were dead weights. "That was an accident, it happened long ago. But my other eye sees just fine. I've fallen from my chair, can you help me?"

Kirsten saw the square shape in the weeds for the second time. It was a wheelchair. One side of her mouth turned slightly. "How do I know you're not some weirdo?"

The man seethed. He seemed ready to let out a string of curses at her, but shut his mouth tight and crumpled back on the ground, unable to hold himself up. "My name's Randolph Leeds. I was out enjoying the night, that's all."

"Randolph Leeds!" Kirsten's mouth dropped. "You're Randolph Leeds? The resident owner of Dead House?"

Randolph bobbed his head up and down. "Yes, the very one."

Kirsten slipped the long blade back into her skirt, flush against her lower spine. She bent over and helped the old man into a sitting position. "Wow, I can't believe this. I'm Kirsten. I live down the street."

Randolph nodded. "That's very nice. Now can you get my wheelchair and place it close to me, please."

"Sure." Kirsten lifted the chair from the weed-choked field. Upon moving it, a small leather bound book tumbled out. Kirsten ignored the book for the moment as she pushed the wheelchair closer to Randolph, fighting the weeds with the wheels. "Here you go."

Randolph said nothing. He used his hands to guide himself into the chair, then braced and lifted his body until he was sitting in the chair. "Ah, that's much better."

Kirsten grabbed the book and tucked it away in her clothing. She would give the book back later. "Okay, now let's get you out of here." Kirsten walked behind Randolph and took the handles of his chair.

Randolph's hand shot out. "That won't be necessary, my dear. I can do it myself."

"Ah, no you can't. If I didn't come along you'd still be lying in the grass. So let me be a good girl and take you home. Or should I just dump you back on the ground and be on my merry way?"

Randolph frowned. "You're a feisty thing, aren't you?"

"Damn straight." Kirsten struggled with the wheelchair at first. Her neck muscles strained, her arms trembled, and as she forced the wheels to roll, beads of sweat speckled her forehead. The chair weighed a ton. Kirsten groaned as she pressed onward, flattening tall weeds and stumbling over small depressions in the earth. "How did you get out here anyway?"

"No one pushed me, if that's what you're thinking," Randolph snapped curtly. He folded his hands together and motioned for her to stop.

"What is it?"

Randolph pressed a tapered finger to his lips. "Listen closely."

A roll of thunder crackled over the mountains.

Randolph's features soured. "Hurry now. It's going to rain soon."

"What's wrong with a little rain?" Kirsten wiped her forehead with the back of her hand. She focused on the swirling black clouds above. The rain would feel great on her hot skin right about now.

Randolph rocked in his chair. He tried to spin the wheels but the weeds were too heavy and he remained rooted on the spot. "Hurry now. Get us out of here."

"Okay already." Kirsten forced the wheelchair a little further and found the road ahead. "Here we go. Good as new."

"Thank you very much, young lady. But I must be getting home now."

"I'll take you," Kirsten said. "If you don't mind, that is?"

Randolph looked at her for seemingly the first time. His single eye was dead and almost motionless. "What's a girl your age doing out here all alone at night anyway?"

Kirsten raised one eyebrow. "I could ask you the same question." The two stared at one another for a full minute before Kirsten put a hand on her hip and replied. "You don't tell and I don't tell, got it? Just let me take you home. I want to see Dead House."

Randolph sneered.

A loud roar of thunder crackled above them and the rain fell from the night sky like black pins.

"Fine, take me home. But be quick about it. I don't want to get stuck in the rain." Randolph's lips went back to a straight, hard line. "Who are you anyway?"

Kirsten grabbed the handle bars and together they rolled down the dark street. "Like I said before, I'm Kirsten. My family moved in last night. We're from Knoxville, Tennessee."

"Tennessee, huh. What the hell are you doing in upstate New York?"

"My father lived here when he was a boy. I suppose he was always homesick as much as he talked about this place. So here I am."

The wind kicked up a strong gale that made the trees sway. Droplets of rain slapped their faces as the storm rolled in.

Randolph pointed out a patch of darkness. "Go down there."

Kirsten slowed down, but only a little. She could see a faint outline of a dirt trail lined by dense brush. "I'm not taking you down there. Are you nuts? I barely got you out of that field."

"It's a short cut. Trust me."

Kirsten heaved the wheelchair off the road. "Okay, but you'd better give me the grand tour of Dead House."

"Why do you care about that heap? The place is falling apart."

Kirsten slipped under the trees and held onto the handles as the wheelchair descended a small hill. Branches struck her face and scratched her bare thighs. They'd only traveled the path for a moment before she caught sight of slick pavement. "Some short cut that was."

Randolph rocked in his chair. "You didn't answer my question, young lady."

"Sorry." Kirsten wrestled a twig out of her long hair. After removing it, she straightened her spine and pushed the wheelchair onto the pavement.

"I've always been interested in ghost stories ever since I can remember. My cousin would read them to me every night before I went to sleep. One of the stories was about an old mansion set on a weathered hill. The Leeds family mansion it was referred to, but the neighbors called the place Dead House." Kirsten let the words roll off her tongue. The tale brought a giddy childhood excitement she hadn't felt in years. "The Leeds house was full of secrets. At night, local people said you could hear strange moans and endless screaming."

Randolph spat a yellow ball of mucus onto the road. "I don't want to hear anymore. That's just a bunch of trash."

"They say it's haunted by ghosts. And Randolph Leeds was attacked by one."

"Enough." Randolph pounded his armrests. "That story was nonsense, cooked up by a loser reporter who wanted a big scoop. She made it up. Lies. All of it."

Kirsten's arms tensed. She'd done it again. She bit her lower lip. "I'm sorry. I just got a little carried away. It's just... I really like that story."

Randolph huffed. "Take me home, please, now."

The rain came fast and hard, sheets of water pounding every inch of bare flesh, drowning out any more potential for conversation. Kirsten began running, shoving the wheelchair along.

She heard no complaints from Randolph, and thought she heard him laughing.

*　　*　　*

Dead House shook with a crash as thunder pounded overhead. In the withered grass, the earth protruded and a skeletal hand slithered to the surface. Black soil gave way to a ragged, melon-shaped head full of worms. A guttural moan escaped from its mouth, as the corpse lifted itself out of the ground.

Victor didn't hear the thunder or the moan. He sat on the couch in the living room, watching static blare across the television screen. It had been four hours since his father's disappearance and the police still did nothing. He couldn't file a missing person's report for eight more hours. Hell, they wouldn't even send a dispatch unit over. Their advice was to stay calm and wait.

He slumped in the couch cushions. It wasn't like his father to do this. He never left the house: not to get groceries, shop, visit friends, nothing; which made Victor believe he was kidnapped. The signs of a fight weren't apparent. But how could a sixty-seven year old man in a wheelchair put up a struggle?

But his work area was a mess. Wasn't that enough evidence? The police didn't seem to think so. And once he gave them his address, they said to call back later. Victor knew what they were thinking. He could hear it in the way the dispatcher's voice grew shaky. Dead House was a place to fear. To strangers, the four-story mansion was a blight on the community, a dark blot to be wiped out and forgotten. But to Victor Leeds, Dead House was a home. Not the kind of home that you hang pictures up or have family gatherings in, but the kind of house where the rooms remain unaltered, as though time itself would never dare to touch it.

The television clicked off.

The storm had knocked out the power. Victor left the couch and walked into the kitchen for a spare flashlight. He found one beneath a baseball trophy he'd won over ten years ago. Back in the good old days, when his mother was alive and his father wasn't bound to a chair. The glory days. He made sure the flashlight worked before leaving the kitchen. A circle of yellow light appeared when he turned it on, shining on the hardwood floor. He exited the kitchen and then left the trophy and its haunting memories behind.

And yet, old memories flashed before him.

His mother cheering as he hit a baseball. His father rubbing his head after losing a game, then taking him out for ice cream. The pit of Victor's belly ached. He pushed the memories away. Yesterday was gone; it was now just a rotting autumn leaf being blow away from a gust of winter's bitter reality.

Victor was halfway to the living room when the doorbell chimed. For a moment, he thought it was his mind playing tricks on him, until the bell rang a second time. When he looked through the peephole, only darkness and falling rain greeted him. He unlocked the door, praying to see his father on the porch. But when he stepped outside, the porch was empty. He panned the yard with his flashlight and caught sight of a dark figure standing in the rain. Victor gasped. The humanoid shape gave a low groan and advanced toward him. Victor's eyes matched with those of the shambling terror and what he saw was pure death. He quickly spun around and dashed inside, locking the door behind him.

A wet thud shook the front door, followed by a bellowing wail. Nails scratched paint, as the corpse tried to get inside.

Victor found himself slowly backing toward the living room. He kept the flashlight's beam trained on the door. "Get out of here! Leave me alone!"

If the walking corpse heard Victor's cries, it ignored them, as again and again fists pounded on the door, rattling the frame, unable to break through.

Victor fled into the kitchen. Lightning flashed throughout the house, exposing every dark shadow in a burst of white light. He emptied the knife drawer until he came upon what he was looking for. His fingers surrounded the black handle of a large meat cleaver.

The relentless pounding continued, filling his ears with dread.

How can this be happening? That *thing*...it can't be real. Victor chased his fears away. He marched toward the front door and raised the cleaver high over his head. He put the flashlight on the floor, and with trembling fingers, he unlocked the door.

The pounding ceased.

Victor's heart thumped like a war drum. He flung the door open and greeted the rotting horror with a downward stroke. But the meat cleaver only severed air. He swung the blade sideways, thinking the corpse had somehow gotten behind him, but this wasn't so. The porch and yard were empty. The only sounds he heard were the lolling of distant thunder and the constant downpour of black rain. Victor grabbed his flashlight. He searched the driveway, the twisted trees, and the withered grass as he became soaked from the rain, but no sign of his attacker remained.

Lightning flashed and a patch of upturned soil caught his attention. He walked closer to examine the small cavity in the wet soil. Heaps of worms writhed in the piled soil along the sides of a deep hole. It was as though a gardener had uprooted an ancient tree during the storm.

Thunder crashed overhead.

He thought someone was calling his name. Victor kicked a loose stone into the hole. A voice drifted on the wind.

"Victor..."

Among the spoiled earth was a small and elegant ring. He picked it up. The ring was gold with a single diamond in the center. Another flash of lightning and he caught movement in the corner of his eye. It was a solid human mass appearing at the closed gate. He dropped the ring as he turned to see the figure better.

"Victor," his father called out to him over the crashing thunder.

35

"Dad?" Victor left the gaping hole and raced to the entrance of the property. His father was waiting for him with a grim smile. Behind him was a dark-haired girl of such exquisite beauty he had to take a second look, just to be sure he wasn't imagining her. But when she lifted her hand and waved, he knew she was real. Recognition slapped him away from the dark-haired girl. He gazed at his father and his voice broke. "Dad, where have you been?"

Randolph pounded the gate. "Don't just stand there boy. Let us in."

Victor unlatched the lock. He embraced his father with a quick hug. "I thought I'd lost you."

Randolph grunted. "This young lady saved me. So why don't you thank her."

Victor's eyes slid over Kirsten's slender body. She was curvy in all the right places, and the way her wet cloths clung to her lithe form made his heart skip a beat. Kirsten caught his stares and they matched knowing glances. "Thank you," he said.

Kirsten nodded. "No problem." She flicked her long black hair behind her. "Can I come in?"

"Yes, yes, of course, my dear," Randolph said. "Come in and have some tea. But let's get out of the rain first." He yanked on Victor's pant leg, speaking lower for him alone. "Now, boy, let's go, it's not safe out here."

Chapter 7

Kirsten took another sip of her green tea and crossed her legs. She sat at the far end of a round table across from Victor and his father. The tea was hot and soothing. Her hair had been toweled dry and she was slowly warming up.

"So tell me about Dead House," she said.

Victor and his father exchanged glances. "I'm afraid there's not much to tell," Victor said. "I can only assure you that it's not haunted."

Randolph gave a gruff laugh. He pulled the heavy gray blanket over his chest. Victor had draped the thick material over his father's shoulders the moment they got inside. Since then, neither one of the two had talked except for an occasional thank you or pleasant nod. Randolph leaned over the table. The burning candles made dark patches on his face, forming his features into a ghoulish mask. "I suppose you want the real history of my house?"

Kirsten set her tea cup down with a clatter. She settled back in her red cushioned seat. "Yes, please." Her voice was distant, even to her.

Randolph unraveled his hands and spun his tale around the flickering candle light. "This house wasn't always a mansion. When I was a boy, all that existed here were a few stone fences and a wooden shed. My father, Brigadier Leeds, bought the property as a means to satisfy his wife, Isabella, who above everything desired land. We lived in a small cottage house in Somers near a small, man-made pond. Every weekend I'd go fishing while my parents worked on this house. You see, my father was a wealthy man. He was a doctor by trade. His only weakness was for Isabella. He spent every weekend working on the house. Placing each stone perfectly, hiring men only when absolutely necessary. Years slipped by and I became a man. My father grew old; his Isabella older. Our aged home was in shambles. The pond had dried up. He sold the old house and moved into this one. I joined the army and didn't return for some length of time."

Kirsten's lips curled downward. "I thought your father was a mortician?"

"Ah, that he was, my dear. After my mother passed away from sickness, my father turned this house into a temporary morgue; simply because the town didn't have the means to hold the deceased that long. And everyone knew and trusted my father. He was a likable man." Randolph sighed. "I do miss him."

Kirsten leaned back and crossed her arms. He was hiding something. She could read it on his face like a cowering dog. "I heard six people disappeared on the property. Is that true?"

Randolph's single eye blazed with fire. "There you go again. Ranting about what those reporters made up."

"Sorry," she said and then shrugged. "Why don't you tell me about what really happened"

Victor stood from the table. He scooped her tea cup and saucer into both hands. "It's getting late."

Randolph agreed. "It is. I'm sure your family is worried about you. Why don't you go home?"

"You haven't showed me around yet. That was the deal, remember? And anyway, you didn't answer my question."

Randolph erupted in laughter. "My, you're a feisty girl. You just don't take no for an answer."

"I guess I don't," quipped Kirsten.

"That's good," smiled Randolph as he leered at her. "I like you, girl. You've got spunk. But I'm older than I look and need my rest. Come back tomorrow and Victor can give you the grand tour." He gave her a wink with his single, dead-looking eye.

"Thanks. That sounds great, but before I go, just tell me if it was true. Did six people vanish from Dead House?" she asked.

Randolph's mouth formed a hard line. He narrowed his one eye and glared at her. "Nobody has ever gone missing here."

*　*　*

"If you ask me, you should leave her there," Lisa said. She blocked the door leading to the Subaru.

Trevor put on a blue raincoat and ball cap with the New York Yankees printed in white on the front. "I didn't ask you. Now move out of the way."

Lisa's expression was one of intense shock, as though he'd slapped her across the face. "Excuse me? What did you say?"

"I said, get out of my way."

"No, before that." Lisa huffed like a dragon preparing to spit fire.

"Look, I'm sorry, okay? I just want to get my daughter. Could you please move."

Lisa shook her head. "Not before we talk. I've put up with a lot of crap from her, Trevor. The black gothic clothes, those skimpy outfits you let her parade around in, not to mention seeing her dead mother all the time, and now this."

Trevor pushed against her, his lips twisted into a snarl. "That's my daughter you're talking about. And she's my first priority, not you. So get the hell out of my way before I make you."

Lisa's jaw dropped. She stepped away from the door. "Go then. Just go. But I might not be here when you get back."

Trevor's hardness melted. His anger dying out like it always did. "Baby, you don't mean that, do you?"

Lisa's lower lip pouted. She pounded her feet into the hardwood floor and raced for the master bedroom.

"Honey?" Trevor called, then heard the door slam shut. He went after her and tried the doorknob but it was locked.

"Dammit." Trevor stalked through the front door and closed it quietly. He was never a man to express his anger. He'd bottle it up for months at a time, letting it eat him inside until a situation would arise when he would explode. He stepped out into the rain. It felt good to breathe fresh air and feel the storm slide off his raincoat.

A few recurring questions nagged at him. Am I doing the right thing? Do I express my concerns and get my views across to others in a friendly manner?

For Trevor, the answers were simple. He didn't know. All his life he'd listened to orders from family members, friends, and lovers. But through it all, he couldn't seem to discern if the actions he took were the right ones, like now. His daughter had knowingly disobeyed him. She'd wandered off and got taken in by strangers. "But it's her life," he said to himself as he jumped behind the wheel of the Subaru. Kirsten was over eighteen and pretty soon she'd be twenty-one. A frightening thought. Trevor started the Subaru and sped down the driveway and onto the street. He could see Kirsten parading in bars, drinking her sorrows until the bottles were empty, then getting knocked up by some guy who would leave her. The signs were there, laid out before him like the road ahead.

But then again, his mind twisted, Kirsten also had the potential as a shut in. He could picture her smooth face aged by wrinkles. She would spend most of her time rummaging through her room and remembering the good times in life. She would cling to old toys and jewelry her mother had given to her, then lock herself in her small room until the day she died. Trevor gripped the wheel as the storm splattered the windshield. Neither one of those fates faired well with him. A growing anger throbbed at the back of his neck. Why was he thinking such things?

Lisa.

Yes, it had to be her. Lisa planted the seeds of doubt in him. And perhaps a part of him believed her.

Trevor gave the Subaru some gas and bore down the twisted roads. A lonely stretch of trees appeared on the passenger's side, followed by rows of black iron fencing. Within a minute, Dead House erupted from the darkness. Lightning flashed behind it, giving the aged home an ominous life for a brief second. Trevor pulled into the driveway. The gate was unlocked so he drove up to the house. Dead House.

What a strange name. Fitting though considering the information Kirsten had told him. He peered through the rain and noticed the cracked wall and aging stone along the house's foundation. In a brief flash of lightning, he witnessed a dark shadow pass by the basement window and vanish. Trevor scratched the side of his head. Surely his daughter wasn't down there.

And she wasn't, as the front door opened; emitting Kirsten, a tall muscular boy, and a gray-haired man in a wheelchair. Trevor stepped into the pouring rain to greet them. "I see you've kept my daughter out of this mess," he said.

Kirsten rolled her eyes as her father came up the steps. "This is my dad. Dad, this is Randolph and Victor Leeds."

Victor shook Trevor's hand. "Hi...uhm..."

The young man had a strong grip, Trevor thought. "Hi, yourself. I'm Trevor, only she calls me Dad," Trevor grinned, looking at his daughter.

Randolph Leeds raised his head and gave Trevor a careful look over with his lifeless eye bobbing up and down. "It's a pleasure to meet you."

Trevor shook Randolph's hand gently, as though it might break. He tried to avoid staring into the empty socket, but found himself powerless not to. Where an eye had once been, now lurked a dark pit, as if the orb had been cored out. Trevor managed to look away. "Nice to meet you." He focused his attention to Kirsten. "I'm not happy with you, young lady."

Kirsten lowered her head. "I'm sorry, Dad."

Randolph spoke before Trevor had a chance. "Don't be too hard on her. If it wasn't for your daughter, I'd be a dead man."

Trevor raised a questioning eyebrow.

"I took a rather bad tumble off the road," explained Randolph. "Your daughter rescued me. So if you're going to blame someone, blame me."

Trevor gave a forced grin. "Well, that's great and all. But Kirsten has rules to follow." He took two steps towards the Subaru. "Come on, Kirsten, it's time to go home."

"Yes, Dad." Kirsten faced the two Leeds men. "Thanks for letting me stay. I'll come by tomorrow sometime." She went down the porch stairs as she followed after her father, making sure to smile at Victor. "Goodbye for now."

*   *   *

As father and daughter climbed into the Subaru and drove away, Victor clenched his fists into tight balls. "Where did you go?" he addressed his father.

"I went out. I'm an old man. I can do what I want." Randolph wheeled inside, making for the elevator, dismissing his son.

Victor slammed the front door behind him and locked it. "Then why was my room a mess? Not to mention the basement? I thought you were in trouble, Dad?"

The elevator opened and Randolph wheeled inside. "I was in trouble. That girl saved me." Before the elevator door closed, Randolph got out one more sentence. "By the way, she likes you if you couldn't tell." The elevator doors closed and Randolph was gone.

Victor picked up the closest thing, which was a tea cup, and threw it against the elevator door, spraying pieces everywhere.

"I hate you."

Victor went to his room and lay in bed, clenching and unclenching his fists. Then, he suddenly sprang upward. He quickly found a blank sheet of paper, snatched a ball point pen off his desk, and began to sketch the walking corpse.

Chapter 8

Victor sat alone on a pew in the Loch Family Funeral Home. He gazed ahead as mourners clad in black silently filled the room. The funeral home was stale like a doctor's office, but dressed up like a church. This was his first wake. He'd refused to attend his mother's. What was the point? The dead are dead. They don't speak. They don't move. They feel no pain. Dead is dead. Of course that was his reasoning back then, but it had taken a different course over the last few days. That thing in the road...

It was dead and yet it moved, even reached for him. Lynn had touched the walking dead woman, and now she lay in a wooden box soon to be six feet under. He stared at the casket for nearly an hour, trying to bore through the intricate mess of metal casing. The lid remained closed as more and more mourners filled the seats. Victor wondered how Lynn looked under the coffin. Did her blonde hair fall past her shoulders? Were her lips the lips he'd kissed a lifetime ago? Only now they were drawn into a thin fine line?

He felt he was being watched, and he looked up to see a face focused on him, bringing him back. It was Jack, Lynn's father. He had dark circles under his eyes from lack of sleep and a sagging frown. Jack parted through the crowd to reach him. "Thanks for being here, Victor. It means so much to me."

Victor offered him a seat. "Care to join me?"

Jack tightened his black tie. "Just for a minute, then I have to get back to my wife." He sat down heavily. "You really loved her, didn't you?"

"Yeah," Victor choked. "She meant more to me than any girl I've ever known."

Jack lowered his head. He dug into his pocket and produced a necklace in the shape of a heart. "Here, take this."

Victor sat on his hands. "No, I couldn't. Please, you keep it."

"You don't understand," Jack said. "She wanted you to have this. We found an unfinished letter on her desk with this on top. She was going to give it to you on your next date."

Victor let the heart necklace fall into his hand. He turned it over. The heart was red and shimmering. He faced Jack, uncertain of what to say.

Jack rose to his feet, a man lost to grief. "I have to go now. Take care of yourself, Victor."

Jack left him. He joined the remnants of his family by the casket. Lynn's mother cried her eyes out while an older woman, presumably her mother, held her close. Jack sat down beside them and pressed his hands to his eyes.

Victor slumped in his seat. He put the necklace around his neck as a priest came down the aisle. He went to a wooden podium and asked everyone to stand as they prayed. After saying the Our Father, the priest had the audience take their seats. He spoke of the glory of God and how He called His servants home when the time was right. Victor blocked out the voice, went through the motions, and sulked. When the priest was finished, Lynn's father took center stage.

Jack's sorrow was plain for all to see. He staggered to the podium and didn't bother to wipe the tears rolling down his cheeks. "I didn't know how short life was until now," his voice cracked slightly. "My future and that of my wife's lies in the box before us." Jack's entire body shook as he broke down in front of the mourners. "I love you, Lynn." He choked on a sob and went back to his seat, lowering his head and crying.

Victor couldn't move. He couldn't breathe. He'd never seen a grown man cry before. And he didn't want to see it again.

Lynn's mother, Rosemary, took center stage. She held the podium close to her chest as though trying to hug it. When she spoke, everyone listened.

"Lynn was every mother's dream. She did what was asked of her and more. She was head cheerleader in her senior year of high school. She acted in three plays, and could perform on a grand piano better than I ever could. She..." Rosemary closed her eyes and dug her fingernails into the podium, trying to find the strength to continue. She wiped her eyes, blew her nose into a black handkerchief, and went on. "Lynn was my heart. My daughter never let me down. I'm proud of her." Rosemary stepped away from the stage and went to the casket. She whispered to Lynn, but nobody could hear her words.

The priest materialized from the side. "All are welcome to say their blessings as we make peace in this time of sorrow."

One by one, the rows of mourners left the pews. They prayed over Lynn's casket and gave console with the grieving family.

Victor tried to leave the scene but was drawn to Lynn's casket like a shark to blood. Memories from nights gone by flooded his thoughts. Lynn had touched the walking corpse, and now she was dead. He recalled the way her hand had turned that sickly pale color, almost like unmolested clay.

43

If he could just get a peek at her, for just a second, to confirm the event did actually take place. Victor had made it halfway toward Lynn's casket when he turned around.

This is wrong.

A banshee's call struck the back of his head as a woman cried out in anger. "You!"

Victor spun himself around in time to see Rosemary racing up the aisle towards him. "You killed my daughter!"

He raised his hands as though under arrest. "Wait, I just came to pay my respects."

She leapt for him, fingernails aimed at his throat like tiny daggers. "Murderer," she seethed as their bodies locked in combat.

Victor avoided her nails but couldn't dodge her as the two clashed head on. Rosemary screamed in his face and wrestled him to the ground. He managed to jut his body to the side so he didn't fall. The sudden movement caught Rosemary off guard. Her legs tripped over his and she toppled backwards. Victor could only watch as she tumbled toward the stage and knocked into the stand holding Lynn's casket. Mourners gaped, but Jack was quick on his feet, rushed to the aid of his wife, and wrapped his arms around her.

Then the worst scenario played out. It was something Victor and the onlookers would never forget. The stand holding Lynn's casket gave way with a heavy thud. An instant later, the casket toppled onto its side and Lynn's lifeless corpse rolled out. Her body was a sunken, pale husk. Where golden hair once fell on smooth flesh, it now adorned dried cheeks and wrinkled skin; it was as though she'd been dead for months. The hall fell silent. No one moved or gasped.

What Lynn's white dress didn't hide was the unnatural color of her skin.

Lynn's mother cried out. "My baby..." She thrashed about the floor like a dying fish seeking the water it would never breathe again.

Jack let his wife go. He went to Lynn's casket, bent down, and eased his daughter back inside. "Rest, my princess. We'll be together again."

The mourners cried as one, cursing Victor and throwing pamphlets and bibles at him.

But Victor was made of stone. He stood rooted in place, his mind trying to rationalize what his eyes had seen. Then his feet were moving, taking him from the funereal home and onto the street. His forehead broke out in a deep sweat. His mind formed the answer he had sought.

This can't be. Can't someone tell me this isn't so? But he'd seen it even if he didn't believe it. He ran halfway home until he stopped to gather more air into his lungs. He gripped his head and paced the desolate Stormville streets.

It was true.

Lynn's body had looked the same as that *thing* she'd touched.

* * *

The gate to Dead House could've resembled the Black Gate guarding Mordor. Iron spikes towered over Kirsten's head as she stood before it.

"Victor? Randolph? Let me in," she called out. She pressed a buzzer seated in a stone pillar, but no one ever came. Kirsten paced the gate like a tiger stalking prey. She lowered her head and assessed the black gate. The spikes were too high to climb over. She could fit her arms through the bars but that was about it. Unless Victor or his father came to open the gate soon, she'd be forced to go home, which was simply something she didn't want to do. After her father had taken her home the night before, Lisa had started yelling at her. Kirsten screamed back until Trevor had ended the conflict by sending Kirsten to her room. She'd accepted. For nearly two hours after that, Trevor and Lisa tore at one another with insult after insult, followed by heavy weeping. Kirsten had put her headphones on, listened to Rob Zombie, and immersed herself in a paperback book titled *30 Days of Night*. She read through four chapters of Andy Grey lamenting after his dead vampire FBI partner before falling asleep. In the morning, Lisa gave her the evil eye so she took a walk, her feet carrying her to Dead House.

Kirsten rang the buzzer again. She caught a long red curtain moving in an upstairs window. "Hey, let me in. You promised a tour!" Kirsten waved. The curtains fell back into place. Kirsten thought it was Victor. He was a quiet guy, kind of cute, and kept mostly to himself. Not her type, but maybe underneath that protective armor he'd be soft-hearted and respectable. Kirsten wasn't interested in any other kind of guy. If he was good looking, had money, but treated her like a prize or someone just to fuck she was gone. She wanted no part in that dance. Her dream man might not have a killer body, and that was okay. Respect and a soft heart went a far greater distance in her book.

She found herself pacing back and forth again as twenty minutes crawled by. They were ignoring her. "Bastards," she muttered as she stepped away from the gate. There had to be another way in, maybe a weakness in the bars?

She saw the curtain in the window flutter once more. She raised her middle finger and walked down the street. "Assholes," she muttered. She followed the fence until Dead House was out of sight. "I'll show them." She curled her hands around the bars and pulled. She repeated the process on every part of the fence. There had to be a weak spot some-where. Nothing was impenetrable; no building, castle, home, or the blackest heart. Everything in the world had a weakness.

Her own was caring too much. Kirsten bit her lower lip and contin-ued to tug at the iron fencing. Her thoughts wandered to her mother. The way she laughed at Kirsten when they went to the animal shelter to pick out a dog. Kirsten had cried. She wanted them all. Not for herself but just so she could set them free, because freedom was a far better fate than being caged and waiting for death. Her mother gave her a kiss and told her to only choose one.

"You can save the world when you're older." So Kirsten chose a large dog with long white hair and brown eyes. She named him Max. The two were together constantly, and when Max died of old age, her mother helped her through it. She was always there, rain or shine. The whole world could fall apart and her mother would shrug and say, "Well, it had to happen sometime."

Kirsten yanked two bars free with ease. She pulled so hard she tum-bled backwards, landing on her butt, the iron bars still clutched in her hands. She got up and dusted herself off. A wide grin crossed her face as she slipped unnoticed through the fence. She was still smirking at her cleverness when Victor stepped out of the woods to greet her.

"My father was right about you." He stopped short and shoved his thumbs into his faded blue jeans.

Kirsten's smile faltered. "I didn't mean to bother you." She motioned to where the two spiked bars lay. "Sorry about your fence."

Victor nodded. "You could've waited at the gate."

She put her hands on her hips. "I'm not the kind of girl you keep waiting."

"I can see that." Victor marched past her. He scooped up the twin bars and set them back in place. "I never thought anyone would find my getaway."

Kirsten scratched her head. "What getaway?"

Victor positioned the bars with a practiced hand. "Right here, I un-screwed them as a boy. Sometimes I would sneak out of my house just to go on nightly walks." His expression sorrowed. "It's been a long time since I've done that."

"Sorry again," she said and meant it. She wanted to give Victor a hug, hold him close to her, and soothe away his sorrows. The feelings made her suddenly angry. She didn't even know this guy.

She crossed her arms and tipped her head. "I'm not coming back later. Either you show me around today or never."

He laughed and shook his head. "I can see how you and my father get along so well. He thanks you again. And so do I."

She stared into his eyes. They were a marvelous shade of blue with a splash of green. She quickly looked at the woods and felt her cheeks burning.

"It was no trouble," she said.

"Before I show you around the place can I ask you something?"

She shrugged. "Go 'head."

"What were you doing out there in that field last night?"

"You're not the only one who enjoys walking the streets at night. And as for being in the field, I heard a moan and went to check it out."

Victor's eyes got big like ping pong balls. "You heard a moan..."

"Uh-huh, it was kind of like from one of those zombie films, only it turned out to be your father, no offense though."

Victor flinched at her mention of the word zombie. The walking corpse that touched Lynn...

He shuddered. That thing was in the field, maybe stalking his father. If Kirsten hadn't come along in time, his dad might have never come home.

"Hey, are you all right?" She touched his arm.

"Yeah, I'm fine. Let's go inside. I'll show you the house." Victor spun around and headed toward a hill side dense with brush.

Kirsten followed closely. Her eyes strayed to a series of thick ropes dangling from an oak tree. "Did you have a few tire swings or something at one point?"

Victor shook his head and let her walk beside him. "No, those are the ropes left over from the hangings."

"What hangings?"

"Way back when. My dad could tell you the story."

Kirsten tugged at his shirt, making him stop. "What if I want you to tell it?"

He looked into her angelic face and quickly looked the other way. He sensed he couldn't run away from her argument or beauty, so he turned inward and recalled the tale his father would spin as a fire crackled in the living room fireplace.

"Back when my dad was a boy and Dead House was only half finished, a group of men kidnapped the mayor's daughter. The men called themselves the Leg Spreaders because they were notorious for raping young girls. They brought the mayor's daughter to Dead House and spent four days on her. She cried so loud that the nearest house, almost a mile from here at the time, heard her cries. The locals came and found the Leg Spreaders taking turns with her. The locals were outraged. In a fit of

47

anger, they beat the four men senseless, breaking their arms and legs, then bashing their genitals with a claw hammer. After the torture, they were hanged. My grandfather watched the men swing and decided to leave the bodies. I don't think they ever took them down. My father said the ropes eventually broke and the bones are still here on the grounds. I've never looked myself."

Kirsten listened with amazement. "What happened to the mayor's daughter?"

"She jumped off the Kent Cliffs. After her ordeal, she didn't want to show her face to any man and took to wearing a black mask. Two years passed before she committed suicide. In her room, they found a drawer filled with rotting male genitals. Apparently she went through town seducing men and cutting off their members after her rape. Nobody came forward as a victim. It was thought that she lured them in as an escort then went to work, perhaps even killing some of them afterwards and then disposing the bodies."

"Poor girl, what was her name?"

"Lily, I think. You can ask my father. He said he met her once."

"Really?" Kirsten was intrigued. She watched as the dry ropes swayed back and fourth from a sudden gust of wind.

"I told you my father can tell the story better than I can." Victor tugged at her arm. His fingers brushed against her bare flesh and the sensation was electric. "Come on, I'll show you the house."

Kirsten followed two steps behind him. She wanted to giggle at how Victor's face flushed red when he touched her, but she stilled her girlish laughter and went up the hill. Her heart fluttered. She was falling in love.

They had only hiked for a few minutes until Dead House rose from the woods like a stone giant. Weathered from last night's storm, the giant appraised them with wicked interest. Kirsten and Victor pressed onward to the house and avoided a large plank of wood placed over upturned soil.

"What's this?" she asked as she tested the board's strength.

Victor took her by the arm with force and led her away. "Don't go near that, it's covering up a deep hole. You could've broken through it."

She pried his hands off with ease. "First thing, buddy; if you grab me like that again I'll crush your face like a soda can. Second, I don't think I weigh enough to break that board, it looks brand new."

"It is." He wore a hurt expression on his face. "I'm sorry. I didn't want you to get hurt."

"I appreciate the gesture, but I'm a big girl. I can take care of myself."

Victor wanted to choke from hearing her words, the way she said it. She sounded so much like Lynn: rebellious, strong, beautiful, confident,

48

and careless. She would make a mistake. He was sure of it. And when she did, Victor would help her. He would save her the way he couldn't save Lynn.

"Your confidence will destroy you," Victor said plainly, as though he were discussing the weather. "You can talk big, but can you back it up?"

"What did you say?" Kirsten huffed. "You don't even know me. Are you crazy?"

"I know you too well, or your type at least." Victor walked to the porch and leaned on a stone pillar.

"My type, huh?" Kirsten poked him in the chest with her middle finger.

"Yeah, you were walking alone last night weren't you?"

"So?" she said.

"Didn't you just move here? How safe do you think it really is out there?"

Kirsten laughed in his face. "Safe enough."

"A girl named Lynn died on those streets just two days ago." Victor tried not to sob but his voice was already breaking.

"What happened to her?"

"I...we...she died, okay? She got sick from being in the rain and died."

Kirsten eyed him with general concern. "You knew her?"

Victor nodded. He bit his tongue to keep his sorrows at bay.

"Were you with her that night?" Kirsten probed.

"Yes." He let the word slip through his lips like a straight razor, painful and scaring.

Kirsten went to him. She tried to put her arms around him, but he eased away from her. "I'm so sorry."

"Don't be, okay?" Victor held up his hands.

"Okay." Kirsten gave him a sheepish grin. "Do you want to walk me home? I don't think I want my tour of Dead House today."

Victor sucked in his lips. "I walked her home, too." He shook his head. "I'm sorry, Kirsten. You're a beautiful girl but..."

"Look," she interrupted. "I didn't ask you to be my boyfriend or lay me down and screw me. All I asked was for you to walk me home."

Victor's heart told him yes, but his mind said no. How could he parade around with this girl after Lynn's funeral? But it was the nagging thought of staying locked in the basement with his father all day long. Having nothing to think about but Lynn's dried corpse spilling onto the carpeted floor. "Okay. I'll walk you home. How could I say no?"

Kirsten swayed her hips in a flirtatious motion, letting her skirt raise just enough to make him curious. "I don't know, Victor. I didn't really think I was that unattractive."

"You're gorgeous." He tried not to roam his eyes over her bare legs, but he found himself doing so until he reached her black mini skirt, it was different from the one yesterday in that it had a rose pattern on the side and was shorter.

She frowned. "Maybe I'll walk home myself."

"No, don't. I'd love to walk you home."

"Good, just don't expect anything."

Victor laughed. His first real laugh since he'd found out Lynn was dead. He nearly snorted and Kirsten laughed along with him.

The two of them left Dead House and it's mysteries behind.

Chapter 9

Lisa waited until Trevor was outside before picking up the phone. She quickly punched in a series of numbers, made positive that her husband was mowing the lawn, and listened for the other end to pick up.

On the sixth ring, a thick male voice cooed in her ear. "Hello, this is Dario."

"Hey, hot stuff."

"Lisa...I told you not to call this number." Dario sounded angry with her, but also amused.

"I miss you between my legs. Are you still coming?"

He lowered his voice. "I'm doing business right now. I can't. I told you I'd call when I reached White Plains."

"I know," Lisa pouted. Her hands slipped to one breast and she rubbed her nipple. "How much longer? I need you here with me. In me."

"Don't worry, baby. Everything's going as planned. I'll be there as soon as I can. Two days, tops, okay? Then we can slip away together and have some fun."

Lisa moaned. "I'd like that. Trevor can't do much for me. And I'm ready to push his daughter down a flight of stairs. I hate that stupid little slut."

Dario chuckled. "Well, we can't have that. Not yet anyway. Just keep playing along. All our planning will be for nothing if you screw up now. And you don't want that, do you, baby?"

"Of course not," Lisa sighed. "I just don't think I can take much more of this good wife shit. We need to kill Trevor and his daughter now and dump the bodies so I can collect on the insurance money as the grieving widow."

"A few more days. That's all. Once we get going this one will be just like the others."

"It better be," Lisa snapped.

"It will. I promise. Look, babe, I've got to go. I'll keep in touch."

"Okay, bye." Lisa hung up the phone. Her hand fell away from her nipple and she let out another long sigh. "God I need a real fuck."

She checked on her husband through the kitchen window. Trevor was pushing a John Deer lawn mower over the tall grass. He wore a stupid grin, obvious to the pain that awaited him in the days to come. She would make Trevor suffer more than the others. He deserved it; the self righteous, kind-hearted bastard. She'd never met a man so nice and caring before in her life. A lump in her throat made her gag. She wanted to throw up just thinking of him. And the way he put up with that trashy looking daughter of his!

Lisa tightened her fists so hard her nails pierced her palms. Kirsten belonged in a nut house, but pretty soon she'd be in pieces and underground. Lisa licked her lips with a sensational thought. Maybe she'd tie Kirsten up and let Dario have his way with her. *I bet the little bitch would like that.* She could even subdue Trevor and make him watch, then fuck him for the last time; it would be an orgy. She squeezed her breasts, wishing Dario was here to slide his dick between them and jack off all over her face. But he wasn't.

With a sigh, she got a Pepsi from the refrigerator. She fingered the can after popping the top and wondered if Kirsten's twenty year old pussy would be as tight?

The lawn mower cut off and Trevor came inside, his t-shirt soaked in sweat and blades of grass. "Hey, honey, can you get me something to drink?"

"Sure." Lisa plundered another soda from the fridge and handed it to him.

"Thanks, dear." Trevor swallowed the cold drink in three quick gulps.

"Sure." *Just playing my part*, she thought as she flashed Trevor a grin.

* * *

On the way to Kirsten's house, Victor wanted to make a detour to the field. Kirsten agreed, saying how she didn't mind the walk. For the duration of their travels, she stayed ahead of him, her flawless legs sliding back and forth like a deli slicer. He couldn't help but stare at her. She was gorgeous, but a bit underdressed. He didn't really understand the gothic look. The music was fine, though. He'd listened to Marilynn Mansion way back when Brian was just a long haired skinny guy singing about a Lunchbox. As far as the crazies who wanted to dress like him? Forget it. Victor knew how to make it in today's world. And it wasn't putting on black lipstick and shopping at *Hot Topic*.

Back in high school, there were only a handful of gothic chicks, but none of them were like Kirsten. Most of them were overweight, pimple-faced wanna-bes with no friends. But Kirsten was trim and her flesh was baby smooth. She certainly didn't belong to the gothic group, yet here she was parading around in a tight mini-skirt and combat boots; sexy as a *Devil's Reject*, or a midnight vixen.

He followed her like a puppy dog until she stopped suddenly and picked up something off the road. For a brief moment, Victor saw a silver thong. Heat rushed to his face and groin.

"Hey, look what I found." She held out a set of keys with a rabbit foot attached to one ring.

His stomach sank as he snatched the keys from her. "I know who these belong to. It's a guy named Jimmy who comes to the deli every Tuesday and Friday."

"What deli?"

Victor jingled the keys. "Where I work. He's a regular."

"You didn't tell me you had a job."

He put the keys into his back pocket. "It never came up. I'm technically on vacation right now. I guess that's what they call a grievance period."

Kirsten's lips curled downward as if recalling the loss of Lynn herself. "Sorry."

"It's okay. We'd better get these keys back to Jimmy. Not that he drives his car much, but if his woman gives him anymore heat, he probably will."

She nodded and flicked her waist long hair behind her like a super-model preparing for the catwalk. "Which way do we go?"

Victor's eyes roamed up her legs then he quickly turned his gaze elsewhere. "Why don't I lead us for a little while?"

"Because you're slow," she quipped. "My grandfather could walk faster than you." She playfully nudged him with her elbow.

"I'm not slow. I just like to take my time, enjoy the scenery, you know?"

She leaned to one side and slapped her butt. "I know. Boys are all the same."

His face turned bright red. She'd known the entire time, and his mind reeled.

And yet she stayed ahead of me anyway, even letting me glimpse her underwear, he thought as he rubbed his cheeks. "Well, it's hard not to stare. That skirt is really short. I bet all the guys look."

Now it was Kirsten's turn to blush. She turned away, hiding her embarrassment. "A girl has to attract a guy one way or another."

"There's other ways. You really don't have to dress like that."

She threw him a flirtatious glare. "Really? And I suppose you'd like me better if I wore thick sweaters and spoke about Homer's Iliad?"

"Well...I guess I might. You're a beautiful girl. I'm sure that no matter what you wore, you'd look great."

Kirsten stepped closer to him. "You really think that?"

"Absolutely," he said. His body was encased in stone, and as she eased forward, an icy chill crept up his spine.

Kirsten put her arms around his neck. "Aren't you going to kiss me?"

He leaned into her. He felt her fingers play with his hair. Her soft breasts pressed against his chest. Victor looked into her eyes and welcomed the feel of her kiss. But an inch away from contact, Lynn's face flashed before him. Lynn, with her golden hair and thin lips. He would love her forever, locked in that moment of pouring rain and darkness.

He twisted his head and broke off Kirsten's embrace. "I'm sorry. I can't."

Kirsten gave a sad smile. She curled her arms about her waist, wishing it were Victor instead. "It's my fault. I didn't mean to. It just sort of happened. I like you."

He lowered his head. "It's too soon. I don't think I could be with anyone after Lynn, not for a while at least."

"I understand," she said. She went to him quickly and kissed his cheek. "Sorry again, we can start off slow if you want?"

Victor seemed to consider this for a moment, then his shoulders sagged and he let out a sigh. "I'm sorry. I just can't right now."

"Okay, that's fine." She began walking down the hill side road. "I'll wait for you. But I won't wait too long."

He laughed at that. "If you can't wait for me then you're not the girl for me." He ventured straight ahead and paused at a road with no sign. "Jimmy's house is this way. Follow me."

* * *

After a round of half-assed sex, Lisa left her husband on the bed and went to the bathroom to masturbate. It wasn't that Trevor had a small dick; by far his was one of the largest she'd ever seen. But Trevor liked to kiss and cuddle, fuck her for twenty minutes, take a nap, and then do it all over again.

Lisa sealed the bathroom door; she needed more than deep kisses and loving sex. Her hand slipped between her legs and she began working three fingers in and out. Lisa needed Dario. She needed his dirty comments seeping into her ears as he pumped his dick in and out, telling her she was a great fuck. And after he came inside her, he would stuff his cock into her mouth. Lisa played with the image until a little moan escaped between her lips. Dario knew how to please her. He knew what she liked. And she liked her sex rough and dripping in warm cum. Trevor played it safe. They were married a year and two months ago and he still wore a condom. It was appalling.

She took her hand away. How she yearned for that warm, white fluid to fill her. She would swallow Dario and let him spread his seed anywhere he liked. Dario enjoyed it. She sure as hell enjoyed the act as well. But Trevor... poor Trevor. He always played it safe. He'd never cum in her, even after all this time. But that was okay. Soon he'd be like the rest of them, a memory in her mind and deep underground.

Lisa licked her fingers. She hummed to herself as she stepped under the shower's powerful spray. The water beat down on her like a thousand small hands coursing over her flesh. She moaned and rubbed her breasts. Wishing Dario was here to chew on her nipple and shove a hard dick up her ass.

Only a few more days, her mind repeated.

The bathroom door creaked open. Trevor stood naked in the doorway. He was muscular for a man of his age, almost cut from marble. He pushed the shower door open and stepped inside. "Do you mind if I join you?"

Lisa withered against him like a flower bending to the breeze. "Looks like you already have."

Their bodies interlocked under the shower's hot spray, as she gave in to him, going to her knees, the water now striking her shoulders. Her thoughts drifted to Dario as she took him into her mouth.

* * *

"Hey, Jimmy, are you here?" Victor called out as he pounded on the flimsy door with his fist. "Jimmy, it's Victor, open up." He listened closely for a blaring television or flushing toilet but heard neither, only silence.

"I'm going to check around the backyard," Kirsten said. She didn't wait for Victor's approval as she stepped off the porch and went to the side of the house. Her feelings were all wrong. She shouldn't be here. Her gut wretched and she heard her mother calling from the woods. "No. Not again. Not here," she said under her breath.

"Kirsten, come to me, darling. Mother misses you very much."

A dark shape formed in the trees.

"Get away from me!" Kirsten screamed. She ran to the back of the house and found the back door lying on the ground. She didn't think twice. She ran into the house, away from the bad feeling, and away from the image of her mother. Upon entering, she stumbled over heaps of dirty clothes.

Her mother's voice sang out from the woods. *"Kirsten...where are you?"*

Kirsten covered her ears and shook her head. "You're not real. You're not real. You're not real!"

A hand grabbed her by the collar and she screamed again.

"Hey, it's only me." Victor stood before her, a look of concern plastered on his face. "Are you hurt?"

She hugged him, curling her arms around his back. "Thank God you're here. I was so scared."

Victor pulled her back slowly. "What's going on? I heard you screaming and then I find you in here. And I know you didn't break that door down."

"I can't explain it. Not right now, maybe not ever." She cleared her eyes. "Can I hold your hand? Please, don't leave me alone."

He did as she asked. "Look, I'm going to look around the house. Can you stay here for a minute?"

She shook her head violently and looked toward the forest. Her mother emerged from behind a tree. She was rotting and wearing a blue dress. Kirsten closed her eyes. *Not real. Not real. Not real.*

"Kirsten? Your really worrying me," Victor said. He placed his hand over hers.

"I'm fine. I'm okay." She squeezed his hand harder. "Let's go inside together. I can't be left alone."

"If that's what you want," he said.

"Yes, please." Kirsten kept her eyes shut, willing the image of her deceased mother to fade.

Victor led her inside by the hand. He flicked a light switch on and turned to address her. "Aren't you going to open your eyes? You don't have anything to worry about. I'm here."

Kirsten's eyes shot open. They were still inside Jimmy's house. She panned the surroundings carefully. A red couch rested in one corner, a fifteen-inch television sat on a card table, and beer cans littered the floor. Kirsten's breathing went back to normal. Her mother was gone. "This place is a mess."

"Tell me about it." Victor kicked empty beer cans out of his way and strolled into a storage room. "Jimmy? Are you in here?"

The house groaned. If Jimmy was among the heaped junk, he didn't answer.

"I'm going to check upstairs," he said.

Kirsten grabbed his hand and held on tight. "I'll go with you." She walked side by side with him. Occasionally, she would look over her shoulder. "Do you think someone broke in?"

"I don't know. It's possible I guess," he said as he reached a set of stairs, climbing up them. There were three bedrooms on the top floor.

One was piled with old chairs and a large cutting table. The other yielded stacks of newspapers and children's toys. And the third door was locked. Victor tapped on it lightly. "Hey, Jimmy? Are you in there? I found your keys."

Kirsten kept her back to the wall, checking the staircase for any sudden movements.

"I don't like this," Victor said. "I've visited here before and someone is always home."

"Maybe they went out for a while?" suggested Kirsten.

He knocked on the door again, louder this time. "He can't. We have his car keys."

"They might have taken another car?"

Victor stepped away from the door. "I'm going to kick it down."

"No, don't," Kirsten pleaded. "You don't know what's going on. They could just be out or something."

Victor ignored her as he reared back and planted his foot a little bit above the door knob. Wood cracked and a horrible stench crept from the room. He willed up enough strength and kicked the door again. This time it broke open with a loud *crack*. "Oh, God..." he gasped.

Kirsten felt herself moving down the stairs. "Holy crap."

Inside the small bedroom were two bodies. Jimmy was facedown and naked on the floor. His wife was half on the bed and half off. Both wore the same sunken eyed expression and pasty skin. Two dried husks, pale as clay.

Victor stepped into the room. "It can't be..."

"I'm calling the police," gagged Kirsten. She ran down the stairs and threw up along the way.

Victor bent over Jimmy's lifeless form. His skin was chalk white. Just like Lynn and the walking corpse. Tears stung his eyes. "Jimmy...I'm so sorry."

He scanned the room for a sign of what may have happened. A broken window, footprints, blood splatters, anything that would suggest what he was forced to conclude. But the room yielded no such evidence. No sign of forced entry or murder, only that the back door was broken in. No other evidence remained. Victor stared into Jimmy's sunken eyes. They were black and solid. He shuttered, recalling the night with Lynn and how that *thing's* eyes had glowed in the darkness. He drew closer to get a better look, but then withdrew from the dead and stood in the doorway. "My God."

Kirsten pounded up the stairs. "I called the police. They'll be here any moment." She pushed her way past Victor and went to Jimmy's body.

"I've never seen anything like this." Kirsten cupped a hand over her mouth and reached for Jimmy's pasty leg.

"No!" Victor yelled. Just before her fingertips touched Jimmy's clay, white flesh, Victor grabbed her by the collar, tossing her backwards.

She slammed into the wall, her breath exploding out of her like a bullet from a gun.

"What the hell do you think you're doing? Don't touch them, ever."

She coughed twice and leaned over, gasping for air.

"Kirsten? I'm...I didn't' mean to hurt you. Are you all right?"

A fist shot out and connected with his solar plexus. He doubled over and slumped against the doorframe. Kirsten stood over him seething with rage. "Don't ever touch me like that again! What the fuck is wrong with you?"

Victor gasped and rubbed his stomach. "Don't touch them. You'll die."

She helped him to his feet and ushered him out of the room, closing the door, which didn't close properly after being kicked in by Victor. "I didn't hit you too hard, did I?" she asked.

"You punch like a girl," he wheezed and straightened his back. "I guess we're even now."

"Yeah, I guess so." She took his hand. Together they went downstairs and out the front door to wait for the police. She sat on the stoop, staring blankly into the forest. "I've seen dead bodies before, you know. But none like those. I wonder what happened to them," she mused.

Victor sat beside her and ran his fingers through his hair. He wanted to tell her all he knew. About the walking corpse, how Lynn looked when she fell out of her casket, and the night before when the shambling terror came knocking on his door. But Victor sealed his thoughts away. They were his problems and he would deal with them himself.

"Jimmy was a good friend. His wife, Tina, wasn't so nice but she loved Jimmy. They'll be missed," he said.

Kirsten leaned against him, her cheek pressing on his shoulder. "Do you think they were murdered?"

Victor nodded.

Twenty minutes later, a police car, and ambulance pulled into the driveway. Kirsten held onto Victor, melting herself with him.

"Whatever happens, Victor, I'll stay by your side."

Chapter 10

After hours of relentless questions from the police, Victor was dropped off at Dead House. The cops stopped at the black gate, unwilling to go any further. Victor would've laughed if two of his friends hadn't died.

Now he sat at the desk in his room, playing with a butterfly knife, his mind still on Kirsten. When the police talked to her, she never broke into tears, her voice remaining strong. Her father picked her up an hour later. She promised to come over one day soon, but the way things were panning out, Victor doubted it. He twirled the blade back and forth, back and forth.

Scattered images of Jimmy and his wife reaped havoc on his psyche. When the cops examined the bedroom with the bodies, they shouted for an ambulance. Victor told them not to touch the bodies. He wasn't sure if they did or not. A black man by the name of Tom assured him that everything would be fine. Yeah, sure. After Tom got a close look at Jimmy, Tom stayed pale until they zipped up the body bags. Victor swung the butterfly knife back and forth. How many is that now? Lynn, Jimmy, Tina, possibly a paramedic or two.

When would it end? What the hell was going on?

He stabbed his desk and left the knife imbedded in the wood. He rummaged through his closet and picked out a pair of black pants and a matching sweater. Tonight he'd find answers. No matter how crazy they were. He opened his desk drawer and took out a mag-light. He grabbed his compound bow and found a spool of yarn. Carefully, he connected the yarn to each of his arrows, then tied the remaining string around the bow.

If he could get a clear shot of that dead thing, maybe he might pull it in. He stared at the yarn. "Shit, what am I doing?" He dropped the compound bow; it fell behind him with a heavy clunk. Grabbing the mag-light, he exited the bedroom. His father had a shotgun in the basement and he grinned. One blast from the double barrel and that walking terror wouldn't be moving ever again.

*   *   *

Trevor sped along Route 52. His knuckles bulged around the steering wheel as though they might rip out of his jacket. Kirsten sat in the passenger seat with her hands in her lap. The Subaru Forester ate the concrete road like a hungry monster, neither speaking until the awkward silence was broken with a single demand. "I don't want you to see that boy again. Do you understand me?"

"Dad. Today was..."

Trevor jerked his head, his eyes boring into her. "Do you understand me?"

Kirsten gulped. She hadn't seen her father this mad since the death of her mother. "No, I don't understand, Dad. He's my friend. We we're just returning Jimmy's car keys. Victor found them."

"Please, Kirsten. You've had enough problems. You don't need this."

She slumped her shoulders. "You're not talking about Mom, are you?"

"Yes I am. Not to mention you're going back to school soon. You are going, aren't you?"

She crossed her arms and rolled her eyes. "Yeah, I am. I want to go."

"Good," he said.

Kirsten chewed her lower lip, knowing she shouldn't bring up her mother again. The pain in her father was evident every time she mentioned her, as though the word itself was a long knife being twisted into her father's heart.

"I saw her again," Kirsten said, hating herself the moment the words poured out.

Trevor answered by pulling into an exit off Route 52. He drove to a Burger King and killed the engine. His jaw slackened as he turned to her with a heavy heart. "You're not well, princess."

Kirsten felt fire rushing to her cheeks. He hadn't called her princess in years. "I know, Dad. I see her more and more now. It's like she's trying to tell me something."

Trevor heaved a long sigh. "Your mother's dead. She isn't talking to you. What you see and hear are illusions your mind is making up."

She shook her head. "But she's real when I see her. I know she can't be real and yet she's there. I take my pills. I'm not crazy, Daddy. Please don't send me away."

"Honey..." he hugged his daughter tightly. He spoke into her ear and kissed her forehead. "I would never send you away. Never. We can work through this. You'll get better."

"But I haven't gotten any better. I've gotten worse. In the back of my mind, I can see you getting sick of it. I know Lisa is. I can see it in her face."

Trevor released his grasp on her. "Lisa loves you. She's just concerned, that's all. I would never let her take you away from me. Ever."

"Daddy!" She wrapped her arms about her father's neck.

"Come on now, princess. No more tears. There's already been enough crying for today and the days before to fill up a lake." He cleared the long strains of black hair hiding her face. "How about you and me go get something to eat? This is the Burger King my parents would take me and my sister to once a week when I was a child. She'd always get a chicken sandwich and I'd get a cheese burger kids meal. What do you say?"

Kirsten pushed her hair behind her ears. "A cheese burger sounds great."

Trevor rubbed his hands together. "Now that's what I'm talking about." He led his daughter to the Burger King and they ate their food happily, conversation falling on better times and promises of a wonderful future.

*   *   *

Night fell with all the glamour of an old hooker in high heels and smoke for breath. Victor deeply inhaled the cool air as he entered the old forest path. His boots crushed the underbrush with ease. The path was littered with tangled roots sprouting from the ground. One false step and he would be sucked into their twisted maze, but he didn't fall or even stumble. He knew the old forest path well enough from years of traversing it as a boy.

The moonlight shone through the trees and he picked up speed. The double barrel strapped to his back bounced up and down in its long leather hostler as he walked. The forest was a living, breathing entity, filled with malice and evil intent. He saw trees form into stalking killers, shadows merging into ghosts. He stayed on the path. His hand circled around the mag-light but he didn't dare turn it on. Tree limbs scratched his back as he raced down the woodland trail. Iron bars of the fence came into focus and Victor halted. He counted the last three spiked bars and twisted, the bars falling away with a metallic scrape. He pushed his way through the opening, his feet sliding onto the pavement.

Victor planted the bars back into place. For a moment he caught a hunched figure watching him from the forest. Instinct took over and he reached for his flashlight. The figure faded into the trees before he had time to turn the beam on.

He crept away from his property, taking safety in the road. He walked around a bend, and when the last remains of Dead House faded into the shadows, he turned his flashlight on.

"Safe," he whispered to himself. He glanced over his shoulder to make sure nobody was following him. Cherry Pit road was deserted. Trees towered overhead like a natural canopy. He swung his light at them and caught the luminous eyes of an owl.

"Don't mind me. I'm just passing through." He focused on the road ahead. A few more turns and he'd be at the field. He pulled the collar of his black sweater over his neck when a cool breeze rustled dead leaves and sent his feet racing. Victor shone the flashlight's beam on every dark shape he came across and was thankful he wasn't being followed. Then, a tiny burst of light appeared down the road. The single orb broke into two and barreled toward him.

"Shit," he said and jumped over a ditch to crawl into the woods.

Car headlights flickered and grew in intensity. The high performance engine from a sleek red Celica thundered toward him.

Victor squeezed himself into a tight ball and buried his head into the ground.

Don't let them see me. Please don't see me.

The Celica slowed down only a few feet away from where he hid. An electric window rolled down. "Hey? Is someone there?" a young man asked.

Don't see me. Please don't let him see me. Victor thought, remaining still. He held his breath, willing himself to be invisible.

"Hello?" The window buzzed upwards and the car door flew open.

Victor lifted his head. He saw a young kid with a crew cut and football jacket looking straight at him.

"Who the hell are you?" the kid asked.

In a panic, Victor leaped to his feet and ran into the forest. He heard heavy footsteps giving chase after him.

"Hey, get back here!"

Victor slipped behind a thick oak tree shrouded in green vines. He flattened his back against the thick oak tree and waited.

The football player didn't make it far. He stumbled through the woods like a giant ox, and after a quick check of the area, he cracked his knuckles and returned to the road. Victor heard him muttering before he climbed back into the Celica.

"I must be seeing things," the kid said. Then the car disappeared with a thunderous roar.

Alone in the dark, Victor breathed easier. "That was a close one," he whispered to himself. He left the comfort of the tall oak and returned to the road. This time he stayed near the forest, far from any other cars that might come his way. He kept a steady pace, made two turns, and before long he stood before the farmer's field. A low fog hung over the tall weeds. He reached behind his back and pulled his firearm free from its hostler. The double barrel felt good in his hands, a sense of security washing through his veins. He'd find the thing that had killed Lynn and blast it to bloody pieces.

DEAD HOUSE

He flicked off the safety and far off in the distance he heard an owl hooting. Victor slipped between the tall weeds, parting them with the shotgun's long barrel. A nagging thought penetrated his mind. *What if the shotgun is useless against the undead? What if this entire search proves nothing?* Maybe his father wasn't lying. Perhaps his father had been out for a stroll and fell into this field by accident. *Yeah, sure, Dad, and I've got some land in Florida to sell you cheap.* This field was the start of everything. It was where Lynn had spotted the walking corpse between flashes of lightning, and where his father had gotten trapped. *Does Dad know about the walking dead? Surely he must. Why else would he have come here?* Victor shoved the jumble of thoughts aside for now. He would question his father later. He flattened the tall grass with his boots. So far the field was proving to be a fruitless journey. He scanned the grounds with his light but discovered nothing of interest. There were small holes here and there, shallow impressions in the earth and the occasional beer can or condom wrapper. But Victor wouldn't be deterred. He filled his head with murderous revenge, gathered all his hate and sadness into a single ball of bottled energy, until it was just begging to be unleashed. Lynn was dead. She was gone forever. Jimmy and his wife died because of him.

Victor choked on his guilt. Had he told the police, his father, or even Lynn's dad what had happened, things might've turned out differently. They would've called him nuts, but maybe Jimmy would've had the incentive to tread more carefully. His house was broken into. The ghoul or living dead probably tore the flimsy door apart before Jimmy stirred in his sleep. The blame couldn't fall on him. And yet it did. The decomposed woman had pounded on his door not long ago. Had she found a way inside Dead House, he would have faced her, too, and paid the ultimate price.

Jimmy and his wife were blood stains on his hands. Victor clenched the shotgun tighter, digging his fingernails into the hard polished wood. That thing...whatever it was, would pay dearly. He reached the end of the field without a single clue or hint. He illuminated a stand of trees and the flashlight caught a reflection off a windshield; a truck lay in the woods up ahead. Vines curled about the tires like green tentacles searching for raw meat. The worn vehicle groaned.

Victor's shoulders tensed. He took slow, deliberate steps forward. Upon closer inspection, he discovered a slender birch tree grew from the ground straight through the driver's seat. The truck was a wreck. The front tires were missing and where the engine should've been was a rusty, hollow core. He approached the ruined vehicle with caution. He kept the shotgun close, ready to blast anything, but the truck was empty.

Whatever had made that sound; mice, snakes, wind, or the living corpse, it was gone now.

He dared to open the driver's side door. It gave way easy enough, but complained like a nagging old man wanting to be left alone. He slid into the passenger's seat, a tiny spring snagging his black pants. He ignored the twisted metal for now and popped open the glove compartment. The small cavity yielded spider webs, stained yellow paper beyond reading, and a pair of silk panties.

"Dammit," he said as he withdrew his hand and wiped it on his sweater. "Useless junk." He was about to depart when the flashlight's beam fell on a cardboard shoe box. The lid was sealed shut with gray duct tape. He scooped up the box with one hand as something jiggled inside it. He drew his pocket knife out and sliced the duct tape off. His face contorted as he looked inside.

Three old notebooks captured his curiosity. He opened the first one, only to discover the notebook filled back to front with a language made of strange circles and numbers. The other ones held the same symbols. When Victor removed the papers, he spotted a large brass key, the kind that fits ancient doors from the 1800s. Victor put the key into the light. On the hilt of the key was a picture of an eye with a red gem as the pupil.

Thunder growled above him, threatening rain.

Victor quickly stuffed the notebooks back into the shoebox and put the key in his pocket. Zeus's lightning bolts painted the night sky. He grabbed the shoebox, slipped the double barrel into its holster, and leaped from the truck and into the field just as the first raindrops fell on his head.

Victor ran. The wind slapped his face and thunder shook the sky like a dozen angels bowling the lanes of Heaven all at once. He ran until he found the road. Lightning darted across the sky in a twisted wire as the rain began to pour.

*　*　*

Kirsten stood in front of a full-length mirror. Her black satin bra and panties showed off enough cleavage and curves to make any boy drool, unless of course that boy was Victor. She'd be surprised if he'd even glanced at her. She straightened her back and swayed her hips from side to side.

Yeah, that might get his attention, she laughed to herself as she put on a pair of pink shorts and a loose fitting white t-shirt. She shouldn't feel this way about Victor. He'd lost his girlfriend and two people close to him. A fresh wash of guilt splashed over her. Why was she so infatuated with him? The moment she looked into his eyes, she knew she was in love. Cupid's arrow had struck true. Aphrodite smiled down upon her.

Then why do I feel so goddamn guilty?

She lowered her shoulders and grabbed her hairbrush off the night stand. Her elbow knocked Randolph Leeds' book onto the floor. She meant to return it today, but after Jimmy and his wife Tina... She forced the grisly picture aside. She picked up the book and flipped through it. The book was no bigger than a thin paperback novel and filled with a language she'd never seen before. There were a few hand drawings toward the end: a cup brimming with dark liquid, odd symbols shaped like numbers but different, and a graveyard lined with tombstones. Behind the cracked slabs were grotesque humanoid shapes missing arms and in rapid stages of decay. She closed the book. She'd seen enough death and old ghosts for one day. The image of her mother haunted her each time she closed her eyes. She always wore a blue dress and beckoned with a skeletal hand. Kirsten shuddered. She reached for her pill bottle, took two, and chased them down with the soda on her nightstand. She lay back on her bed and stared up at the ceiling.

"What do you want from me mother?" To Kirsten's relief, no answer came. She pulled the blankets up to her neck and left the light on.

Outside, tiny raindrops fell against the roof. She captured a brief glimpse of lightning before drifting off to sleep.

* * *

"No, oh, shit, no. This can't be happening," Victor gasped as he heard the moan again; it sounded closer this time. He pumped his legs to move faster. Lurching footsteps slithered after him as rain dug into his exposed flesh like a dozen nails. The flesh walker was getting closer. Victor ran until he reached the edge of Cherry Street then yanked the double barrel from behind his back.

"Come on, where are you?"

The rain splattered along the desolate pavement as a low guttural moan bellowed. Thunder roared, lightning flashed, and the walking corpse emerged closer than before.

He aimed at the figure's torso and pulled the trigger. The shotgun blast was deafening, and it jerked in his hands like a rouge dog trying to break free of its leash. He held onto the shotgun tightly and when the smoke cleared he was astonished.

The walking corpse of the woman was still standing. Half of her side was blown to shit, pieces of cracked ribs jutting out like curved fangs. The corpse hissed at him and advanced.

"Holy shit!" Victor dug into his pockets, retrieved two buckshot shells and loaded the shotgun.

The dead woman leered at him with a haunting smile. Her pale flesh gave off its own whitish glow in the dark. She jerked her body toward him and reached for his throat.

He let the shotgun roar again. The blow caught the abomination in the waist this time, severing the body in half as the two parts dropped to the ground. The legs slumped over, still, but the upper half remained animated. The pale woman clawed at his boots, threatening to make contact with his skin. Victor gave her a swift kick in the head. Once she let go of his boots, he raised the stock of the double barrel and brought it crashing down on her rotting skull. The blow caved in the head like a rotten melon.

The flesh walker jerked twice and remained still.

He set the shotgun on the pavement, letting the rain wash off the filth. He wanted to cheer in triumph, scream out to Lynn and Jimmy that their deaths were avenged. But as he stood over the ruined corpse, a wave of sadness washed through him. Around the dead woman's left hand was a wedding ring. He swallowed the rising lump in his throat. Whatever the woman was, she wasn't a monster. He said a silent prayer for her lost soul, slid the shotgun back into place, and walked away.

* * *

Kirsten awoke to the sounds of something tapping against her bedroom window, which was strange because she was on the third floor. Instead of turning on her light, she took out the long knife from under her bed and advanced to the window. The storm raged outside, as bright flashes of light came and went, then followed by thunder loud enough to shake the house.

A series of taps struck the window pane again.

Kirsten pulled the drapes aside and gasped. "Victor?"

Victor stared in at her. He was dressed in black and soaking wet. He waved his hand in greeting.

She put the knife down and unfastened the window's lock, then slid the window upwards. "How did you get up here? What are you doing?"

"I missed you," Victor smiled. "Can I come in?"

Kirsten smirked. "I don't think my father would approve." She leered over his shoulder, looking at the dark expanse stretching along the bottom of her house. "How did you get up here? Can you fly or something?"

"I climbed. I'm good at that." He lowered his voice. "Can you let me in? This storm is getting nasty."

She moved aside to let him through, closing the window behind him. Her eyes went to the shotgun strapped to his back.

Victor caught her urgent stares. "Don't worry. It's incase I ran into some trouble."

Kirsten crossed her arms. "Keep your voice down," she whispered. "If my father finds you here he'll kill you."

"Sorry," he said just below a whisper.

"What kind of trouble?" she asked.

He sucked in a deep breath. "We need to talk. Or I need to talk. Strange things have been happening."

Kirsten sat down on her bed and crossed her legs. She let her long hair fall behind her back and raised one eyebrow. "I'm listening."

Victor told her everything; about that night with Lynn, the walking dead, Lynn's funeral, and the way Jimmy and his wife Tina looked when they'd found them. He filled her in right up until reaching tonight and how he'd killed the shambling abomination. After he spoke, he heaved a sigh, thankful to be rid of the nightmares and share them with someone he trusted.

Kirsten looked at him for a while, then said, "I believe you."

"Thanks," Victor said, now relieved. "I really didn't think you would."

"After my mother died I can believe just about anything can happen."

His eyes went wide. "Your mother?"

"Yeah, it was six years ago on my birthday. A drunk driver ran into us. The car flipped four or five times. My mother was thrown out of the window. She got pinned down by the car. I tried to help her, but I wasn't strong enough. The gas tank was leaking and the engine was still running. A fire started. She burned alive. I couldn't save her. She screamed for so long." Kirsten sucked in her lips and closed her eyes, fresh tears staining her face.

He went to her then, holding her to his chest and rubbing her back. They stayed that way for a while, neither sensing time.

Victor cleared his throat. "I lost my mother, too."

"You did?" Her eyes brimmed with tears.

He nodded. "We have a lot in common you and me."

She held his hand. "I'm so sorry, Victor. I had no idea. Do you want to talk about it?"

"Not today." He brought her hand up to his mouth and kissed it. "How about another day? There's been too much talk of death lately."

She curled up beside him. "Victor, I really like you."

"I like you, too."

She brushed his cheek with her nose, then planted a kiss on his chin, to quickly pull away. "I'm sorry."

"It's okay." He combed through her hair with his fingers. "Do you think I did the right thing? You know, going after that thing?"

"Yeah, I guess so. What did you do after you shot it?" she asked.

"I left it there. I didn't want to touch it," answered Victor.

"You just left it there?"

"You don't understand. That thing, zombie, or whatever it was, killed Lynn. All she did was touch it and she died. I didn't want to get near it."

Kirsten shuddered. "What if someone else touches it? Will they die, too?"

"I don't know," he shrugged. "That's why I didn't want you to touch Jimmy or his wife. I couldn't let you take that risk."

"But what about the police and the mortician? Surely they'll touch the bodies."

He covered his mouth. "I don't want to think about it. I hope that thing I shot tonight was the last link to whatever poison brought it to life."

She leaned against him. "Do you want to stay for a while?"

"Yeah, if that's okay with you? Just until the rain stops, then I'll go."

"Okay," she said and tossed him a towel. "Here, so you can dry up, you're soaked."

"Thanks," he said as he toweled off.

She lay down on the bed. "You can lie next to me if you want to. But I'm not having sex with you or anything, got it?"

He lay flat on his back next to her. "Got it." He closed his eyes as the rain dripped off the roof. "Thanks for letting me stay."

Kirsten gave a heavy sigh and rested her head on his chest. "You know, if you were my boyfriend, you could be in between my legs right now."

"I might have to change my mind about staying here," he gulped as he stifled a laugh and held her close.

Chapter 11

Officer Brian Kratos was thirty-four, divorced, in great physical shape, and extremely unlucky. For three years he'd worked in New York City as a homicide detective. Too many bad things can happen in three years. And when millions of people live close together, there's always trouble and a body or two in the morning.

Brian wanted out. He needed to get away from all those people, and the dark city. He wanted a life in the country, a quiet life, a good life. He'd started his job in Stormville the day before and already there'd been two murders. His partner, Julie Reeves, said the second worst thing to ever happen in Stormville was when an angry ex-boyfriend opened fire on his lover's house with a twelve gauge. Six people lived there at the time: two children, a mother and father, an elderly grandmother on the father's side, and a female teenager. The gunshots should've killed half of them, but the family was at the hospital at the time of the incident because the grandmother had a bad heart.

But the worst thing Julie said ever happened was the double murder of Jimmy and Tina Vahaugn the day before. Brian hadn't seen the bodies yet, but from what Julie reported, they were in an advanced state of decay. He'd left the city for this? What the hell was he thinking in coming here? Although Stormville did have its benefits, and that credit would go to his partner Julie. She was five years younger than him, never married, no children, and a rock hard body to kill for. The only thing about her that Brian didn't like was her short blonde hair, but despite that, she was still a knock out.

Brian had dreamed of her all night as the storm pounded on his modest, two-story home. He tried to imagine what it would be like to put his hands on her small waist, wondered what she tasted like, and if she knew how to grill a steak. In the morning, as he drank black coffee and watched the news, Julie had called. She had a firmness in her voice that made him pay attention. There was trouble at the local morgue last night. He'd dressed in a flash and raced toward the funeral home. He was almost there when Julie called him again on his cell. She said there was nothing more to do at the morgue and asked if he wanted to grab breakfast?

Brian was quick to agree. They'd meet at Alf's Diner in thirty minutes. He'd found the Mom and Pop place just an hour ago. He sat at a small booth, drank more coffee, and pretended to read the newspaper.

Where is she? Brian read an article about a Doberman pincher biting a small child when Julie tapped him on the shoulder.

"Hey, hot stuff, mind if I join you?"

Brian lowered the paper and greeted Julie's wide smile. "Not at all, are you buying?"

"You're a funny guy." Julie sat across from him. A young waitress came over and she ordered pancakes with sausage and a tall glass of orange juice. Brian decided to get scrambled eggs with five pieces of bacon. No juice. The waitress took their orders and left.

Julie leaned back in her chair. "I've got bad news, partner."

"What now?"

"Do you remember those bodies from yesterday?"

Brian stifled his laughter. "How could I forget them?"

"They're both gone, someone broke into the morgue and took them last night."

"You're joking, right?" He saw the stern look in her eyes. "You're not. It's my second day in this town and everything goes to hell. Are there any leads?"

"We're working on it. So far the only evidence we have are the footprints of the victims."

Brian arched his head up. "What footprints? Did they just walk out on their own?"

Julie shrugged. "It sure seems that way."

The waitress brought two steamy plates of food for them. Brian poured ketchup on his eggs, and after the waitress was gone, he resumed the conversation. "Where was the mortician?" he asked.

"That's another problem," Julie said. "He's missing." She poured maple syrup on her pancakes then cut them into little squares. "At first I thought he was the one who took the bodies, but Mr. Slade is a seventy-three year old man. He can barely walk. So there must be an accomplice, or a totally different party broke in to play a prank."

"Or the dead just got up and walked out themselves," added Brian with a snort. He shoved a fork full of eggs into his mouth. They were warm and tasty.

"This isn't a joke, Kratos. Two bodies are missing and nobody's seen Mr. Slade since yesterday."

Brian stiffened at her mention of his last name. Julie sure knew how to drive the nails in. "Have you questioned the family?"

"Not yet, I wanted you to come with me."

He nodded and took big gulps of his coffee, then started in on the strips of crispy bacon.

"There's something else," Julie said a bit hesitantly.

"What is it?"

"I saw those bodies yesterday, Brian, and well, they were like nothing I've ever seen before." She bent over the table and lowered her voice to a whisper. "Their skin was chalk white, like they'd been floating under a dock for about a week. I don't know what happened to them, but it's not natural."

Brian finished his bacon. "Bad things can happen to good people. I've seen plenty of cases before, believe me. We'll get to the bottom of it."

"Yeah, well, I just thought you should know." She finished her orange juice and left half the pancakes untouched. "Let's go down to the Slade family's property and see what we can dig up."

Brian's waist radio blared to life. "Dispatch 50-72 respond."

"That's us," Julie said. She paid the waitress with a twenty. "Let's roll."

Brian left a five dollar tip on the table and answered the call.

*　*　*

Brian and Julie arrived at Memory Lane Cemetery at the same time. They parked their cars along a grassy knoll fitted with hundreds of tombstones. A middle-aged man in coveralls and a bald head greeted them.

Julie advanced on the man. "Are you Mark Parks?"

"That's me. You two got here fast."

Brian joined them. "What can we assist you with, Mr. Parks?"

"Mark. Just call me Mark. There's no need for formalities here." Mark spit on the grass. "Follow me. I want you both to see this."

Brian and Julie exchanged glances.

Mark led them up a slight incline. They strolled by a giant oak tree and came upon a ruined piece of worm-turned earth.

"What happened here?" asked Brian.

"I found it this morning."

"Whose grave is this?" pressed Julie.

Mark shook his head. "Lynn Turner. She was buried only a few days ago. It's a damn shame."

Brian loomed over the upturned soil, pieces of Lynn's casket laid scattered about the cavity. "Do you have any security cameras or someone who might've seen what happened?"

"I don't have any cameras. I don't even keep a guard on duty. There's no need. People tend to stay out of here at night. I still get a few kids that run through every now and then. But they never do anything except drink and have sex."

71

"Where's the nearest house?" asked Julie. She gave the grave an examination and clenched her fists.

"That'd be Joy's place. It isn't far from here. She's an old lady," Mark said. He spit on the grass again. "I don't think you'll have much luck there, though."

Brian rose from the grave. "Does she live with anyone?"

"Only a bunch of cats, and believe me she has plenty of them."

"Thank you, Mr. Parks. We'll keep you informed on what we find."

Brian and Julie filed the case, took photographs, and reported to headquarters. As the two went back to their patrol cars, Julie nudged her partner with an elbow. "I want to stop by the cat lady's place."

"Sure." Brian waved Mark over. "How far away does Joy live?"

Mark pointed across the graveyard. In the distance, the outline of a little red house with a green roof could be seen through the trees. "Just over there."

"Let's walk," Julie said. "I could use a little exercise."

Brian snickered. "If you exercise anymore some things are liable to pop."

"Watch it, mister," she grinned.

When the two officers approached Mark, he advised them on how to reach the cat lady's house. "She doesn't like visitors," Mark said. "But tell her that I sent you and she'll warm up."

"Thank you, Mr. Parks." Brian said as he and Julie ascended the incline and headed for the house.

"Hold on," Mark called after them. "I forgot to warn you. Don't eat any of her muffins; they're hard as a rock."

Julie stifled a laugh as she led the way through countless marble slabs. "So what do you think?" she asked.

"About the missing body? Odd isn't it? Jimmy Vahaugn and his wife disappeared last night and now this happened. I think they're linked."

"Me, too," agreed Julie. "I'd like to find the morgue owner and see if we can get some clues."

"Do you think he did it?"

"You don't?"

Brian shrugged. "I've followed cases before where I was positive I had the suspect nailed, only to discover later I was wrong. I don't like to guess."

Julie nodded. "Smart guy, I'm glad you're my partner." She brushed away a group of branches and revealed a clear cut path where Mark said it would be.

"Ladies first," Brian said.

She rolled her eyes and ducked under the branches, then held them long enough for Brian to pass. As they approached the house, three cats, one black, the others brown, yowled at them. Julie stopped dead in her tracks.

"Are you all right?" he asked.

Julie never took her eyes off the black cat. "I have a confession to make."

"I'm all ears."

She chewed her lower lip. "I'm afraid of black cats."

Brian didn't laugh. He didn't even crack a smile. "You're kidding, right?"

She shook her head. "I'm afraid not."

"We could just walk by it together, or I could scare it away."

Julie took a step back. "I can't, okay?" She kept her focus on the black cat. The feline watched her with curiosity, then started easing toward them. Julie shrieked. "I'm out of here." She ran through the forest the way they came in.

"Julie, wait!" called Brian.

"I'll meet you back at the patrol car!" she answered and then disappeared behind a row of dense trees.

He chuckled. "I would've never guessed." He shook his head as the black cat rubbed itself against his leg. "How could anybody be afraid of you?" He petted the cat between its ears and approached Joy's humble red house. It was a small single story country home with a rocking chair on the front porch. Fifteen or so cats were racing about the lawn or guarding the porch as he approached. These cats weren't skinny or diseased in any way. All of them were taken care of and had flea collars. Brian reached the door and knocked twice. Inside, he could hear a television blaring.

"Just a minute," replied the voice of an aged woman.

Brian waited patiently. He stepped away from the door so he wouldn't seem threatening.

Three locks unlatched before the door opened. A guard chain allowed just enough room to see a thin old woman with long silver hair appraise him. "Who are you? What do you want here?"

Brian cleared his throat and held up his badge so she could see it. "My name's Officer Kratos, I'm with the county Sheriff's department. I was wondering if I could ask you a few questions. I promise not to take up too much of your time."

Joy eyed him with caution as though he might strike her. "What kind of questions?"

"It's about a robbery in the graveyard. Mark Parks sent me."

Joy's hard face lightened. "Mark sent you." She closed the door, unhinged the chain guard, and opened it wide. Joy was barely five feet tall. She walked with a weathered cane and wore baggy pants and a heavy gray sweater. "Well, don't just stand around, Officer. Come in, come in."

Brian grinned and stepped inside. Even more cats greeted him as he passed through the doorway. The television was an old black and white set resting on a large wooden chest. Hundreds of small dishes lined the living room, each bowl containing milk or cat food. Brian carefully stepped around the mess and followed Joy into the kitchen which, to his surprise, was actually quite clean. A round, wooden table sat in the center of the kitchen surrounded by four chairs.

"Have a seat at the table and tell me your name, Officer," Joy said. She busied herself by getting two plates from a cupboard above the sink.

"My name's Officer Kratos," Brian said again, as he took a seat. "I don't mean to bother you. I only have one question, really."

"Nonsense, you're not bothering me. I don't get many visitors here besides Mark, and he's not much for company." Joy set the table with two glasses full of milk and a tray of chocolate chip cookies surrounded by a mound of blueberry muffins. "I hope you can have a little snack while you're on duty?"

"This is very kind of you Ms..."

"Jones, Joy Jones. I've been a widow now for twenty-seven years."

Brian's stomach growled. Breakfast seemed so long ago and the cookies smelled like the ones his grandmother would make back home. He grabbed a handful of them and a muffin or two for good measure.

"So, Officer Kratos, what brings you here?"

Brian quickly ate two cookies and chased them down with a gulp of milk. "It's nothing pleasant."

"Oh, dear." Joy snatched a large orange tabby from the floor and cradled the cat in her arms.

"Mr. Parks had a disturbance at the cemetery last night. I was wondering if you saw or heard anything out of the ordinary."

Joy's face contorted. She looked frightened. "How out of the ordinary?"

"Someone dug up a grave last night. The body is missing."

Joy put the cat on the floor and went to the sink. "Oh, dear." She started cleaning dishes with a wet wash rag. "Would you like some more cookies, Officer? I have some vanilla ice cream in the freezer."

"Ms. Jones, you didn't answer my question," Brian said in a firm tone.

Joy closed her eyes and dropped the dish rag into the sink. "You won't believe me."

"Please, anything would help right now."

"It was raining last night. I always let my babies in before sunset, but one of them, a white cat named Whiskers, wouldn't come in. I called and called but that damn cat just stayed near the woods close to the graveyard. So I put on my raincoat and went after him. And I saw it."

"Saw what?"

Joy closed her eyes again. "A girl with blonde hair crawling out of the earth. She moaned like the wind when she saw me. I grabbed Whiskers and ran inside."

Brian took a muffin and bit into it. His teeth bounced back as though he'd tried to eat a rock. He cleared his throat and put the muffin back on the tray.

"Could you have mistaken her for someone else, perhaps a gravedigger taking her body out?"

Joy's lips curled downward. "Not a chance. She got herself out of that grave." Joy turned away from the kitchen sink. "The dead walk."

*   *   *

Back at the car, Julie scratched her head as Brian related the story. "Yep, she's crazy or senile or both. I'm glad that I wasn't there," she said.

"Yeah." Brian looked over the bone orchid. "She sounded so sincere, and she fed me, too."

"She fed you? What, milk and cookies?" asked Julie with a smirk.

"How'd you guess?"

She laughed. "Sounds like a nut job. I bet my badge she saw that mortician dig up Lynn's grave but won't report him, and that's our next lead."

Brian nodded in agreement.

Julie's eyebrows fluttered. "Brian, you don't actually believe her, do you?"

"No, but I'm sure she saw something."

She hopped into her patrol car. "Come on, tiger, we've got work to do now. I'll meet you back at the department."

Brian gave the graveyard one more glance over.

He thought he witnessed a dark shadow pressing close to an oak tree in the distance, but when he looked again, it had vanished. The cemetery offered no answers, only questions. Brian got behind the wheel of his car and followed Julie out.

The image of Lynn Watterson forcing her way from the worm-turned earth haunted him, and Joy's words were stuck in his head like a long nail.

The dead walk.

Chapter 12

Kirsten adjusted her short pleated skirt down so that her underwear wasn't showing. She made sure her pink halter top wasn't too revealing then knocked on the front door of Dead House with her knuckles. The sound of hard bone rapping against the worn wood sent a chill rushing down her spine. She straightened her posture and waited.

Victor said for her to be here at noon, it was five minutes before. She counted to thirty and knocked on the door again. Dead House offered no answers.

"Victor, are you here?" she called. Kirsten rapped on the aged wood once more.

The crunch of dry leaves caught her attention.

"Wow," Victor said. "You look amazing." He stood near the side of the house with a shovel in his hand. His white t-shirt had dirt and sweat stains on it.

Kirsten leaped from the porch to meet him. "How else would I look?" She wrapped her arms around his neck and planted a kiss on his lips.

He kissed her back, but he refrained from touching her. "Don't get too close. I'm really dirty."

She brushed against his chest. "I don't mind."

He grinned and escaped her grasp. "I didn't think you'd be here so soon."

She tapped the pink watch on her right wrist with a red fingernail. "I'm right on time."

"Let me see." He glanced at her watch. "Shit, I'm sorry, Kirsten. I guess I lost track of time."

"What are you doing anyway?"

Victor wiped sweat from his forehead. "I was covering up a hole in the yard."

"And a hole is more important than me?" she asked with a hand on her hip.

"No way, you're more important than yard work, believe me."

"I'd better be," she smiled and leaned on his chest with her breasts. "Are you still sorry about last night?"

His face flushed red. "A little, you know I really wanted to, it's just that..."

"Too soon," she finished for him. "I know. I wanted to tell you I was sorry for teasing you like that, although I wasn't really teasing. You could've had me, and you still can." She rubbed her soft body on his.

Victor moaned. "I meant what I said last night. I want to be your boyfriend. I just need more time."

She pulled away from him. "Okay, but don't make me wait too long or you might miss me."

He laughed. "Don't worry. I don't think you'll be waiting long." He stepped toward her. "I really like you. You're a very attractive girl and a smart one, too."

"Damn straight," she replied. "I've got an idea. Why don't you get cleaned up so you can give me the grand tour of Dead House."

"That sounds great." He leaned the shovel against the house and led her to the porch. "I'm surprised my father didn't try to chase you away today."

"Why would he do that? I saved him."

Victor plucked a key from his back pocket. "He's been acting strange lately. I don't know what's gotten into him. My father's never liked people, but he always recognizes a friend."

Kirsten thought about the strange book she'd discovered and how she meant to give it back, or at least tell Victor about it. If there was a time to tell him it was now.

"Victor?"

"Yes?"

"What does your father do for a living?" she asked, silently cursing herself for not asking the real question.

Victor frowned slightly. "He was a microbiologist a long time ago, but now he's retired. Sometimes he drags out old files and a microscope and goes through data." Victor fit the key into the lock and twisted the knob. "After you, my lady."

The door squeaked open.

"Thank you." Kirsten stepped into Dead House and immediately felt cold air slither up her naked thighs like groping fingers. "It's cold in here."

He followed her in. "Sorry about that. Why don't you sit on the couch while I get cleaned up?"

"Can I have something to drink?"

"What do you want?"

She sat down on the couch in the living room and crossed her legs. "Water's fine?"

"Coming right up." He went to the kitchen. "Do you want ice with that?"

77

"Sure." She grabbed a throw pillow and held it for warmth. "Where's your father?"

"He's probably in the basement. Don't worry, I told him you were coming for the grand tour today." He came back with two tall glasses of ice water. He gave one to her and took the other for himself.

"Thank you." She sipped the water and put it on the small table beside her after she was done.

Victor downed the water quickly and sighed. "That was refreshing." He saw her clutching the throw pillow and chuckled. "Are you cold?"

"Hell, yeah, I'm cold. Why don't you come over here and warm me up?"

"I'd get the couch dirty."

She rolled her eyes.

"I'll be right back," he said and disappeared down a hallway

"You'd better be," she called after him.

Two minutes later, Victor returned with a heavy blue blanket and a small cardboard box. He threw the blanket over Kirsten and placed the box on the table. "I want you to look at this while I'm getting cleaned up. Tell me what you think."

Kirsten curled herself in the blanket. "Okay."

He kissed her on the forehead, raced upstairs, and a moment later the shower was running.

The shoebox sat on Kirsten's lap. She put it on the coffee table for now as she wrapped the blanket around herself like a second skin. She didn't want to wait for him to get back, her curiosity peaked. She left the living room and went upstairs. She'd just go by herself and explore.

"And maybe I'll take a peek in the shower while I'm at it," she snickered to herself. An ornate metal railing led the way upstairs, the cast iron decorated with interlocking brass leaves. Kirsten gripped the railing and began to climb. The steps groaned under her feet. She tried to soften her footsteps but the aged wood continued to protest. Undeterred, she reached the top. A long hallway was spread before her. She could hear the shower running, but couldn't tell which door it came from. She curled the thick blanket around her shoulders. The first door she came to was opened slightly and dark inside. She pushed it open and stepped inside. The room smelled like mothballs. She swatted a cobweb clinging to her hair.

"Yuck." With the hallway's dim light behind her, she could pick out the outline of a queen size bed and five rows of dolls staring at her with unblinking eyes. She counted twenty of the ancient dolls on the first row alone. They would've been beautiful if someone dusted them off every once in a while instead of leaving them to rot. For a brief moment,

Kirsten wondered why the Leeds Family would have such a girlish room, then she remembered Victor's mother. She was dead just like hers, but not completely.

Kirsten imagined that Victor kept this room the way his mother had it before her passing, maybe she had wished to have a girl? The room was a shrine, a reminder. Just as Kirsten was haunted by her mother's ghostly presents, Victor was haunted by this room.

Kirsten walked out and closed the door.

A ragged voice roared behind her. "What were you doing in there?" Randolph Leeds asked. He sat in his wheelchair only an arm's reach away from her.

Kirsten yelped. She slammed herself against the wall and panted. "Jesus, you nearly gave me a heart attack."

Randolph gave her a cold, plastic stare. "Why did you go in there? Who the hell do you think you are?"

"I was just looking around a bit. I didn't touch anything."

Randolph snarled at her. "If you were anybody else I'd have blown you in half right about now."

It was then that she realized a double barrel shotgun was propped on the wheelchair's side. "I'm sorry. I really am," she said. "I just wanted to see the house."

"Where's my boy? Where's Victor? Victor, get your ass out here!"

"He's in the shower. He told me to wait downstairs, it's not his fault."

Randolph snatched her hand and squeezed. His grip was strong for his age, like the talons of a vulture. "Let me tell you something, girl. One day that curiosity is going to be your end." He let her hand go and wheeled down the hallway without looking back.

Kirsten rubbed her hand. "Jerk off," she muttered and went back downstairs, falling onto the couch in a huff.

The shoebox on the table was missing.

* * *

Victor led Kirsten to the third floor. "And this is the parlor where my grandfather once worked on the dead bodies. The drain on the floor is where all the fluid goes."

Kirsten crossed her arms. She'd given the blanket back after being scolded. The parlor was so cold it was as if it was frozen in ice. The floor was a dull marble color and the walls were painted green. Victor offered her no warmth. He barely even looked at her after his father gave him a tongue lashing for letting her roam unattended. He'd yelled at Victor so long that Kirsten had covered her ears to block out the sounds.

"I haven't come up here in years. My dad keeps some of his old equipment up here," explained Victor. He ran his index finger along a worn work table. It came away caked in dust.

Kirsten didn't touch anything. She took the parlor in, absorbing it like a sponge. "What are you going to do with this place?"

"My father wants to keep the parlor the way it is. I say rip everything out, put up some new walls, and change this place into a walk-in attic."

"Don't you already have an attic?"

He glared at her. "How did you know? Did you look up there, too?"

The harshness of his tongue left her bleeding. "No, I didn't. I've researched Dead House for years now. And I'm sorry about earlier, okay?"

"Well, sorry doesn't cut it," he spat. "You should've stayed downstairs." He threw his hands up and seethed. "And where the hell is that box I gave you?"

"I told you. I left it on the table."

"Are you sure you didn't steal it?" he pressed.

She uncrossed her arms, showing off her pink halter top. "Does it look like I can steal anything? I'm in a skirt, for God's sake."

"Well, the thing just didn't disappear." He pressed a hand over his face.

"Maybe it fell, or your father took it." Kirsten took in a deep breath before she spoke. "Don't go blaming me. I didn't even look inside your stupid box. I went upstairs to surprise you in the shower, but I got distracted. And I'm sorry, okay? You said I could have a tour of the house so I thought I'd check out a few rooms myself."

Victor sealed his eyes shut in sheer frustration. "You didn't look inside the box. Don't you remember what I told you last night? Didn't you hear what I said? It's not normal for a dead body to walk around and I don't care who the hell she was; the dead stay dead. Inside that shoebox were two pieces of paper with strange writing on them and a brass key." He pulled out a thin chain from around his neck. A large brass key dangled on the end. "I found this in the glove compartment of a beat up truck. It was in the same field where you found my father, and where Lynn and I first saw that dead thing."

Kirsten examined the key with her eyes. The brass was tarnished along the key's notches and the handle had the markings of an eye with a red gem for its pupil. "I wonder where it fits."

"I don't know." Victor put the key under his shirt. "It's all linked together. I know it is."

She nodded to herself. She thought about the book on her desk at home and wondered if the writing matched those on the papers? If so, then Victor's dad was behind the mystery. "Victor, why don't we ask your father? Maybe he's seen the shoebox."

"You just don't get it, do you?" He paced the floor. "He's crippled. He can't walk. Hell, he's only got one eye. If you're suggesting my father has anything to do with this then you'd be dead wrong."

"I wasn't saying that he did. I just thought he might've moved the box."

Victor stopped pacing. "This is crazy. The whole damn world is upside down." Victor was on the verge of screaming. He clenched his fists and grimaced instead.

"I'm sorry about this, Victor. I don't know what's going on." She gave him a quick hug, pressing her breasts against his chest. "Please don't be angry with me."

He looked into her eyes and then looked away. "I'm not. I'm just frustrated." He kissed her forehead and broke the embrace off. "Come on, I'll show you the rest of the house. We'll talk to my father, too."

"That sounds nice."

She took his hand and Victor led them down two flights of stairs. "The only places you haven't seen yet are the backyard and the cellar," he said.

"Show me the cellar first. That's where all the ghost sightings took place."

He held back his laughter. "I've lived here my entire life and I've never seen a single ghost. How about we check out the backyard? I wouldn't mind some fresh air, and I think my father needs some time to cool off."

"Okay, sounds great."

Kirsten followed him past the kitchen and through the back door. From a window, she spotted an old storage building, a wood shed, and a gazebo covered in vines. She squeezed his hand. "I've always wanted a gazebo, that and a pool, too."

He slipped outside and onto a faded wooden deck. "We have both. They're in bad shape, though. The pool is the worst off." He pointed to a concrete structure surrounded by thick bushes. "The pool's over there. The water was attracting too many bugs and blood suckers so my father drained it."

Kirsten stepped off the deck and went to the gazebo. The eight sided structure was crumbling inward, and vines curled up the supports, trying to reclaim the wood. She ran underneath the crumpling mass.

"Hey, don't go in there! It's not safe," he called out, chasing after her.

Kirsten spun in circles under the gazebo like a girl at the prom. "This is fantastic."

Victor grabbed her. "We need to get out of here, it's not safe."

"Is anywhere safe?" She put her arms around his neck. "Dance with me."

His hands slipped to her slender waist line. "If this falls on us I'm blaming you."

"Shhhh." She pressed her lips against his and let her head sink onto his shoulder. "Just try to relax. Have you ever danced before?"

He eased his shoulders down. He gripped her waist as they drifted back and forth. "No. Never have. I didn't go to my prom."

She nuzzled her nose against his neck and whispered in his ear. "Me either."

"Why didn't you go?"

"I have my own reasons. Why don't you tell me where you were that night instead?"

"I didn't have a date," he grinned

She smiled up at him. "Nobody asked me, so I didn't go." She gave him a long kiss then broke off their dance. "We're very much alike you and me."

"I'm beginning to notice," he replied. "How about I show you the rest of the backyard?"

She took his hand. "Lead the way."

The backyard was choked with weeds, but Victor took a well used path and navigated through the tall grass with ease. He stopped at a small building with no windows.

"What's in there?" she asked.

He pulled her closer. "Why don't you follow me and find out."

She hiked up her short skirt. "I hope you brought protection."

Victor laughed. "I don't need protection to go in here."

She rolled her eyes.

The door gave way with a slight nudge. The first thing she saw was a row of cages and small bones. "What the hell?"

Victor yanked a string dangling from the ceiling and brought the building to life with a dirty halogen bulb. "Here we go."

The building housed over a dozen empty cages. Each wire mesh unit contained a standard water bottle and tiny bones.

Kirsten cringed. "Gross, what did you keep in here?"

"Not me or my father, it was my grandfather's bunny house. He apparently took very good care of them, but when they died he wouldn't burry a single one."

She stuck her face toward one of the cages; inside were tiny white bones and matted fur. "Why didn't you clean up after him?"

"My grandfather's will requested they not be removed. So we never touched them. He loved those rabbits to death."

She frowned. "Yeah, I can tell." She sneezed on one of the cages.

"Bless you."

"Thanks," Kirsten sniffed. "Why don't you show me the rest of the backyard?"

"Sure thing." He opened the door and she bolted out, coughing and gagging.

"Are you okay?" he asked.

"Yeah, I guess." She took a purple hair band from her wrist and put her long hair into a pony tail. "I'm not so sure I want to see the rest of your property."

"It's not so bad. There's just an old storage building in the woods."

"I hope your grandfather doesn't live there now," she said.

"No, don't be silly. My grandfather passed away over thirty years ago, or at least as passed away as you can get these days." Victor had a far away look, as though he was dwelling on the past.

Kirsten took his hand. "Are you feeling okay?"

"Yeah, it's nothing. I was just thinking about something my father used to say about Dead House."

"What?"

"It's stupid, but he would always scare me. He'd say that the bodies never left. That the dead were still here, waiting to get me."

She didn't laugh. She leaned her head on his shoulder. "Why don't you show me that building in the woods?"

He shook his head. "You don't want to go in there."

"Why not?"

"It's just a building for leftover machine parts," he explained.

Kirsten rubbed herself on him. "Is it secluded?"

His breath grew hot. "Yes."

Her hand drifted to his crotch. She rubbed him between his legs, feeling him grow excited. "Maybe you could show it to me?"

Victor gulped. "I..."

She rubbed harder. "I'll make this real easy for you to decide. You can either watch me on my hands and knees as I give you a blow job, or you can watch me walk back home. Which will it be?"

Chapter 13

"Jeffery York," Julie said. "That's the mortician's name."

Brian swallowed a big gulp of Pepsi. "Good work. Now, where do we find the son of a bitch?"

Julie typed more keys, her fingers jabbing like they'd taken on a life of their own. "He's on 617 Maple Street," she replied and twirled out of her chair. "Let's roll."

"Hold on a second. We can't just barge in on this guy and start asking questions."

"And why not?"

"Because we don't have any leads. The only thing we do have is guess work. We don't have a single fact."

Julie tightened her utility belt a notch. She looked amazing, prepared to kick ass and take names later. "It's common sense. He's a suspect. He saw the bodies last," she said.

"And disappeared afterward himself," Brian finished. "I know, but what could he do?"

"Look," Julie said. "You're either with me or not. This is my town and I don't let criminals walk my streets." She snatched a set of keys from her desk. "Are you with me?"

"I guess. Someone has to look out for you."

Julie threw the keys at him.

Brian caught them in a flash.

"Good reflexes," she smiled. "You're driving."

* * *

When the patrol car pulled onto 617 Maple Street, Brian tapped the brake pedal. He passed two and three story houses set far back in the woods, each one nearly identical in the same reddish cedar paint. "Which one is his?"

Julie pointed to a large red brick colonial. "That's it. Pull in there."

"Right." Brian squealed into the paved driveway. He parked beside a sleek midnight-colored Corvette. "Damn, I should quit the force and work on cadavers instead."

Julie lightly punched his shoulder. "Don't hold your breath. I saw the way you eyed that graveyard. I don't think working with the dead is your forte."

Before Brian could respond, the front door swung open. A heavy-set, bearded man in stained blue coveralls stumbled from the house with a beer in each hand.

Julie nudged Brian's ribs. "Heads up, we've got a live one."

The man swaggered toward them with a dreamy smile. "Julie? Is that you?"

Julie stood her ground. "Please state your name, sir, and don't come any closer."

"Shit, Julie. You know me. I'm Tom. Tom Roberts. I was the star quarter back in high school."

Julie's jaw dropped. "Tom? What're you doing here?"

Tom downed the rest of his beer. "What does it look like I'm doing? I'm partying."

Brian went for his cuffs.

Julie held up her hand.

"What are you two here for?" Tom asked. "I didn't do anything. I haven't done anything since fumbling that ball in my senior year. Do you remember that night, Julie?"

Julie's lips formed into a straight line. "We came here to question Jeffery York. Is he here?"

"You're here for York? That guy has less of a life than me." Tom threw back a hasty laugh. "York's not here. I haven't seen him since he disappeared."

Brian stepped in. "What *are* you doing here, Mr. Roberts?"

"I told you," Tom leered. "I'm partying. Old Jeff has a stash of alcohol like you wouldn't believe. Every now and then I come over and we drink. He gave me a key to his house. I kind of thought if York showed up he'd come here first."

Julie pushed Brian aside. Her way of saying, *I'll take this one*. She cleared her throat. "When was the last time you saw Jeffery York?"

Tom scratched his scruffy beard. "Last week was the last time I saw him. We had a couple of drinks. He bitched about his job. I bitched about losing you. Same old shit."

Julie took a step closer to Tom. She gave him a hard stare that bore straight through him. "First off, don't ever address me like that again or I'll cart you off for a night in the slammer. And secondly, you didn't lose me, Tom, you never had me."

Tom tipped his head back. "Ha!"

Julie poked his chest with her index finger. "Look, asshole, you've got about five seconds to take that back before I run you in."

Brian stepped in front of her.

"Back off," Julie said to Brian. "This is between him and me."

"You're out of line," Brian stated. "We're on an investigation and you're taking care of an old grudge."

Tom looked back and forth at them. "What investigation?" he slurred.

"We've got work to do." Brian tapped her shoulder. "Pull yourself together."

Julie raised her upper lip. She directed her attention toward Tom. "If you see Jeffery York tell him we stopped by."

"He won't be here," Tom said. "But if I see him, I'll call you, babe."

"Don't push your luck." Julie turned away and went back to the patrol car.

"I think I pissed her off," Tom chuckled to Brian.

Brian's narrow gaze stopped him cold. "That's my partner back there." Brian cracked his knuckles.

"I didn't mean anything by it. I promise."

Brian lowered his voice. "Good. If you see York, tell him we've got a few questions to ask." And with that said, Brian walked back to the patrol car. He saw Julie leaning against the driver's side. She wouldn't look at him.

"Hey, wait," Tom said.

"Yeah?" Brian asked.

"I have something to tell you." Tom chugged the rest of his beer. He wiped his mouth before speaking. "I did see Jeff."

"When?"

Last night I saw him in the rain. He was moving really strange, kind of jerky, like he couldn't move his limbs. I called out to him but I don't think he heard me, and then he was gone."

"Where did he go?" Brian asked.

"I don't know. He just vanished. One minute he was there and the next poof, gone." Tom scratched his beard again.

Brian tried to look appreciative of the information, but he knew he wore a face full of disgust. Tom was a drunken liar. "Thank you, Mr. Roberts."

"No misters here. I'm only Tom."

"I'll keep that in mind." The men exchanged glances and Brian turned away.

Tom slipped back inside the house.

"Where to next?" Julie asked.

Brian shook his head. "I don't know. We're at a dead end."

Julie stuck her hand out. "Give me the keys. I'm driving."

"Sure." He slipped the keys into her waiting hand. "Do you have any ideas?"

"Just one," Julie said. "Did you hear about that girl who died of the flu last week?"

"No, what happened?"

"She was walking in the rain with a friend, a boyfriend maybe. The next day she's found dead in her bedroom."

Brian slid into the passenger seat as Julie got behind the wheel. "Do you think they're related?"

"It's a possibility," she said. "I don't think the friend can help much, but his father might have a lead. They live in a mansion called Dead House."

"Dead House, what kind of name is that?"

Julie started the car. "It was once a morgue."

Chapter 14

Kirsten licked her lips. She savored the sweet taste in her mouth. "Did you enjoy that?"

Victor brushed errant hair away from her face. "That was..." A wide grin cut his lips as he tried to catch his breath. "Wonderful."

"I thought you'd like it." Kirsten got off her knees and stood.

Victor massaged her breasts.

She moaned with pleasure but she moved his hands away. "That's enough for today. Why don't you show me the rest of the house now?"

"Are you sure? We could stay here for a little longer?"

She grabbed his crotch. She zipped his pants and rubbed between his legs with eager fingers. "I don't want it for a little while. If you're going in me it had better last all night."

"I look forward to that," Victor said, and gave her a kiss.

She sucked on his lips and shoved her tongue in his mouth. When they ended the embrace, she gave him a wink. "Come on, lover boy. Show me your house. I want to see the cellar."

"Okay." Victor led the way out of the storage building and toward Dead House.

Kirsten latched onto his arm. "I've only done that once before."

Victor's eyes shot open. She had worked on him like a pro. "I enjoyed it. You know I consider you my girlfriend now."

"I would hope so," Kirsten laughed. She playfully smacked his chest.

Together, they crept into Dead House hand in hand. Once inside, Victor guided her to a shabby door set on rusty hinges. "This way." Victor swung the door open. A set of cobweb strung steps led downward. The bottom stairs were shrouded in darkness.

She hugged him from behind. "Did you bring a flashlight?"

"Flashlight? This is my house. I don't need a flashlight. Besides, it would take away from the tour."

"Right."

"Just hold onto the railing and follow me down," he said. "There's a light switch at the bottom."

Kirsten did as he said. She held onto the metal railing and descended into the darkness. "Is your father down here?"

Victor stayed three steps ahead of her. "He might be. His office is down here." When they reached the concrete floor, he flicked a switch on the wall.

A single bulb flashed and died out.

"Dammit." Victor squeezed her hand. "Stay here. I'll see if I can find the other light."

Kirsten saw the last bit of Victor's body swallowed by the thick gloom. She crossed her arms across her chest. "Don't make me wait too long."

"I won't." Victor's voice trailed off. He sounded far away.

"Sure, okay."

A cool draft raced downstairs and up her bare legs, causing her to shiver. *Did they forget to shut the back door*? She couldn't see the cellar's entrance from where she stood. *We didn't go that far down, did we*? She braced her arms tighter, wishing she'd put on something less revealing. *Victor had enjoyed the view though. He couldn't keep his eyes off me*, she smiled in the dark. She could still feel his large shaft in her mouth as she had bobbed her head back and forth.

A disturbing sound ended her daydreaming; footsteps echoed in the cellar. Not the heavy thumps that Victor made, but more of a dragging motion.

"Victor?" Her voice came out in a squeak.

The footsteps drew closer.

"*Kirsten...*" It was the familiar tone of her dead mother.

Gooseflesh spread across her arms. "No, you're not real. Go away."

The terrible lurching motion of skeletal feet scraping concrete grew louder. "*You've been a dirty girl, Kirsten. Didn't I raise you better than that*?"

Kirsten pressed her hands to her ears and closed her eyes tight. "Not here, Mother. Not now. I'm not running this time." Even with her ears covered, Kirsten could still hear her getting closer and closer. "Not real. Not real. Not real."

Hands suddenly grabbed her and shook hard and she screamed. Her eyes fluttered open and Victor stood in front of her.

"Oh my God," she said and embraced him, pressing herself into his chest.

"Kirsten...you're shaking. What's wrong?"

"I'm fine," she quivered.

Victor held her close. "What's not real?" He rubbed the small of her back with soothing hands.

"It's nothing," Kirsten said and ended the embrace. "I'm fine. Just don't leave me alone down here, okay? I'm afraid of the dark," she lied.

"Yeah, all right." Victor held two cylindrical objects. He gave a blue flashlight to her. "I found two of these, one for me and one for you."

She snatched the flashlight from his hand. She immediately turned it on and scanned the area. Four massive shelves filled with books and labeled glass jars greeted her, in addition to an empty desk littered with papers. The cellar was enormous and the flashlight's beam couldn't reach the end. Kirsten felt her heart return back to its natural rhythm. Her mother was gone, back to the nether world of dreams and phantoms.

Victor rubbed her shoulders. "Are you sure you still want to go through with this?"

"Yes, I'm fine." She walked toward the desk, her combat boots slapping the concrete floor like a hammer driving nails. "What did you say your father did again?"

"He was a doctor, retired now. Sometimes he comes down here and pulls out old files to work on."

Her flashlight shone over stacks of memos and data entries. A worn patch of tan paper caught her attention. "What kind of doctor was he?"

"Microbiology, germ research, stuff like that. He doesn't talk about it and I don't ask."

Kirsten snatched the tan paper from Randolph's desk; it felt like beef jerky. Printed in red ink was a blueprint of a series of connecting rooms. One of the passages was marked with an asterisk.

She handed the rough map to Victor. "Do you know what this is about?"

Victor studied the paper carefully and shrugged. "I don't know? It feels weird." He tossed the paper back on his father's desk. "Come on, I want to show you the rest of the cellar."

She obliged but before they left, she scooped up the map and looked it over once more.

"I don't come down here much anymore," Victor explained as he led her across the room. "My father doesn't like me snooping around his work area."

Kirsten focused on the paper. There was a large octagon room which connected to a narrow hallway to then spread into two separate rooms. An asterisk was marked at the end of the hall.

"Hey, I think this is a map of the cellar," she said.

"Really? Let me see that again." Victor shone his flashlight on the paper. His eyebrows connected in thought. "I think you're right. But where this mark is leading into a hallway, there's just a wall."

He took the map from her. The large room they walked through narrowed into a hallway only fit for one person. Kirsten followed close behind him. She held onto his shirt tail and wouldn't let go. When the passageway ended, another room appeared with two wooden doors flanking both sides. Ahead of them was a stone fountain, no water ran through it, and mold grew along the sides.

Kirsten came up from behind him. "The map showed a hallway beyond that fountain."

He stared at the sketch. "That's impossible. There's nothing but brick and dirt behind that wall."

"What about those two doors? What do you keep behind them?"

"Old toys, machine parts, broken televisions, stuff like that."

Kirsten ran her index finger along the water fountain's edge. "Did the fountain ever work?"

"A long time ago," Victor answered. He went to her side and placed a warm arm around her shoulders. "I don't remember it working. My father said the fountain stopped running with water after my mom died, but I know that's a lie 'cause I came down here to play near it all the time. The fountain never worked."

She peered into the fountain's center then began to clear away bits of stone and cobwebs. "Victor, come look at this."

"What is it?" he asked, moving closer.

She moved out of his way so he could see. "Just look."

The beam of the flashlight danced over the center of the fountain and revealed a large notch. "It's a keyhole." He traced the hole with his fingers.

Kirsten's eyes widened. "Your key, try it."

"The key..." He dug out the brass instrument from the chain around his neck. "I found this in that field where you saved my father."

"I know. I bet it's his. Go 'head and test it," she urged. She shone the light at the key; the red emblem on its hilt sparkled like a watchful eye.

Victor held the key in his palm and clenched his hands into fists. "I can't, it wouldn't be right."

"Why not? Your father is behind everything. Don't you see? He's connected. Hell, he might even be the cause of those walking corpses."

Victor laughed. "Don't be silly. He probably crawled into that truck and left it there by mistake."

"Like those papers you tried to show me?"

Victor's smile crumbled. He squeezed the key so tight a trickle of blood seeped from his palm. "I don't want to know." He turned his back on her and headed down the hallway.

"Where do you think you're going?" She yanked him back by his shirt tail, then spun him around. "What about Lynn, and Jimmy, and his wife? That's three people dead, gone forever because of this. You have a chance to discover the truth and you're going to just walk away?"

"He's my father. If he's a part of this mess I don't want to know."

Kirsten never broke eye contact with him. "It won't end. Another day, another week, more and more people will suffer, maybe die. How can you let that happen?" She pressed herself to him. "Just try the key. If it doesn't work then I'll leave you alone."

His upper lip rose. "Fine, I'll try it once." He went to the fountain's facade, drew the key overhead like a Spartan with a spear, drove it into the center, and twisted.

The grinding of ancient gears spun behind the wall. A trickle of dark water flowed down the fountain's tip.

Victor withdrew the key.

The wall behind the fountain slid open, revealing a dark pit laced by cobwebs and dust.

"Holy shit," he gasped.

Kirsten gripped his hand. "Oh my God, Victor."

"Where's that map?" he asked.

She handed him the map then aimed the flashlight beam down the hidden passageway. "I can't see anything," she said.

Victor pawed over the map. "If this is correct, then there's an entire level below the cellar."

"I didn't think it would really work."

Victor ventured to the entrance. "Well it did. Shall we go?"

She paused. "No way, we don't know what's down there."

"We can find out."

"We're not prepared. What if that thing is down there?"

"Kirsten, I blasted it to bits, it's dead."

"What about the others?"

Victor walked into the passage. "There are no others, and if Lynn turned we would've seen her by now."

Kirsten stomped her feet. "We have seen it. She turned Jimmy and Tina. You saw them. And what about the paramedics that handled the bodies, that's at least three or four more people." She crossed her arms. "What if all of them are down there, waiting in the dark?"

"I'll protect you. Look, we won't go in very far. I just want to look around." He handed her the map. "Here, you can navigate for us."

Kirsten took the map. She traced the secret hall until it forked into separate paths. "I don't want to go in too far."

"We won't," he said.

"Okay."

Victor gave her a quick kiss. He penetrated the darkness and cut through the cobwebs beyond the wall. Kirsten kept one hand curled around his belt loop, the other on her flashlight.

When they'd traveled only a few feet, the floor under them sank.

Kirsten jumped.

"What's going on?" Victor wailed.

Gears spun and the wall sealed behind them.

Kirsten pounded the solid mass with her tiny fists. "Dammit." She kicked at the wall and cried out. "Shit, we're trapped!"

Victor went to her like a rock bracing a river about to overflow. He eased her away from the wall and into his arms. "We're okay. I'm here with you. We'll find another way out."

She wiped her eyes on his shirt. "Sorry I freaked out."

"Don't be," he said and squeezed her. "Let's find out what's down here." He broke apart from her. Together they made their way down a sloped floor. The cobwebs were thicker here, too. He made sure to break the spider webs before advancing. The concrete floor gave way to gravel, and when the passage ended, two rooms appeared on either side. Victor shone his light into both of them. The room on the right had strange runes inscribed on the walls. The other held only more darkness.

"Which way should we go?" Victor asked.

"Let's go right," she said.

"What's down the other way?"

Kirsten stared at the map. Her lips curled downward. "It's a dead end."

"Do you want to check it out?"

She shrugged. "I don't think we'll find much, but as long as you go first..."

"Got it," he said as he headed into the right hall. Upon entering, he choked on the foul air. "God, what's that smell?"

Kirsten held her nose. "I don't know. I left a cheeseburger under my bed for three weeks once and it smelled like that."

Victor pressed onward. The flashlight trembled in his hands. "Oh my God."

"What is it?"

Kirsten came up behind him and gasped.

Along the walls were uncovered tombs. Fleshless bodies were stacked onto one another in a haphazard way. Limbs were entangled, heads meshed as one, and the lingering scent of death was overpowering.

Victor advanced. His light scanned over more and more rotting carcasses. The catacombs seemed to stretch on forever. Kirsten held onto to him. Together they ventured into a large room fitted with concrete slabs in the center, strapped to the tables were dismembered corpses.

Kirsten tugged at Victor's shirt. "Let's get the hell out of here."

A low groan from behind caught them off guard.

Victor's flashlight illuminated the skeletal remains of countless dead remains. They were still and lied crumpled together like used husks drained of life.

"Who's there?" Victor asked.

A rotting arm moved, a head turned, and the dead pulled away from each other and onto the floor.

"Victor, get us out of here!" Kirsten yelled.

Shambling bodies dislocated from their restless sleep, sightless eyes focused on the intruders, and hungry groans echoed down the narrow passageway.

As the rotting corpses fell upon them, Kirsten let out a shrill scream.

Chapter 15

Lisa sat in the Subaru Forester, putting the finishing touches on her makeup, at the moment, applying blue eye shadow in the rearview mirror.

Dario always liked this color, she mused. The parking lot was half-packed with other cars. She didn't notice any of the people coming in or going out of the grocery store. It was mostly single mothers with two or three children crying and whining. She hated that sound, so she twisted the key in the ignition just enough for the radio to play. The Rolling Stones, *Sympathy for the Devil* drowned out the screams of youth.

When she was finished with her eye shadow, she puckered her lips and kissed a short red stick. She enjoyed the sensation of the lipstick gliding against her open mouth. "God I wish you weren't so late, Dario," she pouted as she crossed her legs. With her makeup done, she eased back and let the radio soothe her. She hadn't listened to The Rolling Stones in years and wondered how old they were now? The last time she could remember seeing them was on MTV. Mick was strutting down a city street where the buildings were as tall as he was.

How long ago was that? Her mind reeled. It was before Trevor and his bratty daughter, she was positive.

Dario would put a stop to them. She blushed in the mirror with the idea of finally escaping those two bastards. After all these years of dealing with their crap, she'd make sure personally that both of them paid the ultimate price. Lisa blew a kiss to herself. Their deaths would be sweet, just like the others.

She spotted a sky-blue Corvette turning into the parking lot. "Dario," she grinned, "late as always." She checked herself in the mirror one more time, gave a wink, and exited the Subaru.

The Corvette purred like a lion. Dario saw her waving and pulled in beside her. He was wearing a black business suit and a red tie. He got out of the sport's car in a flash.

Lisa ran to him and smothered him with kisses.

"Miss me?" he asked as he gave her breasts a squeeze.

"Did you miss me?" she laughed. She rubbed herself on him. "We have to go. I don't have much time."

Dario stopped caressing her. "What did you tell the sap?"

"That I was going shopping."

He gave her a crooked smile. "What's the hurry then? We have the rest of the day." He pinched her left nipple and she flinched.

"Not funny, my shopping expeditions don't last all day," she said.

"They do when you're with me."

"Did you find a place for us?" she moaned in expectation.

"I did. Why don't you get your little ass in my car and I'll take you there?"

Lisa giggled. She opened the passenger's side door of the Corvette and slipped inside. Her feet got caught in two large duffel bags.

"What's this?"

"Why don't you open one up and see," he said.

Dario got behind the wheel. He brought the Corvette to life with a simple twist of his wrist.

Lisa put one of the bags on her lap. She was surprised at how heavy it was.

"Go ahead, open it up," he urged.

"Okay." Lisa opened the bag and saw black leather straps, a mask with a zipper where the mouth should be, thick ropes, handcuffs, her Uzi, three long serrated knives, a handheld blowtorch, bullwhip, fishing hooks in a zip lock bag, leather gloves, four dildos, and an assortment of prescription drugs.

"Oh, Dario!" she squealed in delight and kissed him. "This is wonderful."

Dario pulled out of the parking lot and onto the street. "I thought we could try that one out ourselves." He pointed to the black straps.

"What is it?"

"It's a sex swing."

"Kinky, I like it." She stuffed the contents of the duffel bag inside and zipped it up. "I wouldn't mind using that on the brat." Lisa rubbed his upper thigh. "You can fuck her hard baby. I can't wait to see that," she moaned.

Dario's upper lip curled. "I love it when you watch."

"But I want in on her, too, after you're done of course."

He licked his lips. "Hell, yeah."

"I can lick your dick while you fuck her." Lisa rubbed his crotch and felt a sudden rise. "Would you like that?"

"You know I would. I loved it five years ago when we did that teenager and her mother."

Lisa unzipped his pants as he drove. "Then you'll love this." She yanked his slacks down low enough so she could free his hard member. She jerked him up and down for a minute before shoving him in her mouth.

96

Dario groaned. "Oh, yeah, baby. Suck it good."

Lisa's head bobbed up and down, faster and faster until a warm fluid filled her mouth. She was barely aware he had pulled the car over on the side of the road. Lisa finished him off, then lifted her dress and planted herself on top of him.

"When will we kill them?" Lisa groaned as she eased herself down on his throbbing cock.

Dario moaned as he thrust deep inside of her. "Don't worry, baby. They'll die soon."

Chapter 16

"Run, dammit!" Victor yelled as he slammed into the nearest rotting corpse, a dried out shell of a woman with a black hole where her stomach should've been. She collapsed in a mass of bones and withered flesh. He caught another living dead in the upper torso and knocked it down.

Kirsten stayed behind him. Her eyes were wide and a shrill squeak erupted from her mouth.

"Don't touch them!" Victor instructed. He spread his arms wide to protect her from the approaching undead horde.

The dead shambled toward them, groaning and hungry for the living.

Victor snatched a chunk of rubble from the floor. He heaved it over his head and brought the rock down upon a hairless skull. The zombie's head caved in like a rotten melon and the body tumbled backward into the attacking crowd.

Victor bashed in another zombie skull, then another until the bodies piled up around him. "Come on you fucks." The sea of animated corpses moved in closer. Victor charged into the mass of walking dead. Skeletal arms clawed his back and shoulders, drawing blood. Victor smashed the rock into the heads of the fleshless zombies, each one crumpling under his blows. But the dead were many and soon filtered past him.

"Victor, help me!" Kirsten screamed.

Her screams caught him off guard. He looked back only to find her surrounded. They tore at her top and ripped her short skirt. Kirsten thrust herself upon them, striking two attackers with her fists, but she was being pulled deeper into the passageway. "Victor!"

Victor threw a large chunk of heavy ruble, striking one of the zombies holding her in the lower back, breaking it in half. Despite his effort, the dead swarmed around her and dragged Kirsten into the darkness.

Victor roared and slammed through the shambling terrors, heedless of his own safety. The dead bit and scratched his shoulders. One latched onto his arm, driving nail-like fingers into his flesh and wouldn't let go. He pounded the corpse with his fist. It broke away from him, but left a deep wound on his forearm. "Kirsten!"

The only response he got were groans and shuffling feet from a sea of decaying shades.

He tore through the dried husks like a provoked boar. He rammed and kicked, punched and elbowed until he reached the hallway.

"Kirsten!" He couldn't see through the blanket of darkness. His flashlight lay on the floor somewhere in the hallway. He pressed forward. He used his hands to feel the wall, it was cold and damp. The further he went, the wetter it got. A constant drip assailed him. The gravel below him gave way to soggy earth. Shuffling footsteps followed after him. The dead were closing in. Victor ran into a body lying prone in the dirt. He tripped right over it and fell flat on his face. "Kirsten?" He felt a leg, then a thigh. The flesh was gone. The leg was thin like a twig. His fingers found an eyeless skull. He jumped back in shock and disgust. "Shit!"

Hungry moans echoed down the narrow passageway, eager claws scraping along the walls as the undead gave chase after him.

In the darkness, he could depict an endless flow of corpses heading his way. There would be no escape. Kirsten was surely dead by now, and he would be, too. He rose from the dirt. He ran blindly down the passageway with his arms outstretched. The hall went on forever. Then the wet earth sloped upward and dirt transformed into concrete once again. Victor pressed forward. Cobwebs stuck to his face and arms like thick ropes. He ripped through them, then clawed up the slope on hands and knees.

Above him was a circular ray of light and he reached for it. His hand pressed against a rusty set of bars.

From behind him came a guttural moan.

Victor curled his hands around the bars and twisted. The metal gave a chalkboard squeal.

A sharp hand suddenly gripped his ankle, digging long fingernails into his flesh.

Victor screamed. He kicked the corpse away and forced his energy on twisting the bars free, but the rusty metal wouldn't move.

"Dammit." He was vaguely aware of the walking dead surrounding him. They crawled and shuffled, lurched and dripped, but every one had the same mission in mind. Skeletal hands encircled his legs, crooked teeth bit into his thighs, as a shrill cry of agony split his lips.

He yanked the bars with every last bit of strength left. His forearms bulged, his biceps nearly tore. The bars slowly twisted and the circular door creaked open all the way.

A flood of brilliant sunlight bore down upon him, and as if afraid of the light, his attackers groaned and faded back into the bowels of the earth. Victor crawled out of the tunnel only to find himself in a wooden glen. A crisp breeze cleaned the sweat from his brow. He crawled from the pit and lay on the long grass. Warm fluid ran down his legs. The scratches on his arms stung and throbbed. He could still hear the ceaseless demands of the dead below. Their impatient groans brought him to his feet. He lifted the circular entrance and put it back in place. A small keyhole lay in the center.

He found himself reaching for the key around his neck, but it wasn't there. Panic seized him. "Where is it?" he said as he tore at the ground. The brass key wasn't among the grass. He slipped his fingers into his jean pockets and felt the key's handle. He slipped the brass key from his pants and thrust the thin metal into the hole. He turned the key four times before hearing a reassuring click.

He slumped onto the ground, tears spilling down the sides of his face. He had failed again.

Kirsten was among the dead.

Chapter 17

Dusk twisted the sky into a red hue as Julie and Brian took the long way to Dead House. Julie wore a hard grimace and jerked the steering wheel at every sharp curve.

Brian bounced in the passenger seat. "Are you sure you don't want me to drive?" he asked.

"I'm positive," she said as she took a turn around a bend and the tires cried out.

Brian put his hand on her shoulder. "What's going on? I've never seen you this upset."

"Tom, that's what. He's an asshole." She shook her head. "I would've kicked in his teeth if you hadn't been with me. And that's no way for a professional cop to act."

"You did the right thing," he said. "You listened to what he had to say and you walked away. It takes more guts to do that then beat the crap out of somebody in my book. I admire you."

Julie eased off the gas pedal. "Really?"

He gave her shoulder a little squeeze. "Really. You were terrific. I nearly hit the guy myself."

That got her laughing. "I saw the way your fists shook. Tom almost wet himself."

Brian leaned back in his seat. "All in a good day's work, what happened between the two of you, anyway?"

Julie gave a sigh that made her shoulders lower and breasts shake. "He was my boyfriend for a little while, back in high school. Tom was a star quarterback for the Eagles and I was on the cheerleading squad."

"You were a cheerleader? Give me a break," he smiled.

"I'm being serious," she grinned. "I was a cheerleader. I loved doing the cheers and always executed my flips perfectly. The only thing I didn't do that Tom hated was have sex with him. I was a virgin and wanted to stay that way."

Brian felt heat flushing to cheeks. "There seems to be a lot I don't know about you."

"Maybe you should ask me to dinner sometime and we could share."

Brian patted her leg. "I'd like that."

"Me, too," she said.

Brian cleared his throat. "So, what happened to Tom?"

"He tried to do me and I declined. So the day before our senior prom, he found a girl who liked to spread her legs and he screwed her." Her eyes teared up just a little. "The girl he had sex with told me the next day. She had been my best friend since middle school. So I dumped them both that day and stayed at home eating mint ice cream and watching *Near Dark*."

"At least it wasn't a total loss. I love that movie. It's with the vampires living in the van right?"

She nodded. "That's right." She drove the patrol car along a black iron fence that stretched out for at least a mile or two. "This is the property."

Brian watched as the black fence zipped by like hundreds of long spears. "Looks like a friendly place."

"Yeah, they're really nice. When I was a girl scout I tried to sell them cookies."

"What happened?" he asked.

"An old man with one eye screamed at me and I ran away."

Brian shook his head. "So you were a girl scout and a cheerleader? That's a winning combination."

"Watch it, mister. I'm the one driving the car. You wouldn't want to upset me and make me wreck us, would you?"

Brian chuckled. "Yep, you were definitely a girl scout. A pushy one, too, I bet."

"You know it," she grinned as she pulled into the driveway to the house.

A large black gate guarded the entrance.

"Is this the place?" Brian's gaze fixed on the weathered house in the background. It looked like a dark patch of evil among the surrounding forest.

"Sure is," Julie said. "I'll get them to open the gate. You stay here."

"Better you than me."

She shook her fist at him. "Keep it up." She exited the patrol car and approached the black gate. A heavy duty lock and chain secured the thick bars together. There was no intercom or ringer to press and Julie put her hands on her hips. "That's just great."

Brian stepped out of the car. "What's up?"

"There's no doorbell or intercom. The place is locked down tight."

Brian went to the fence. He gave the bars a tug. "I can hop over this easy."

She crossed her arms. "Sure, go for it, city boy."

He spit onto his hands and rubbed them together then grabbed the bars firmly and eased his feet sideways along the bars. "This is just like old times."

"Is there something I should know about you?" Julie snapped with a tearing smile.

"My high school was surrounded by a fence like this. I had a habit of skipping class from time to time," he said.

"Sounds more like you just took the day off a few times to me."

Brian shrugged. "Who likes high school, anyway?"

Julie was about to respond when the front door of Dead House swung open.

A ragged man in a wheelchair rolled out and started screaming. "Get the hell off my fence!"

"Whoa." Brian slipped from the bars and tumbled. He bumped into Julie who caught him just in time.

"Are you all right?" she asked.

Brian straightened his shirt. "I'm good."

The man in the wheelchair raced toward them. "What the hell do you think you're doing? This is private property, dammit."

Julie stepped closer to the fence. Her face was hard like marble.

"That's him, isn't it? That's the guy who chased you off?" Brian asked.

"It looks like him. He's older now." Julie whispered as the man drew near. "He looks smaller, too."

The material of the crippled man's dark blue bathrobe flew under his arms as he came to the gate. "What is it? Can't an old man get a little peace and quiet without some hooligans climbing his fence?"

"We're police officers, sir," Julie said. "And you'd do well to remember that."

The old man looked her over with his single, roving eye. "Do I know you? You look familiar?"

"I live in the area," Julie replied.

"I thought so." His gaze fell on Brian. "You're not so familiar. Why were you on my fence? I've done nothing wrong."

"Your gate is locked. We need to ask your son a few questions. Mr...?" Brian asked.

"I'm Randolph Leeds. What do you want Victor for? He's a good boy, a hard worker, too. So what did he do, huh?"

Julie raised her palms in an attempt to calm Randolph down. "Your son hasn't done anything, but he was with a girl last week who recently passed away. We need to question him about that night."

103

Randolph nodded and withdrew a large key ring from his side. It clanged together like a jailer's collection as he searched through a series of different keys. Finally, he picked out a silver one. "Ah, here we are."

Julie and Brian stepped aside as Randolph unlocked the gate and opened it. "I'll fetch my boy. He'll be out in a moment. You two can wait outside."

Julie and Brian jumped back into the patrol car. They both watched as Randolph raced toward the dilapidated old mansion.

"He seems friendly enough," Brian said.

Julie smacked his leg. "He's just an old, grouchy man. I hope his son is a little more hospitable."

"We can hope."

Julie drove the car into the driveway and parked, the two staying inside the vehicle. "This place sure is creepy," she said.

"It looks like the Adam's family house. I wonder if they have a Lurch," he mused.

Julie stifled her laughter. "Why don't you ask? If they don't, you can always work here part time."

"Hey now, don't be cruel."

"Who's being cruel?" She nudged his shoulders. "You are rather tall, but I must admit, you're too muscular to play Lurch."

"Thanks." Brian stared at Dead House with a gaping jaw. "So this place was a morgue once?"

"Yep, sure was." Julie patted his leg, almost resting it there. "Come on, partner. Let's go."

Brian got out of the car, and where Julie's hand had been, there was now a lustful warmth. He waited for her. She looked great in her police uniform. The way her breasts jutted out from her chest made Brian wish her uniform showed a little cleavage.

Julie caught him staring. She nudged her breasts against him as she moved past him and up the porch steps. He was speechless. He watched the way her round butt bounced a little as she reached the stairs. A rush of heat flooded both his cheeks.

Julie threw her head back to look at him. "Are you coming?"

"Yeah."

Brian reached the porch without incident. He stood beside Julie and faced the front door. "Have you ever met his son before?"

"No. I've heard he keeps to himself," she said.

"Wasn't he the one who found Jimmy and Tina Vahaugn?"

Julie nodded. "He's had a really bad couple of days. I wasn't there when they questioned him, but it seems like he's always at the wrong place at the wrong time. He was with Lynn Watterson before she died and now the other two."

"I see where you're going. It sounds like a suspect to me, or at least some sort of lead," Brian suggested.

Julie paced the porch. Everywhere she stepped the boards under her feet would groan. "What do you suppose is taking them so long?"

"It's a big house, maybe he's still looking for him."

She grabbed the door knocker and was about to use it when the door opened.

A well built young man blocked the entrance. His eyes were wide and his face was very pale. Along his arms were scores of bandages. "My name's Victor," he said in a rather lost manner. "You wanted to speak with me?"

"Yes," Julie said. "Can we come in?"

Victor stepped onto the porch and shut the door behind him. "We can talk out here."

"Victor, how old are you?" Julie asked.

"I'm almost twenty."

"So why do you still live here in this house? You're out of high school and talk around town says you're a hard worker."

Victor shrugged his shoulders. "There's no need for me to leave." He turned and stared at the crooked windows of the house as though seeing someone there. "I can't go. Not yet." He faced Julie with deep, sunken eyes. "It's expensive to get your own place in New York."

Julie nodded, knowing this was true.

Brian cleared his throat. "I don't believe you have our names yet. I'm Brian."

"And I'm Julie," she added, wanting to keep things informal.

Victor looked them both over.

"Victor, we need your help," Brian stated. "We're on a case where more than a few people have wound up dead or missing."

"Missing?" Victor drifted off.

Julie interrupted. "Do you know Lynn Watterson?"

"Yes, she was my girlfriend before she died."

"I'm sorry for your loss," Julie said. "When you saw her last, did she say or do anything strange or out of the ordinary?"

Victor's gaze narrowed. His lips formed a hard line. "I was already questioned by the police about what I knew."

Julie didn't let up. "The night you found Jimmy and his wife, I already know about. I've read the report. But I'd like to hear it from your mouth. What happened that night?" Julie softened him with a smile, showing her straight white teeth. "Anything you say will be off the record. Isn't that right, Brian?"

Brian nodded. "Please, Victor, we need any information you can give us."

Victor's shoulders slumped in defeat. He looked like he'd aged twenty years in that single moment of time. "You won't believe me, but someone was following us that night. I can't tell you who it was, only that it was dead and stalking us. Lynn touched it and the next day she was dead."

Julie and Brian exchanged glances.

"I can't prove it, but I think my father's behind it. I was down in the basement today and..."

"The dead stay dead," Brian said, dismissing Victor's words as silly. "Could the person you saw have been wearing a mask or a body suit?"

Victor shook his head. "It was a walking corpse, dammit. A real-life walking corpse."

Julie stepped in front of Brian. "Calm down, no one here is questioning what you think you saw that night."

Victor took a few deep breaths.

"That's better," Julie said. "Why don't you let us speak with your father now?"

"You don't believe me, neither one of you do." Victor went back inside and called for his father. "He'll be here in a minute. Just tell me one thing then."

"What is it?" Brian asked.

"Is Lynn the one who's missing from her grave?"

*   *   *

Julie eased the patrol car onto the road, and watched Randolph lock the gate in the rearview mirror, as they left Dead House behind.

"I never want to go back there again," Julie said.

"You said it."

Brian scribbled notes down in a small pocket notebook. He tapped his pen against the last line he wrote.

"What do you have for us?" she asked.

"I think we've got a psychopathic mortician dressed like a corpse injecting victims with a slow acting poison. Either that or the dead really are coming back to life."

"I think I'll stick with the first one, though both sound nuts," she said.

"Yeah," Brian agreed. "But it's the fact that someone dug up Lynn's body for some sick purpose that's got me bothered." Brian heaved his head back. "And I thought I'd left all the crazies behind in New York."

Julie laughed. "Where there's people there's trouble. Believe it or not, the country has worse crazies than the city does."

Brian pressed his fingers to his temples. "I'm starting to see that."

"So, tiger, where are you taking me to dinner tonight?"

"Whatever restaurant sells Chinese and leaves a tall glass of coke and rum on the table."

Julie grinned. "I know just the place. How about I drop you off and you can get changed."

"I could meet you there," Brian said and instantly regretted saying it. He tried to act casual but his palms were sweating.

"I'd rather go together, unless you don't want to?"

"We'll ride together," Brian agreed. "But this time I drive."

Chapter 18

Fleshless hands clawed at Kirsten's long hair.

"Get away!" She batted the ghouls with her fists to no avail. Skeletal hands sliced her upper thighs and sought purchase under her mini-skirt.

"*Kirsten...*"

That voice. She knew that voice. She tore away from the mass of surrounding dead only to see her mother gliding toward her in a blue dress. "Mother, is that you?"

"*I've been waiting for you, Kirsten.*" A long hand of yellow bones and shredded flesh reached for her.

Kirsten tried to run, but her legs were pinned down. Her mother curled thin arms around her mid-section and lifted her away from the sea of dead bodies.

"Let me go!" Kirsten cried, but her mother held her tight against her belly. A rotting stench of decay overwhelmed Kirsten's senses as she thrashed in her mother's grasp. Kicking her legs wildly, she sent the ghouls chasing her flying backwards.

A haunting skull eased close to Kirsten's ear. "*I'm taking you with me, darling. There will be no escape this time.*"

Kirsten managed to scream one last time before her mother flung her into an empty room and closed the door, thus sealing her inside. Outside, the dead groaned and hissed. The ghouls thumped against the aged wood, but none of them broke through.

Kirsten's mother straightened her dress. It was lavender and blue, but stained yellow around the edges and tattered with holes below two ragged breasts.

"What do you want from me?" Kirsten quivered. She backed into a gritty wall lined with cobwebs.

The haunting skull replied. "*I want to hold you again, my darling, to hear you laugh, to kiss away all of your bruises, and to tear the hair from your head.*"

"No, don't, Mom!" Kirsten screamed. "I tried to save you. I really did. But I wasn't strong enough. You were trapped, and the fire started. I went for help."

"*None came.*" Her mother clamped a fistful of Kirsten's long hair in a pale, thin hand. "*You will listen to me and you'll listen well.*"

Kirsten yelped as the specter that was once her dear mother yanked her hair so hard that her neck almost popped from her shoulders.

"You were the cause of my death. I didn't raise you to be such a weakling. Why didn't you pull me from the fire? Where was your father?"

"I told you, I couldn't help! It was over eight years ago. I was just a kid; a scared little kid." Kirsten swung her head back. She head butted her mother in the chest and heard a splitting sound akin to breaking dry sticks.

The phantom let her go. *"What have you done?"*

Kirsten felt her hair slipping through the skeletal hand and she ran toward the door and tried to open it. But the door was sealed tight and refused to open. On the other side, she could hear fingernails scraping the heavy wood's surface.

The dead were waiting.

Her mother gripped Kirsten's chest where she had butted her, a few ribs now poking through her blue dress like curved fishing hooks.

"You little tramp, look what you've done. Just look, you've ruined my dress."

"Shut up! You're not my mother! She's dead! She died eight years ago!" Kirsten screamed at the wraith.

The corpse's shell glided toward her. *"I'm your mother, child."* Her fleshless skull bobbed up and down. Where loving eyes once dwelled were now twin, yellow orbs. She stopped before Kirsten.

"Your favorite color is black and orange because you like the way the leaves look on the ground in autumn. We had a German shepherd named Elmo, after the character on Sesame Street. I drove you to school everyday and gave you a butterfly kiss because you always said...."

"The boys could tell I'd kissed someone and wouldn't want to talk to me," Kirsten finished. She turned away from the door.

"I'm your mother, Kirsten. I've come back for you."

Tears welled and flooded down Kirsten's cheeks like rainwater.

"Oh, Mom." She wrapped her arms around her mother's back and cried into the stale, blue dress. "Why did you die? Why did you have to leave me and Dad? I was so scared without you. And Dad...he had a gun to his head one night. I saw him. I ran up to him and yelled at him. He was there to take care of me, I told him. If he died, then who would be there for me?"

"And he has," her mother soothed. She ran a sharp nail through her daughter's long hair. *"He was a wonderful husband. He took great lengths to make you happy, but he's in danger."*

Kirsten stayed in her mother's arms. "I know. Lisa's a bitch."

"She's not very kind. I don't see why your father ever married that woman."

"Mom, I can't stay here with you. Can you let me go?"

"And feed you to those abominations out there? Never, you're my daughter, my darling. I'd never let anyone hurt you."

Kirsten wiped her eyes on her mother's blue dress. The stench of rot filled her nostrils and brought her back to the situation at hand. "Let me out, Mom. I can fight them off. Victor needs my help."

"Victor, ha, your boyfriend ran away. He got his pleasure and left you here to die."

"No, he wouldn't, and if he did run, it was only to get help. He'll return."

"Just like you did for me?"

Kirsten didn't turn away from her mother's piercing gaze. "I did what I could. I'm sure Victor did the same. And I did come back for you, Mom."

"Too late, though." Her mother drifted toward the door. *"But it's not too late for you."* Her fleshless hands curled around the door knob.

Kirsten's mind raced. She suddenly didn't want the door open. The fear of countless animated dead bodies piling through the opening made her scream. "Please don't, Mom."

"And why shouldn't I? This is what you wanted. You said you could fight them off."

Kirsten could hear the guttural moans seeping under the door. "I can't. Please, keep it shut."

"I thought you couldn't stay here?"

"Not forever. I don't want to die. Not yet. If you love me, Mom, you'll step away from that door. Please."

The yellow glow in the back of her mother's skull flickered, then her hand twisted the door knob. Kirsten's heart beat in her ears like a war drum. She set her feet into the dirt and prepared to launch herself at the door.

Her mother's hand slipped from the knob.

"I can't. I love you."

"I love you, too, Mom."

The wraith glided in front of her. *"If you're to survive, there are things you must know."*

Kirsten took her mother's hand, it was cold and frail. "I'm not afraid."

A sudden gust of wind separated them. Her mother pressed her skull of a face against Kirsten's cheek. Arms curled around her waist, lifted her off the ground, and leaned in with stained, yellow teeth.

"What are you doing? Stop it." Kirsten's instinct was to avert her head, but it was no use as a lipless mouth connected to her own. She gave a muffled scream. All around her, the room shifted and twirled. It reminded her of a roller coaster ride. The room was changing before her eyes. As it spun faster, the dirt rose to her knees. The door opposite her was flung open, revealing a passageway, not littered with walking corpses, but clean and full of candlelight.

Her mother pulled away from her death kiss, leaving Kirsten shivering and dizzy. She tried to focus on the door. The blurry images straightened out after a few minutes and Kirsten suddenly realized that her mother had vanished.

"Mom, where are you?"

Soft whispers echoed down the hall.

Kirsten lifted herself out of the mound of dirt. Her mouth gaped open. The room was completely altered. The cobwebs were gone and all traces of the walking dead were erased. She stumbled through the doorway, careful to avoid the low ceiling. "What the hell is happening?" She could recall taking her mother by the hand, and the feel of rotting teeth pressing on her lips, then the room had changed. Kirsten wiped her mouth.

The incessant whispering continued down the hall.

"Mom?"

Kirsten stepped into the passageway and took comfort in the candlelight. Dozens of red candles lined both sides of the wall in brass holders. As she made her way past them, her mind reeled. *The cellar is smaller than before.*

A chop, akin to an ax splitting wood sang out.

Kirsten jumped. She waited for the sound to return, but only heard more of the indecipherable whispering. "Hello? Victor, is that you?"

Another chop made her jump, a wet splatter soon followed.

She advanced. The hallway merged with a larger room lined with rusty cages. She stepped on a pair of tattered jeans with flowers imprinted on them. The pants were ripped at the crotch. She kicked the clothing aside and continued along the room's outer edges, peering into the cages as she went by them.

Behind one of the bars came watery gurgles. She took a closer look, but inside she could only see darkness.

"If he doesn't come tonight, he'll come tomorrow," whispered a voice in the black ink.

Kirsten tapped the bars with her fingernail. "Excuse me? Is someone there?"

KEITH LUETHKE

The voice repeated itself. "If he doesn't come tonight, he'll come to-morrow."

Kirsten backed away from the rusty cage.

Two pale limbs jerked out from the bars. A ragged head emerged; it was a woman with seaweed hair and no nose. She rocked back and forth with glassy eyes as though Kirsten wasn't there. She repeated herself over and over.

Kirsten found herself turning her back on the woman. She passed the other cages at a steady gait. Sometimes she saw humanoid figures jumping in and out of the dark, but often times nothing stirred beyond the reach of the candle light.

The wet chopping had ended.

She continued onward; past the jail cells was a small corridor leading into a well lit room. Kirsten's eyes immediately fell on a heavy set man in a white apron smeared with blood. He darted to and from the surgery table and a shelf full of glass jars. On the table was a long-haired blonde woman. Where a face should've been there was a flat mass of gore. Her breasts were removed and her belly was split open.

Kirsten's stomach churned. She held back a warm gush of vomit and eased toward the table. "What the hell is going on here?"

The man ignored her. He wiped back his gray locks and went to the shelf to fetch a jar filled with green fluid. "Just a dab of this, my pretty, and you'll be fine."

Kirsten saw a silver medical tray littered with scalpels and an odd assortment of sharp devices. She snatched the largest scalpel and advanced on the large man. "I want answers, and I want them now."

The man opened the jar, scooped out some of the green fluid, and smeared it on the woman's empty chest, eliciting a low moan as he rubbed it on. "You like that now, don't you?" he breathed heavily.

Kirsten swiped the blade at his hands. To her astonishment, the scalpel passed right through. She struck again, hard and deliberate. The blade wouldn't cut him, it was like striking air. Kirsten dropped the scalpel on the floor and it made a metallic sound.

The man jerked his head up. "Hello? What's this?" He bent down and picked up the scalpel, looked it over, and licked the flat side of the blade. "Tasty." He put the instrument back on the tray and continued working on the corpse.

Kirsten watched him dab the green fluid on every part of the dead woman's missing flesh. A low buzzing noise raced around Kirsten like an electrical charge. She turned just in time to see bony fingers clamp down upon her shoulder.

Her mother's gleaming skull brushed the back of Kirsten's hair. "*It's time to go. I have more to show you.*" She wrapped herself around Kirsten like a cold blanket.

The room spun round and round like before. The man moved in and out of the room in a flash, like a movie on fast forward. The corpse was placed in a coffin under the floor, other women were brought in, live ones; they were brutality raped, dismembered, and buried in the walls. The room grew larger still. Horrible screams raced about like wailing banshees from a nightmare.

Kirsten covered her ears to the sounds. Her mother held her fast from behind.

The room stopped spinning. The cruel man was gone, and Kirsten was alone once more. The medical table was caked dark red; its holding straps lay on the side, cut in half.

Kirsten lifted her boots from the floor; they peeled away with a sickening sound. She avoided the medical table and searched the room for clues.

Why did she bring me here? What do I need to know? That mad man had something to do with the walking dead, but what?

The room was unchanged by time. Scores of jars still lined the shelves, and the tray full of scalpels remained the same, sharp and gleaming under the floodlights glaring down from above.

Where did those come from? Kirsten felt a prickle at the back of her neck. She'd witnessed a passage of time without being altered herself. Where flickering candles once melted wax, now electric lights took their place.

Quick footsteps came from beyond the room. "Daddy?" asked an innocent boy's voice.

Kirsten could see no one in the room with her. She saw the long tunnel behind her and shivered as though a cold steel knife had penetrated her belly. She knew what dwelled in those walls; the horrors of countless women suffering well beyond the grasp of death.

"I'm not going back there," she called, hoping her mother might hear her.

The boy's voice echoed once more. He sounded like he was trapped in a well. "Daddy, I know you're in here. Mommy wants you to come upstairs for lunch."

The voice was coming from behind the wall. She walked toward the sound and immediately spied a long vertical slant along the bottom edge, split light shimmering through.

It's a door, she thought as she pushed through and gasped at the sight that greeted her.

113

A hairy butt bounced between two smooth legs chained at the ankles. The man was the doctor from before. He was much older now, with wrinkled skin and bald on top. Beneath him was a young girl no older than sixteen, bound and gagged. She was dressed in a sexy French maid outfit, and terror struck as the man pumped in and out of her.

"Daddy, where are you?" the boy's voice cried out.

The doctor gave a little moan and thrust deep inside the girl. Beneath him, the girl's eyes widened, tears staining her cheeks.

He pulled out of her with a sigh. "Sorry, love, I've got to go now." He gave her breasts a hard squeeze and laughed when she tried to scream. "You like that, don't you? Don't you worry, love, I'll be back later tonight. We'll have a grand time, too."

"Daddy, where are you?"

The man cleared his throat. "I'll be there in a minute, son. Tell your mother I'm coming."

"Okay," the boy answered. "But where are you?"

A wicked grin crossed the doctor's face as he pulled up his pants. "Wait right there for me, son. There's something I want to show you."

"No, don't," Kirsten gasped. She stared into the girl's eyes and saw pure terror dwelling within both orbs. Kirsten looked away. She couldn't save her. She could only watch.

These things have already come to pass, Kirsten told herself. *There's nothing I can do.*

The doctor went to the wall. He felt along the cracked bricks and pushed one in. The wall gave a groan and slid open. A little boy with shaggy dark hair froze in shock at the scene before him. "Daddy, what's going on?"

Kirsten recognized the kid immediately, the same jaw, the same forehead. He was Randolph Leeds, Victor's father.

"Go, run," she whispered.

"Come on in, son, don't be frightened." The doctor waved his hands, urging his son inside. Randolph didn't move. His mouth formed a giant O as he saw the half naked girl on the floor.

"Come in closer, son. Have a good look. She's a cute one. Would you like to touch her?"

The girl gave a muffled cry.

Randolph stepped into the dark room. "Who is she?"

"A girl from the supermarket, I think it was the Grand Union. I picked her up late last night. She's very horny and wet. Why don't you see for yourself? I know you want to. I've seen those dirty magazines you keep hidden under your bed."

The boy blushed.

"Come on, son, take a little peek."

Randolph moved closer, taking small steps until he stood over the frightened girl. "She's beautiful," he said.

The doctor smiled and patted him on the back. "Isn't she?" He reached for the brick and pushed it back in. The wall slid shut again. "Why don't you stand over here, that's it, stand between her legs. Have a good look."

The boy's eyes grew huge and he said, "Molly, her name's Molly. I've seen her working at the register."

Molly shrieked. She began twisting in her bonds in a feeble attempt to break free.

Randolph took three steps backward in panic.

"Don't worry, son. She can't escape. You can do anything you want to her and she won't escape." The doctor grabbed her breasts with both hands and gave them a good squeeze. A single tear drop rolled down Molly's cheek as she silently pleaded with her eyes for the young boy to help her.

The doctor unbuttoned her top. "Go ahead now. Why don't you get a little feel."

Randolph looked stunned. "I...I don't know. She doesn't seem to like it."

"She likes it. They all do. They'll cry and beg to be let go but then they moan with pleasure and plead so that it doesn't stop after a while. Believe me, she likes it."

Randolph rubbed his hands together. His face turned bright red. "I. . .I can't." He turned to leave, but his father snatched him around the waist and threw him on top of the girl. Randolph grunted, falling right between the girl's smooth thighs.

"There you go, see, nice isn't it?" his father said.

Randolph used his hands to get off of her, but they went straight for her breasts. He looked at his father for instruction.

"Go 'head." He patted his son on the back again and exited the room. "Lock up when you're done with her. And don't feel bad about what you do. She's just like the naked girls in the magazines. She's begging for it."

Molly shook her head.

Randolph's hands moved on instinct. He rubbed her breasts gently and opened up her shirt. "Wow," he gasped as he kissed one of her nipples, and then began sucking on it like a newborn searching for milk.

"That's my boy," the doctor said. pleased, just before he disappeared down a dark hallway. A door opened and closed.

Kirsten stood amazed. *This can't be happening. How could he?* She tried to shove Randolph off the trapped girl but her hands passed right through him.

Randolph stopped sucking. He unbuttoned his pants. "You're so beautiful. I wish you were my girlfriend," he breathed heavily.

The girl shrieked as Randolph took off his pants and underwear, his erection jutting from between his legs. He planted himself on top of her. "Oh, man, this is going to be good."

Molly struggled against her bonds, thrashing wildly.

Randolph backed off for a moment, still nervous. After he realized she couldn't break free, he rubbed his dick between her legs until he found his way inside her.

The girl screamed.

Randolph pushed himself inside with all his might. A bright smile formed on his face as he pumped in and out of her. The girl strained her right hand, bringing it up with all her strength.

The leather strap broke free.

Randolph didn't notice as he thrust inside of her wetness and had an orgasm, his eyes squeezed shut in pleasure. The girl's hand reached for a thin piece of metal lying on the floor, but her fingers couldn't seem to reach it.

Kirsten raced toward the object. She gave it a little push.

The metal slipped into the girl's hand and she reared back and shoved the metal into Randolph's eye.

"Arrarrah!" Blood and clear ooze seeped from Randolph's eye socket. He tore at the metal, but couldn't pull it free. The girl shoved him off of her with her free hand. Then she went about trying to unfasten the gag around her mouth.

"You bitch!" Randolph roared. He got a firm grip on the metal spike and yanked it free with a sickening *pop!*

Heavy footsteps raced into the room. "Son, what's the matter, are you hurt?"

Randolph spat out a flood of red ooze seeping into his mouth. He towered over the girl with an evil grimace, then shoved the metal spike between her legs.

The girl's eyes nearly bulged out of their sockets. She tried to cry out but the gag restricted her.

Randolph shoved the object further into her, beaming at her pain with his single eye.

"My God," the doctor muttered. He marched into the room and closed the wall behind him. He barreled toward the girl. "My boy, my God, what have you done to my boy?"

The girl shrieked as the metal disappeared inside of her. Fresh blood leaked onto the concrete as she kicked her legs in agony.

The doctor snatched an axe from a table, and before Kirsten could scream, "No", he severed the girl's free arm at the elbow. Blood shot out to spray the walls like a firehouse, the flow soon slowing to a sputter.

The doctor grabbed his son and carried him to the medical table.

"What did she do to you? How could she? Son, say something."

Randolph seemed to gaze at Kirsten with his single orb. "I want her to suffer," he said through gritted teeth.

The doctor snatched a long needle from a drawer, filled it with a clear liquid gel, and injected his son with it.

"She will, son. They all will."

Chapter 19

Trevor paced his kitchen back and forth, a cell phone clamped in one giant fist. Lisa had been missing for half the day.

She just went out for groceries, he kept telling himself. *Groceries don't take that long.* The Grand Union was only twenty minutes away. He'd driven there earlier in their second car, but hadn't seen the Subaru Lisa had taken that day. And now it was getting dark. Trevor went to a small cupboard and picked out a bottle of wine. He fetched a glass and filled it. Slowly, he drank, letting the wine seep down his throat and warm his belly.

The phone rang.

Startled by the sound, he dropped his glass. The wine splashed onto the kitchen floor, but the glass was unbroken and rolled under the kitchen table. Trevor took the phone into his trembling hands and pressed it to his ear. "Hello? Lisa?"

The phone went dead.

"Hello?" Trevor made sure that the line was disconnected before hanging up. He looked at his watch, it was a little past seven. *Kirsten should've been home by now. What if she's in trouble? Maybe that was her?* Trevor knelt down and retrieved the glass from under table. *She's fine. She's with that new guy, Victor. You know how girls are at that age. She'll be home before ten.* Trevor ran cold water into the glass to rinse it out and left it in the sink. He was mopping up the wine with a paper towel when the phone rang again. This time he let it ring a couple of times before picking up.

"Hello?"

A pause, followed by a loud buzzing.

Trevor pulled the phone away as if it had become a large, hairy spider with fangs. When the buzzing subdued, he put the receiver to his ear.

"I...?" a voice began but paused.

Trevor grasped the phone. "Hello? Who is this?"

"I'm so sorry about your daughter."

A cold lump sank down his throat. "What's wrong with her? Where is she? Who is this? If you hurt her, I'll..."

The line went dead.

Trevor hung up and dialed zero for the operator.

"Operator, how may I help you?"

"Yes, please, could you trace the last phone call to my house? It's an emergency."

"Just one moment, sir."

He waited for what felt like hours. The operator asked him a series of questions concerning his home phone number, address, and company policy. Once he answered, she gave him the number that called him. Trevor scribbled it on a notepad.

"It's in your network," the operator said. "Shall I connect you to the caller?"

"Yes, please. Thank you."

The phone gave a series of clicks and started ringing. On the forth ring, an aged man grunted into the phone.

"Hello?"

"Who is this? Where's my daughter?"

The person on the other line hesitated; a seething breath muffling the speaker. "I don't know what you're talking about."

"Who is this? Answer me," Trevor demanded.

"I'm afraid you have the wrong number. This is Randolph Leeds, goodbye."

The line went dead.

Trevor called back but received no answer. He typed in 9-1-1.

A firm woman answered. "9-1-1, is this an emergency?"

"Yes, my wife and daughter are missing."

"How long have they been gone, sir?"

Trevor checked the clock. "At least ten hours. They went separate places." He explained the situation to her without pausing for a breath of air.

"I'll send the police over right away."

"Thank you." He hung up. His palms were sweating. He ran to the master bedroom and snatched his house keys from the dresser.

As he dashed to the front door, it swung open and, Lisa's voice stopped his heart. "Honey, I'm home."

He slipped on the hardwood floor trying to get into the living room. "Where have you been all this time? I've been worried sick." He gaped at his wife. "Why are you dressed like that?"

Lisa slapped the tight black, bondage suit and rubbed her breasts. "Do you like it?"

"It's a bit extreme," he blinked, not understanding.

"Do you want to touch me?" Lisa licked her finger up and down.

He swallowed hard. "We don't have time for this. Kirsten is missing." He gave her a quick kiss on the cheek and raced through the front door. "Why don't you stay here? The cops are coming soon. I'll take the Subaru and return in a little while." Trevor prepared to step through the door with keys in his hand.

And a large shovel slammed into his forehead.

Stunned, Trevor wobbled from side to side. The shovel struck him on the head again. He tried to block the blow with his arms, but couldn't react fast enough. He sank to his knees and dropped onto the living room floor.

Dario threw the shovel into the living room. "Damn, that asshole wouldn't go down."

Lisa ushered Dario inside and closed the door. "I wish he was like that in bed." Lisa kicked Trevor in the side. "He'd better not be dead already. I still want to have some fun."

Dario bent over Trevor's crumpled form. He pressed two fingers to his victim's neck. "Don't worry, he's still alive."

"Good, let's go. We can dump him into the trunk," she said.

"What about the kid? I thought..."

Lisa grabbed his crotch. "Don't worry, honey, you'll get to screw her. The slut isn't here, but the cops will be so we've got to hurry."

"Cops, how?" Dario looked worried.

Lisa shrugged. "Something about the brat being missing, it has nothing to do with us." She rubbed his groin. "Come on, hard guy. Let's move it. We'll find her ourselves."

Dario unzipped his leather pants. "Get on your knees," he breathed.

"We don't have time for this."

"I'll be quick," he grinned.

Lisa stopped massaging his crotch. "Look, I'll blow you in the car. But let's get this stupid asshole in the trunk, okay?"

Dario zipped up his fly. "All right, but you'd better suck it good."

"I will," Lisa said. "You know I'm good for it, baby."

The couple ushered Trevor through the door and toward Dario's Corvette. Lisa made sure to bang Trevor's head on the trunk as they dropped him inside.

"That's for bringing me to this shit-ass town," she hissed.

Dario snatched a roll of electric tape from the truck and wrapped Trevor's wrists and legs together.

"Make sure it's tight. We don't want him to get free," Lisa instructed.

Dario used half the roll. Trevor's bonds were so tight around his wrists his hands turned red. "Is that tight enough?"

"It looks great to me, baby."

Dario broke off four inches of the tape and went to slap it on Trevor's mouth but

Lisa took his hand away. "No, wait, I want to hear him scream when he wakes up. I want him to plead and beg for mercy. Then, after we rape his daughter in front of him, I want to watch him cry."

Dario smiled, a white-toothed, luminous grin reserved for new clients and investors with heavy wallets. "I like the way you think, baby." He squeezed her ass playfully.

Lisa grinned. She leaned over the trunk and gave Trevor a kiss on the lips. "Sleep well, darling, for it'll be the last peaceful slumber you'll ever know."

Dario slammed the trunk shut. He climbed into the driver's seat and undid his pants. "I hope you're thirsty, baby."

Lisa got into the car and pressed her face into his hardness. "Start the engine, and drive out of here," she said as she slid his member free. She ran her tongue along the shaft before easing it into her wet mouth.

Dario put the key into the ignition, started the car, and pulled onto the road. A quick moan eased through his lips as Lisa's head bobbed up and down.

*   *   *

Julie straightened her red dress and tossed her flowing brown hair behind her back. She squeezed Brian's arm. "This is the place."

Brian took his eyes off her for a second. They stood in front of a tall brick building with high arches and stained glass windows. The florescent green letters above the restaurant read **Chinese Buffet**.

"All right, I could go for some grub," he said.

Julie patted his stomach playfully. "Me, too, but save some room, okay? You just might get dessert." Julie licked her lips and smirked.

His face flushed. He looked at her tight-fitting dress and imagined taking it off. She caught him staring. "Sorry," he said.

Julie's laugh was musical. "Don't be." She took his arm and slid up close to him.

Brian got the door.

"Thank you, kind, sir," she purred.

"My pleasure." He tried not to watch her butt as she walked. An image of her ridding him flashed through his mind and he felt heat rush to his face.

Only in your dreams, pal, he thought.

Inside, the restaurant wasn't that big. There were only two sides to sit on; one for smoking, the other for non smoking. In the middle of the room was the buffet bar. Brian could see fresh snow crab legs, fried rice, wanton soup, crab cakes, egg rolls, and a seafood salad. Steam rose from every selection and fogged the glass above.

A young Chinese woman came from behind the counter. "Hello, table for two?"

"Yes please," Julie said.

"Would you prefer smoking or non smoking?"

"Non smoking," replied Julie and Brian at the same time.

The young lady nodded. "Right this way please." She led them under rows of low-hanging paper lanterns and past the buffet bar.

Brian eyed the crab legs. His stomach growled. "It looks delicious."

The young woman sat them at a table with cushy chairs. "What would you like to drink?"

"You go first," Brian said to Julie.

"I'll have coke and rum."

"And for you, sir?"

"The same," he answered.

The woman nodded. "Enjoy your meal." She walked around the bar and disappeared through a kitchen door.

Julie pressed Brian forward. "Move it, mister, I'm hungry."

"Lady's first," he said as he side stepped her. He put his hands on her sides as they walked. She didn't push him away. She went to a pile of plates, and after wiping two off with the back of her hand, she gave one to Brian. "Fill it up, please."

"Trust me, I will," he said.

Brian headed straight for the crab legs while Julie piled a heap of fried rice on her plate. When they had their food, both returned to the table.

"I see you found the crab legs," she commented.

Brian put a side plate of lemons and melted butter on the table. "And I see you found the rice."

She kicked his shins under the table. "A girl has to eat sometimes."

The young Chinese woman came with their drinks. She set down two large glasses; each had a lemon slice hanging off the side. "Will there be anything else for you?"

"No thanks," Brian replied with a pleasant smile.

"Do you have straws?" Julie asked.

The woman produced two straws from her apron. "Enjoy."

Julie and Brian unraveled their straws and placed them into their drinks.

"To us," Julie said.

"Here, here."

They clinked glasses together and drank. The coke was cold and bubbly; the rum was tangy and warm.

Brian tipped his head back. "Ah, I needed that."

Julie had put her drink down and already filled her mouth with rice. She gave a thumbs up for approval.

"You must be starving," he mused and she nodded.

He broke off a crab leg, crushed it with a nutcracker, and dipped the meat into the melted butter. He savored the taste as he put it in his mouth and chewed.

They ate in silence for a few minutes.

A bare foot rubbed Brian's calf.

Julie sucked on her straw, draining her coke and rum around her lushes red lips.

A throb came from his crotch at the feeling of her foot. He broke off another crab leg, separated the meat, and offered it to her. She opened her mouth wide, devouring it. She sucked on Brian's finger and licked the tip.

"Mmmm," she purred and Brian felt his pants becoming confining. He wanted to adjust himself but Julie's foot crept higher and higher until it rubbed between his legs. She never broke eye contact with him as she sucked his finger deeper into her mouth.

Brian moaned. He was ready to burst.

"Is there anything else you need?" the Chinese girl asked.

Brian's finger withdrew from Julie's mouth and her foot went away in an instant, leaving a warm spot on Brian's crotch.

Julie cleared her throat. "No thank you, we're fine," she said to the waitress.

The young girl blushed. She spun about and went through the kitchen door while giggling.

Brian and Julie locked eyes and laughed, too.

"Maybe we should go back to my place," Brian smiled.

Julie shook her head. "You promised me a date, mister. After a night on the town, then maybe I'll spend a little time alone with you."

Brian adjusted his seating position. "I think I'd want to spend more than a little time with you."

"Same here, but you'll have to take what you can get." Julie leaned over the table to kiss him.

Brian didn't hesitate. He did the same and placed his hand behind her head, pressing his lips to hers. Julie's lips were soft and moist. He sucked her bottom lip and let go.

"Wow," he breathed.

She grinned. "You're not so bad yourself, tiger." She gathered a spoonful of rice and slipped it between her lips.

Brian went back to his crab legs. After Julie finished eating, she pushed her plate away. "Maybe when we're done here you could show mc your place?"

"I thought you wanted a night on the town?" he said.

"I can't think of a better way then spending the night under your sheets."

Brian nearly choked on his drink.

"Are you okay, there?"

"Yeah, it just went down the wrong hole," he said, his voice hoarse from almost choking.

"I hope it doesn't happen again. Just remember, you're not allowed access to the back hole. You can stick it anywhere but there," she said bluntly.

Brian felt his face turning red. He cleared his throat. "I'll try to remember that." He reached for Julie's hand and she gave it willingly.

Just when they were about to kiss again the radio on Brian's belt blared to life.

"Dispatch car 114."

Brian sighed and pressed the com button to speak. "This is car 114, go 'head dispatch."

"There's a disturbance on Ritter Road over, a teenage girl never returned home. Her name's Kirsten Tucker. Her father reported the incident a few hours ago, but I've lost contact with him, over."

Julie wiped her mouth with a napkin. She mouthed two words, "Dead House."

"We're on the way, over and out." Brian put the radio back on his belt. "Dispatch normally doesn't report like that."

"That's because dispatch is a new college intern with little training. She doesn't know better yet. We'll work on her." Julie frowned and her shoulder's fell. "Time to go back to work?"

"It sure looks that way."

"Yeah," she said.

"Did you get enough to eat?" he asked.

"I could go for a take out box," Julie suggested.

"That's not a bad idea."

"Now what do we do about our attire?" he asked.

She grinned. "Well, I always carry a spare uniform with me, how 'bout you?"

"It's in the trunk."

Julie clapped her hands together. "Great minds think alike. Let's roll out, partner."

*   *   *

When Brian reached Dead House, the gates were already open. "That's odd," he said.

Julie managed to chew a mouthful of fried rice from a take out box and talk at the same time. "Maybe they have a visitor?"

"Yeah, maybe."

As Brian drove through the black gates, Dead House materialized on the hill. Seeing the ancient stone work made his teeth grind. The house was a blight on the land, a stain that should be condemned and torched. "How can anybody stand to live in there?"

Julie finished her meal, chasing the last of the rice down with bottled water. "I don't know, nothing good ever came from that house that's for sure."

Brian parked the car. He straightened his uniform and loosened a notch on his belt. "Are you ready for this?"

"I'm always ready," Julie said and jumped out of the patrol car and marched up the cracked stone steps. Brian followed after her until they were standing in front of door. Julie knocked on it with her fist. A hollow thud echoed down hidden pathways and vacant rooms bloated with stores of useless furniture.

The door creaked open.

Randolph Leeds stared up at her from his wheelchair. His single orb scanned her. "Yes?"

"We're here to see Victor," Julie stated.

"He's in his room. I'm afraid he's become violently ill," Randolph said.

"What's wrong with him?" Brian asked.

Randolph folded his hands like a poker player with a full house. "I'd rather not say. It's disturbing me greatly, of course. Why are you here?"

Brian opened his mouth to speak but Julie was quicker to respond.

"A girl came here earlier today. Her name is Kirsten Tucker. She was due home over eight hours ago and this is her last known location," Julie said.

"Ah...yes, my son's girlfriend. She's a very beautiful girl, but she left over an hour ago on foot. I'm surprised that you didn't run into her out on the road."

Brian stepped forward. He towered over Randolph and bore down on him. "Mr. Leeds, we're coming inside to see your son, sick or not."

"Very well, but don't track any mud on the rug. I spent all evening vacuuming." Randolph wheeled out of their way and raced toward the staircase. "Victor! Come down here."

Brian and Julie stepped inside Dead House. They closed the door behind them as a caretaker shuts a coffin lid.

"Victor?" Randolph called again.

"What's wrong with him?" Julie questioned.

Randolph craned his head around to look at her. "He tried to attack me with a fork earlier. I sent him to his room. He keeps talking about dead people in the basement."

Brian raised his eyebrow. "Step aside, sir." He brushed past Randolph and climbed the staircase.

"Hey, you can't go up there. This is my house. Mine. I make the rules and you can't just come in here and go wherever you want."

Brian ignored him. He reached the third floor and paused. The hallway ahead of him was shrouded in darkness. Four closed doors lined one side.

"Mr. Leeds, we're officers of the law. We're here to protect you. If your son threatened you, then we have just cause to speak with him."

Randolph rocked in his chair. His fingernails dug into the arm rests. "He's a good boy. He would never hurt me."

"Which room is he in?" Brian called down from the top of the stairs.

"It's the second on the left," Randolph answered, though not pleased about it.

Brian eased his way down the hall. His footfalls slapped the wooden floor like a wild horse. When he reached Victor's room, he pressed his ear flush against the door. From the other side came a metallic scrape and clink. Brian knew the sound by heart. Victor was sharpening a knife. He tapped on the door lightly with his knuckles. "Victor? This is Officer Brian Kratos with the Sheriff's Department."

The metallic graining stopped.

Brian heard bed springs rising, then the door was unlocked. He stepped back, his fingers wrapped around a can of mace just in case there was trouble.

The door slid open halfway and Victor's head popped out. His eyes were large and bloodshot. "How did you get in here? Are they in the house? Did they climb through the tunnel? They're here, aren't they?"

Brian uncapped his mace and pulled it from the holster. He kept the small can behind his back, ready to use it at a second's notice. "I want you to come out of there slowly, Victor, and keep your hands behind your head."

"They're here for me. I can hear them...you...you're with them, aren't you?"

Brian put his foot under the door so Victor couldn't close it. "I'm an officer of the law, and I'm here to help you, Victor," Brian said in a soothing voice.

Victor swung the door open the rest of the way. He was only wearing a pair of faded blue jeans. His torso was decorated with claw marks. He held a long knife by his side. "Where is she? Did you find her?"

"Find who?" Brian asked. He could hear Julie making her way upstairs.

"Kirsten, they took her."

"Who took her, Victor? What's going on?"

Victor backed onto his bed, the knife clattering to the floor. He put an arm over his face and scratched his chest, digging his nails into the flesh. "They almost had me, almost. Black spots, there on me, aren't they? They touched my skin. I'll be one of them soon."

Brian kicked the knife into the hallway. He saw Julie come up behind him. She drew a bead on Victor with her pistol. Brian signaled her to stay in the hallway. "Victor, I want to help you. I want to find Kirsten, too," Brian said.

Victor's body trembled. He clawed at his back and neck. "I don't know where she is. They took her. They took her."

Brian put his mace back into its case and withdrew a pair of silver-plated handcuffs. "Calm down, we'll find her. I promise."

"She's dead. They're all dead." Victor rocked back and forth. He lay down on the bed, shivering. "Dead. Dead. Dead."

Brian grabbed his hands and put them behind his back. Victor didn't seem to notice nor did he struggle as Brian slapped the cuffs on him.

"Come on, Victor, on your feet. You're coming with us," Brian said.

Victor jerked his body upright but refused to move. "Dead. Dead. Dead."

Brian dragged him out of the room. He nodded to Julie. "Can you give me a little help?"

"But you're doing so well," Julie quipped. She put her gun back. "Why ruin a good thing?"

"Just grab his legs and we'll carry him out."

Victor's body turned limp. His eyes drifted off into space and his tongue lolled out. Julie took his legs while Brian held onto his shoulders. Together they managed to lift Victor and bring him downstairs.

"My boy, what have you done to him?" Randolph cried out.

"We're taking him in," Brian said. "You're welcome to come with us, too."

Randolph's lower lips sagged. "Where are you taking him?"

"To the station," Julie replied. When she reached the bottom of the staircase with her burden she found Randolph had blocked the way with his wheelchair. "We'll give you a call once we've figured things out. If you don't move out of my way, I'm going to arrest you along with your son, your choice."

Randolph's face burned but he wheeled his chair out of the way. When Brian and Julie were passing him, Randolph stroked his son's arm. "Victor? Can you hear me? Victor, answer me."

But Victor remained catatonic.

Brian and Julie exited through the front door with him, Julie opening the door with one hand and then her foot. She looked back at Randolph. "I'll call you in half an hour. Your son will be fine, I promise."

Randolph watched them go. He wheeled onto the porch as Brian put his son into the back of the police car. As they drove away, a wicked smile crossed the old man's lips.

"Goodbye, Victor. I wonder if there's anything left of your girlfriend for me to play with."

Chapter 20

Trevor opened his eyes to darkness, his head throbbing as though he'd drank two six packs of beer the night before. Trevor struggled to sit up, but he couldn't.

"Help!" he screamed. It was in that moment he realized his arms and legs were bound. He came to life, stretching his legs as far as they would go, his shoes pounding a ceiling less than a foot from his face. Tail lights flashed and he saw in the red glow he was in the trunk of a car.

His body was tossed about suddenly as the car went over a bump in the road. His head whacked the floor and pain exploded below his right eye. He could feel a long gash there begin to sting and bleed. Trapped and battered, he forced himself to remain calm.

I'm alive. Wherever I am? Whoever kidnapped me didn't kill me. He sucked in air through his nostrils. *I'm breathing. I'm still alive.* He tried to recall what had happened. The memory was a faded blur. He was worried that Lisa was missing as was his daughter. He'd phoned the police then Lisa showed up. *Was Kirsten with her? No. Lisa was alone but she was dressed oddly with black leather straps; very kinky and deadly. I went to open the door...no, it was already open and then bam! Something hit me.* Trevor couldn't picture what the object was, maybe a cement block or a shovel? He didn't know and it didn't matter. All that mattered was breathing and waiting out the darkness to escape.

He sealed his eyes tight and began kicking the underside of the trunk, hoping someone might hear him.

*   *   *

"Slow down, darling. We've got all night," Lisa said. She caressed Dario's leg and moved her hand to his crotch.

Dario kept his foot on the gas petal. He turned the steering wheel to maneuver around the sharp curve of the lonely, deserted road. The Corvette handled like a dream. "Well, I don't want to wait all night, and stop stroking me."

She sat back and crossed her arms. "What climbed up your butt?"

He sped even faster as the empty road straightened out. "The cops, that's what."

"The cops?" She laughed loud and hard. "Oh, dear, we're miles away from the house. Nobody'll suspect a thing, unless of course we get pulled over for a speeding ticket."

A wide grin cut Dario's lips. "If we did, we can just do what we did last time."

Lisa huffed. "We? You mean me. I don't blow pigs anymore, it's my new rule. Deal with it. If we get pulled over the cop is dead meat. Besides, this isn't California."

"No, I guess you're right," he nodded. "You'd have to ride one of these Yankee fucks just to get us out of a ticket."

She frowned. "The only one I'm riding tonight is you, that asshole in the trunk, and his twat of a daughter."

Dario scratched his chin in thought. "Where do you suppose that little bitch is?"

"I don't know. Probably spreading her legs for some sex-starved, teenage boy."

"I hope he's saves some for me," Dario grinned.

Lisa shook her head. "Don't worry, darling. Your precious little slut will be tight and ready for you. She may dress like a whore, but she hasn't been screwed in years."

"Good," he said and leaned back in his seat. "Maybe we should pull over and see if sleeping beauty knows where she is."

"I doubt he does. You saw the look in his eyes. She's staying out late, or she ran away from home."

Dario sighed. "That's a pity."

The Corvette's headlights illuminated a hitch hiker up ahead.

"Hello? Who's this?" he wondered.

As the car approached, they could make out the figure of a short female wearing short, cut off jeans and long blonde hair draped over a leather jacket. She had her thumb stuck out and the girl looked no older than thirteen.

Dario slowed down and rubbed his hands together. "That's some easy pickings, right there."

"Be nice now," Lisa said and winked.

As Dario stopped on the shoulder of the road, the young blonde ran to the passenger side window. Her face was thin and the most striking feature about her was her small, petite nose; it was almost fairy like.

Lisa rolled down her window. "Hi, stranger, you need a lift?"

The young girl put a hand on her hip. "It depends, where're you going?"

"North," Dario replied. "We're going camping."

The girl nodded. "That's too bad. I'm heading south." She pulled the zipper down and opened her leather jacket. "That is unless of course you've got some money?"

Dario's mouth hung open and Lisa chuckled.

The young girl sported a lacy black bra that barely covered her nipples. "How about it? Thirty for a blow and forty for a screw. I'll even eat some pussy, too, no charge."

Lisa and Dario matched wild stares.

"We don't have any seats in the back," Lisa explained and pointed to the low wall behind them. "But you can sit on my lap."

The youth leaned into the window. "It looks inviting; you've got to pay up first though."

Dario slipped his wallet from his boot. He forked a fifty dollar bill out. "We'll take it all."

The girl snatched the money and stuffed it into her bra. "I'll give you all of it, you sick perverted fucks." She slapped Lisa across the face and ran for the cover of the dark forest.

"Bitch!" Lisa cried as she opened her door and jumped from the Corvette to give chase after the blonde runaway. Dario swung the car around so that the headlights cut through the dense woodland. "Kill the little bitch!" he screamed.

The girl crashed into the forest head on, ducking and weaving under low branches and hopping over tree roots. She was quick on her feet and getting away.

Lisa didn't let up the chase. A few branches cut her face as gnarled limbs dug into her ribs. She roared in fury and reached for a handful of long blonde hair. "I've got you now, slut!" Lisa's hand now clutched a fistful of golden hair and she yanked back with all her might.

The young girl yelped like a kicked puppy, twirled backward, and fell down.

Lisa pulled her hair even harder. "You'll pay for running like that, bitch."

The girl got to her knees as Lisa yanked. She cried and thrashed like a fish on a hook. "Let me go."

Lisa kicked her in the stomach, her boot heel sinking in deep. The girl wheezed in pain. She toppled over in a fit of coughing, gasping for air. Lisa stood over her in triumph. She drove her heel into the small of the girl's back.

"Let's see you run away now," Lisa spit.

The girl sobbed and yelped, squirming under the pressure to her spine. She eased her fingers into the front of her cut off jeans, and then her small hand flashed with sharp steel. The blonde youth drove three inches of stainless steel into Lisa's calf.

Lisa screamed and immediately released her hold on the girl as she slumped to the forest floor. "You fucking slut!" Lisa yelled, her eyes flaring hatred.

The girl leaped to her feet but stumbled a bit. She soon gathered her wits and made a run for it.

Lisa wrapped her fingers around the knife's black handle. She bit her tongue and ripped the blade free. In one swift movement, she threw the knife at the girl's head. The blade spun end over end until it made contact with the back of the blonde-haired girl's skull. She tumbled face forward.

Lisa howled in glory, amazed at her luck with throwing the blade. A steady flow of crimson ran down her calf, soaking her boots and staining her socks. Lisa ignored the stinging throb and dragged herself closer to the fallen girl.

The girl didn't get up. She stayed put with her face in the dirt. When Lisa approached, she found the knife beside the girl's head.

"You got real lucky, bitch," Lisa breathed. She grabbed a fistful of hair and yanked until that sweet angelic face came into view. "You'll be wishing that blade had killed you in about an hour."

The girl spit in her face, a big white glob landing on Lisa's nose.

"You fucking bitch!" Lisa snarled and backhanded her.

The girl's head jerked from the blow as Lisa planted her fist into the youth's belly. "Do you like that, you dirty whore?" She punched her side and lower back a few times. The girl doubled over in pain as a groan seethed through her clenched teeth.

"Is that all you've got, bitch?" the girl said groggily.

Lisa reeled back her fist, preparing to knock out a few prize teeth.

A dark figure appeared on top of the hill. Dario looked down in surprise. "Did you get her?"

Lisa snarled, "I got her. But the bitch cut me."

"Good, you needed a little sport, bring her up here and don't mess her up too much."

Lisa lowered her fist. She grabbed the girl by her jacket collar and picked her up.

The youth gripped her naked belly and threw up. Lisa snatched the knife from the forest floor. She planted the tip of the blade into the girl's back, drawing out a thin line of blood. "Get moving, now," Lisa ordered.

The girl wiped her mouth and marched up the slope. When they reached the road, Dario was waiting for them with thick nylon rope. His eyes roamed over the youth's bare legs, and thin belly, then came to rest on her grapefruit shaped breasts.

"Damn, we've got a looker here." He tossed the rope to Lisa who quickly went about tying the girl's hands and feet. Dario opened her leather jacket. "Would you look at that?" He popped opened her shirt and massaged her breasts with both hands.

The girl averted her head. "Please, don't," she whimpered.

Dario bent down and spread her shirt wide. The fifty dollar bill fell out. "I guess you can collect that later," he grinned and pocketed the money. He placed his mouth over her left breast and began sucking the nipple.

Lisa finished tying the bonds. She rubbed herself against the young girl, placing her hands between her legs. "You like this, slut?"

"Stop it. Please stop," the girl begged.

Lisa laughed. She dug into the girl's front pocket and withdrew a pink wallet and a cell phone. "What have we got here?" Lisa tossed the cell phone under the Corvette's front wheel. "You won't need that anymore." She flipped the wallet open. "Ah, here we go. Nice picture, Sybil. Do you still live at this address?"

Sybil's body shook. Dario sucked on her nipple and pinched the other nipple between a forefinger and thumb as tears stained Sybil's face.

"Answer me." Lisa smacked the back of her head.

"Yes I do, sometimes."

Lisa withdrew the knife. She placed the long blade between Sybil's legs. "Sometimes you say? You'd better be straight with me, honey," Lisa warned.

"I only stay when my parents are away. I have a key."

"Are you a runaway?" Lisa asked.

Sybil clenched her jaw tight as Dario sucked her nipple harder. His hands unbuttoned her mini-skirt. Sybil gasped for air. "No, don't..."

Lisa stabbed her left butt cheek. "I asked you a question, slut."

Sybil yelped, as a small dot of blood formed on her butt cheek and pooled into a quarter size mark. "Yes, I'm a runaway."

Lisa grinned. "I thought so."

Dario slid the mini-skirt down to her ankles. The road was pitch black, and the odds of someone driving down it were next to none. It was the perfect place to have some fun. In the trunk of the car, Trevor still kicked, though his actions were futile.

"Do you want to get her started?" Dario asked.

Lisa licked her lips. She eyed the pink satin panties the young girl wore. "I would, very much so, but not here. We need to go, love."

Dario sighed and rubbed Sybil's breasts harder. "Why not right now? She's hot and ready, aren't you slut? This road is safe."

Sybil looked away and pleaded. "Please, just let me go. I'll do whatever you want. I won't even charge you. Just let me go, please."

"Did you hear that?" Lisa giggled. "She wants to be let go."

Dario joined her laughter.

"Please," Sybil begged. "I'll do anything you want, wherever you please. Just let me go afterward, okay?"

Dario stood up. His dick was nearly poking through his pants. "Wherever I want, huh?" He unzipped his fly and let his member free.

Sybil gasped. His dick was pierced with a silver stud. She averted her eyes. "Do what you want with me."

Lisa kicked the back of Sybil's legs and she fell on her knees. Her mouth gaped open in surprise, and before she could close it, Dario was inside of her mouth. He shoved in deep as Sybil gagged. She tried to pull her head back, but Lisa shoved her forward until the entire member was down her throat.

"Suck it, bitch," Lisa laughed as Dario motioned his hips back and forth.

Sybil thought about biting it off, but as Dario worked in and out, she decided to give him what he wanted. Hopefully, after they had their fun, she'd be free to go. It would be just like with her father. Just give him what he wanted then he'd go away. Sybil moved her head back and forth, rolling her tongue around his shaft, sucking as she went.

Dario moaned. He placed his hands on her shoulders. "That's right, girl, blow me good."

Lisa watched with glee. She went behind Sybil and began rubbing her breasts as Dario groaned louder. Sybil's head jerked up and down until a warm, salty fluid filled her mouth. She swallowed quickly, trying not to think about it.

Dario pulled out. "Wow, I think you might have some competition, Lisa."

Sybil lowered her head as tears fell from her eyes.

"You always liked the young ones, don't you?" Lisa squeezed Sybil's breasts. "I'll have to see how well she likes tasting me."

Dario pulled up his pants. "I can't wait to see that. It's been years since we've had a good threesome."

Lisa yanked Sybil's skirt up and unbuttoned her shirt. She gave her a kiss on the cheek. "How would you like my main man to ram you between the legs while I suck on your pussy? Won't that be fun?"

"Please, just let me go. I did what you wanted me to," Sybil pleaded.

Lisa yawned. "What do you think, love?"

Dario hiked his thumb to the Corvette. "I think the trunk sounds like a great place for her."

"That works great for me." Lisa wrapped her arms around Sybil and lifted her.

Dario opened the trunk, and two feet smashed his face in. Dario stumbled backward and fell. "Shit!"

Sybil found herself screaming as a bound man crawled from the Corvette's trunk.

Lisa's grip on her tightened.

"You piece of shit!" Dario roared. He got to his feet and kicked Trevor in the head.

"Get him good, baby," Lisa cheered as she forced Sybil closer to the Corvette.

"What're you doing? Let me go!" Sybil yelled as she fought to escape.

Lisa slapped her a few times with the back of her hand. "Don't start on me now, you little slut."

Dario's boot rose and fell until Trevor had blood flowing out his nose. "Asshole, you can't escape us." Dario gave Trevor a kick in the stomach and then picked him up. "Back in you go," Dario said as he lifted a bloodied Trevor like a wrestler and threw him back into the trunk. "That's one down."

A wicked smile cut across Lisa's face.

"What are you thinking, darling?" he asked.

"Take off his pants," Lisa ordered.

Dario nodded as he leaned into the trunk. His hands flashed with steel, and a moment later he held up a pair of ripped jeans and underwear. "He's in his birthday suit."

"Good, now undress the slut." Lisa shoved Sybil to him.

Dario smiled. The knife slid down Sybil's skirt, cutting fabric and a layer of skin.

Lisa stuck her head inside the trunk. "Hey, honey bunch. Remember me?"

Trevor's face was covered in blood. His lips were puffy and one eye was swollen shut. "Fuck you," he mumbled.

"No, dear, *fuck* you." Her mouth went to his limp member. She worked him up and down like she had so many times before, sucking and nibbling until he was hard.

"Why are you doing this?" Trevor asked.

Lisa ignored him. "Okay Dario, bring on the slut."

Dario tossed Sybil into the trunk. He made sure her naked body was pressed against Trevor's hardness. "Have fun, love birds."

Lisa wiped her mouth and waved. "Bye, bye." She slammed the trunk shut. "I hope they get along well together."

Dario grabbed Lisa's butt and gave it a squeeze. "I'm sure they will. Now let's go find Trevor's brat so we can really party."

They hopped into the Corvette and sped down the lonely country road.

Chapter 21

Dr. Alvin Tandy puffed on a Marlboro cigarette and leaned back in his soft leather chair. The case before him was the worst he'd seen in years. He let the smoke cloud his mind, it felt good to relax for a minute. The file on his desk read #8042, patient Victor Leeds. Dr. Tandy thumbed through the file and rubbed the bite mark on his hand.

The orderlies had brought Victor in only yesterday. He appeared completely catatonic. Two police officers had said he was babbling about dead people kidnapping his girlfriend in his house. He had heard about the troubled youth and made sure that Victor ended up under his watchful care. The police officers, whose names had abandoned him, said Victor Leeds was a primary suspect in the missing girl's case. Kirsten Tucker had gone missing three days earlier and surprisingly so had her father and step-mother. The officers relinquished Victor into his care after questioning the young man for hours.

Victor's story never changed. The dead seeped from the walls of his home and out of ancient tombs and had taken Kirsten away. An investigative search had taken place in the Leeds home to find the girl. The neighborhood turned out in force to watch, peering through the black gates that surrounded Dead House, hoping the search would yield gruesome details and a few rotting bodies. But nothing of the sort happened. No bodies were unearthed and no shreds of evidence linking Victor or his father to the missing girl were uncovered. There was nothing. The crowd dissipated. The police climbed back into their cars and drove away. And Randolph Leeds slammed his front door.

The only hope for the lost girl was Victor, and he only spoke three words: *the dead walk.* Yesterday, Dr. Tandy had approached Victor on the subject. He asked about his childhood, his dead mother, and why he thought the deceased walked? Victor answered the questions with his middle finger while staring off into space. It wasn't until Dr. Tandy asked why he thought these things that Victor had tried to escape. He was a strong young man and shoved Dr. Tandy into a wall with such force that it left an indentation in the sheetrock. It had taken four orderlies to subdue him. Dr. Tandy attempted to give him a sedative, but before the needle punctured Victor's skin, the young man took a bite out of his hand. The teeth were sharp and left purple marks afterwards. Dr. Tandy jabbed the needle into his patient's shoulder and after a while Victor became limp. Then he was strapped to a bed in a room with only one wire mesh covered window.

Dr. Tandy looked over the photos of Dead House.

"The place should be condemned," he said as he closed the files and snuffed out his cigarette.

A quick rap struck his door.

"Dr. Tandy?" came a young woman's voice. "Can I come in?"

"Yes, of course, Alice."

Alice entered the room. She was a tall, slender woman with a short crop of brown hair and a straight line for a mouth. "Dr. Tandy, I need to speak with you, it's urgent."

"By all means, come in and sit down."

Alice pulled up a chair and sat down in front of the long oak desk. "It's about patient #8042."

"Victor Leeds. Yes, I was just looking over his file, very troubling." He gazed into her hazel eyes and quickly turned the other way. His heart still ached for her, but their love was one that couldn't be. "What seems to be the problem?"

Alice sensed his eyes and crossed her legs. "No trouble. He's talking more coherently though," Alice said but then seemed hesitant to continue.

"Go on."

She cleared her throat. "I don't like him."

Dr. Tandy laughed hard at that. "You don't have to like him. Just get the job done. You've always been good at that."

She nodded and folded her hands on her lap but then rubbed her thumbs against her temple.

He knew the gesture all too well. "Do you have a headache? Would you like two Tylenol? I'd ask you to call me in the morning but you'd probably take it the wrong way."

"I would," she said.

Alice lowered her hands and began to twiddle her thumbs together. "Have you listened to him, Doctor? I mean, really listened when he's not repeating himself?"

Dr. Tandy leaned back in his chair. He opened his second drawer and plucked out a thick book.

Alice knew what it was and nodded.

He opened the book to a pint of scotch placed beside two shot glasses; it was their shared secret. Dr. Tandy set both glasses on the table and filled them to the brim. "I have listened to him, and I don't believe a word of it."

137

Alice took one of the shot glasses, pressed it to her thin lips, and downed the liquor in a single gulp. "I believe him," she said. "Not about the dead people in his house. I think that's a delusion or a group kidnapping, but the woman in the rain is true."

Dr. Tandy raised his eyebrows. "What woman?"

Alice motioned for another shot. Dr. Tandy obliged. He drank the scotch in his own glass quickly.

"He hasn't told you?" she asked.

"No, I'm afraid not. Should I go ask him about it?" Dr. Tandy made a move to stand but Alice's left hand landed over his forearm.

"He told me not to say anything. He said that you would lock him up forever."

Dr. Tandy withdrew his arm and rubbed the aching bite mark on his hand. "I still might."

Alice chewed her lower lip. "Promise me you won't tell."

"Alice, you can't honestly expect..."

"Promise me."

Dr. Tandy arched his back. "Very well, I promise I won't tell another soul, and it will go unrecorded."

Alice nodded, looking appeased. "He told me about the night of Lynn Watterson's death."

"His ex-girlfriend," Dr. Tandy confirmed. "Yes, go on."

She nodded. "Victor was walking her home in the rain when they saw a woman. She had long hair and disappeared in the distant only to reappear even closer. This woman, this thing, whatever it was, came after them. Lynn touched its flesh. Then she passed away in the night."

Dr. Tandy grunted. "Poison I guess. I have a colleague who wanted to exhume Lynn Watterson's remains but they've vanished; someone dug her up. Her killer I presume, it's a very sad case."

"I believe Victor's story, Doctor."

Dr. Tandy didn't reply. He stared at her from behind wire-rimmed glasses and sat motionless. "Why would you believe in such things? What proof do you have?"

"I saw her," Alice choked. "I saw Lynn Watterson. I was taking out my trash and she walked by my house. I knew who she was instantly from all those pictures in the newspaper. Her skin was pale and her face gaunt. She had strange eyes. I called out to her and she came towards me. I ran inside my house before she reached my front porch." Alice's eyes began to tear up. "I've never been so scared in my life."

Dr. Tandy went to comfort her but Alice recoiled. He reached into his pocket and produced three pills: one blue, the other two white. "Take these please, calm yourself."

Alice took the pills from him. She slipped them into her mouth and chased them down with a sip of scotch.

"Are you better now?" he asked.

Alice wiped her mouth. "I will be, thank you. I didn't expect you to take me so seriously. I just wanted you to know what I saw." She rose from her chair and stood in the doorway, about to leave. "It's just possible that Victor might not be crazy after all."

Dr. Tandy watched her go. He tried to avoid looking at her shapely butt as she went down the hallway, but found he couldn't. It wasn't so long ago that she was on top of him, moaning with pleasure. Dr. Tandy pushed the thoughts aside with the bottle of scotch. He cleared his throat, put the bottle and glasses away, and headed towards Victor's room.

* * *

"Victor," Dr. Tandy said softly. He was sitting in a chair he'd brought in with him, holding a notebook and a blue pen. Victor was lying on his bed in cuffs, staring at the ceiling as if he could see beyond it to the sky above.

"I have to ask you some questions about Kirsten."

Victor didn't respond. He continued to bore holes into the ceiling. Dr. Tandy was about to ask another question but Victor's lips parted.

"Kirsten," he whispered.

"Yes, go on."

"I love her," Victor said, nearly inaudible.

"If you love her you should want to help her. What happened back at the house, Victor?"

The cuffed man dug his nails into the bed. "I already told you. They took her."

Dr. Tandy made a few quick notes. "Who took her? Was it your father, or a group of men?"

"The dead grabbed her."

"How do you know they were dead? Was it dark? Perhaps you didn't see them clearly."

Victor turned his head to Dr. Tandy. "They were dead, all of them. Kirsten and I found a tomb under my house and they were down there...hundreds of them."

"A tomb?"

"Yes," Victor snapped.

"The police searched every corner of that house. If there was such a place surely they would have discovered it."

"It was hidden. My father's doing. He's the one behind all this."

139

Dr. Tandy made another brief note. "Do you love your father, Victor?"

"That's not the issue." Victor rocked back and forth on the bed, now agitated as he tried to escape from the cuffs.

"Calm down now, please, you're safe here. Would you like me to call the orderlies? They're right outside the door."

Victor stopped his rant. "I'm not crazy. I know what I saw."

Dr. Tandy lowered his voice. "It doesn't matter to me what you did or didn't see. My concern is with your mental health, and the fact that a young girl and her parents are missing."

"Kirsten's parents are gone?"

Dr. Tandy sighed quietly, cursing himself for letting the information slip. "Yes they are. The police suspect foul play. The only lead they have is you, however."

Victor lowered his head to his pillow like a beaten dog. "I told you everything I know."

"No, I don't believe you have."

Victor gripped the bed sheets. "Yes, I love my father. He would never harm me."

"Would he harm someone else?" the doctor asked.

Victor seethed. "No, it's not in his character. He's an old bitter man, but not a killer."

Dr. Tandy stood up. "Victor, I want you to do something for me." He placed four sheets of notebook paper on the young man's lap. "I'm going to let the orderlies release you. Will you promise to behave yourself?"

Victor nodded.

"Good. I want you to do a few drawings for me of anything you want. I'll be back to pick them up later tonight." He withdrew a package of thick colored crayons--similar to what a preschool would use--from his white coat and set them on the bed.

Before Dr. Tandy left the room, Victor addressed him. "Doctor"

"Yes?"

"I'm sorry I bit your hand."

Dr. Tandy gave him a tired smile. "Apology accepted. Just make sure it doesn't happen again." He left the room and strolled back to his office, content in the day's progress.

Chapter 22

Sybil's body was slick and warm. Her breasts jiggled as the Corvette ate concrete. Trevor tried to think of the blood oozing from his nose, or his three missing teeth, but his dick was still hard. He lay on top of her, his hardness pressed against the juncture of her thighs. He could feel her heat.

"I'm so sorry," Trevor wheezed. He tried not to let his blood seep out of his mouth and onto her.

"Who are you?"

"I'm that bitch's husband. She's trying to kill me, but I don't know why?"

Sybil squeezed her knees together, making sure he couldn't slip inside her wetness.

"I'm sorry," Trevor repeated.

"I know, it's not your fault."

Trevor imagined her tear-stained face and felt himself going limp in the darkness of the trunk. "My name's Trevor. What's yours'?"

"It doesn't matter. We're both as good as dead. They'll have their way with us and toss us into a ditch when they're finished."

Trevor rocked his hips from side to side. His head bumped against the underside of the trunk. There was no way around it; he was forced to lie naked on top of her in the cramped confines.

"How did they get you?" he asked.

Sybil's voice sounded like a child's in the dark. "They thought I was a hooker."

Trevor swallowed blood. His lips were dry and he licked them.

"Are you?"

"Sometimes I am."

"It doesn't matter. We need to get out of here." Trevor planted his elbows down and smashed against Sybil's breasts in an attempt to kick his legs up.

"Ouch, you're hurting me."

"I'm sorry," he said as she shifted position.

"I know you mean well, but haven't you learned after the beating they gave you? There's no escaping."

"I got out before I can do it again."

"Yeah, like I just said, they beat your face in for your trouble."

"He did. My wife didn't do anything."

"But she's with him."

Trevor spit a mouthful of blood over Sybil's head. "Yeah, I can see that." He adjusted himself, thankful that his hardness had shriveled away. "Please tell me your name. We can help each other."

"Sybil, my name's Sybil."

"Sybil...I like that. I have a daughter a few years older than you. I'm sure you two would be great friends."

Sybil said nothing.

"Do you have anything in your shoe?" he asked.

"If you mean like a knife, then no, I don't. I had one but that bitch took it. If you're her husband what does she want from you?"

"I'm not sure? I don't think she was happy to move to New York."

"Have you ever seen that man before?" Sybil asked.

"No. We were a happy family. My wife, daughter, and I. Things were great. I don't know why she's doing this?" Trevor tried to sound brave but his voice failed him. Sybil spread her legs and hugged him close. "I think we're going to suffer before the end."

Trevor held back a sob. He focused on the pain in his lips and mouth from his beat down. "We're getting out of here, Sybil, just you and me. We'll find a way. We have to."

With a squeal of brakes, the Corvette came to a sudden halt.

"We've stopped," Sybil quivered, her body shaking beneath Trevor.

"Be strong, we'll get through this," he whispered.

The engine died and it grew silent.

Lisa howled like a wolf as car doors slammed, shaking the vehicle slightly.

Trevor attempted to kick his legs out. If he could connect with a swift kick to one of them, especially the man, it might give him a chance to escape again. He pressed down on Sybil and lifted his legs, preparing for his chance.

But the trunk swung open before he had time to gain any force behind the blow.

"Your husband doesn't know when to quit," the man said while looking down on his two captives.

"Tell me about it," Lisa said. "He always gets me ready to explode in bed and then he rolls over and falls asleep, the selfish bastard." Lisa pushed Trevor's legs down with her hands.

Trevor withdrew. "I'll kill you, Lisa. You're a dead bitch for what you've done to me. And you too, asshole," he said, glaring at Dario.

"Such a mouth," Dario said.

"I thought we gagged him?" Lisa asked.

"Well, you said you wanted to hear him scream," Dario shrugged.

"Maybe I'll fit one on him," Lisa said.

"Don't bother, darling. I want to hear him scream now."

"Fuck you," Trevor snapped. He eased himself off from Sybil enough to see the man. He was tall, muscular, and had a dead stare like double zeros.

"My name's Dario by the way. I guess it doesn't really matter since you'll be bleeding out of your ass and wherever else I like in the coming hours we'll be sharing together."

"Just try it, pal." Trevor spat a thick glob of mucus; it flew from his mouth and splattered onto Dario's boots.

Dario's grin faded. "You're going to pay for that one, dipshit." He reached inside the trunk; grabbed Trevor by the nylon rope wrapped around his wrists and ankles, and jerked him out. "I hope you had a good screw back there because it was your last." Dario tossed him onto a gravel driveway.

Trevor smacked on the loose stones like a heavy weight, his breath exploding from his lungs.

"Can you get the slut, Lisa? I've got some unfinished business to handle," Dario said as he cracked his knuckles.

"Sure, darling." Lisa took Sybil by her long hair and tugged. "Out of the car, whore, it's party time."

Sybil yelped like a wounded puppy but she didn't put up a struggle. Lisa got her to stand and pressed her mouth to Sybil's ear. "Are you ready, slut?"

Sybil was motionless.

Trevor cried out as Dario's boot crushed his right foot. "How do you like that, cowboy?" He pressed his boot down even harder. "Answer me when I ask you a question."

A loud scream from Trevor deafened the night as bones ground together, threatening to break and fracture.

"Fuck!" Trevor screamed, his leg jerking in pain. Nothing seemed broken but that didn't change the fact he was in serious pain.

Dario removed his boot. He nudged the broken toes. "I don't think your going to be running away anytime soon."

Lisa suddenly gasped and Dario lifted his head to see car headlights cutting through the tiny stretch of lonely roadway they had chosen for their fun.

"Shit," Dario cursed. "Who the fuck could that be?

Lisa shook her head. "It doesn't matter. Just get them to the house and keep them out of sight. If they call out, break their goddamn jaws."

Dario went into action. He snatched Trevor off the gravel and tossed him into the forest. Then he reached for Sybil around the waist and tossed her over his right shoulder. "It's time to go, baby."

The car headlights drew closer, illuminating Lisa's lithe figure.

She lowered her leather suit, making sure that one of her nipples showed slightly.

The car was a gray Corsica. It moved at a slow gait but didn't stop. Lisa patted the small of her back, making sure Sybil's knife, now hers, was secure. Her fingertips brushed the black handle. Out of the corner of her eye she saw Dario slip beyond the hillside. He was well hidden and their human play toys were out of eye sight.

The car rolled forward slowly, never pausing as it headed straight for the Corvette. Lisa stood in the way of the car. She twisted her hips and flipped her hair. "Are you looking to get laid tonight, stranger?"

The Corsica rolled onward, heading straight for her.

Lisa leaped out of the way.

The car tapped into Dario's Corvette, punching a fist size dent into the rear bumper. Lisa bared her teeth as she approached the driver's side door. "Buddy, you just made the worst mistake of your fucking life."

The driver was a middle-aged man with a crop of shaggy brown hair, and skin the color of unworked clay. His face was planted on the steering wheel. Rock music blared from the car speakers like a primate beast.

Lisa tried to open the car door, but it was locked. She flipped her knife out, reared back, and smashed the window with its black handle. The glass flew inward, covering the man's shoulder. He didn't seem to care. Lisa reached into the opening she'd made and unlocked the door.

Guns and Roses' *Welcome to the Jungle* pumped from the speakers. Axel was halfway through the song.

"Okay, asshole, you've got about two seconds to live," Lisa hissed but the driver sat motionless.

Lisa poked the back of his head with the knife but the man still didn't move. She thrust the blade in deep enough in the back of his skull to draw blood. A thin red line ran down his pale cheek. Lisa wiped her knife clean on the man's brown leather jacket. This guy was already dead.

"Huh? Who killed you?"

The man suddenly slipped from the steering wheel as Lisa yelped and leaped out of the way. The man tumbled out of the car to land in the road. His eyes were sunken into the back of his skull and he wore an awful grimace.

Lisa kicked his lifeless body. "Crazy shit, you scared me half to death."

Dario called to her from the forest. "What's going on, baby?"

144

"This asshole ran into your car."

"What?"

She could hear Dario crashing through the woods. "Don't worry, darling, he's deader than shit."

"You killed him already?"

"No, believe it or not, I found him that way."

Dario emerged from the darkness. His chest and face were splattered red. "Wow, he is dead. I wonder what happened to the loser."

"Who cares, let's pop his lungs and sink him in the pond we passed on the way here."

Dario nodded. He turned the man over with his boot. "I don't see any entrance wounds."

Lisa's face contorted. "Who cares? He's dead and anyone could come down that road any minute and find us standing over him. So what, you're going to debate how he died?"

"You've got a point. I'll ditch the body and you take care of the car."

Lisa bowed like a servant. "It'll be my pleasure." Before she hopped into the driver's seat, she kissed Dario like a long lost lover. When they broke apart, she patted his chest. Her hands came away smeared with blood.

"What did you do to our guests?"

"I gave them some northern hospitality." Dario soaked his fingers in the blood and shoved the digits into Lisa's open mouth. She welcomed the gesture and sucked his fingers dry.

"Are they still alive?"

"Barely."

Lisa kissed him on the cheek. "Let's clean this mess up and finish the job."

"What about his daughter, Kirsten?"

Lisa rubbed Dario's crotch. "We'll find her, darling. We always do."

* * *

Kirsten cowered in a dark corner of the basement with her hands over her ears and her eyes sealed shut. The lasting image of Randolph Leeds raping the teenage girl while streams of blood dried on his face was a picture she'd never forget.

"*Kirsten,*" her mother called. "*It's over, honey. Open your eyes and stand beside me.*"

"Go away."

Cold fingers clutched Kirsten's wrists and she screamed at the fleshless skull hovering above her.

"*Honey, it's only me.*"

Kirsten pulled her arms toward her chest, but the skeletal hands were too strong. "Let go of me."

"*As you wish.*"

Her mother released her and Kirsten tumbled into the wall. She was vaguely aware of her mini-skirt rising above her hips.

"*I see that you've turned into quite a classy lady.*"

Kirsten yanked the skirt down as she got to both feet. "Don't you ever do that again."

The hollow corpse leaned over her. The familiar structure of her mother's face was eroded by time, now just a rotting skull leering at her.

"*Do what, dear?*"

"The kiss, showing me the past, and grabbing me like that." Kirsten's face burned red. Her fists were like twin hammers by her sides.

Her mother reached for her face. Kirsten was slow to react and the boney fingers soothed her cheeks and tucked her long hair behind her ears. "*My poor daughter, I always loved you. I never stopped caring you know, even now, but these are things you must see, places you have to be. I can't hide you from the world's horrors forever.*"

Kirsten closed her eyes. She tried to picture her mother as she once was, warm, caring, always smiling down at her. Kirsten kept the image sealed in her head as the boney fingers played across her face. "I'm sorry, Mom. I'm just scared."

"*You shouldn't be,*" her mother soothed. "*I'm here with you.*"

"I know." Kirsten opened her eyes. There her mother stood; a rotting image of her former self. Kirsten stared into the yellow flicker of light where lovely blue eyes once dwelled. "What do you want from me?"

"*Close your eyes again, honey. I have something else to show you.*"

Kirsten did as she was told. She stood ridged and flinched when naked bone pressed against her lips. The world was ice and black. She could sense the room changing around her, but she dared not open her eyes. Then, her mother's cold embrace drifted away. Kirsten slowly opened her eyes only to discover she was now outside. The moon shone above her in a crescent shape and Dead House sat behind her like a wretched giant in slumber.

"Tried to get away did you?"

Kirsten didn't move. The voice belonged to that of a man, though she couldn't tell where it had come from.

"I had you pegged from the start, my finest catch yet."

Randolph Leeds came up the hillside. He was dressed in blue coveralls and dragged a black body bag with him.

"I can't stand this!" Kirsten tugged at her hair. "Mom, get me out of here!"

The wind blew through autumn leaves, it almost sounded like giggling. Randolph continued to drag the heavy bag toward the house. "Almost there, my pretty, you'll be the best one yet."

Kirsten approached him. She watched his arms strain and a vein pulse on his forehead. "I hope you have a heart attack, you son-of-a-bitch," she yelled but Randolph didn't seem to hear her. He lifted his head and seemed to gaze at her from his single orb.

A booming voice came from behind. "Ah, I see you've brought the last one. Your mother will be very pleased."

Kirsten spun around in time to see the doctor stomping down tall weeds. He walked right through her. Kirsten felt a cold shiver racing through every one of her limbs as her teeth clattered.

"We're almost done then?" Randolph asked.

The doctor bent down. He fumbled with the bag's zipper before opening it.

Kirsten wanted to turn away. She couldn't bear to witness another half-dead girl pleading for her life. But her feet were encased in stone. She couldn't seem to avert her eyes no matter how hard she tried.

"Still fresh I see," the doctor grinned.

Kirsten peered over the mad doctor and her jaw dropped. The body inside was that of a little girl. She was no older than nine or ten, her face bruised and bloodied.

"You're monsters," she hissed at them.

"She'll do just fine, son, throw her down the chute," the doctor said approvingly.

Randolph tugged the corpse hand over fist across the dewy grass. The vein in his forehead looked ready to burst. He stopped before a black patch of earth and ran his fingers along a metal latch. The earth opened on rusty hinges and Randolph hauled the body over the pit. "Bombs away, bitch," he chuckled.

The young girl came to life in a burst of sucking air. Her face twisted into a heartbreaking sob. "No, let me go!"

The corners of Randolph's mouth lifted and he tossed her down the hole without a care, the girl's screams trailing off into blackness.

The doctor clapped his hands. "Good work, my boy. Why don't you wash up before we get started, tonight is our night."

"Yes, Father," Randolph said and shuffled away.

Kirsten followed both of them into Dead House. Upon entering, she saw that the interior was the same as it had been that morning; the red couch in the living room, book shelves touching the ceiling, and the same Oriental rug taking up space below a small television set with rabbit ears.

Well, at least the television has changed, she thought as she kept pace with the father and son, careful not to get too close. She buttoned her shirt all the way, not that anybody could see her cleavage, but she didn't want to take that chance.

Randolph unlocked the cellar door with a large key and descended down the stairs, his father following after him.

"I'm quite proud of you, son. You've grown up to be a fine man."

Randolph said nothing in response.

Kirsten trailed them into the blackness. Their shapes merged with the midnight, and as the two disappeared, Kirsten continued walking.

"Your mother would be so proud," the doctor said.

Kirsten went to where the voice came from. She put her hands out before her. "Where are you bastards?" Then Kirsten's arms were freezing. She pulled back, shivering with the onset of cold.

"It's a bit drafty in here," the doctor snapped. "I'll turn on the heater."

A light flickered above them and Randolph stood beside a switch. His face could've been chiseled from granite. "I want to work alone tonight," Randolph said.

"Alone?" The doctor raised his eyebrows.

"Yes, Father, alone. Don't disturb me." He turned his back and walked toward the fountain.

"Randolph, come back here this instant."

Randolph stopped in his tracks. "What?"

The doctor rushed down the hallway so fast Kirsten leaped a good four feet back. He grabbed Randolph by one arm and spun him around.

"Don't ever walk away from me again!"

Randolph twisted out of his grip with ease. "I'll do whatever the hell I want. You're getting old, Father, too old. You can't even go after them anymore and your scalpel shakes every time you go to make an incision." Randolph breathed heavily with anger. His nostrils flared as he bore down on his father. "You'll take none of the glory tonight. I did the work. I captured the girls. I prepared them. What have you done? Hump one or two and then plant your body in front of the television? You're pathetic."

The father smacked the son across the face. He then grabbed his son by the throat and squeezed. "I was researching this project before you were even born. Never speak to me in that way again."

Randolph's face turned a dark shade of red as he fought to breathe. His arms shot to his father's face, two thumbs digging into two eyes.

The doctor screamed and let go. He back peddled and rubbed his eyes. "You ungrateful ingrate. I taught you everything you know and this is how you treat me?"

Randolph sucked the dusty cellar air into his lungs. His hand slipped to the front pocket of his coveralls and he withdrew a pair of brass knuckles fixed with four long spikes. "I appreciate all you've done for me, Father; the young girls, the experiments, and for tonight." Randolph slipped the weapon over his knuckles. "Your wife won't be lonely this night."

The doctor stumbled over a stack of Playboy magazines. He fell on his back and groaned. "I'll get you for this; you won't get away with it."

Randolph reared his fist back. "When you see him, tell Satan I'll see him soon, but not too soon." His fist crashed into his father's forehead, knocking it backward. The spikes left four small dots upon his father's head. Randolph hit him again and again. As the doctor's body fell to the floor, Randolph straddled him, planting fist after fist into his face.

Kirsten flinched at every wet crunch. She stood behind Randolph and hugged herself, it had become so cold. When Randolph was out of breath, he rose from the limp body of his father. Where the doctor's grinning face once dwelled, it was now reduced to a splattered mass of leaking gore. Randolph wiped the sweat from his forehead as he smiled widely. "Rest in pieces, you stupid bastard."

Kirsten watched him head for the fountain entrance. His hands dripped blood like a leaky faucet. Suddenly, a rush of cold air blasted her face.

"Kirsten, you must go."

"Mom, where are you?" Kirsten looked for the disembodied voice but only saw black. "Was that what you wanted me to see?"

A shambling figure edged along the cellar wall. Her mother's blue dress gave off a radiant light of its own. *"No, not all of it, but the ones underground have broken through. They're coming for you."*

Now knowing her mother meant her no harm, Kirsten instantly put out her arms and let her mother embrace her. A rush of a thousand icy blades stabbed her body as the cellar twisted and morphed around them.

Kirsten closed her eyes. She was torn back and forth through the fabric of time and space. When she came to, she was once again alone in the dark room where she'd hid in the present.

The door was partway shattered, pieces lying on the cellar floor, and leering skulls and boney fingers poked through the wood eagerly.

Kirsten gave a single shrill scream before the door broke apart.

Chapter 23

A soft knock struck Dr. Alvin Tandy's oak door caused him to look up. The taps of knuckles were delicate and quick, like summer love.

Dr. Tandy adjusted his reading glasses. "Come in, Alice."

Alice eased through the door. Her blonde hair was unraveled and trickled down her arched shoulders. She set a manila folder on his desk.

"This is from patient #8042, Doctor."

"Victor Leeds," he said.

Dr. Tandy took the folder into his hands. "I asked him to do some drawings for me. Have you looked at them already?"

Alice nodded as both corners of her mouth dropped into a frown. "Yes, I have. It's terrible." She walked out of the room, closing the door quietly without saying goodbye.

Dr. Tandy opened the folder. Upon looking at the first drawing, he choked in shock. "What the hell?"

The sketches were done in pencil and akin to nothing he'd ever seen before. There were four in total. The first one was of a long dark hallway littered with ancient tombs and desiccated bodies. The next picture was of a group of dismembered bodies with the skin peeled off their bones, seeming to be rotting away. It was almost as if they were clawing out of the sketch. Dr. Tandy flipped over to the third drawing. It was the most disturbing one so far. The pale body of a lovely girl hung out of her coffin at a wake. Dead eyes looked out of a once beautiful face.

He swallowed hard and looked over the last drawing; this one was of a woman with dark shaggy hair, sunken eyes, and a groping hand curled like a hawk's talon.

He set the sketches back into the folder and left them on his desk. "My God..." He was just about to pry the last of his concealed stash of liquor out of his desk when the telephone rang.

Dr. Tandy cleared his throat before picking up. "Hello?"

"Is this Dr. Tandy?" a male voice inquired.

"Yes, this is he. What can I do for you, sir?"

"I didn't mean to call so late, but your secretary said you were still in." The man paused briefly as though searching for the proper words to say. "This is Officer Brian Kratos with the Sheriff's Department. I was calling about Victor Leeds. Have any breakthroughs taken place yet?"

Dr. Tandy eyed the manila folder and looked to the far wall. "None so far, I'm afraid to say. It's a slow process, Officer. The mind is a delicate machine and sometimes it likes to hide the truth from its owner."

"Has he talked about the missing girl? Has he said anything about Kirsten Tucker? Or said anything about her parents?"

Dr. Tandy heard the sharpness in the officer's voice and didn't like it one bit. "No, he hasn't spoken. I still need more time. It's only been less than two days since he was released into my care."

"People are missing, Doctor," Brian said. "I need answers, and I think he's the only one with them."

Dr. Tandy took the receiver away from his mouth and sighed. *Don't get angry with him now, he's only trying to do his job*, he thought. Dr. Tandy eased the phone back to his ear. "Look, Officer, I'm afraid I have no new information at this time."

"Then what information do you have? Please, Doctor. One of my best leads has also disappeared."

"And who might I ask was that?"

Brian hesitated.

Dr. Tandy waited for the inevitable *none of your business* line to unfold, but the officer surprised him.

"His name is Mark Parks. He's..."

"The local caretaker at Memory Lane Cemetery," Dr. Tandy interjected. "Yes, I know him. What happened?"

"Nobody knows. He phoned the station earlier to complain about a stranger on his property. I drove over there with my partner, but we couldn't find a trace of him."

"That's a pity," Dr. Tandy said.

"It's still under investigation, and with any luck, we'll find something soon. That's why I need your help, Doctor. Has Victor told you anything? It doesn't matter how small it might seem."

Dr. Tandy uncapped a bottle of scotch and gulped a mouthful. The strong liquor burned going down but warmed his body and eased the throb growing between his eyes. "I'm afraid the only thing Victor's told me is about dead people in his basement who kidnapped his girlfriend." Dr. Tandy tapped the folder on his desk. "He's very disturbed. When I have more information you'll be the first to know."

Brian sighed, knowing his call had been for nothing. "Thank you, Doctor, I'm sorry if I've bothered you."

"No bother, goodbye now." He placed the phone in its cradle, finished off half of the scotch, and exited his office. Alice was in the hallway smoking a cigarette. She stared at the white wall across from her, her gaze making her look like she was seeing into oblivion.

"Alice, you know smoking isn't allowed inside the building."

Alice took another drag before snuffing it out on her high heel. "Sorry, I just didn't want to go outside. It's pouring rain."

"How's Victor doing?"

"He's watching the rain from his window."

"No problems?"

Alice shook her head. "Not since he bit you." She eased closer to him. "I don't trust him and those pictures he drew are terrible."

"Yes, I saw them. There's no question the boy is having a breakdown. I'm going to speak with him now." Dr. Tandy reached for Victor's door but Alice stood in the way. "What is it?" he asked.

She suddenly wrapped her arms around him. "Hold me, just for a little while."

He found his arms caressing her back; it didn't seem so long ago when their bodies were intertwined in a fit of passion in his office. Alice snuggled into his chest and a soft moan escaped her lips. She pressed herself closer; her grip all consuming.

Dr. Tandy felt a rise in his pants. He cleared his throat and eased her apart from him. "I'm sorry, my dear, are you all right? This isn't the time for this."

"No, I'm not all right," she replied as she crossed her arms and leaned against the wall.

"You're upset. Can I get you something to drink?"

"No thank you."

"How about a valium?"

Alice gave a hysterical laugh and covered her face with her hands, sighing slightly.

"You're going to think I'm crazy, Alvin."

"Never, my dear, you're under a lot of stress, and it's getting late. Why don't I drive you home after I finish with Victor?"

"I have a car these days, you know. I can drive myself."

Dr. Tandy smiled. "That's good to hear. I'm glad you're taking care of yourself."

Alice's lower lip quivered. "Do you believe him?"

"You mean patient #8042?"

Alice rolled her eyes. "Yes, of course. Who else would I be talking about?"

"No, I don't. I think he's delusional and suffers from prior childhood trauma."

Alice nodded as he spoke, as if she'd already heard his answer before he opened his mouth. She stepped away from the wall.

"He has something to show you when you go see him." Alice gave him a quick kiss on his cheek. "Goodnight, Alvin."

Dr. Tandy pushed his wire-rimmed glasses back onto his nose as he watched Alice leave. "Perhaps another night, Alice?"

She paused and glanced over her shoulder. "You bet," she said, then was out the door.

With Alice gone, Dr. Tandy focused his attention on Victor's door. He knocked twice, unlocked it, and entered.

Victor was leaning on the window sill on his elbows, staring out the window through the metal mesh covering the glass. The rain fell in thick sheets.

"Good evening, Victor."

Victor continued to stare out into the rainy night, unresponsive.

"I looked over your drawings, very creative." Dr. Tandy shut the door behind him. "Would you like to turn around?"

Victor's voice was cold and distant. "I can't, I'm watching someone right now."

Dr. Tandy lowered his glasses so they sat on the brim of his nose. "And who might that be?"

"A dead woman. It's Lynn; she's come to get me."

Dr. Tandy cleared his throat. "Why don't you sit down for a spell, Victor? You must be tired."

"She's right there, standing in the rain. She's waiting for me."

"Should I call the orderlies, Victor?" The question hung in the air like shriveling brown leaves before a strong November wind.

Victor twisted his head around. He had dark circles under both eyes. "She's right there, under that willow tree. The rain animates her somehow. I don't understand it, but Lynn's come here to finish me off. She's one of them now."

Dr. Tandy went to him. He loomed over Victor's shoulder and looked out into the storm. Heavy sheets of rain pounded the desolate street. A river of water crept along the front lawn of the building. The willow tree swayed in the wind, empty underneath, devoid of shape or form.

The doctor placed a hand on Victor's lower arm. "I won't repeat myself."

"Don't you see her? She's standing under that damn tree."

"Victor, please come and sit down so we can talk some more."

Victor suddenly twirled around, breaking contact with the doctor. "Just look, dammit!"

He grabbed Dr. Tandy by the collar and slammed him against the wire mesh, banging the top of his head against the glass.

153

Dr. Tandy struggled in his captive's grasp. He was about to cry out for help when a dark form parted from the aging weeping willow. A woman, drenched and pale like the underbelly of a great white shark, stumbled into view. Where a lower stomach should have dwelt there was an empty cavity choked with dirt, maggots and ragged strips of flesh.

"My God..." Dr. Tandy muttered in disbelief.

"Do you see her?" Victor asked. His grip was an iron vice. "I'm not crazy, she's really there. Lynn has come back from the dead to kill me."

"Yes, I do see her."

Victor released him.

Dr. Tandy never broke eye contact with the disfigured woman. "It's an abomination." He took off his glasses, wiped the lens on his white coat, and placed them over the bridge of his nose, to glaze out the window again.

This wasn't a joke or a prank, somehow this was real.

The walking corpse who was once Lynn Watterson opened her mouth as though calling to him and Dr. Tandy held his breath.

Like a wraith, the dead woman drifted back under the weeping willow, melting into the darkness.

Victor sat down on the bed, his arms crossed over his chest.

"Should we talk now, Doctor? Maybe it's you who should take a seat."

Chapter 24

"Are we dead?" Sybil's soft voice snapped Trevor into consciousness. His elbows sank into the damp earth as he tried to rise. The black straps that Dario had bound him in were still in place. Trevor had to blink his eyes a few times before they came into focus. Sybil was nailed to a half exposed chimney. She seemed to smile, but Trevor soon realized he mistook her grinning lips for a line of dried blood. They were in the basement of a burned out house in the country. The dark sky looked down on both of them as droplets of water fell on Trevor's head.

"No, we're not dead, not yet."

Sybil's voice was hoarse, like she'd been screaming for hours. "They'll be coming back soon."

Trevor moved his neck from side to side and a lightning sharp pain shocked him between his shoulders. He eased himself across the damp earth and let the rain wash his pain away. The last memory he had was of being dragged through the woods by a nylon cord tied around his neck. Sybil had been limping ahead of Dario, and each time she slowed down, he kicked her lower back. When they'd reached the remains of an old colonial house, Dario had tied Trevor up. He was too weak from blood loss to fight. Dario had whispered something in his ear before bringing a concrete block down on his head.

"We have to get out of here," Sybil said.

Trevor turned to watch her frantic struggle. Dario had nailed her hands to the chimney and tied ropes under her armpits to hold her in place. The only piece of clothing she wore was her pink panties. Trevor's mouth was dry like a burning desert at high noon. He opened his mouth and took in the rainwater.

"I think I can get my hands free," she said. Sybil eased her right hand back and forth, opening the wound even wider; tendons, flesh and bones ripped and cracked. She cried out in anguish when she tore her hand from the nail, her right arm swinging free.

Trevor just stared at her, amazement filling his heart. He got onto his elbows to get a better view of his own situation. Three black straps were across his mid-section, and both his arms were held back by unseen bonds. Trevor's legs were free to move, but his feet gave a lightning stab of pain when he tried to move so much as a single toe on either one. He waited a moment and tried again and this time it was easier, less pain shooting up his legs.

He pushed his shoulder blades back and felt a heavy chain press against his skin. The braided metal links were fashioned around a plastic PVC pipe and then curled around his arms and shoulders like a live snake.

"Goddamn it!" Sybil shrieked as she jerked her left hand free. The nail tore between her middle and ring finger, creating a large gap in her hand. Sybil cried out even louder. She swayed on the ropes and cradled her misshapen hands to her naked chest as blood dripped from the wounds to splatter the dirt floor.

"Sybil..." he said.

She didn't seem to hear him. Her head sagged and she began to sob.

Trevor rocked in his bonds, testing how long the encased chain length held him. To his surprise, he discovered he could drag himself a good distance. But his crippled foot limited his movement greatly, and before long, he sank back into the dirt. The rain felt like a thousand needles stabbing his body.

"I think I can break free," Sybil grunted.

She swayed her arms back and forth like a scarecrow caught in a tornado. The thick ropes holding her suspended against the chimney were not willing to let her go. She tucked one arm behind her back and swung from side to side. When her body had gained enough momentum, she slipped her arms free of the ropes. In a flash of twisted limbs, she dropped through the air and landed with a hard thud.

Trevor gasped with hope. She was face down in the mud, but she was free.

"Sybil?"

A hysterical laughter welled up from her naked body. She used her elbows and knees to rise and now smeared with wet earth and bloody from the waist down, she crawled to her feet.

"I did it," she said, amazed. She spun around in circles, raising her head to the heavens. "I'm free!"

"Shhhh," Trevor hissed. "Lower your voice. Don't be so loud."

Sybil stopped spinning. She looked to the forest through the crumbling foundation and then to Trevor. For a split second, she took a step toward the woods, her mind deciding if she should just run for it and to hell with Trevor.

Her eyes darted to his ruined face, and when she saw his pain, she quickly switched her path and headed for him.

"I have to get you out of here," she said.

Relief flooded his face like the torrent of rain falling from above.

"Hurry, find something to get me out of these chains."

Sybil was two feet away when a dead branch snapped in half behind her. Dario and Lisa materialized from the darkness, blocking the only clear exit. Each of them carried a black bag in one hand and a can of gasoline in the other. Dario dropped both items at his feet and began to clap. "Bravo. Who'd ever guess a two-bit teen hooker would have so much stamina," he joked.

"I bet she'll put out till dawn, too," Lisa added.

Dario unbuttoned his leather pants; he then slipped out of his pants and began to stroke himself. "I can't wait."

"Please, let me go. I already pleased you," Sybil said. She hid behind Trevor, her breath coming in and out like ocean waves.

Dario rubbed himself harder. He was sticking straight out now. "I don't think so, bitch. This time you're going to get it, and you'll get it real good."

Lisa giggled with excitement.

Sybil shook her head. "Please, I'll do anything. Just let me go. I want to go home. I want to go back to school. Please."

Dario pressed closer.

Lisa caught up to him. She whispered something in his ear which brought a shark's grin across his mouth.

"Well, there's one thing you can do," he grinned lecherously.

Sybil backed away until she came up against the chimney. She covered her breasts with her bleeding hands. "Anything, I'll do anything."

"Have sex with Trevor," Dario said.

Sybil's hands trembled. "Trevor? No, I can't. No."

In a flash, Dario had both of her wrists locked in his large hands. He squeezed right above her bleeding palms. "Have it your way, bitch." Dario rubbed his giant member between her legs. "I figure I'll see how the back door feels first. This is gonna hurt."

"No, please," she begged.

Dario kicked her legs out from under her and Sybil fell to the wet earth. He parted her legs with ease, a wicked grin painting his face.

"I'll do it," Sybil cried out. "Just get off of me."

Dario looked toward Lisa for approval.

"It's your call, darling," Lisa answered with a shrug of her shoulders. "Either way the bitch is screwed...literally."

Dario nudged his cock against Sybil's upper thigh.

"Please...don't do this," Sybil sobbed. "I'd rather be with Trevor than you."

Dario's hand slapped her cheek and made it red. "Shut up, slut." He rose from her like a tiger holding down its prey. "Go to him, but play any tricks and I'll skull fuck you with this." Dario shoved his dick beside her eye socket, whacking his member against her face like it was a small baseball bat.

Sybil quivered in fear. She got to her hands and knees and crawled over to where Trevor lay staring into the star-filled sky. Dark storm clouds rolled across the night, scattering the flecks of moonlight piercing the cloud cover and bringing more rain.

"Trevor?" she said.

His eyes were wide open. "Don't do this. They'll kill us anyway," he told her.

Sybil hovered over him. Her hair was brighter than the sun. She edged closer to him and her smooth legs brushed against his.

"I have to, it's my only chance," she sobbed. Her soft breasts bounced as tears streamed down both of her cheeks. "They'll let me go afterward. They just want a little show."

"They're rapists and killers." Trevor lowered his voice to a whisper. "I can't believe I was married to Lisa. She's a monster. You need to make a break for it. Get Dario to come over here and I'll bite his leg. While he's dealing with me you can escape."

Dario snapped his fingers with impatience. "Hey, get it on over there. I don't have all night."

Sybil whimpered. "I'm so sorry. I have to do this. There's no other way. Please don't hate me. I'll be gentle."

Lisa laughed like a jackal. "Fuck him good, honey."

Sybil curled her hand around the base of his dick. She attempted to jerk him up and down, but quickly stopped, as she cradled her wounded hand to her belly.

"Sybil, don't do this. They'll never let us go. He'll rape you. He'll kill you," Trevor said.

Sybil eased her face to Trevor's shriveled member. "At least I'll have you before he gets a chance at me. It's the only mercy I deserve." Without another word Sybil's tongue slid down his shaft.

"Don't..." Trevor's pleas for her to stop soon turned into moans as her mouth encased him. She worked him hard, better than she did Dario. Her head bobbed up and down until she was rewarded with a mouthful of warm white fluid. She swallowed every last drop. Trevor laid back in ease. His chest rose and fell like a war drum.

"Damn," Dario said.

Lisa watched in awe. "That girl has a mouth on her."

"Not as good as yours, baby," Dario replied.

Lisa acknowledged the compliment but her face turned to doubt.

Sybil parted her legs. She slipped her underwear off, the dirty pink satin fabric gliding off her legs. She went to Trevor as a lover would, full of passion and desire. Sybil placed her knees against Trevor's hips. Her breasts jiggled in his face as she leaned over to kiss him.

Trevor didn't fight her. He kissed her back. Gentle at first, then he was sucking her lips and probing her with his tongue.

Sybil rocked back and forth over his limp shaft. She kissed Trevor's cheek until her lips reached his ear. Her voice was soft and warm. "If we make it out of this alive, will you be my lover?"

A quick intake of breath made Trevor choke. "Yes," he replied. "God yes."

Sybil arched her back, feeling the tip of his hardness as he grew excited once more. She used her bloody fingers to guide Trevor inside her. For a moment, it seemed like Trevor was too big for her. But Sybil thrust down upon him; up and down, wet and moaning until at last she was full of him. Trevor grunted as he slid himself inside her.

Sybil and Trevor slowly rocked to a hidden rhythm only the two knew the lyrics to. Their bodies melted together, moving quicker all the time. A wet sucking sound matched in time with Trevor's urgent thrusts. Sybil pounded on his member as her breasts shook in his face and she moaned with angelic pleasure. Trevor filled her, panting after each time he slid deep into her. They were enjoying themselves so much that when Dario's shadow passed over Sybil's backside, in the moonlight neither one of them noticed.

"Faster," Trevor moaned in a heated whisper.

Sybil picked up the pace as she bounced up and down. Her pleasure soared into the night sky.

"Oh God, yes!" she cried out.

But before she had a chance to finish, Sybil was shoved aside. Her bond between Trevor was broken immediately. She tumbled into the mud and landed on her back.

Dario stood over her, naked from the waist down. "Now it's my turn."

"Get away from her." Trevor fought to break free of his chains. He shook violently, straining every muscle till they nearly popped free of his flesh.

Lisa giggled. "Oh, darling, have fun with her, she sure is ready now."

Dario leaped upon Sybil, smashing her deeper in the slick mud.

Sybil kicked her legs, tried to bite him, and even managed to rake her nails across his face, but all acts proved hopeless.

Dario struck her twice in the jaw and sank his knee into her stomach. In the end, Sybil laid spread-eagle, defeated.

"Leave her alone, damn you," Trevor ordered, but was ignored as Dario eased himself between Sybil's smooth thighs, and began banging away.

Chapter 25

Dr. Tandy twiddled his thumbs together. It was a nervous childhood habit he could never break. Back in his high school days, the other kids would call him Tandy thumbs. The teasing got so bad that one fateful day he purposely slammed a truck door on his right thumb, snapping it like a twig. Teenagers were so wacky. Even that stunt didn't work though, and after the thumb healed, he was right back at it again. Just like an itch begging to be scratched.

When Victor's story came to an end, Dr. Tandy's thumbs rubbed together faster than before.

"And these...corpses," Dr. Tandy said clearing his throat. "How many are there?"

"Two that I know of," Victor replied. "But it's possible that more people could've gotten infected."

"What about the ones in your basement?"

Victor shrugged. "I don't know. They scratched me and took Kirsten away." He lifted his shirt, showing off three long red lines across his belly and lower spine. "I haven't turned, so I'm not sure what those things in the basement could've been? They certainly were dead, but not like the woman in the rain. The woman was pale like clay. She was a rain walker."

"This is very interesting, but I still can't release you," Dr. Tandy said.

Victor sprang off the bed with a start. "Why the hell not? What, you don't believe me even now? Kirsten is alive. She needs my help."

Dr. Tandy's speech took on a soothing tone. The voice he reserved for delicate situations. "It's not that I don't believe you, Victor."

"Then what is it?" His face was right in front of the Dr. Tandy's. "You don't trust me?"

"Victor, I can't let you go. Not only would I lose my career, but the police would go after you." Dr. Tandy's breath stank of scotch as he exhaled. "They would find you and then where would you be?"

Victor broke free of the doctor's steady eyes. He went to the window and rapped his fists on the glass. "Kirsten's in trouble. I have to get out of here and save her."

Dr. Tandy placed a caressing hand on his shoulder.

The door to Victor's room swung open suddenly and three bulky orderlies stood behind Alice. They wore hard expressions. Alice had a straight jacket in hand. "I called for back up," she said. "I didn't want you alone with him."

One of the orderlies, a large three-hundred pound man with a shaved head, cracked his knuckles. "Would you like the patient restrained, sir?"

"No." Dr. Tandy fiddled with his front pocket. "I was just leaving." He sidestepped Victor and stood in front of the window, peering out into the rain. His gaze went to the willow tree where the dead woman had been, but now the area was empty. "Please take care of yourself, my boy. I have great faith in you." As he moved away from the window, he left a small silver object on the window sill. None of the orderlies saw him do it, and Alice was too busy watching Victor to notice.

"Come along, Alice, it's late and I think it's time for you to go home." The group walked into the hallway and Victor's door was closed and locked.

When he was alone, Victor examined the window sill.

On it was a small silver key.

*   *   *

Fred Schwartz stuffed another jelly doughnut into his mouth and changed the channel on the small twelve-inch television. The rain pattered on his security shed like millions of annoying insects. He flipped the channel until *The Simpsons* came on. Homer was trying to sell bags of stolen sugar with glass shards in it. Fred chomped his doughnut and laughed at Homer's antics. "Another shitty shift in the loony bin," he chuckled.

His two-way radio blared to life in a buzz of static. "Fred, are you there?"

It was Maury and he sounded scared.

Fred decreased the volume on the television. "I'm here boss, what do you need?"

"We've got a situation in here. A patient escaped. We're going on lockdown. Nobody enters and nobody leaves, got it?"

Fred's stomach churned. He hoped it was only indigestion. "Copy that, boss. Complete lockdown."

The radio went dead.

"Maury you're such an ass. Lockdown," Fred sneered. "I've been on lockdown three times this week. What's his problem?" Fred increased the volume on the small television. "He acts like something bad happened, jerk off." Fred finished the rest of his doughnut and reached behind his chair for a beer. A sudden movement grabbed his attention from the corner of his eye. A jerky flash of twisted limbs edged into view. Fred wiped a mess of jelly from his mouth and as the figure approached, he saw it was a woman. Her face was hidden behind long scraggy, yellow hair. Fred checked to make sure his service revolver was still strapped around his utility belt, the handgun set on safety. Fred turned off the television and left his security shed.

The woman was about thirty feet away and closing in. She had an awkward gait as though her legs were too stiff to bend at the knees.

"Excuse me, lady. We're on lockdown right now. I can't let you go any further."

The woman ignored his orders and kept edging closer in that jerky, zombie-like motion.

When she was closer, Fred could see her skin through the falling rain; it was a sickly white color. He could only match the tone with cottage cheese. She was dressed in a stained white dress, and the right side of her shoulder was ripped and revealed a grievous wound filled with yellow pus.

"What the hell?"

The shambling terror shuffled closer. She extended a blackened hand toward him. Fred leaped backward, withdrawing his firearm, and drawing a bead on her. "F...f...freeze, lady," he stuttered.

The wind blew across the tree tops and chased the woman's long hair from her face. Where eyes should've dwelled were twin hollow sockets. She opened her mouth to speak but worms and dirt fell out.

"Jesus Christ on a cross." Fred's stomach twisted in knots as rainwater slid into his mouth. Volcanic vomit exploded from his mouth like a fountain gushing water. The walking corpse drew within an arm's length of him. Fred aimed for her and pulled the trigger, but his hands shook in terror. The bullet smashed into her neck, punching a quarter-size wound in her jugular.

"Shit." Fred aimed again but he never got off the shot.

The corpse yanked him by the hair and lifted him from the ground with strength the frail wraith should never possess.

"No, no!" Fred's oversize legs kicked out. His fingers slipped on the handgun as the zombie lifted him even higher. "Help!" Fred cried out as the revolver landed on the ground.

A pale undead skull bore into him. The dead woman once had a face that would've been pretty in life, but death had taken all her beauty away. She touched the side of Fred's cheek with a long, tapered finger and then dropped him.

Fred tumbled onto the concrete and rainwater soaked into the seat of his pants.

The corpse walked past him without a care. She was headed for the asylum.

Fred searched the pavement for his firearm but in the darkness and rain, the pistol blended in too well.

"Come on, dammit, where the hell are you?" His foot kicked an object large enough to be the gun. Fred spun around, felt for the handgun and found it. He lifted it, prepared to blow five holes into the trespasser but his mouth dropped open. He lowered the gun. The dead woman was gone. The straight concrete path leading to the building was empty. And at the slow gait the woman was using, she should've been in plain sight. Fred's cheek itched. He scratched it and ice crawled up his spine. Right where the woman had touched him was now going numb.

He raced for the security shed and once inside, he looked in a small mirror on the wall. His cheek was turning a sickening white color. Choking back a terror-filled sob, he grabbed the radio.

"Code red, perimeter is breeched, repeat, code red!"

*　*　*

Victor was sorting through a laundry bin when the sirens blared to life. His immediate response was to duck behind the bin and wait for the alarm to stop, but as he hid, time passed very slowly. The sirens didn't cease their piercing ring. He peered down the hallway. Two men in white uniforms were running. They disappeared around the corner and didn't return. Victor continued his search through the laundry. He found a white coat that fit but no pants. And each pair he came across was either so large that both his legs could fit, or only small enough to fit a shoe in. His ears throbbed as the siren continued to shriek. Was it getting louder? Then he came across a pair of pants that looked just right. When he held them up to his waist, he noticed a large blue ink stain on the hip. Beggars can't be choosers so he ducked behind the bin again to get dressed.

Heavy footsteps approached.

"She went this way."

"No," answered another man. "This way, I saw her. Trust me."

Victor crouched down even lower; under the laundry bin's crusty wheels he saw four pairs of feet. He arched his back, ready to sprint if need be. The pants were only up to his calves, and he still had to fight to get them on around his shoes. There would be no escape, and running was out of the question with his pants half on. He held his breath. His heart beat in sync with the blaring sirens.

"How about you go down that hall and I'll check the rooms?"

"Okay, got it."

One pair of feet disappeared. The other stayed in place.

Please don't see me. Please don't see me, he thought.

"Hello? What's this here?" The man leaned over to examine something in the laundry bin. Victor could see the top of his gray thinning hair. He snatched a dollar bill from the bin, pocketed the money, and turned away.

Victor watched him walk to the nearest door where he produced a set of keys on a ring and flipped through them. The minute the graying man unlocked the door and slipped inside, Victor was pulling the pants over his shoes and thighs. Within seconds the pants were on. They fit like a snug pair of jeans he had at his house. He quickly put the jacket on, buttoned it up and stood.

The hallway was still empty and there was no sign of the man with the gray hair. He let the shirt hang out and left his hiding place to head toward the closest stairwell.

"Hey buddy? Where're you going?" came a voice from behind.

Victor fought the urge to break into a run. The tone in the man's voice seemed curious, not alarming. He turned around to see the gray-haired guy with the keys.

Does he recognize me? Victor wondered. Victor had never seen the man prior to a few minutes ago.

Victor realized the man was still waiting for an answer.

"I'm heading downstairs," Victor said, trying to act like he belonged.

The man drew closer. He had a gruff, wrinkled face. His name tag read **Justin**. "We already searched the bottom floors. Where have you been?"

Victor's face and ears grew hot. "I was in the bathroom; the ham sandwich I had for lunch was spoiled."

"Ah, well." Justin checked the name tag on Victor's shirt. "Alice, huh?"

Victor looked down to see his name tag did indeed say Alice. Thinking quickly, he grinned at the man. "Uh, yeah, my father wanted a girl."

Justin nodded, not quite understanding but too busy to really care. "Whatever, look, we're checking the last two upper levels now for the escaped patient. Why don't you come with me, uhm..." He wanted to say Alice but seemed hesitant.

"Just call me Al for short," Victor said, trying to hide his embarrassment. He followed Justin to the next locked door. "How far do you think the patient got?"

Justin huffed. "Not very far, we're not that concerned with patient 8042. He'll turn up eventually. So how long were you in the can for?"

"Almost half an hour," Victor lied. He gripped his stomach. "It's still kind of tender."

Justin shook his head. "I had a tuna sandwich last week that did a number on me, too, but my wife made that one." He unlocked the door and turned on the light switch. "Man, I wouldn't eat any ham for a while if I were you. Anyway, in case you didn't know, some crazy broad with chalk white skin snuck in the ward a short time ago."

Victor's feet transformed to stone. He couldn't move a muscle. "A woman...did you see her?"

"No I haven't seen her yet. The cops are on the way, though." Justin eased inside the small room, it housed stacks of unmarked boxes and a couple of mop buckets. "Hey, Al, snap out of it and check the back room, huh?"

Victor felt the hard lump in his throat ease down his gullet. "Yeah, sure okay." He slipped into the adjacent room. Upon entering, he saw someone in the corner. He flicked on the light and breathed easier. It was only a janitor uniform hung on a nail peg. He found more mop buckets in addition to a few bottles of cleaning solution.

"Find anything?" Justin asked. He poked his graying head inside.

"Empty," Victor said.

"Right. Let's search the next one." Justin headed for the door. "You know I think I've seen you around here before. Do you work for Dr. Tandy?"

Victor's hands drifted to an unattached wooden mop handle hanging nearby. "Dr. Tandy? No, I don't think so, but then it's a big place, right?"

Dripping water echoed from the hallway and Justin averted his attention. "That's strange, there's a trail of water..."

He didn't have time to finish as Victor brought the mop handle down on the base of his neck. Justin went limp and dropped to the floor, but he remained awake and breathing. Victor snatched the keys from the man's hands.

"Sorry about this. No hard feelings." Victor stepped over him.

Justin reached out, his fingers scraping Victor's shoes. "You!"

Victor slipped from his grasp. He darted into the hallway, turned, and locked Justin inside the room. "You'll be safer in there." Victor saw the long trail of water and flinched. "Believe me."

A long wail echoed down the hall as the lights above began to flicker.

Victor fought the urge to run in the opposite direction. He stood firm and tightened his grip on the mop handle. Now was the time for choices. He could flee, exit the building, try to steal a car, and smash it into the side of Dead House, but what then? Even if he found Kirsten, the dead woman would still be after him. There was no doubt in his mind she was here for him.

And how many innocent people would the corpse turn in an attempt to get him? He clenched his jaw shut. Run or hide, he couldn't do it forever.

The lights above him died.

A faint drip, like a leaky facet, rattled in his ears. He was faintly aware that the alarm system had cut off. "Come on, you bloated piece of wet meat," he rasped.

A rank odor drifted down the hallway; it smelled like rotten eggs or rancid bacon left on the sidewalk in the heat of summer.

He walked toward the smell, his shoes slapping the water as he went. The hall arched to the right and he made out a pale figure slumped against the wall. It wasn't the dead woman. As Victor drew closer, he made out the white of an orderly uniform and the man who wore it. "Hello? Sir, can you hear me?" Victor asked hesitantly.

The man was heavy set and in his early thirties.

"Thank God you came." He tried to stand but both his legs buckled under him.

Victor saw a flash of his skin; it was turning from a healthy hue to a grayish white. "Where is she?" Victor asked.

"You're patient #8042, you're Victor Leeds. How did you escape?" the man asked. The tag over his upper left breast read, **Mike**. He tried to grab Victor with both hands but fell over before getting too far.

"The woman, where is she?" Victor asked again.

Mike laughed long and hard, a crazy man's laugh. "You mean the walking corpse?" He chuckled to himself. "And they called you mad. I bet those doctor's are shitting themselves right now."

Victor raised the mop handle over his head, knowing what he had to do. "She touched you." The statement hung in the air like an autumn leaf about to be blown from a tree.

Mike sluggishly crawled down the hall. He slid along the newly waxed floor, unaware there was no escape. "Please...mercy."

"You're rotting away. I have to kill you before you turn into one of them."

Mike raised his hand in a feeble action to defend himself. "Please don't kill me. I have a wife at home. We just got married last month. Please..."

Victor could feel his resolve slipping further away. The mop handle lowered, if only a little. "You'll be dead in a few hours, you know."

"Please, spare me," Mike pleaded.

"I'm sorry." Victor lifted the wooden pole high over his head.

"Just let me call my wife. I want to hear her voice before I turn. Let me say goodbye to her."

Victor sucked in his lips.

"Please, she means the world to me," Mike begged.

Victor's nostrils flared, but he lowered the mop handle to his side. Though the man was doomed, he was still human at the moment.

"Thank you. God, thank you." Mike lowered his head and groaned.

Victor grabbed him by the shoulder. "I don't know how long you have, but you're going to turn, and when you do, I'll find you. I swear to God I will. I'll hunt you down, every last one of you." He let Mike go, snatched the mop handle from the floor, and walked down the hall.

Mike sobbed. He crawled on his forearms like a soldier through thick brush behind enemy lines, going off in the opposite direction.

Victor held the mop pole in two hands as rage coursed through his veins. He followed the constant dripping down the hallway. The water trail was getting thicker as he went. He made a left turn and the hall ended at a set of doors. The water pooled below the twin double doors and he felt himself growing nervous. He approached the doors as he would a coiled snake. The water soaked through the sides of his shoes and made his socks wet.

There was a faint light seeping through the crack at the bottom of the doors. Victor took a deep breath and flung the doors open and stepped inside.

The room was wreathed in gloom and was octagon shaped and decorated with plush red chairs with circular end tables. Large, country style windows served as the wall. The rain was pounding on the glass in Spartan heaves.

Lightning flashed, and for a few seconds the room lit up. There, behind the red curtains he saw a humanoid shape, a puddle of blackish water pooled below the form.

Victor held the mop handle like a baseball bat. He approached with caution at first, but as rage, fear, and hate burned through him, he found himself charging toward the shape like Achilles on the battlefield. This thing, whatever it was, wherever it had come from, was responsible for Lynn's death. Hate boiled in his veins. He swung his shoulders back, let out a roar, and swung with all his might. The mop pole smacked something soft. Victor struck again and again until the mop pole cracked in half.

A pale figure slumped to the floor and landed by his feet.

Victor took the time to catch his breath.

The crumpled humanoid shape twitched. Lightning flashed, thunder rumbled as Victor flung the red curtain out of the way. His mouth formed into a silent O.

The crumpled shape before him wasn't the decaying corpse of the fiendish rain walker, it was Doctor Tandy. Where Victor had struck him, there were grayish bruises. The doctor had been tainted by lady death.

Victor stood apart from the limp body, tears already blurring his vision. Dr. Tandy had been good to him, had treated him fairly. A scrap of dried bones tugged at Victor's pant leg. He spun around in time to see a familiar sunken face grinning into his.

Lynn's rotting corpse reached for his exposed arm.

Victor was too shocked to move; everything was going in slow motion. The skeletal hand got closer to his warm flesh.

Then, all hell broke loose.

The double doors exploded inward. Two cops, a man and woman armed with high caliber pistols, addressed the situation in a split second before firing. Victor didn't know which one shot first. He guessed it was the man. The bullet smacked into Lynn's arm, taking it off at the elbow.

Victor shoved the animated corpse away from him with the mop handle.

Gunshots deafened the small room. Some hitting Lynn, others whining past Victor's ears to hit the windows behind him. The glass panes shattered and strong gusts of wind and rain sailed in.

The walking corpse edged toward the police officers, not affected by the impact of the bullets.

Victor didn't waist a moment of time, he wanted out, now, away from Lynn and the bullets buzzing around him. It was only a matter of seconds before one round found his body. He was running on instinct, and when he leaped toward an opening in the shattered window, his only thought was of how far he would fall before meeting the ground.

Chapter 26

Sybil lay in the mud like a used rag doll. Her eyes were glassy and her mouth was a straight thin line. She was wet and slick.

Dario was peeing on the remains of the chimney. "Hey babe, get me a smoke," he asked Lisa.

Lisa slid up next to him and pinched his bare bottom. "Sure thing, stallion, did you save any for me?"

"I sure did. That slut can handle anything. She was already loose before I got in."

"You never minded sloppy seconds before," Lisa laughed. She withdrew a pack of Camels from her back pocket. "Do you remember that time those three college guys screwed me on the beach?"

Dario finished peeing. "Yeah, that one guy humped you like a damn rabbit."

"Mmmm, he was nice." Lisa paired off two cigarettes, cupping her hands so they wouldn't get wet, and lit both. She handed the two of them to Dario. "Hold mine for a minute, would you?"

Dario took a drag off one. He breathed smoke like a volcano spewing ash.

Lisa got on her knees and began to suck him off.

"That's really nice." Dario sighed as he shoved his dick deep down her throat. "God, I love you."

After Lisa finished the job, Dario gave her the cigarette he'd been holding. The two of them smoked in the rain with leering grins.

Trevor had come across a dark comic in Kirsten's room one day. Inside were vampires that smiled like sharks. It was titled *30 Days of Night*. Looking at the two of them standing in the darkness, the image was complete. They looked identical to those vampires.

"Why, Lisa? You seemed so nice when we first met. What happened to you?"

Lisa matched knowing stares with Dario, as though this had happened countless times before. The two of them broke out into laughter.

"Darling, Trevor," Lisa said. "You were played from the start."

Dario dropped his smoke on the ground and stomped it out. "I'm going to tie the whore up until you're ready for her."

Lisa waved him away as she addressed her husband. "You didn't honestly believe I loved you, did you? Sure you had a nice car and a steady job, but a girl of my talent needs more."

"How long have you been doing this?" Trevor growled.

Lisa looked toward Dario but he had his back turned as he bound a limp Sybil with nylon rope. "I don't know really." Lisa shrugged and her perfect breasts jiggled a bit. "If I had to make an estimate, I'd say fifteen years or so."

"Fifteen years?"

"Does that sound right, dear?" Lisa asked Dario.

"It's more like seventeen, baby." He finished binding Sybil and proceeded to lick her between the legs.

"See, there you go," Lisa said. "Seventeen years, give or take." She sucked on her cigarette and delighted in watching Dario in action.

"And how many lives have you taken? How many deceived husbands? How many daughters? How many, you bitch!"

"Ten husbands and six daughters," Lisa snapped. "And you make eleven, darling."

Dario's head popped out from between Sybil's legs. "That reminds me, when are we getting his daughter? Now that's a nice piece of ass."

"Shut up, you sick fuck!" Trevor roared. "You'll never touch her. You hear me? I'll break every bone in your body before I kill you."

Lisa laughed and pressed her boot over Trevor's mouth. "Like we've never heard that line before?" She forced the heel further into his mouth. "Please, Trevor. You're nothing but dog meat now."

Dario wiped his mouth with the back of his hand. "This girl's gone dead on me." Dario squeezed Sybil's nipples between his thumb and forefinger.

Sybil blinked. She hadn't made a sound since the rape began.

"Leave her alone for now," Lisa instructed. "Let's pry some information from lover boy here." She gave Trevor's face a good stomp. Blood sprouted from his nose and one of his teeth on the bottom jaw chipped off.

Dario left Sybil in a hurry. He went to his black duffel bag and pulled out a pair of steel pliers while Trevor spit blood.

Lisa leaned down and kissed Trevor's forehead.

"Would you like an oral compliment or a straight screw while being tortured, darling?" Lisa whispered in his ear.

"Fuck you," Trevor spat and growled, a wad of clotted blood smacking her chin.

Lisa didn't seem to mind.

"Fine, then I'll just start you off with the oral and end with the screw while my assistant here removes your ears and pops your eyes out."

Dario leaned over Trevor's bruised face with steel pliers. "It'll be my pleasure," he grinned.

*   *   *

Victor stomped on the gas pedal of a new silver Mustang convertible while red and blue lights stabbed the darkness behind him. He'd found the car sitting next to the security shed after his fall from the window. It looked like a silver bullet in the parking lot, the heavy rain and lightning bouncing right off its sleek outer shell. Victor found the sport's car unlocked and had discovered the bonehead who drove the thing had left the keys in the ignition. The engine roared like a lion being unleashed. The Mustang eased away from the curb and onto the road.

He was driving for only a few minutes when the flashing police lights appeared. He simply stomped on the gas and let the Mustang take him home.

"Dead House," Victor muttered. A sliver of glass was wedged into his collar from his fall out the window, but every time he fingered it the object dug in even deeper. "Dammit, why did I jump out of that window?" He recalled the events leading up to his current situation. The sirens blaring inside the ward still throbbed in his eardrums. Lynn's animated body. The two cops storming inside, and the gunshots zipping by his head like angry hornets. The walking corpse had been taken apart. The bullets severing her bit by gory bit until she was a lifeless husk of used flesh.

And now he was free and there was only one thing to do.

Kirsten was alive. Lynn was dead.

Kirsten was alive and trapped in Dead House. The police wouldn't have believed him; he knew that for a fact. They would've locked him in a stale room and grilled him for days. *Hell, maybe even a week.*

Dr. Tandy had seen Lynn for himself and she had gotten to him. With him dead, too, there was no other option but escape.

"Kirsten," he whispered.

The police car gathered up enough speed to pull alongside him. A rather attractive young lady with short hair addressed him firmly through a speaker.

"Pull over."

Victor gave her the finger and smiled politely. He pressed the gas pedal all the way down and zoomed ahead. Rain splattered the windshield like a hail of bullets. The road ran straight and Victor watched in the rearview mirror as the red and blue lights trailed off. He didn't lose them, but they weren't on his bumper anymore.

"Almost home, just two more turns and I'll be..."

From the backseat came a low groan as two hands shot out from under a blue quilted blanket.

171

"Holy shit!" he screamed.

Victor jerked the steering wheel. One minute he was on the road, the next he was in the air. For a moment, time slowed down to a crawl. The hands yanked his shirt tail and a pale man in a security uniform rose from the backseat. The Mustang flew over a bare hill and crashed into a chimney. Victor was thrown forward, but his seatbelt prevented him from flying through the windshield. The air bag deployed and saved his life. But the man in the back seat wasn't so lucky. He was thrown forward and forced through the front windshield. Then, as suddenly as it had happened, it was over. The Mustang came to rest on the passenger side, demolishing the chimney; blowing gray smoke into the rain.

Victor loosened his grip on the steering wheel. Dizzy and disoriented, he unfastened his seatbelt and climbed from the Mustang.

A dark figure raced toward him.

Was it Lynn? But how, he saw her destroyed.

Victor couldn't see her clearly in the rain and darkness, but when she came close to him, he decked her in the jaw. She dropped at his feet like a sack of potatoes. Victor closed his eyes as he slumped against the car's roof. He could feel the rain trickling down his face, flattening his hair. The wind felt great on his cheeks.

Someone was shouting at him.

"You son-of-a-bitch, asshole, no good fucker." The man's voice sounded very close and Victor felt himself straighten out, woozy from the blow to the head from the airbag and crash. The sensation was akin to spinning around in circles and trying to walk afterward.

"Hey, fuck face."

Victor snapped out of oblivion. He focused on the situation at hand. To his surprise, the lady at his feet wasn't Lynn's walking corpse but an attractive, brown-haired woman dressed in a kinky leather bondage outfit. One of her breasts had popped out and her butt cheeks were showing. Under other circumstances, Victor would've blushed, but his immediate reaction was a gripping fear.

"Hey lady, are you all right? So sorry I hit you, I didn't know who you were."

Victor bent over and checked her wrist for a pulse. He found a steady beat.

"Of course she's not all right, dick head. You nearly punched her head off." The screaming man yelled and cursed an even longer series of words than before. And Victor quickly found out why. The man was dressed much like the lady, and was trapped under the front tire of the Mustang.

"Oh my God, Victor gasped at seeing the trapped man." Who were these people, what were they doing out here in the country in what appeared to be an abandoned and destroyed house?

"Get me out of here, you shit head. Christ, it hurts." The tire covered his mid-section just below the ribs. Victor suddenly noticed two other people. A naked teenager that kept staring at him and a bloodied middle-aged man with dark hair. Both of them were bound by their hands and feet with nylon rope. The dark haired man had two leather straps across his chest in addition to being chained to a PVC pipe. Victor's mouth dropped open and rainwater spilled into his mouth. "What's going on here?" Victor asked no one and everyone.

The angry man under the tire screamed and tried to force the car off of him to no avail. Then, like a light switch being turned off, his screams were silenced. Victor was about to check on him, see if he was still alive, when the girl spoke up.

The teenage girl was shivering. "Who are you?" she asked with a quiver. "Are you our angel here to save us?"

"My name's Victor Leeds. I'm definitely not an angel. Why are you two tied up? Whats going on here?"

The dark-haired man in the corner spoke. "Those two sick bastards captured us. We were being tortured before you showed up." He gave a weak smile. "Thanks, now do you mind setting us free?"

Police sirens whined in the distance and soon blue and red lights would be flashing down upon them. Victor wondered if he should just run into the woods, but with the rain and utter darkness, he'd never find his way out again. He'd never reach Kirsten in time.

"Oh, shit," Victor mumbled. "It's over." He stumbled to the car, still a bit disoriented from the crash as he hid from view.

Two blinding streaks of light shone down like twin suns, cutting through the trees.

"I see you've brought some help," the dark-haired man said as he shifted on the ground.

Victor dropped down next to the woman he'd knocked out.

"This isn't my best night." He cupped his hands over his head. "I'm so sorry, Kirsten. I failed you."

Chapter 27

An endless array of rotting fingers and arms clawed through the shattered oak door the way sea waves devour a cliff side; slowly and in great numbers.

Kirsten screamed for her life. She screamed for Victor, for her dead mother, her father, for anybody. But when the door splintered and cracked in half, she simply recoiled into the darkness, clutching the tattered blue dress for protection.

The shambling horrors piled in. Some walked with a shuffling gait, others stiffly, and a handful were legless and crawled toward her on their fleshless elbows. All of them were rotting; chunks of dried meat hung down from bellies bloated with nestling maggots. One of the female corpses wore the remains of a shirt around its waist. The breasts were dried and hung low, a few strains of brown hair trickling down the desiccated chin.

"Molly?" Kirsten recognized the female corpse immediately for what she had been in life, before Randolph and his father discarded her. The image of Randolph bent over her lithe body, blood still oozing from his destroyed eye as he thrust in and out haunted Kirsten. Molly halted. Her lower jaw eased open to speak but all that came out was a raspy hiss.

"Molly, please don't hurt me. I'm trapped in here like you. Randolph did this to you. Not me."

Molly advanced with the rest of the undead, only a few feet away now.

A cocky old man beckoned to her from the door. Kirsten couldn't see him but knew it was Randolph Leeds. "Shall I call them off?"

Kirsten's upper lip twitched in a snarl. "I'll kill you! I swear it!"

"I don't think so," Randolph replied calmly. "If you want to survive this current mess you're in, I'd suggest you make me an offer."

Kirsten found herself backing into a corner. She wrapped her mother's blue dress around her waist and put up her fists, awaiting the onslaught of dead flesh.

The dead were mere yards away from ripping into her when Randolph croaked. "Halt."

Kirsten shoved away the closest of the walking terrors; it was a woman missing her lower jaw. The corpse fell back and tumbled into three others, knocking them down as well.

"It's useless to fight, my dear. Even if you manage to escape this room, there are countless others roaming the house as we speak." Randolph laughed quietly to himself. "It seems I was finally able to wake them all up."

Kirsten caught sight of Molly edging closer. She sank her fist into Molly's face. The skull snapped apart and the meat fell away as Molly toppled over and remained still.

"I'm not afraid of you," Kirsten said.

"No? Tell me, how did you think Victor's last girlfriend died so suddenly?"

Kirsten pounded the corrupt flesh of another decaying victim. Her fists sunk right through the frail form and the corpse turned to a lifeless husk before it struck the floor.

"When I get my hands on you, I'll make sure to take your other eye out, you sick bastard. I know what you did to them. I saw what your father made you do. They were just girls, lost little girls. How could you?"

Randolph didn't respond for a moment. She could hear the squeaking of his wheelchair as he rolled into view behind the legion of the dead.

"It was easy, my dear. When something you desperately want is laid before you, ready to open and play with, why it's like getting a Christmas present. I never knew any of them. Sometimes they told me their names, but most of the time they only screamed." Randolph wheeled into the room. His long tapered fingers played over a double barrel shotgun. "And it's been a long time since I've heard anyone scream." Two barrels pointed at Kirsten's chest. "Will you come quietly or should I blow your legs off?"

Kirsten's insides twisted, but she didn't let it show on the outside. She narrowed her eyes and put on her game face. "Go to Hell."

One minute Kirsten was frozen to the ground, the next she was side-stepping into the undead horde. The shotgun roared, deafening in the small room and riddling the air with buckshot. Kirsten sank to one knee. The corpse behind her was blown apart at the waist. For a minute, the legs stood in place, then they toppled over. Kirsten shoved two of the mindless zombies in front of her and raced for the door. A shotgun blast leveled the two corpses like they were hay-filled scarecrows. Kirsten's left shoulder burned as the blast grazed her. She was halfway to the door when Randolph shouted an indecipherable word. But Kirsten's ears were ringing and she couldn't quite make it out.

Skeletal hands wrapped around her arms and legs, and cracked teeth sunk into her collar. Kirsten thrashed with all the strength left in her body. She struck down three of her attackers before the warm barrel of Randolph's shotgun poked into her lower back.

"Make one more move and I'll pull the trigger."

Kirsten's back itched. She didn't move a muscle.

"I surrender...for now."

Randolph let out a rasp of laughter. "There's that spunk again. Even in defeat you still think you stand a chance." The barrel slid lower, pressing down the elastic of her black mini-skirt. "There's no escape, my dear. And after I have my way with your body again and again, you too, will walk among the dead. But don't shiver too much, dear. I'll be sure to place you in the higher order of things."

"You're crazy," Kirsten replied. "Victor will come back. He'll find me."

Randolph seethed. "My son is gone. He'll never return."

Kirsten twisted her head around enough to see him. "What did you do to him? I'll kill you right now, so help me."

"You're in no position for threats, my dear." Randolph rammed the shotgun hard against her spine causing her to cry out in pain. "This baby's got a hair trigger and I wouldn't mind blowing you apart right now."

Kirsten's lower lip trembled. When she spoke her voice broke. "What have you done with Victor?"

"He's locked away for the murder of Lynn Watterson." Randolph produced a long needle filled with a dark, yellowish liquid. He lifted Kirsten's skirt and jabbed the needle into her left butt cheek. "And now, my dear, he'll be responsible for your death, too."

Kirsten tried to speak, but her mouth went slack. It became hard to breathe and seemed like she wasn't filling her lungs with enough air. Kirsten slumped to her knees like she was made of jelly.

The last thing she witnessed before drifting off was Randolph Leeds boring down on her with his single eye.

Chapter 28

"Kirsten," the bloodied man repeated. "Do you know her? She's my daughter; black hair, gothic looking."

Victor lifted his head. "Kirsten's my girlfriend."

The man shook in his chains like a puppet attached to strings. "Where is she?"

"They took her," Victor said. The rain matted his hair and poured down his face. He didn't bother to wipe it off. "I tried to help her but there were too many of them."

"Too many of who?"

Victor looked to where the two headlights were approaching. The police were still a bit away, but closing in fast. "The dead," Victor finally answered. "We were at my house and the dead came out of the walls and took her." He pressed his hands to his forehead. "I couldn't save her."

"So you're Victor." The chained man didn't wait for a reply. "I'm Trevor, Kirsten's father. I need to find my daughter. Please, get me out of here and take me to Dead House. That's where you live, right?"

Victor gave a silent nod.

"You're being chased by the police, aren't you? I heard the sirens. Free me, and I'll help you deal with them. I only ask you to bring me to your home so I can find my daughter."

Victor stared at him blankly.

Flashlight beams cut across the forest.

"Please, Victor. We don't have much time," Trevor pleaded.

Victor righted himself and came toward Trevor. "What can I do?"

"There's a black bag over by the chimney." Victor went to it. "Yeah, that's the one, open it up. Maybe you'll find something useful inside to get me out of these damn chains."

Victor held up a pump action shotgun.

Sybil jerked her head, coming awake. She propped herself on hands and knees and slowly rose to her feet. Though covered in blood, and her hands were bleeding, Victor still gawked at her. Though young, her body was hard and trim. She had a little bit of weight around the stomach, but other than that she was beautiful. He looked away immediately when she caught him staring at her breasts.

"I'm sorry. I didn't mean to," he said.

Sybil stepped up to him, a little shaky on her feet, and snatched the shotgun from his hands. "Thank you for saving us." She kissed him on the cheek like a pixie. "I'll help you, too."

Victor nodded. He dug into the black bag and discovered a hack saw, claw hammer, long serrated knives, and an Uzi with two lengthy clips. He took the automatic weapon and shoved the clips into his pockets.

The police were close enough that he heard the approaching officers crushing wet twigs and stirring autumn leaves as they moved through the night.

Sybil aimed in their direction with the shotgun.

"No," Victor said. "Don't hurt them."

Sybil lowered the weapon so it pointed to the ground. "So what do we do? Let them find us and take us in to figure out what's happened here?" she asked.

Trevor spoke up. "No, there's no time for that." He rattled in his chains. "Hide yourselves. I'll distract them, catch them off guard, and if it works, we'll high-tail it out of here."

Two dark figures appeared on the hill.

"Let's go," Victor said and motioned for Sybil to follow him. He hid behind the remains of the chimney, but Sybil wasn't with him. Instead, she slipped under the smoking Mustang on her backside, disappearing from view.

Both remained still and quiet as the police approached.

"Damn," a woman gasped. She held a standard pistol and flashlight. When the light passed over Dario's limp body, she paused. "Brian, come down quick. We've got bodies."

Victor silently cursed from behind the brick remains. He'd forgotten all about the creep he'd flattened on the way down.

Was he dead? Victor thought, hoping he was.

"Is he alive? Brian asked coming over the hill.

The female bent down, checked the man under the tire for a pulse and nodded. "Barely, but he needs medical attention. The station is still jammed, isn't it?"

Brian passed his light over the wrecked Mustang. "I don't know what's going on in town but I don't like it one bit. The station shouldn't be non-operational." He checked the driver's seat. "It's empty. He couldn't have gone far."

A low bellow sent both of them jumping. Trevor rattled his chains and spit blood. "Help me, please!" he cried out.

Brian was the first to reach the prone and chained man. "Cover me, Julie." He shined the beam into the Trevor's face as he approached.

Between the caked blood and broken nose, Trevor attempted a grin but it came out more of a grimace.

"Jesus," Brian gasped.

"Help me, please," Trevor said again.

Brian kept his gun trained on the man. "Who are you and what are you doing here?"

"My name's Trevor Tucker. I live on Ritter Road with my wife and daughter. My wife's over there on the ground. She and the man under the car tried to kill me. And my daughter's missing." Trevor felt real tears rolling down his cheeks. He cried for his traitorous wife and for Kirsten, wherever she might be. "Please, get me out of here."

Julie nodded to Brian. "I don't know what happened here but his daughter is missing, that much is true."

Brian put his revolver back in its holster. "Keep me covered," he told her and then addressed Trevor. "Where did the driver of this vehicle go?"

"He went into the woods, that way," He used his chin to gesture. "He was limping badly."

"Okay," Brian said. He went behind Trevor and sighed at the network of chains. "Somebody did a number on you, pal." He took out his lock picking tools.

"My wife, or soon to be ex-wife, started this mess," Trevor added.

Julie walked toward the Mustang. The radiator smoke had dissipated and was replaced with the strange calm that settles after a car crash, only the rain hitting the metal causing noise. Her flashlight illuminated black boots, two legs, and then the rest of Lisa's crumpled body. She was facedown in the mud. Julie checked her pulse, satisfied she was alive, she turned the woman onto her back. "Can you hear me?" Julie asked.

Lisa's eyes stayed shut. She was knocked out cold.

"What happened to her?" Julie asked.

At that moment Brian set Trevor free. "There you go." He threw the chains off. "We'll get an ambulance here for you, as you need medical attention."

Trevor stretched his arms as his back tensed and popped like a crushed soda can. "Thanks, I never thought I'd get out of there. And I'm fine. All they did was kick me around a bit. I've been through worse in schoolyard fights when I was a kid, thanks."

"Don't mention it," Brian said.

"Sir," Julie repeated to Trevor. "What happened to this woman?"

Before Trevor replied to her, he turned casually to the old chimney and nodded. "Now, Victor," he said curtly.

Before Julie had time to react, a fully loaded Uzi pressed against her temple. Then the sound of a pump action shotgun being cocked came from under the car and was quickly followed by Sybil pointing it at Brian.

"Don't move," Victor said. With his free hand he took Julie's gun from her hand and tossed it aside.

Brian tensed and his fingers began sliding to his pistol.

"Don't do anything stupid," the girl said from under the car. "Make one wrong move and I'll blow your head off."

Trevor grabbed Brian's gun and shoved the barrel between his shoulder blades. "I'm really sorry about this, Officer. But there's no time to explain everything right now. You'll just have to trust me that we're all on the same team. You just arrived at the worst possible moment."

Brian put his hands up. "What can I say? We're cops, that's what we do."

That made Trevor chuckle; he felt Brian move as though he could've spun around and ripped the gun from his hands, but Brian didn't dare try it with his partner in danger.

"Come on out, Sybil," Trevor said. "We've got them covered."

Sybil crawled out from beneath the Mustang. Mud had caked her breasts and stomach. She pointed the shotgun toward Brian. "What now?"

Victor nudged Julie hard with the barrel of the Uzi. "We take them with us." He bored into Julie like she was a worm drowning in a black puddle after a rainstorm. "I'll prove to you we're the good guys and that I'm not crazy."

Julie's neck stiffened. "I don't think you're crazy, Victor." She shook her head. "Do you know what happened after you jumped out that window back at the asylum?"

Trevor moved away from Brian. "Watch him closely," he instructed Sybil as he went to his wife.

"What?" Victor sneered. "You chased me and I got away, so?"

Brian spoke up then. "The corpse we shot, Lynn Watterson, she got back up," he said. "I emptied an entire clip into her head before she stopped moving."

Julie addressed Victor. "What was that thing?"

"I don't know," Victor said. "But my father has something to do with it. There's more than one of them. I know that much. If they touch your skin you get infected and turn into one of them."

"I believe you," Brian said and Julie agreed.

Victor kept the Uzi trained on Julie's head. "Good, but that doesn't change a thing."

"Hey," Trevor said. "Can one of you pass me your cuffs?"

Brian's hands slid to his utility belt.

"Don't move," ordered Sybil with steam pouring from her mouth. She advanced on Brian and shoved the barrel into his chest. Her hands slipped with expert practice around his belt and unbuckled it. She winced with the pain of her torn hands but she ignored it.

Brian saw her wounded hands and he winced in sympathy. "What happened to your hands?"

"Nothing," Sybil said, not wanting to talk about it.

When the belt fell around Brian's ankles, Sybil backed off. "Toss them to him."

Brian bent down slowly and did so and Trevor caught the belt. He took off the cuffs and snapped them around his wife's wrists. His mouth twisted upwards on one side. "Have them go stand by the car," he told Sybil.

"You heard the man," Sybil said. "Move it."

The two officers went to the Mustang as the rain splashed down on them in sheets. Both wore the same hard expression.

"Now, I want you to lift this car and let it fall so we can save that man," Trevor directed them.

"Save him?" Sybil snorted. "I'd rather shoot that no-good rapist bastard now and be done with it."

Trevor repeated his statement and Sybil gave in.

The two officers gripped the side of the Mustang and dug their heels into the muddy ground. On the count of three, Julie and Brian pushed. The Mustang groaned and toppled over like a metallic giant taking a nap.

The motionless body lying underneath stirred. Dario's breathing came in and out, and became steadier, but he didn't regain consciousness.

"This man needs help," Julie said. "We have to get him to a hospital immediately."

"Not on your life," Trevor said. "He's going to suffer for a long time."

"Yeah," Sybil added.

"But he's hurt. He'll bleed to death internally," Julie said.

"He raped me," Sybil said. "I fought him, but he raped me."

Julie closed her mouth.

Trevor started to say something but Sybil shook her head and said softly, "I didn't count our time together as forced. I rather enjoyed it." Then she spoke up for the two officers. "He's a bad man. And if Victor hadn't come along when he did, this bastard would've killed us. Just look what they did to my lover," Sybil said.

Trevor's eyes got big. *Lover?* "I...yeah, they hurt me, too. Before all of this happened I had a caring wife, I guess what they say is true about you never really knowing someone."

Brian cleared his throat. "Look, I don't care what happened between everyone right now, we can sort that out later. But I do care for this man's health and his life. I'm sorry if he raped you, but he needs to be brought to a hospital. Until then it's all conjecture. It's their word against yours."

Sybil's eyes blazed, realizing what Brian said was the truth. It was very possible Dario could walk from any and all crimes. With her jaw set, she strutted over to where Dario lay and shot him in the crotch. The gun blast was a mini explosion in the valley as blood shot out to mix and dilute with the rain. But it wasn't as bad as the screaming that came chasing after it. Dario woke up then and howled and jerked like a squished bug.

Brian turned pale and Julie gasped.

"There, he's going to die now, so justice is served." Sybil poked Brian in the ribs with the barrel. "Get him and the girl off the ground."

Brian didn't hesitate. He lifted Dario to his feet as Julie went to Trevor's wife.

"Carry them to the car," Sybil instructed.

"What are you going to do to them?" Julie asked with a hard face.

Sybil looked toward Trevor for answers as Victor stood silent.

"Does your patrol car have a trunk?" Trevor asked.

"Of course it does," Brian replied.

"Perfect, put them in there," Trevor said with a pained grin.

*   *   *

Before Victor got into the back seat of the patrol car, he scanned the forest for any sign of movement. The pale man who'd flown through his windshield earlier had vanished after the impact. Had he stood behind a tree and watched as the havoc played out? Or had he simply gone deeper into the woods searching for new victims? The rain made it hard to tell if someone was walking around in the dead leaves. He saw a barn owl in a tree looking down on the patrol car.

"Hey, Victor, you coming?" Trevor asked. He was behind the wheel already, bruised and beaten like a wadded piece of gum. His face looked like raw hamburger meat.

"Yeah, just give me a second." Victor searched the forest, hoping to spot a pair of pale limbs. But he found only shadows.

"Move it," Sybil said from the back seat. She had the two officers covered with the shotgun. Not that either of the officers would try anything at this point though. By the way both hung their shoulders and held hands, Victor could tell they were willing to play along for the moment.

"Okay, I'm coming," Victor said and he climbed into the passenger seat and aimed the Uzi in Brian's direction. "Okay, let's go."

"It's about time." Trevor backed out of the forest clearing and onto the roadway. He stomped on the gas pedal. "How far away is Dead House from here?"

"Not very far," Victor replied. "Maybe ten, fifteen minutes from where we are right now." He caught Brian staring at him. "What?"

"How long have you known about them?" Brian asked.

Sybil poked Brian in the ribs with the barrel of the shotgun. "Be quiet," she said.

"No, it's okay," Victor told her.

Sybil narrowed her eyes and she pulled the barrel away, but only by an inch or so.

"The first time I saw one was the night Lynn showed up at the deli where I work. When we saw that thing it was far away, but within a few seconds it was right next to us. Lynn was curious and wanted to touch it."

"And now she's one of them," Brian said.

Victor nodded and his eyes grew sad. "There was nothing I could do."

Julie squeezed Brian's hand. She tried to look friendly toward Victor. "How many exist?"

"I don't know. I mean, I can't say for certain, at least five."

"Five?" Brian gasped.

"Yeah five: Lynn, Jimmy, Tina his wife, the guy at the ward, not to mention the one I saw first."

"We finished off the one who tried to grab you. So that's minus one," Julie said.

Victor thought back to the man in the Mustang. He should've told them about him. "I never got to tell you both thanks."

"Don't mention it," Brian said.

"Hey guys. I hate to break up your conversation, but the road is blocked," Trevor said.

Everyone turned their attention to the long stretch of roadway in front of them. A silver tractor trailer with a BP symbol on the side was turned over, blocking both lanes. As the patrol car approached, two figures appeared from out of the gloom.

"Oh, shit," Trevor said under his breath.

The shapes took form as the police car edged closer. They were two men; one was heavy set and had a beard. The second was considerably thinner. He held a woodsman's axe and at the very tip was a chunk of dripping, red meat. Both of the men were dead, very pale, and welcomed the travelers with unnaturally wide grins.

"Go around them," Victor ordered. "Or drive through them."

Trevor put the car into reverse. He backed up and slid off the road.

"They're coming!" Julie said.

"Shit." Trevor slipped the transmission into drive. He stomped on the accelerator, but the vehicle only roared and didn't move forward. "What the hell?"

"Get it back into gear!" Julie cried.

"You'll have to shoot them," Brian added.

Victor rolled down the window, agreeing with Brian's assessment of the situation.

The skinny man with the axe was first to reach the car. He walked like a man with a serious injury, and upon his arrival, it was clear his left foot was missing below the ankle. The wood axe came crashing down on the hood of the patrol car, leaving a deep gash.

Before he could jerk the axe free for another blow, Victor aimed the Uzi at him and pulled the trigger. The automatic weapon cracked and popped out bullets like the fourth of July. Victor's mouth opened to yell, but the firearm silenced him. The skinny man was hit with the full force of the rounds from almost point blank range. He danced around until Victor stopped shooting, then slumped over the hood of the patrol car in a steaming heap of ruined flesh.

"Damn." Victor's hands were still shaking. "That's one down, right?"

"Good work!" Trevor shouted above the ringing in his ears.

Victor's ears buzzed. Wisps of pale smoke swirled from the Uzi's short barrel. "Where did the other one go?"

Trevor slid the car into drive and the car moved. He spun the head-lights to face the forest. "I don't see him." He drove onto the wet grass and the car kicked up mounds of dirt. "Shit." Trevor cursed as he put the car into reverse. He turned the wheel and pounded on the gas pedal. Overgrown weeds and wet earth splattered the side windows as Trevor drove forward. The wheels began to spin. "Damn it, I think we're struck."

Trevor, Sybil, and Victor looked to the two officers at the same time.

Julie crossed her arms. "I'm not going out there to push." She nudged Brian with her elbow. "And neither is he."

"Well, somebody has too," Sybil said.

"Did you try putting it into four wheel drive?" Brian asked Trevor.

"This heap has four wheel drive? But it's an automatic?"

"The Sheriff turned all of the patrol vehicles into manual four wheel drive two years ago after he got trapped in a mud pit," Julie explained. "That's your tax dollars at work."

"Where's the switch?" Trevor flicked on the overhead light and stared at the shifter. "I don't see anything."

"It's the button below the hood release," Julie said.

"Ah, here it is." Trevor pressed in a circular black button. He shut off the overhead light and tried again. "Here we go."

The patrol car spun for a few seconds then made it out of the mud. Trevor got back onto the road; the tractor trailer now lay behind them.

"I still don't see him anywhere. How does a fat man move so fast?" Trevor mumbled.

"Don't worry about him. We need to attack the source," Victor stated. "Take us to Dead House."

Chapter 29

Dead House was like a large tomb settled into the earth. Silence dwelled within as though the entire world could crumble and fall apart and it would still be there, waiting in the rain.

Trevor parked outside the black gate. "Wait here. I'll get us in." Before anyone could object he was out of the car. Trevor went straight for the wood axe embedded in the hood. The entire drive to Dead House, he'd focused on it, no doubt remembering the shambling corpse who wielded it before Victor blew it back to Hell. With two hard jerks, he freed the axe. He went to the lock, the axe gleaming in the lightning as he struck it. The first blow made sparks, the second left a dent, and the third broke the lock down the middle. Trevor threw the chains off and shoved the gate open.

Inside the car, Sybil was shaking badly. "This...this is where you live?"

"Yes," Victor answered. "My father is behind everything. I know it."

"You don't know that," Brian interrupted. "I agree that something bizarre is going on here, but I don't think your father is the sole one responsible."

The shotgun jumped up and down in Sybil's hands. "You're not from around here, are you?"

Brian gave a slight nod and focused on the dancing barrel.

"Dead House is haunted. I mean really haunted. I'm not going in there," Sybil said.

Trevor climbed back into the car. The rain had washed away most of the blood on his face, but the deeper bruises stayed the same color. Despite the rain and cold, he was sweating. "Piece of cake, let's do this. My daughter's in there." He saw fear in Sybil's eyes and retracted. "What is it?"

"I...I can't go in there," she stuttered. The shotgun jumped up and down like a live snake.

Brian's hand reached out, slow and easy. "Calm down now. You don't have to go inside." He was aware of Victor pointing the Uzi at him, but his hands continued to progress toward the shotgun. "You're safe here." He wrapped his fingers around the barrel and pointed it up. An awkward silence followed. Brian addressed the others. "Look, you don't have to hold us at gun point. We're here to help."

Victor's upper lip rose in a snarl. "Oh, yeah? And how do we know that for sure?"

"Because we could've escaped by now," Julie stated. "Do you really think we only carry one lousy handgun a piece?"

Brian held up his hand. "Look, I want to get to the bottom of this. We've had strange reports coming into the station all night. And now there's no signal. I'm concerned for this town and its people. I never really believed in the afterlife, but even I know it's pretty damn unnatural to rise from the dead."

Trevor shrugged. "I trust them. Hell, we need their help."

"I don't," Victor said.

"What do you think, Sybil?" Trevor asked. "Should we trust them or keep them at gunpoint?"

The shotgun still pointed at the ceiling. Sybil made a vain attempt to cover her naked breasts by crossing her arms. "Let them go. The town's lost anyway."

"Why do you say that?" Julie asked with concern.

"Before the two crazy assholes in the trunk kidnapped and raped me I was running away from one of those things." Sybil paused for breath. The anticipation for her to continue was apparent in everybody's face. "She had long stringy blonde hair, like spaghetti. And she walked crooked. Have you ever seen *The Ring 2* when Samara is crawling out of the well? It was like that. I freaked out. That's why I flagged down their car; then I realized they were a couple of loonies. I took their money and ran away but they caught me," she nodded toward Trevor. "I might be a hooker for the right price but I'm not stupid."

Trevor reached over the seat and patted her arm. "You're safe now. You don't have to go in with us. I'll give you the keys and you can stay here in case things go wrong."

"I'd like that," Sybil grinned nervously. She arched a thumb to the trunk. "What about them?"

"They're coming with us," Trevor answered. "I'm not leaving them alone with you."

Brian and Julie frowned.

"I want them close by. They're dangerous," Trevor explained. "Do you think I tied up myself and had Sybil beat the crap out of me before you showed up?"

Brian opened his mouth to speak but Julie squeezed his hand and answered for him. "We don't doubt what happened. But we can't keep them cuffed and not even arrest them."

"Then you arrest them," Sybil snapped. "Place them under arrest before I smash in that rapist's face with the butt of this shotgun."

Brian's shoulders tensed. He knew fully well that the young girl would do it. And so did the rest of them. That was apparent the minute she blasted his manhood into pieces with the 12-gauge.

"You do realize," Brian said to Sybil. "If that man in the trunk dies, you'll be up on murder charges."

"Like I give a damn. He got what he deserved," she said defiantly.

"That may be but once this mess is over, we'll bring them down to the station and you can press charges, but for now..." Brian was cut off by Victor.

"Oh, shit," Victor breathed. His face was pressed against the passenger window as he stared at Dead House. The others turned their attention to the house and gasped.

From the surrounding forest came dozens of pale, twisted shapes. Some were men wearing tattered garments drenched in fresh blood; others were women stumbling along on broken legs, and a few without legs at all.

Julie immediately recognized a few of them as locals. "Oh my God, what happened to them?"

Spellbound, the dead headed toward Dead House in a massive horde, completely ignoring the police car and its occupants. Once they reached the front porch, the door swung open seemingly on its own accord to welcome them inside.

Sybil's fingers twitched and the shotgun went off with a deafening bang! She screamed at the top of her lungs as a fist-size hole appeared in the roof of the patrol car.

"Shit!" Brian took the firearm away from her. He held the weapon in an upward position. "You could've killed somebody."

Sybil started to cry.

The last of the walking corpses dragged themselves into the house and the door closed behind them.

"What the hell is going on in there?" Trevor asked. He rubbed his ears and took Sybil's hand.

"I don't know," Victor said. "Those looked like people from town." He sucked in his lips as a ripple of fear coursed through him. "I have to find out. My father could be in trouble. And Kirsten's in there somewhere, too."

Brian's hand eased over Victor's shoulder. "I'm coming with you."

Victor nodded.

"Me, too," Julie said.

"No, you're not. You need to stay here with Sybil and those two in the trunk," Victor said.

"But...I can't let you go alone," Julie pleaded to Brian. She wore a puppy dog look. The kind girls could turn on when they wanted you to stay an extra minute or two, or for one more kiss.

"He won't be alone," Trevor said. He slipped the car into gear and drove through the black gates. "My daughter's in there and I'm not leaving until I find her."

Julie's slumped shoulders told everyone she accepted their decision. "Fine."

"Sybil needs you," Brian told her. "And I need you here. If something goes wrong in there we'll need a backup plan."

Julie let out a hysterical laugh. "And what plan is that? Run like hell and drive away?"

Trevor parked the car facing the gate. "I'm not leaving here without Kirsten. If things get bad we'll send Brian back for you." Trevor lifted the axe from between his legs. "You have my promise." He killed the engine and gave her the keys.

Victor stepped out of the car first, next was Trevor. They moved to the front of the car and stood side by side as they addressed Dead House.

Julie wiped her eyes. She wrapped her arms around Brian and sobbed. "I know you have to go. Just be careful. We have some unfinished business to address when all this shit is over." She gave him a passionate kiss and embraced him. "Just a small taste of what's to come."

Brian nudged away from her gently. "Well, hell, that's certainly an incentive to stay alive," he breathed, the kiss still on his mind. "I'll be back soon, Julie. Keep the engine running." He stepped out of the police car and into the night.

Victor was reloading the Uzi. He rammed a clip into the bottom and spit on the ground. Trevor saw this and Victor shrugged. "What? I like guns. I used to go shooting on the weekend."

"I didn't say anything, its good to know you can handle that, is all," Trevor said.

"So what's the plan?" Brian asked.

"We go in fast, shoot anything that's already dead, and stay together. I'll lead the way," Victor stated.

Brian checked the shotgun's cartridge holder. "Do you have anymore ammunition for this?"

"I'm afraid not." Victor reached around his back and pulled out two handguns. He handed Brian the two pistols he had in the car with him. "These are yours and your partner's, I made sure to pick them up before we left where you found us."

Brian took them both. He checked the rounds and made sure his utility belt had spare bullets. It did. "I'm ready."

Victor climbed the porch stairs like he'd done a million times in the course of his lifetime. Trevor followed close behind and Brian took the rear.

"When I open this door, will you two be ready?" Victor asked.

"We've got your back," Brian said.

Trevor twirled the axe back and forth impatiently. The way his face was marked he could've passed for one of the undead.

"Okay, here goes." Victor twisted the door knob. "Damn, it's locked."

"Step aside." Trevor arched the axe between his shoulder blades. Victor got out of the way as the heavy blade bit into the door. Trevor yanked it free and struck again, this time a vertical split cut down the middle. He pulled the axe free.

Brian motioned for him to move. "Save your strength. I've done this many times before." He bent his knees, ran at the door, and shot his boot heel under the lock.

The door broke open and slammed against the inner wall.

"Good job," Trevor said.

"It was my pleasure." Brian pulled out a medium size Mag-light from his belt and directed the beam inside.

The house looked normal under the circumstances. No furniture was out of place or books missing from the wooden shelves. The only sign of the dead passing through was the drops of water trailing into the living room and splotches of mud.

Victor pushed past Brian, sending the flashlight dancing along the wall. "What the hell is that?"

Brian shone the flashlight at the wall again. Bizarre words were scribbled in a deep red texture.

Abathan Kirdovin Ka Thrith.

Victor touched the words and his hand came away smeared. "It's recent."

A sudden crash of breaking glass in the kitchen grabbed their attention. Victor advanced through the tiny room and around the corner. He spotted three dark figures standing near the refrigerator. The light from the open door revealed three pale corpses. Sunken eyes glared at him. Without hesitation, Victor pointed the Uzi at them. "Get out of my house!"

But before he could pull the trigger, Trevor appeared. "Don't shoot them, it's too noisy. We need to be quiet. There's only three of them, we can take them out easily."

"He's right," Brian agreed as he slid into the entrance to the kitchen.

The corpses shambled toward them. One was missing an arm the other two had gaping head wounds, like a giant worm had bore through both of their skulls.

Trevor arched the axe back and swung at the one with the missing arm. The axe sliced into the first walking dead at the collar with a sickening, wet thud. The axe split its body in a vertical half.

Brian had two long steak knives in his hands taken from the kitchen counter. The two guns were now both in his lower back and in his holster. Victor recognized the blades immediately. His father had used them last Christmas to carve a fifteen pound ham.

Everything was suddenly kicked into high gear as the action unfolded. Brian drove the steak knives into the eye sockets of one of the head trauma corpses, while Trevor decapitated the last one in a single blow.

Victor found his mouth hanging open and quickly shut it. He'd eaten in this kitchen with his mother, had celebrated birthdays on the small table next to the microwave. And now three nameless bodies littered the kitchen floor.

"Victor, hey, you okay?" Brian asked.

"Uh, yeah, I'm fine." He gave one of the lifeless bodies a swift kick. "You know, Kirsten's been here for days. I don't think she'll be alive when we find her."

Trevor wiped the axe head with a dishtowel near the sink. "She's here and she's okay. I know it. We'll find her. By God we'll find her." He twisted the axe in his palms. "Lead the way, Victor."

Victor stepped over the dismembered bodies and jumped when boney fingers brushed his ankle, but when he looked down the dead stayed dead. They were just a few lifeless corpses rotting away on the floor.

"I want to check upstairs first, then make our way to the basement," Victor said.

The others agreed and followed him. Victor guided them down a narrow hallway, and was halfway up the staircase, when a terrible cry erupted from outside.

It was a female scream and by the sound of it someone was in horrible pain.

*   *   *

"I can't believe they did that to you, I'm so sorry," Julie said. She placed her hands over the car's heater and rubbed each of her fingers. "Who are they?"

191

Sybil sat beside her in the passenger seat. She wore a blue t-shirt that was too big for her, and a pair of green boxers. The clothing belonged to Brian; they'd found them under the seat crammed in a plastic bag. Julie said he wouldn't mind and Sybil didn't want to be naked for the remainder of the night. She kept her hands between her legs like a little girl, as she spoke timidly.

"Trevor said the woman was his wife. He didn't know the man who raped me. I have no reason not to believe him."

"Are you two a couple? You called him your lover earlier."

Sybil lowered her head in shame. "They made us have sex with each other, Trevor and me. I had to. They told me if I gave them a show they might let me go. I've never seen Trevor before tonight. I'd like him to be my boyfriend though."

Julie put an arm around her and held Sybil close.

A sudden pounding shook the car and was followed by a woeful moan and yells of anger. Julie's hand slipped into the glove compartment. She withdrew a large service pistol as the car bounced up and down.

Sybil hugged the seat. "It's them in the trunk, Lisa and Dario are their names. I wish the bastard would just bleed to death."

Julie checked the side of the patrol car; making sure the movements weren't caused by something else. Outside, the night was cold and damp. She decided to have a look to be sure. Her door was halfway open when Sybil wrapped her arms about her waist.

"Don't go, please," Sybil begged, the tough girl now gone and only a frightened child remaining.

"I'll be right back. I just want to check things out," Julie said as she tore away from Sybil and shut the door.

Sybil pressed against the glass. "Be careful."

Julie saluted her. First, she inspected Dead House. The front door was open and moved back and forth in the wind, the latch broken thanks to Brian.

"I hope you're all right in there, Brian," she said as she gazed at the house and the surrounding forest, hoping another horde of walking dead wasn't on the way. The woods were dark.

For a moment she listened, only hearing the rain splattering on fallen leaves scattered by the storm. She half expected to hear the sorrowful moan again, but it didn't repeat itself.

"This is silly. You know there's nobody out there." But Julie still continued to roam the surroundings with prying eyes.

The car started bouncing once more. The trunk heaved up and down like a wounded wild animal was trapped inside, which wasn't far from the truth.

Julie switched the safety off the pistol. "Get a hold of yourself, Julie. It's just the two rapists you stuck in the trunk," she snickered to herself.

Two rapists in the trunk was a truer reality compared to what she'd been trying to comprehend this night.

The dead walked.

She shuddered at the thought and went to the trunk.

"Hey, quiet down in there," she said, rapping on the trunk.

A crying woman responded. "Let us go," Lisa begged.

Julie planted her fist on the trunk's lid. "I said, shut up in there."

A soft whimpering seeped out.

"You killed my love. My Dario, you killed him, you bitch!"

"I said shut up in there!" Julie pounded on the trunk so hard a dent formed beneath her blow. She rubbed her hand. "Dammit."

Inside, Lisa sobbed and whined. "What kind of monsters are you?"

Julie didn't reply. She stared at Dead House, willing Brian to come back.

What the hell are they doing here with these people? she thought. *By law they would've been carted off to the station and had separate cells and received medical attention.* But the station wasn't responding. Julie pressed the emergency button on her radio; only static answered her.

A flash of lightning scattered across black clouds. The sky opened up and the steady drips of rain turned into a downpour.

"Let me out. Let me out! Please, I need air. I can't breathe in here!" Lisa cried.

Julie let out a long sigh. *This is wrong. Even if they were rapists like Sybil said. Tossing a mortally wounded man with a disorderly woman into the trunk of a police car wasn't right.* A sickness curled up in her stomach. "What am I doing?" Julie went to the driver's side and when she opened the door, Sybil looked at her like a lost puppy.

"What's going on?" Sybil asked.

Julie snatched the car keys from the ignition. She peeled off the spare for the trunk and kept the engine running just as Brian requested. "I'm checking up on our prisoners."

"You're not letting them out, are you?" Sybil's voice broke on the last word.

"I might put the woman in the backseat." She frowned. "Hey, don't give me that look. This is my job. You'll be fine. Don't worry. She won't be able to touch you with handcuffs on."

Before Sybil could complain, Julie was out of the car again and plunged the key into the trunk. When the trunk opened, she drew her gun out, but it was too late.

KEITH LUETHKE

The trunk lid flew open immediately, smacking Julie's gun out of her hand. The man, Dario, was leaning up on his side as intestines seeped out of his stomach like hanging sausage links, his groin a mess of torn and burnt meat. He was gut shot, and though painful, it would still take him quite a while to die.

In his hands was a small handgun. He pulled the trigger with a wicked grin, the gunshot loud over the driving rain.

Stabbing heat slammed into Julie's left shoulder and she was on her knees in seconds.

Lisa howled and leaped on top of her. "It's time to pay, bitch." She dove at Julie head on.

Julie twisted her waist and planted her right fist into Lisa's belly. Julie could hear Lisa's breath bursting out and Julie hit her again for good measure, driving her elbow deep into Lisa's chest.

"Stay the fuck down or I'll knock you're head off," Julie sneered.

The trunk lid opened all the way and Dario aimed the gun at her. He tried to speak, but a thick mess of crimson drooled out instead. The hand gun went off with a bang louder than before. The bullet grazed Julie's inner thigh. Had his aim been a little higher, the bullet would've severed her femoral artery.

Julie leaped toward the car and dropped to the ground, determined to get under cover where Dario couldn't shoot her. She was halfway under the car when the hammer of his pistol pulled back.

"If you go any further, bitch, you're dead," Lisa said. She had scooped Julie's pistol off the ground.

Julie froze.

"Come out of there nice and slow."

Julie obeyed. She crept backwards on hands and knees, her pants soaked from the rain. Her shoulder throbbed where the first bullet passed through.

"That's it, good. Now stand in front of Dario so he can get a good look at you," Lisa ordered her.

Julie did as she asked. Through his bloodied face, Dario looked her up and down, undressing her with his eyes. Julie looked away. She saw the gun Lisa pointed at her, and looking at the wide barrel, she felt a tremor race down her spine.

"So what do you want to do with her?" Lisa asked Dario.

Dario lowered his gaze. He leaned over and put a hand between his legs. His black pants were soaked in blood.

The woman sniffed and a tear drop raced down one pale cheek.

"Don't worry, darling. I'll take care of you." She went to the passenger side door. "Where's the slut?" Lisa demanded.

Julie could see through the back windshield and Sybil was missing from inside the car.

"What did you do?" Lisa pointed the gun at her head. "Where's the slut? We could hear her talking from the trunk." She suddenly looked around. "Where the hell are we?"

At that moment the wet dirt swelled up around Julie's feet. She ran to Dead House, uncaring of the gun aimed in her direction. She gave a silent prayer that Lisa was a terrible shot as she waited to feel the punch of a bullet between her shoulder blades.

Fleshless hands poked through the soil where Julie had been standing.

Lisa couldn't keep her eyes away from the hands, unable to believe what she was seeing. "What the hell is this?" Lisa gaped.

The hands became arms, then ragged heads, and finally hollowed-out torsos, all pushing through the wet earth. When the corpses regained their feet, the shambling figures moaned and advanced toward the patrol car.

"Holy shit!" Lisa screamed and fired, taking the head clean off one of the walking dead.

Julie ran toward Dead House and when she reached the porch, three figures popped out of the front door.

Julie screamed.

Brian's arms were around her waist in seconds, pulling her inside. His firm voice cut through the panic and gunshots. "What's going on, Julie?"

The men saw the living dead attacking the patrol car and knew at once what had happened.

Victor raised the Uzi and pointed it at the horde of fleshless corpses.

"No, don't shoot. You might hurt the woman," Brian explained.

Julie pointed to the blood pooling from her left shoulder. "She tried to kill me, shoot away."

Victor's eyes widened. His lips rose into a snarl and he squeezed the trigger. A hail of bullets shredded two of the corpses but didn't stop them.

The flesh walkers reached for Dario and fell upon him in unison. His gun went off twice, both shots going wild. Yellow teeth sunk into his neck. One of the creatures forced a clawed hand inside his gut and withdrew ropey cords covered in bile and blood. Within moments, Dario was ripped apart, his body turned into a twisted mess of severed limbs and lumps of flesh.

"No, no!" Lisa screamed and fired her last bullets into the undead horde. She managed to bring one down before her gun clicked on an empty chamber.

Trevor raced to his wife's aid, only wanting to save her so he could kill her himself. He heaved the axe into a shambling terror missing an arm. The axe blade cleaved off the corpse's head, and he smashed another with the handle. Then Victor was beside him, knocking the last attacker down with a swift kick to its knee. Trevor fell upon the corpse, splitting the zombie in half. He rose from the foul remains, breathing heavily in the chill night air.

Lisa pointed her gun at him. "Stay back. I'm warning you." She pressed the trigger but only got a dry click as the hammer fell on an empty chamber. She threw the gun at his feet. "Go ahead then. Kill me. Do it."

For a moment the axe rose above Trevor's shoulder but then he paused. "Lisa, what happened to you?"

Lisa wept. She pressed her palms to her eyes and sank to her knees. "I hate you. God I hate you." Lisa scooped up a handful of mud and threw it at him. But her aim was off and the clump of earth plopped near his feet. "I hope you rot in hell, you fucking..."

Trevor sank his fist into her face before she could finish.

He knocked her back three feet and she landed on her back, weeping and sobbing.

"What should we do with her?" Victor asked as he came up by Trevor's side, but his voice seemed far away.

"We'll take her with us. She still needs to pay for what she did tonight," Trevor said.

A shrill scream pierced the night. The group turned around just in time to see Sybil being dragged into Dead House by a pale, grinning corpse.

Chapter 30

With Lisa in tow, the group headed back into the house to finish the job and find Sybil as well. They continued the search, and a few minutes later met back in the main foyer, all but Julie who was still in the house somewhere.

"Empty. The whole damn upstairs and downstairs is completely empty," Brian said angrily. "I can't believe it. Where could they be hiding?"

Victor took the lead once more. "They must be in the cellar and maybe further underground than that. My dad knows we're here. He's waiting for us."

Lisa thrashed in Trevor's arms. If she wasn't cuffed things might've gotten rough. "What the fuck are you talking about? Where are we?" Lisa demanded.

Victor whipped the Uzi at her face. "If she says one more word Trevor I'm going to blow her goddamn head off." He urged Lisa on. "Just say...one...more...word...please."

Lisa's mouth snapped shut.

Trevor held her tight. "She's in my care. Get that gun out of her face. She's still my wife, no matter what she's done."

Brian's hand eased over the tip of the Uzi. "Settle down, we're here to save people, not kill them."

Victor lowered the weapon. He narrowed his eyes at Lisa and she did the same. "Do you really want to know where you are?" Victor asked.

Lisa sucked her lips in a mock gesture. "I'm not talking to you, remember?" She shrugged her shoulders.

"We're at my house."

Lisa burst out in laughter. "You live in this shit hole?"

Victor lifted the Uzi, but Trevor was faster. He threw a cloth rag over Lisa's head and forced it in her mouth, tying the cloth in a knot behind the base of her skull.

"There, that'll keep her quiet," Trevor said.

Lisa gave a muffled grunt and Trevor grinned from ear to ear.

Brian ran a hand through his hair. "Julie should be back by now." He exited the room and headed down the hallway. "I'm going to check up on my partner."

Julie materialized from the shadows, catching him off guard. Her hands were soaked in blood all the way to her elbows.

"Jesus Christ," Brian gasped.

Julie tried to remain calm but her voice was breaking. "When I went to use the bathroom, I heard sounds from the shower, behind the curtain..." Fresh tears dribbled down her cheeks. Brian took her into his arms as she wept and shook.

Victor stepped past them. "I'll check it out." Then he was racing down the hallway before they could argue. His feet recalled every curve in the woodwork, every creaky floorboard, and every small indent before reaching the bathroom. The light was on and the door was shut. He twisted the knob and stepped inside.

An overpowering stench of old sweat mixed with sour decay blasted his senses. He pressed forward. The single bulb flickered above him. Nothing was out of place; the toothbrushes were in order, a bar of soap rested in a blue cradle, then his eyes focused on a single drop of blood on the counter. He found four more, and each penny size spot led him closer to the curtain and the shower. The sky colored curtain was closed. He reached out and flung it open. The scene in front of him would stay with him until his dying days. Three corpses lay over the partially devoured remains of a young teenage girl wearing a blue t-shirt and green boxers.

It was Sybil.

"Oh, God, Sybil..." He reached for her. Her eyes were wide open in death. Her legs and arms were gnawed off, the bottom of the tub filled with her blood. He closed her eyes and leaned against the sink. "I'm so sorry." He shut the curtain and before he could stop, his stomach heaved and he threw up in the toilet.

"Victor?" Julie stood in the doorway. Her arms were crossed and her head bowed. The others had gathered in the hallway with her.

After Victor was finished, he turned to the sink and rinsed his mouth out with water.

Julie patted his back.

"Did you find her like that?" Victor asked.

"No," she answered. "They were eating her when I came in," Julie sobbed. "I bashed their heads in with the cover for the back of the toilet. I don't even know what it's called?"

Victor glanced down to the top of the toilet and realized the cover for the reservoir was missing. He saw the brownish water and his stomach twisted in knots.

"Will you be okay? We really need you now," she asked.

Victor stood up straight. "Yeah, let's get out of here." He leaned in close to Julie and whispered. "Does Trevor know?"

Julie nodded her head. Together they withdrew into the hallway to collect their senses.

Trevor leaned against a wall, his features a mask of dark shadows. Victor shut the bathroom door.

"You found Sybil? She's dead?" Trevor asked.

"I'm so sorry," Victor said.

Trevor's shoulders sagged. His grip on Lisa lost its vigor. "I want to see her." He pushed his wife aside. "Please."

"I don't think that's a good idea," Julie said.

"Let her go, Trevor," Brian added. "There's nothing you can do for her."

Trevor pushed by them, shoving Victor out of his way like a grizzly bear does a small shrub. He entered the bathroom and headed directly to the shower.

"Trevor, please don't look," Julie pleaded. Her voice was tiny and didn't travel far.

When Trevor slapped open the curtain, he froze. "Oh my God..." He sank to his knees. The axe dropped to his feet.

Julie was the first one to reach him and she put her arm on his shoulder.

Brian and Victor hurried in and Brian went to close the curtain but Trevor stopped him.

"Don't. We can't leave her in there. She deserves better," Trevor said, his voice ready to crack

Brian backed away.

"I'm sorry about what happened," Victor said from the door way. "But we don't have time to deal with her right now. We need to find your daughter."

Trevor was back on his feet, chasing away a few stray tears. "I know that. I just want her out of there." He gripped Sybil's torso and yanked. Her body came out easily enough. Trevor set her down on the toilet seat then closed the shower curtain. He addressed Victor first.

"I don't want her in there with those things, that's all, she deserves better," Trevor said.

"I understand," Victor replied.

"For Christ's sake, kid, give the man a few moments," Julie snapped. She rubbed Trevor's backside. "She was a nice girl, I liked her."

Trevor's lips quivered when he focused on Sybil's quartered body. He reached up and tore the shower curtain off its track and used it to cover the body with. Then he lowered his head in grief.

No one spoke for a few seconds and then Victor cut through the silence. "Ah, guys, do you notice anyone missing?"

The group turned their attention toward him and he showed them the empty hall.

"Lisa...that bitch," Trevor said upon realizing his wife had snuck away while they had been dealing with Sybil. He scooped his axe off the bathroom floor, gave Sybil one last look, and then barreled out of the room and downstairs while roaring in anger.

* * *

In the dark, Lisa slipped away silently. Her first inclination was to run downstairs and get the hell out of this haunted house. So far, none of them knew she had escaped. They were too busy crying over the little slut.

Pressing her head to the wall, it wasn't hard to get the hood off her head so she could see.

She dashed down the hallway and faced a flight of stairs. She glanced over her shoulder but didn't see Trevor and the others coming. "Idiots." She grumbled as she took the steps as quick as her feet would allow. When she reached the bottom, she sat down on the first step and worked the handcuffs from behind her back to her front, sliding her arms under her legs like a gymnast.

A loud roar filled the hallway upstairs.

"Lisa!"

It was Trevor

Lisa got to her feet and raced for the front door. She was halfway there when two pale figures emerged from the shadows. Both were women; one had a split face and missing lips, the other had long wet black hair in front of her features and looked like a drowning victim. They blocked the exits. The split-faced girl opened her mouth and maggots fell out to dance on the floor.

Lisa found herself screaming and running away at the same time. She heard a group of footsteps pounding down the staircase, but that seemed of little concern right now. She sprinted through the living room, leaping over the couch, and darting into the kitchen where she found dismembered corpses strewn about the floor. Stepping over the bodies, she found an unlocked door leading to the basement. Moving on instinct, Lisa dove into the darkness.

The door slammed shut behind her.

A buzzing light danced from the basement ceiling like a dying firefly as she made her way down the stairs and toward the light. She paused briefly, testing the door behind her, it didn't open. "Those assholes are probably dealing with those two guarding the front door by now." Gunfire erupted overhead and she smiled under the dying bulb. "You'll never catch me."

She ducked under the light and felt along the walls. "Now, to find my way out of this shit hole." She followed the wall for what seemed like an everlasting amount of time. Her breath became ragged, the sound of her beating heart pounding in her ears. She never liked the dark, it hid too much. The darkness could be a useful tool at times, but in her case the door swung both ways. As she continued in the inky blackness, a startling memory from the past came into focus.

She was five years old and had to go to the bathroom in the dead of night. As a child, she'd rather wet the bed or pee in the pink trash can in the corner of her room than travel to the bathroom at night. But the last time she wet the bed, her father had beat her so hard that purple bruises had formed on her legs and back. Her room took on a whole new meaning at night. Shapes became distorted. Dolls opened their eyes. And her teddy bears got off the shelves to prepare for a midnight picnic. She left her bedroom.

To reach the bathroom she had to climb the stairs, which wasn't so bad, it was the coming back down that scared her the most. That was when the tall man came after you. The man in the ragged hat who ate your eyes if you saw his face. Lisa had glimpsed him on two occasions, and each time she'd outran the night phantom; never looking back to see how close he was, or daring to peer into his face. Her older sister, Chelsea, had told her about the tall man. Chelsea even had a long scar on her inner thigh to prove he'd hurt her. Lisa ran up the stairs and into the bathroom. She did her business in the toilet and sat in the dark, fearing the journey back to her bedroom. The old memories of that night brought goose bumps crawling along her arm. She continued to rub her fingertips along the walls and search for a light in the darkness.

The tall man didn't get her that night, but someone else did. Sitting on the toilet with her underwear around her ankles, she heard quick gasps of breath, rustling sheets, and soft moans. When she stepped into her sister's bedroom, her vision adjusted to the scene. Her father was on top of Chelsea thrusting in and out between her thighs. He wore a ragged hat and his eyes matched with Lisa's thoughts of the tall man. She screamed but couldn't get away as the tall man grabbed her. Then it was her turn.

That was the longest night she'd ever known.

"Just like this damn long hallway," Lisa said to herself. She pushed the past behind her where it belonged. Further ahead, she spotted flickering candlelight. Lisa drifted toward the amber glow. She passed a marble fountain and eased into what looked like an old medical room. There were glass jars on wobbly shelves, sharp implements, dusty books, and a stretcher with a blanket over a limp body. She could tell from the form that it was female as she stepped into the pale light of the one anemic bulb. Besides the body on the stretcher, the room was empty.

Curious, she went toward the stretcher and peeked under the blanket. Smooth, muscular legs greeted her. Lisa lifted it higher. A leather mini-skirt appeared, and when she got a good look at the silk pink panties underneath, she grinned.

"Oh, my, I like that." Lisa decided to fling the blanket off completely. Before the blanket drifted onto the basement floor, Lisa was grinning more than she had all night. "Now what are the odds I'd find you here?"

Strapped to the stretcher was her step-daughter, Kirsten.

No bruises adorned her body, she was unconscious and unmarked. Her chest rose and fell at slow intervals. And other than the fact her breasts were exposed, she was unmolested. She was divine. Lisa gripped the two beautiful breasts in her hands and fondled them with pleasure. She squeezed the round mounds and gave the nipples a little pinch. "Yeah, that's nice." Lisa moaned to herself. "I've been dreaming of this day for a long time. Too bad Dario isn't here to enjoy this. He really wanted to meet you."

Kirsten remained unconscious, but her breathing became heavier.

"Do you like that?" Lisa reached between her thighs. "Then you'll really love this." She was pulling Kirsten's panties down when a loud bellow arose behind her, followed by boots stomping down the cellar stairs.

"Where are you? I'll find you! Just wait. I'll find you, you bitch!"

It was Trevor.

"Shit." Lisa scanned the room for somewhere to hide, cursing herself for being distracted when she should have been escaping. She spotted the shelf full of glass jars. No good.

Urgent footsteps came from down the hall.

"Damn it." Lisa grabbed the blanket and ran into a dark corner. She covered her head and shoulders and waited.

The footsteps ended. "Oh, God. Kirsten?" This was a new voice. She knew immediately it was Victor. That snot nosed bastard. It was because of him this had happened to her. He mortally wounded Dario with the Mustang and had then brought the police with him. Lisa gripped the sheet. She grounded her teeth together. He would pay for his deeds in blood, as would Trevor.

"Kirsten..." Victor wept. "What did my dad do to you?"

Trevor was crying as he held his daughter. "Oh my God, my baby, no," he sobbed.

Victor sobbed for a while too. Lisa heard him put a heavy object on the floor, maybe a gun? Then he was screaming, "Father!"

Lisa dared to lift the blanket over her head. She must've looked silly sitting in the dark under the blanket. Victor had his head buried in his hands as Trevor cradled his daughter. The automatic Uzi was on the floor beside the stretcher as was the axe. She licked her cracked lips. That was her gun; it was a present from Dario on her last birthday. He said he got the Uzi from a drug kingpin along the East coast.

Lisa had always wanted one so he had gotten it for her. *Sweet Dario, he always gave me what I wanted. And now he's dead, eaten alive by...don't even think about it,* she warned herself. Lisa focused on the Uzi. If she could just reach the weapon, the two men would be reduced to shreds.

Victor let out another sorrowful wail and cried over his beloved as Trevor brushed Kirsten's hair from her forehead.

A chunk of concrete was next to Lisa and she picked it up, weighing it in her hand. Then she waited for her moment. It came five seconds later when both men had their backs to her.

Now, go now! Lisa screamed in her head as she slipped from under the blanket and rushed at Trevor. The chunk of concrete came down and Trevor dropped to the floor, dazed and on the verge of passing out.

She spun and came at Victor with her elbow pointed like a spear. The poor bastard never saw it coming. Her elbow jabbed into his solar plexus. One minute he was weeping over Kirsten, the next he was on the floor gasping for air and holding his stomach. Lisa bashed him in the side of his head with her knee for good measure. She delighted in the hard smack of bone against flesh. Victor toppled over, cursing incoherently. Lisa bent over and picked up the Uzi. She aimed at Victor's head as he stumbled to gain his senses.

"Play time's over, honey."

Victor got to his feet. He staggered a little but remained still. He'd been caught unawares and he knew it. He glanced down to Trevor but the man was out of it.

With a snarl, Lisa pulled the trigger, but the Uzi didn't fire. She squeezed the trigger again until she realized the clip was empty. The idiot hadn't reloaded the weapon when he ran out of bullets!

"Bastard!" Lisa launched herself at Victor. Her nails ready to claw out his eyes.

But Victor was ready for her. He sidestepped and threw her into the direction she was going. Lisa was flung head first into a wooden door. She made a sickening crunch and the door popped open as she fell to the floor.

"Bastard, I'll kill you. Kill you!" she hissed.

Victor moved to her. "You shouldn't have come down here."

Lisa's hands fell on a cold piece of metal. She glanced down to find a bent fireplace poker.

"Come on, kid. Let's finish this." Her hand curled around the base of the poker, but as it was behind her back, Victor didn't see her grasp it.

Victor cracked his knuckles. "The others will be here soon. I suggest you stay put."

Lisa's lips rose in a snarl. "Do you think Kirsten took off her bra by herself? I found her that way, you know. I wonder what your dear father did to her."

Victor's face turned pale.

"Do you think he stopped there? Her skirt is really short. Maybe you should check under her panties?"

"Shut up." Victor yelled as he ran at her, arched his fist back, and ready to strike.

But Lisa struck first. She swiped the curved metal at his side and yanked him forward. He gave a surprised yelp when the sharp edge drove into his lower spine. Lisa dragged him to the room behind her. "Say goodbye, asshole." She shoved him inside with the palms of her hands, leaving the metal poker in his back. When he was swallowed by the darkness, she closed and locked the door. Lisa waited a moment for him to cry out or start banging against the frame, but he did neither. Lisa wiped her hands. "Easy as pie."

Heavy footsteps raced down the hallway toward her.

"Damn." Lisa ducked into the same corner she was in last time. "Come on, you fucks." Then, to her astonishment, overhead lights from the ceiling flickered on. Four sets of them were in the medical room alone. She could see two forms huddled together as they entered the chamber and Trevor was slowly getting to his feet, though he had a new scalp wound on his head.

He looked even worse than before. His face was black and blue from where Dario had beaten the shit out of him, but now a long trickle of blood slid down his cheek. Thin trails of blood flowed down his face and splattered on the floor like rain. Trevor held the axe again.

Brian and Julie stayed behind him with their guns drawn. Both of the cops wore uniforms that were tattered from head to toe, and their faces were covered in dark blood and bits of dried flesh.

Must've been ambushed, Lisa thought to herself as the trio approached.

Trevor went straight for his daughter again, checking to see if she was still alive. He sighed when her pulse was steady.

Brian spotted Lisa in the corner and aimed his gun at her. "Don't move or so help me I will shoot you dead."

Lisa raised her cuffed hands. "All right, easy, don't do anything hasty, you got me." She lowered her shirt, making sure her cleavage hung out a bit. "What are you going to do to me?"

Julie pointed a large pistol at her head. "Shoot you where you sit, if you don't shut up."

Lisa gave Brian a puppy dog look as she batted her eyes. Despite her ragged look, she was still a beautiful woman. "You wouldn't hurt me? You're the police. You're supposed to protect me," Lisa purred.

Brian pulled back the hammer of his service pistol. "Lady, the world has gone to Hell in a hand basket in one night. Make one wrong move and I'll blow your goddamn head off."

Lisa snapped her mouth shut.

Trevor covered Kirsten's nakedness and then turned and narrowed his eyes at Lisa. "Who did this to her?"

Lisa remained mute.

Trevor grabbed the wood axe. "Answer me, bitch. Who did this to her?"

"How the hell should I know? I don't fucking live here!"

"Bullshit, who did this to her?" Trevor repeated as he pointed at Kirsten.

A low groan filled into the small room, coming from the doorway, and the undead began to pour in like a wave of water. When the group looked over their shoulders, it was apparent they were now surrounded by the living dead.

All but one of the horde was dead, however.

There was one man sitting in a wheelchair, who was watching them like a scientist might analyze a microbe under a microscope. And when he smiled, showing rows of cracked yellow teeth, the group shivered as one.

"I did," Randolph Leeds said. "And now you will all die." He clapped his frail hands together twice and the shambling terrors advanced.

Chapter 31

Brian unloaded four rounds into the attacking corpses before pulling back. They were dried husks and shattered like an ancient vase when the bullets ripped through them. Julie did the same, cutting three of the horrors down with her pistol.

"Retreat, dammit!" Brian roared above the gunfire.

Julie fired two more rounds and eased backward. "How much ammo do you have left?" Julie asked while reloading her gun.

A large undead woman with a gluttonous belly threw herself at Brian. He sidestepped her assault and shot her at point blank range. Her head was blown apart in an instant, dried brain matter flying off in all directions.

"I'm okay. We can hold them off. I know we can," he yelled back as gun smoke filled the cellar.

Julie snapped a loaded clip into her pistol and got in front of Brian. She cut down the horde by a small fraction as Brian reloaded his weapon. Trevor stood behind them with his daughter clutched in both arms. He stayed in the center and looked for a way out.

"We're trapped!" Lisa roared over the gun blasts. She pounded on Trevor's back. "Get me out of here, you fucking idiot!" Lisa wanted to say more but didn't have time as the dead came at them like the sea to the shore. They reached Lisa first, dragging her from Trevor's back and devouring her flesh within seconds. Her arms were torn from their sockets and her head was ripped off as teeth sank into her throat, while ghouls began working on her legs.

She had time for one brief scream and was silenced forever.

Brian and Julie were overrun; their guns were lost in a tidal wave of maggot infested corpses.

Then a strong voice overrode the chaos. "Enough!"

The dead ended their rampage.

"Chain the live ones to the wall," Randolph Leeds instructed

Brian and Julie were dragged to a set of metal clasps connected to the wall. Both of their hands and feet were locked into place.

"Get the hell away from me." Trevor already had his back pressed to the wall, his axe lost after becoming embedded in a rotting skull. He guarded Kirsten with what strength remained in him, bashing the zombies with his bare knuckles until they overpowered him in sheer numbers. He struggled to fight them off, kicking and even head butting to keep the flesh eaters at bay, but in the end they surrounded him and he was mounted beside Julie.

The dead remained still after the task was completed.

Randolph split the dead horde in half as he wheeled himself toward Kirsten's limp form.

"You sick bastard! Get away from my daughter!" Trevor jerked his arms and strained the muscles in his neck. "I'll kill you!"

When Randolph reached Kirsten, he spoke only one word, "Rise."

Kirsten's eyes fluttered open and her limbs twitched as she sat up. Soon she stood before Randolph like a sleepwalker, not fully dead or alive, but lost in a dream state.

Randolph checked his watch. "It's almost midnight. Soon, my darling, you'll stand before me as my bride."

"Never, you fucking bastard!" Trevor wailed.

"Silence!" Randolph instructed in a tone stronger than what it seemed his frail body could produce. "You should be honored I've chosen your daughter for the final resurrection." He ran his forefinger across Kirsten's cheek. "My dear bride, we will be together at long last."

Kirsten continued to stare off into space as her head nodded slowly. "Yes."

"Kirsten, this is your father. You listen to me. Run away! Get out of here now!" Trevor yelled but Kirsten heard none of it

Randolph tossed his head back in laughter. "She's your daughter no longer. Like the ones before her, she'll take her rightful place as my bride, as a *storm walker*." Randolph took Kirsten's hand. "We'll be together for all the long years I have left. I won't botch this one, my dear." Then, Randolph did what should be impossible. He rose from his wheelchair and walked towards his victims with a wicked grin.

Chapter 32

The door slammed shut and Victor fell backward. He groaned in pain when he landed; the chunk of metal sticking from his back like a tail.

A pale light appeared behind him.

Before he knew what he was doing, he grabbed the end of Lisa's makeshift weapon and ripped it out. He screamed in pain, warm blood dribbling down his backside.

The pale light pulsed twice as a cyclone of wind came from nowhere. He squeezed the metal poker in his hands and swung his arm back, prepared to strike at whatever formation took shape.

The cyclone gathered a ragged blue dress from the wet earth. The dress spun round and round and a soft female voice called his name. "*Victor.*"

The dress began to fill out slowly; first, the chest then the stomach, next legs and arms. The skin on the body was gray and corrupted, but not like the corpses. This body had aged from natural decay. A head, twisted in a mass of scraggly black hair took shape before him. The phantom spun in circles until the transformation was complete. The cyclone died down to a chilling breeze that slapped him in the face. The wraith looked him over with yellow eyes sunken in her skull.

Victor's weapon slipped from his sweaty fingers and fell to the earth.

"Who are you?" he asked.

"*I was once known as Shirley Tucker. But that's not important now.*" She held out a skeletal hand for him to take. "*Come with me, Victor. There's something you need to see.*"

Victor grasped her hand and immediately tried to pull away; it was a numbing cold. But Shirley held onto him and wouldn't let go.

"You're so cold," he said.

She hovered near him and leered over his face. Her other hand pressed hard against the base of his neck. Before he could react, Shirley forced her lipless mouth over his. They were wrapped in a blue light and the cyclone returned and carried him away. Then Shirley released him and vanished without a trace.

Victor found himself in the same small room Lisa had thrown him in, but it was different now. An overhead light cut through the darkness, revealing an assortment of tools cluttered about his feet. He picked through a series of rusty wrenches, hack saws, long nails, screws, and a broken power drill. Then, a wooden box at the far end of the room caught his attention. It was half buried in the earth and covered in cobwebs. He tore off the cover without trouble, and when he peered inside, he discovered a chainsaw.

It was the largest he'd ever seen and he imagined it was the kind of saw lumberjacks would use to zip through the Redwood forest.

A loud bang shattered the silence causing Victor to stand erected.

"Did you really think you could kill me?" asked a man with a deep throaty voice.

Victor recognized the voice instantly.

"Dad, is that you?" He went to the door, found it unlocked, and when he stepped out of the tool room, he found he was standing in a dirty basement. It was the same place as before, but changed. The strange assortment of bottled animals still lined the shelves, but where Kirsten once lay there was a man he'd never seen before in her place. He was young and had a kind face. Randolph leaned over the man like a snake ready to strike.

"Dad, what's going on? Who is this?" Victor asked but his father ignored the questions and continued to address the young man.

"There's something I forgot to tell you." Randolph gripped his face and yanked on it the way kids do with a Halloween mask. The skin peeled apart to reveal rotting dead flesh and lifeless eyes. Randolph laughed, his face now a death mask of horror.

The man strapped on the table gagged at the sight. "No! What have you done?"

Randolph laughed long and hard. "I've perfected life and discovered the ultimate fountain of youth." He pressed his decayed face right up to the man's nose. "What do you think?"

The man didn't turn away. He stared right back. "You sick bastard. I hate you, father. I hate you!"

Victor stopped breathing.

"No," Randolph said with a sinister grin. "I'll be your father no longer." Randolph produced a long serrated knife the length of his forearm and placed it over the prone man's throat.

Victor snapped into action. "Dad, don't do this!" He ran to his father and tried to wrestle the blade from him, but his hands slipped right through Randolph as though Victor was touching a holographic image.

"What the hell?"

Randolph averted his dead eyes to the basement hallway. "Erica," he called. "Come in here."

KEITH LUETHKE

Soft footsteps pattered down the hall in response. "I'm coming." A tall slender woman with short, brown hair and a swollen belly stepped into the room.

Randolph grinned. "Do you see that woman there? She's mine. And the child she carries with her will be my new son. He'll be stronger and better than you ever were." Then Randolph drew the blade across the man's throat.

Erica screamed. "David!" She pounced on Randolph's backside. "You promised you wouldn't hurt him! You promised!"

Randolph made sure David was dead before withdrawing the knife, the man's life's blood shooting out to spray the nearby wall red. He slapped Erica across the face and she ended her assault. "I've just thought of a name for my new son."

Erica sobbed as she rested her head on David's chest, her hair and shoulders now covered in his blood.

Randolph's decayed hand rubbed her stomach. "I'll call him Victor."

Erica wept and Randolph laughed, his voice echoing through the stone halls.

Victor heard his name being called over and over again. Not by his father, but the wraith named Shirley. He continued to stare at Randolph Leeds, boring through him.

A cold hand pressed on his shoulder. *"It's time to go, Victor. You've seen what you must."*

Tears poured from his eyes but his face remained hard. "It's a lie. What the hell is this? A sick trick? A joke?" he snarled.

The boney hand dug deep into his arm. *"This is the past. It wasn't meant for your eyes to see, but I was forced to show you."*

Victor smacked the claw-like hand away from him. "Why? Why me? I didn't need to see this. Everything I've ever known is a lie. That was my real father on that table, wasn't it?

Shirley hovered over him. *"Yes, it was. The man was named David and he was your true father."*

"He'll pay for this!" Victor roared. "Randolph Leeds will die tonight."

Shirley took Victor by the hand. *"It's time to exact your vengeance. Those captured by Randolph Leeds need your help."* Shirley glared at him, her yellow eyes flickering like candlelight. *"My daughter needs you."*

Victor's anger turned into shock. "You're Kirsten's mother?" The phantom kissed him once again, the room faded to black, and Victor was swept up in the cyclone once more.

Shirley's ragged teeth pressed against his lips. Victor closed his eyes as his body fell into space. He seemed to drift on clouds, and when he opened his eyes, he was back where he started from, locked in a dark room. A worn blue satin dress lay at his feet and the memories of his father and mother flooded back to him. Victor's muscles throbbed for release. "I'll kill that son-of-a- bitch," he growled.

Crackling laughter seeped in from the adjacent room.

Victor knew exactly what to do. He went to the corner where the wooden box had been stored. All the tools from the past were missing. "Dammit," he cursed.

He discovered a mound of hard earth in the back of the room. He raked his fingernails across the surface until he could shovel the earth away by the handfuls. After minutes of ceaseless digging, he recovered the wooden box. He eagerly ripped the crate free and feasted his attention on the chainsaw. It was covered in spider webs and stained by time.

He ran his index finger over the blade. A small niche appeared on the tip, followed by a few drops of blood. He studied the blood for a moment.

"Good, still sharp." He grabbed the chainsaw by the handle. The weight of the saw dragged his arms down but he held it to his chest and faced the door.

I wonder what he's doing in there, Victor thought. *He's not my father. He killed my father and kidnapped Kirsten. She might be dead by now, too.*

He held the chainsaw in one hand as he leaned it against his stomach to pull the cord. The first tug did nothing. Victor made sure the choke was on and tried again. Still nothing. Quickly he checked to see if there was fuel and he nodded in relief to see there was still some, though not much. With luck, it would run for a few minutes if he was able to start it. Saying a silent prayer and pressing the priming button, he pulled the cord again and was rewarded by a small rumble.

His spirits higher, he pulled the cord yet again and this time he got a little more of a growl. "Come on, baby. Come on." He pulled again, quicker this time and the chainsaw roared to life, as smoke poured from the engine, creating a thick haze, as the old fuel burned. Victor coughed and slowly eased the choke in. He pressed the trigger. The saw gave a metallic whine. Victor squeezed the trigger once more, delighted at the sound.

He let the saw blades rip through the door, bits of wood flying off in layers. He split the door down the center. He aimed for the handle and within seconds a pile of wood lay at his feet. He could now see the other room clearly.

What seemed like hundreds of rotting dead faces watched him with sunken, blank expressions. None of them resembled the storm walkers, and none of them moved. They were a legion of dead awaiting command, a mass of animated flesh and nothing more.

Victor stepped into the room. He saw Kirsten, naked except for her black mini-skirt, standing beside Randolph. His father had Kirsten's breasts clutched in his crooked hands and Victor was amazed to see the wheelchair was tipped on its side and left abandoned. Then Victor saw the others chained to the wall; Brian, Trevor, and Julie.

All eyes were focused on him as Randolph roughly squeezed Kirsten's breasts and grinned. He motioned for Victor to join him. Victor's upper lip twisted. He let the chainsaw idle as he made his way forward.

Randolph's voice boomed over the noise. "Victor, put that old toy away and come here. I have a few things I need to show you." He had no fear of the saw, or of his adopted son. "I said put that down! Obey your father, damn you."

Victor raised the chainsaw high over his head and brought it screaming down onto Randolph's collar.

"You're not my father! I know the truth!" The blades tore through flesh and bone with ease. Randolph's eye widened in disbelief but still retained its same lifeless quality. Victor sliced him from his collar down to his groin, blood shooting out in all directions to bathe the room in red. And when Randolph was a mere shadow of his former self, Victor quartered his limbs and took off the head last, the single orb still staring at him accusingly. The room exploded in sudden activity. The horde of ghouls separated. Disjointed, they turned as one and left the basement, stumbling upstairs, their master now dead.

Victor kicked Randolph's head against the wall. In the end, there were no witty comebacks or vengeful cries, only judgment and death. The chainsaw slipped from his hands, red stained and quenched for the moment. He felt light headed and sank to the floor on all fours. "What have I done?"

"Victor? What's going on?" Kirsten knelt down and shivered at his side. She was covered in blood now, her eyes peering through the crimson mask.

Victor turned to gaze into her eyes. He wrapped his arms around her.

"Thank God your alive!" he said and squeezed her tighter.

She put her fingers through his hair. "Of course I'm alive. You didn't think you'd get away from me that easily, did you?"

Victor laughed. He took off his shirt and let Kirsten wear it.

"Hey, love birds," Trevor groaned. "Do you mind getting us down from here? My wrists are starting to hurt."

"Daddy is that you?" Kirsten turned to see her father secured to the wall. Now that Randolph was dead, his spell over her was broken. She ran to her father and smothered him with hugs and tears. "What did they do to you?" she asked between hugs.

"It's a long story," Trevor said as he withstood the onslaught of his daughter's love. His face was sore and it hurt each time she kissed him, but he took it in stride. "And not one I want to tell about in my present condition."

"That's goes for us, too," Brian added and Julie nodded her head in agreement.

Victor searched through the scattered remains of Randolph Leeds and came upon a small notebook and a silver key. After cleaning it of gore, he pocketed the book and fit the key into Trevor's locks first. The cuffs snapped open and he did the same for Brian and Julie.

"Thanks," Brian said.

"Yeah, thanks a lot, Trevor. I'm sorry I ever doubted you," Julie added and gave him a kiss on the cheek. When the five of them had gathered themselves Julie addressed them. "I think we should go hunting."

Brian agreed. "She's right. There must be a hundred of those things out there at least."

"But why did they leave?" Trevor asked. They had us cold.

No one knew the answer, though each of them had their own ideas.

"It must have had to do with Randolph's death; he was controlling them somehow." Brian suggested.

No one argued, it was good an explanation as any other.

Victor picked up his chainsaw. "Let's go finish this. I think I have enough fuel to take down a few more." He led them out of the basement and they searched the entire house and came up empty handed.

As the dawning sun rose to greet them, the rainstorm dissipated.

Dead House remained quiet.

* * *

Authorities from Putnam and Westchester County were called in to investigate the bizarre murder spree that had occurred the previous night. Over thirty citizens were missing and only four bodies were discovered, each partly eaten. The storm had knocked down telephone poles and lightning was reported to have caused accidents, one being a tractor trailer, causing the driver to rollover on a back road. The incident was front page news in the Putnam Journal and forgotten by the surrounding counties within a week.

The local weather channel advised another storm was on the way and to expect heavy rain.

But that wasn't anything new to the residents of Stormville.

Epilogue

"I wish the three of you would stay for the reception," Julie said. She fiddled with the white lace on her wedding dress, clearly feeling uncomfortable.

"I wish we could," Trevor sighed. "But we're getting out of here." He put an arm around Kirsten. "Isn't that right, kiddo?"

"Damn, straight," Kirsten replied. She gave Julie a long hug goodbye. "Come and visit us sometime, okay?"

"I will," Julie proclaimed.

Kirsten turned to Victor. He and Brian were busy loading the last boxes into the U-haul. "Thank you for everything. You two should really get back inside. I'm sure your guests must be wondering where you are."

Julie waved her hand, as though swatting away a buzzing fly. "They'll be fine. I see my relatives enough as it is."

"I thought you said they only come to visit once a year?" Trevor asked.

"Like I said, I see them enough," Julie grinned.

The five of them laughed together.

Trevor took on a serious tone. "Are you sure you want to stay here?"

Julie nodded. "Yes, I'm positive. We haven't had any reports for months now."

"That doesn't mean they're not out there," Trevor quipped.

"I'll take my chances," Julie said. "Besides, who the hell else is going to protect this town?"

Trevor grinned. "I can't think of anyone better for the job."

The U-Haul cargo hold slammed shut and Brian and Victor came out from behind it, laughing and joking with each other.

"Are we set guys?" Trevor asked.

"Ready to roll," Victor replied.

Brian gave his wife a quick kiss as he hugged her. He looked quite handsome in his tuxedo. "I love you."

"I love you, too," Julie smiled, and their lips connected again.

"Well, we'd better get going." Trevor shook Brian's hand and hugged Julie. "Nevada's a week's drive from here."

"I just wish you weren't moving so far away," Julie frowned.

Victor held Kirsten's hand and her engagement ring sparkled in the afternoon sunlight. "Yeah, but it doesn't rain much where we're headed."

Brian patted Victor's shoulder. "We'll visit next year. Julie really wants to hit the slot machines."

"You want to also, you said so last night," Julie said and elbowed him in the ribs.

They finished saying their goodbyes, made promises for the future, and went separate ways.

Victor and Kirsten took the Subaru Forester while Trevor drove the U-Haul. Victor drove at a slow pace along his hometown streets, remembering simple times when his mother drove him to McDonald's every Friday. Despite everything, he would miss this place he called home.

Kirsten rubbed his thigh. "Are you going to miss this place?"

"How could I not? This is my town, but I'll come back one day," he said to himself, staring at the long road ahead.

Kirsten smiled. She admired the ring on her finger and gave a happy sigh. "I hope our wedding is like Brian and Julie's. There were so many people, and that church was huge."

Victor nodded and smiled back at her. He was quiet for a moment before speaking. "I feel like a coward, like we're running away from our problems."

"There's nothing left here, Victor. Dead House is boarded up and we haven't seen or heard any reports of the storm walkers or the others for a long time."

"That doesn't mean they're gone," he said. He took her hand, kissed it, and pulled onto route 52. "If Brian and Julie run into trouble..."

"We'll hop on a plane and be there in no time," Kirsten finished for him. "Now, let's talk more about our wedding. I think I want to wear a black dress."

He rolled his eyes as he began to laugh, and she joined in, the two lovers now one.

THE NEXT EXCITING ADVENTURE IN THE DEADWATER SERIES!
DEAD SALVATION
BOOK 9
by Anthony Giangregorio

Henry Watson and his band of warrior survivalists roam what is left of a ravaged America, searching for something better.

HANGMAN'S NOOSE

After one of the group is hurt, the need for transportation is solved by a roving cannie convoy. Attacking the camp, the companions save a man who invites them back to his home.

Cement City it's called and at first the group is welcomed with thanks for saving one of their own. But when a bar fight goes wrong, the companions find themselves awaiting the hangman's noose.

Their only salvation is a suicide mission into a raider camp to save captured townspeople.

Though the odds are long, it's a chance, and Henry knows in the land of the walking dead, sometimes a chance is all you can hope for.

In the world of the dead, life is a struggle, where the only victor is death.

RANDY AND WALTER: PORTRAIT OF TWO KILLERS
by Tristan Slaughter

Randy Barcer lived his life the way he wanted to, joyfully slaughtering innocent women and children.

But sometimes he did much worse to them and those that died would be considered the lucky ones.

That is until he met Walter Brenemen, and he soon found out that this man who claimed to be his brother, was far more dangerous than Randy could ever hope to be.

"I'll give you the name of a woman and tell you where to find her. Then we'll see which one of us can get to her first. If you win, I'll leave you be. But if I win...well, I guess we'll just have to wait and see."

With those words, Walter changed Randy's life forever.

It was a simple game.

Whoever kills the most, wins; with a small town caught in the middle.

Forget what you know or think you know about horror. Let go of everything you've ever been taught about serial killers. Step into the world of Tristan Slaughter and discover what it is that makes a killer.

This is not your typical slasher novel.

This is:

Randy and Walter: Portrait of Two Killers.

You will never look at a man the same way again.

Welcome to a world of despair, desire, cruelty, punishment, pure evil and most of all...Death.

BOOK OF THE DEAD 2: NOT DEAD YET
A ZOMBIE ANTHOLOGY
Edited by Anthony Giangregorio

Out of the ashes of death and decay, comes the second volume filled with the walking dead. In this tomb, there are only slow, shambling monstrosities that were once human. No one knows why the dead walk; only that they do, and that they are hungry for human flesh. But these aren't your neighbors, your co-workers, or your family. Now they are the living dead, and they will tear your throat out at a moment's notice. So be warned as you delve into the pages of this book; the dead will find you, no matter where you hide.

CHRISTMAS IS DEAD: A ZOMBIE ANTHOLOGY
Edited by Anthony Giangregorio

Twas the night before Christmas and all through the house, not a creature was stirring, not even a. . . zombie?

That's right; this anthology explores what would happen at Christmas time if there was a full blown zombie outbreak.

Reanimated turkeys, zombie Santas, and demon reindeers that turn people into flesh-eating ghouls are just some of the tales you will find in this merry undead book.

So curl up under the Christmas tree with a cup of hot chocolate, and as the fireplace crackles with warmth, get ready to have your heart filled with holiday cheer.

But of course, then it will be ripped from your heaving chest and fed upon by blood-thirsty elves with a craving for human flesh!

For you see, Christmas is Dead!

And you will never look at the holiday season the same way again.

REVOLUTION OF THE DEAD
by Anthony Giangregorio
THE DEAD SHALL RISE AGAIN!

Five years ago, a deadly plague wiped out 97% of the world's population, America suffering tragically. Bodies were everywhere, far too many to bury or burn. But then, through a miracle of medical science, a way is found to reanimate the dead.

With the manpower of the United States depleted, and the remaining survivors not wanting to give up their internet and fast food restaurants, the undead are conscripted as slave labor.

Now they cut the grass, pick up the trash, and walk the dogs of the surviving humans.

But whether alive or dead, no race wants to be controlled, and sooner or later the dead will fight back, wanting the freedom they enjoyed in life.

The revolution has begun!

And when it's over, the dead will rule the land, and the remaining humans will become the slaves...or worse.

DEADFREEZE
by Anthony Giangregorio

THIS IS WHAT HELL WOULD BE LIKE IF IT FROZE OVER!

When an experimental serum for hypothermia goes horribly wrong, a small research station in the middle of Antarctica becomes overrun with an army of the frozen dead.

Now a small group of survivors must battle the arctic weather and a horde of frozen zombies as they make their way across the frozen plains of Antarctica to a neighboring research station.

What they don't realize is that they are being hunted by an entity whose sole reason for existing is vengeance; and it will find them wherever they run.

VISIONS OF THE DEAD
A ZOMBIE STORY
by Anthony & Joseph Giangregorio

Jake Roberts felt like he was the luckiest man alive.

He had a great family, a beautiful girlfriend, who was soon to be his wife, and a job, that might not have been the best, but it paid the bills.

At least until the dead began to walk.

Now Jake is fighting to survive in a dead world while searching for his lost love, Melissa, knowing she's out there somewhere.

But the past isn't dead, and as he struggles for an uncertain future, the past threatens to consume him.

With the present a constant battle between the living and the dead, Jake finds himself slipping in and out of the past, the visions of how it all happened haunting him.

But Jake knows Melissa is out there somewhere and he'll find her or die trying. In a world of the living dead, you can never escape your past.

KINGDOM OF THE DEAD
by Anthony Giangregorio
THE DEAD HAVE RISEN!

In the dead city of Pittsburgh, two small enclaves struggle to survive, eking out an existence of hand to mouth.

But instead of working together, both groups battle for the last remaining fuel and supplies of a city filled with the living dead.

Six months after the initial outbreak, a lone helicopter arrives bearing two more survivors and a newborn baby. One enclave welcomes them, while the other schemes to steal their helicopter and escape the decaying city.

With no police, fire, or social services existing, the two will battle for dominance in the steel city of the walking dead. But when the dust settles, the question is: will the remaining humans be the winners, or the losers?

When the dead walk, the line between Heaven and Hell is so twisted and bent there is no line at all.

DEAD MOURNING: A ZOMBIE HORROR STORY
by Anthony Giangregorio

Carl Jenkins was having a run of bad luck. Fresh out of jail, his probation tenuous, he'd lost every job he'd taken since being released. So now was his last chance, only one more job to prevent him from going back to prison. Assigned to work in a funeral home, he accidentally loses a shipment of embalming fluid. With nothing to lose, he substitutes it with a batch of chemicals from a nearby factory.

The results don't go as planned, though. While his screw-up goes unnoticed, his machinations revive the cadavers in the funeral home, unleashing an evil on the world that it has not seen before. Not wanting to become a snack for the rampaging dead, he flees the city, joining up with other survivors. An old, dilapidated zoo becomes their haven, while the dead wait outside the walls, hungry and patient.

But Carl is optimistic, after all, he's still alive, right? Perhaps his luck has changed and help will arrive to save them all?

Unfortunately, unknown to him and the other survivors, a serial killer has fallen into their group, trapped inside the zoo with them.

With the undead army clamoring outside the walls and a murderer within, it'll be a miracle if any of them live to see the next sunrise.

On second thought, maybe Carl would've been better off if he'd just gone back to jail.

ROAD KILL: A ZOMBIE TALE
by Anthony Giangregorio
ORDER UP!

In the summer of 2008, a rogue comet entered earth's orbit for 72 hours. During this time, a strange amber glow suffused the sky.

But something else happened; something in the comet's tail had an adverse affect on dead tissue and the result was the reanimation of every dead animal carcass on the planet.

A handful of survivors hole up in a diner in the backwoods of New Hampshire while the undead creatures of the night hunt for human prey.

There's a new blue plate special at DJ's Diner and Truck Stop, and it's you!

DEAD WORLDS: Undead Stories
A Zombie Anthology Volume 2
Edited by Anthony Giangregorio

Welcome to a world where the dead walk and want nothing more than to feast on the living. The stories contained in this, the second volume of the Dead Worlds series, are filled with action, gore, and buckets and buckets of blood; plus a heaping side of entrails for those with a little extra hunger.

The stories contained within this volume are scribed by both the desiccated cadavers of seasoned veterans to the genre as well as fresh-faced corpses, each printed here for the first time; and all of them ready to dig in and please the most discerning reader.

So slap on a bib and prepare to get bloody, because you're about to read the best zombie stories this side of Hell!

THE DARK

by Anthony Giangregorio
DARKNESS FALLS

The darkness came without warning.

First New York, then the rest of United States, and then the world became enveloped in a perpetual night without end.

With no sunlight, eventually the planet will wither and die, bringing on a new Ice Age. But that isn't problem for the human race, for humanity will be dead long before that happens.

There is something in the dark, creatures only seen in nightmares, and they are on the prowl. Evolution has changed and man is no longer the dominant species. When we are children, we're told not to fear the dark, that what we believe to exist in the shadows is false.

Unfortunately, that is no longer true.

SOULEATER

by Anthony Giangregorio

Twenty years ago, Jason Lawson witnessed the brutal death of his father by something only seen in nightmares, something so horrible he'd blocked it from his mind.

Now twenty years later the creature is back, this time for his son.

Jason won't let that happen.

He'll travel to the demon's world, struggling every second to rescue his son from its clutches.

But what he doesn't know is that the portal will only be open for a finite time and if he doesn't return with his son before it closes, then he'll be trapped in the demon's dimension forever.

SEE HOW IT ALL BEGAN IN THE NEW DOUBLE-SIZED 460 PAGE SPECIAL EDITION!

✓ DEADWATER: EXPANDED EDITION

by Anthony Giangregorio

Through a series of tragic mishaps, a small town's water supply is contaminated with a deadly bacterium that transforms the town's population into flesh eating ghouls.

Without warning, Henry Watson finds himself thrown into a living hell where the living dead walk and want nothing more than to feed on the living.

Now Henry's trying to escape the undead town before he becomes the next victim.

With the military on one side, shooting civilians on sight, and a horde of bloodthirsty zombies on the other, Henry must try to battle his way to freedom.

With a small group of survivors, including a beautiful secretary and a wise-cracking janitor to aid him, the ragtag group will do their best to stay alive and escape the city codenamed: **Deadwater**.

✓ DEAD END: A ZOMBIE NOVEL
by Anthony Giangregorio
THE DEAD WALK!

Newspapers everywhere proclaim the dead have returned to feast on the living!

A small group of survivors hole up in a cellar, afraid to brave the masses of animated corpses, but when food runs out, they have no choice but to venture out into a world gone mad.

What they will discover, however, is that the fall of civilization has brought out the worst in their fellow man.

Cannibals, psychotic preachers and rapists are just some of the atrocities they must face.

In a world turned upside down, it is life that has hit a Dead End.

✓ DEAD RAGE
by Anthony Giangregorio

An unknown virus spreads across the globe, turning ordinary people into bloodthirsty, ravenous killers.

Only a small percentage of the population is immune and soon become prey to the infected.

Amongst the infected comes a man, stricken by the virus, yet still retaining his grasp on reality. His need to destroy the *normals* becomes an obsession and he raises an army of killers to seek out and kill all who aren't *changed* like himself.

A few survivors gather together on the outskirts of Chicago and find themselves running for their lives as the specter of death looms over all.

The Dead Rage virus will find you, no matter where you hide.

FAMILY OF THE DEAD
A Zombie Anthology
by Anthony, Joseph and Domenic Giangregorio

Clawing their way out of the wet, dark earth, these tales of terror will fill you with the deep seated fear we all have of death and what comes next.

But if that wasn't bad enough to chill your soul, these undead tales are penned by an entire family of corpses. The zombie master himself, Anthony Giangregorio, leads his two young ghouls, his sons Domenic and Joseph Giangregorio, on a journey of terror inducing stories that will keep you up long into the night.

As you read these works of the undead, don't be alarmed by that bump outside the window.

After all, it's probably just a stray tree branch...or is it?

The Lazarus Culture

by Pasquale J. Morrone

Secret Service Agent Christopher Kearns had no idea what he was up against. Assigned on a temporary basis to the Center for Disease Control, he only knew that somehow it was connected to the lives of those the agency protected...namely, the President of the United States. If there were possible terrorist activities in the making, he could only guess it was at a red alert basis.

When Kearns meets and befriends Doctor Marlene Peterson of the Breezy Point Medical Center in Maryland, he soon finds that science fiction can indeed become a reality. In a solitary room walked a man with no vital signs: dead. The explanation he received came from Doctor Lee Fret, a man assigned to the case from the CDC. Something was attached to the brain stem. Something alive that was quickly spreading rapidly through Maryland and other states.

Kearns and his ragtag army of agents and medical personnel soon find themselves in a world of meaningless slaughter and mayhem. The armies of the walking dead were far more than mere zombies. Some began to change into whatever it was they ate. The government had found a way to reanimate the dead by implanting a parasite found on the tongue of the Red Snapper to the human brain.

It looked good on paper, but it was a project straight from Hell.

The dead now walked, but it wasn't a mystery.

It was The Lazarus Culture.

END OF DAYS: AN APOCALYPTIC ANTHOLOGY
VOLUME 1

Our world is a fragile place.

Meteors, famine, floods, nuclear war, solar flares, and hundreds of other calamities can plunge our small blue planet into turmoil in an instant.

What would you do if tomorrow the sun went super nova or the world was swallowed by water, submerging the world into the cold darkness of the ocean?

This anthology explores some of those scenarios and plunges you into total annihilation.

But remember, it's only a book, and tomorrow will come as it always does.

Or will it?

DEADFALL

by Anthony Giangregorio

It's Halloween in the small suburban town of Wakefield, Mass.

While parents take their children trick or treating and others throw costume parties, a swarm of meteorites enter the earth's atmosphere and crash to earth.

Inside are small parasitic worms, no larger than maggots.

The worms quickly infect the corpses at a local cemetery and so begins the rise of the undead.

The walking dead soon get the upper hand, with no one believing the truth. That the dead now walk.

Will a small group of survivors live through the zombie apocalypse?

Or will they, too, succumb to the Deadfall.

DARK PLACES

By Anthony Giangregorio

A cave-in inside the Boston subway unleashes something that should have stayed buried forever.

Three boys sneak out to a haunted junkyard after dark and find more than they gambled on.

In a world where everyone over twelve has died from a mysterious illness, one young boy tries to carry on.

A mysterious man in black tries his hand at a game of chance at a local carnival, to interesting results.

God, Allah, and Buddha play a friendly game of poker with the fate of the Earth resting in the balance.

Ever have one of those days where everything that can go wrong, does? Well, so did Byron, and no one should have a day like this!

Thad had an imaginary friend named Charlie when he was a child. Charlie would make him do bad things. Now Thad is all grown up and guess who's coming for a visit?

These and other short stories, all filled with frozen moments of dread and wonder, will keep you captivated long into the night.

Just be sure to watch out when you turn off the light!

BOOK OF THE DEAD
A ZOMBIE ANTHOLOGY
VOLUME 1
ISBN 978-1-935458-25-8
Edited by Anthony Giangregorio

This is the most faithful, truest zombie anthology ever written, and we invite you along for the ride. Every single story in this book is filled with slack-jawed, eyes glazed, slow moving, shambling zombies set in a world where the dead have risen and only want to eat the flesh of the living. In these pages, the rules are sacrosanct. There is no deviation from what a zombie should be or how they came about.

The Dead Walk.

There is no reason, though rumors and suppositions fill the radio and television stations. But the only thing that is fact is that the walking dead are here and they will not go away. So prepare yourself for the ultimate homage to the master of zombie legend. And remember... Aim for the head!

DEAD TALES: SHORT STORIES TO DIE FOR
by Anthony Giangregorio

In a world much like our own, terrorists unleash a deadly dis-ease that turns people into flesh-eating ghouls.

A camping trip goes horribly wrong when forces of evil seek to dominate mankind.

After losing his life, a man returns reincarnated again and again; his soul inhabiting the bodies of animals.

In the Colorado Mountains, a woman runs for her life, stalked by a sadistic killer.

In a world where the Patriot Act has come to fruition, a man struggles to survive, despite eroding liberties.

Not able to accept his wife's death, a widower will cross into the dream realm to find her again, despite the dark forces that hold her in thrall. These and other short stories will captivate and thrill you. These are short stories to die for.

THE PLACE TO GO FOR ZOMBIE AND APOCALYPTIC FICTION

LIVING DEAD PRESS

WHERE THE DEAD WALK

www.livingdeadpress.com

LaVergne, TN USA
12 March 2010
175757LV00004B/22/P